## NIGHT WITHOUT MORNING

The million-dollar robbery would have gone off without a hitch except that two of Willie Madden's partners decided to shoot it out with the cops. Now there are only five of them left—three in prison, one on the loose and presumed dead, and Willie. He had kept his cool, outsmarting them all and living a new life on the Coast. But there was an eighth member, Johnny Quait, an old cripple but still a formidable foe. He intends to find Willie. And to do that he enlists the one who got away—crazy, unpredictable Carol Benedict—to help in his search. Slowly Willie's perfect world begins to crumble. And then he meets Dorothy...

## ROUND THE CLOCK AT VOLARI'S

Jim Chase's legal career had flourished during the last administration. But the reformers are in now, and he's hit lean times. After losing another case, he heads over to Volari's, the nightclub where he used to reign supreme in the good old days. Judy's there, the pretty young waitress he left his wife for. And Al Patton, the new owner. But something is up tonight. Judy's worried, and Al's a jittery wreck. The Grand Jury is going to subpoena his brother Tom, and he needs to get Tom's money to him from the Volari vault. Jim agrees to help, but when the guys who are supposed to deliver the cash to Tom disappear, his job becomes a lot more complicated.

T0279086

# Night Without Morning
# Round the Clock at Volari's

## W. R. BURNETT

### Introduction by David Laurence Wilson

**Stark House Press • Eureka California**

NIGHT WITHOUT MORNING / ROUND THE CLOCK AT VOLARI'S

Published by Stark House Press
1315 H Street
Eureka, CA 95501, USA
griffinskye3@sbcglobal.net
www.starkhousepress.com

NIGHT WITHOUT MORNING
Copyright © 2024 by the Estate of W. R. Burnett. A substantially different
version published as *The Cool Man* by Fawcett Publications, Inc.,
Greenwich, 1968. This edition restores the author's original title and text.

ROUND THE CLOCK AT VOLARI'S
Originally published and copyright © 1961 by Fawcett Publications, Inc.,
Greenwich, in a heavily edited and re-written version. This edition
restores the author's original text.

Reprinted by permission of the Estate of W. R. Burnett. All rights
reserved under International and Pan-American Copyright Conventions.

Prepared for publication by David Laurence Wilson.

"W. R. Burnett: The Iron Knight Who Won the Long Game"
copyright © 2024 by David Laurence Wilson

ISBN: 979-8-88601-111-1

Book design by Mark Shepard, shepgraphics.com
Proofreading by Bill Kelly
Cover photo by Henrik Mårtensson

First Stark House Press Edition: November 2024

# W. R. BURNETT: THE IRON KNIGHT WHO WON THE LONG GAME

By David Laurence Wilson

"Ho hum ... oh, for the life of a Chicago gunman."
Anthony J. Casey in "The Brooklyn Citizen," June 9, 1929

"Finally the racing became too expensive," Burnett said. "I went broke. I owed everybody. Then I wrote *High Sierra*, I had another big seller, I sold it to Warner Brothers, for a good price, and that got me started all over again. Fine timing. Just right. I'm lucky, I tell you. I'm a lucky bastard. I really am."

"Long Game"—the Webster's Dictionary definition: "Something that takes time and will bring success far into the future, rather than in the present or near future."

A lot of it was just a matter of luck. W. R. Burnett, a writer and baseball fan, twenty-nine years of age, hit a home run in his first time at bat. More like a hundred home runs—and counting, because *Little Caesar*, the book in this mixed metaphor has had a knack for staying in print. It happened to "catch on," Burnett would say, years later: "*Little Caesar* (Dial, 1929) came out at exactly the right moment." From that moment on, from the beginning of his career, readers would always be reminded that Burnett was the author of *Little Caesar*.

It would be Burnett's *Moby Dick* (Harper and Brothers, 1851), the novel he would forever he associated with. It was, the story goes, his fifth or sixth attempt at a novel and it was submitted to the Dial Press without the aid of a literary agent. Burnett had the rejected manuscript in the back of his car, under his golf clubs, until he decided to give it one last pitch and Dial accepted it.

Burton Rascoe, was a well-travelled literary critic who was probably best known for his cryptic observation: "What no spouse of a writer can ever understand is that a writer is working when he's staring out of the window."

Rascoe called Burnett's story: "the novel that has been waiting to be written about the Chicago gangsters. This Burnett is a discovery."

According to the nearly delirious but surprisingly perceptive literary
critic, Anthony Casey, in "The Brooklyn Citizen," "Every act of (Burnett's)
characters reveals something about the person who performs it and at
the same time every act of a person contributes to build up the picture
of a world, an underworld, which has its own binding customs, if not
laws, which the inhabitants must not trifle with."

"Burnett does not apologize for his criminals nor does he glorify
them, but tells their story with staccato precision, economy, edge and
force."

Way back in 1929 Casey was already describing Burnett as
"cinematic."

□ □ □

If words on paper were tallied up, the editions and critical writing
surrounding *Little Caesar* would dwarf the rest of Burnett's career.
With *Caesar*, Burnett became the O. G.—the original "gangster" writer,
a fellow who lucked out in many ways. Luck of all varieties.

*Little Caesar* was selected as the June, 1929 choice for the Book-of-
the-Month club. Six months later his second novel, *Iron Man*, was the
January, 1930 selection of the Literary Guild. Then Burnett's short
story, "Dressing Up," published in *Harper's* magazine, received the
1930 O. Henry award for the best short story of the year. It was the
astonishing debut of a new writer.

Burnett had arrived like an unexpected storm. *Little Caesar* marked
the beginning of modern writing; if you read Burnett—if you studied
his choices—you learned how to write.

But hurry along. Nothing to see here that you haven't seen before.
We know that story, and for once this will not be that familiar recap.
This story is not about the rapid rise of Burnett ... and it's not really
about his fall because Burnett didn't choose to imagine or admit that
he would be absent from the writing game for 13 years. He had never
expected THAT! and he probably hadn't been counting the years, either.
Given the long perspective this was just a matter of timing.

And now, a century later, Burnett is back! The important thing is
that he always kept writing.

However delighted or reconciled he may have been with the idea of
success—big success—Burnett never claimed that *Little Caesar* was
the best of the 35 novels he published during his lifetime. That would
be, possibly, *Captain Lightfoot (Knopf, 1954)*, or *Goodbye to the Past
(Harper, 1934)*, or *Underdog (Knopf, 1957)*. The western *Bitter Ground
(Knopf, 1958)*, he said, was one of his "most human" novels, though a
disappointment in sales. To this day, none of the books on Burnett's

short list have been reprinted while *Little Caesar* goes on and on and on.

According to Burnett, "The criminal ... is undoubtedly a great menace to society, but he is at a least an unstandardized male in an over standardized civilization and, as such, interesting."

Few books have received the success of *Little Caesar*, but well before it's publication Burnett put notoriety aside and went back to work, beginning a decade of hits both within and outside the category of crime fiction: *Iron Man* (Dial, 1930), *Saint Johnson* (Dial, 1930), *The Silver Eagle* (Dial, 1931), *The Giant Swing* (Harper, 1932) *Dark Hazard* (Harper, 1933) and *Goodbye To The Past*. Then skip ahead to *High Sierra* (Knopf, 1940). This is one of the most sustained and substantial stretches of work by any American writer.

□ □ □

As is so often the case, we know little about Burnett's early years, though certainly he was surrounded by a prominent Midwestern family. He was born November 25, 1899, in Springfield, Ohio, the family's first grandchild of his generation. The family member he was closest to was his grandfather, the first William Riley Burnett, a Civil War veteran and former mayor of Springfield. As a young boy, Burnett Jr. loved to hear his grandfather's stories. He would draw pictures and talk about becoming an author.

After the publication of *Little Caesar*, the *Springfield News-Sun* looked back into the past and quoted the young writer. "'Grandfather,' he would say, as he settled himself comfortably on his grandfather's knee, 'sometime I am going to write stories. Some day I am going to write stories for a book ... and some day, I'll write about you.'"

At the age of 13 he wrote a short story that won a contest in a Montgomery, Ohio newspaper.

Between 1916 and 1917 Burnett attended the West Point accredited Miami Military Institute in Germantown, Ohio. After graduation he spent a year as a student at Ohio State, where he took journalism classes. His interests included boxing, vaudeville and jazz musicianship.

Burnett's goal had been an appointment to West Point, though after his years at the Miami Institute he was ready to walk away from the severity of the system's discipline. According to Burnett: "It was rough, really rough, but it was alleviated for me by sports, which is about all I thought about then." Primarily, it was football. He played four years as a blocking halfback in prep school and one year on Ohio State's freshman team.

At five feet, eleven inches, Burnett was under-sized for football. Math classes were another challenge. He quit college after a year. On July 6, 1920 Bill married Marjorie Louise Bartow, an Ohio native and friend from high school who was working as a clerk with the civil service. As a married man he stayed in at night and read. The world of books and words became a great love.

Burnett had a succession of day jobs, working as a mechanic's helper and as a clerk in the chain department of the Jiffy Manufacturing Company, which produced mining equipment. After three years at Jiffy he went to work for his father in a business insuring livestock. That lasted for about a year. Then a bank failed and both the Burnett men were out of work. Later his father helped Bill obtain work as a statistician in the Ohio Department of Industrial Relations. He worked there four years.

Burnett began writing at night: short stories, plays and novels, composing on the typewriter. "I'd arranged my life so I didn't have to write for money," he said.

By 1927 or 1928, Burnett was sending his novels and short stories to publishers and magazines but still nothing had been published. After six years then he was passed up for a promotion that would have doubled his salary. Consequently he quit his state job and moved to Chicago for two years, where he wrote. His daytime activities included selling books as an employee of the Marshall Field's department store. He also did accounting work. More importantly, by the middle of 1929 he had completed the novels *Little Caesar* and *Iron Man* and was signed for a 4-book contract with the Dial Press. Bill and Margorie spent six weeks in New York, a first-time visit that coincided with the June publication of *Little Caesar.*

Two months later Burnett went west on a working vacation. Actually, he was on his way to Tombstone, Arizona but the heat chased him all the way to the West Coast, where he'd take a breather. He was not seeking celebrity or improvement but he remained because he liked the weather. He swam with the lifeguards and ultimately he swam in the murky industry of the Hollywood studios. For now Burnett was a name, precocious and salable.

By 1930 *Iron Man* was published. Burnett was compared to Hemingway, Ring Lardner and Sinclair Lewis. During this time the family lived at two rentals, St. Adams Place, then Nolerden Boulevard in Los Angeles. It was a multi-generational household with Bill, Marjorie, and Burnett's parents. By 1931 Burnett had purchased a home and they were living on Hillcroft Road in north Glendale, where they looked out at the rolling and cooling hills of Forest Lawn, a rather contradictory name for a cemetery, since a blade of grass is not quite a tree.

"I really bought it for my mother and father," Burnett said. "I didn't intend to stay because we thought we'd travel, my wife and I, but we stayed. And I had a place at Redondo Beach. It was all we needed for the summers." Burnett's parents would continue their residence in Glendale until their passing.

The studios had called early on, having heard he was in town. Burnett was a good employee. He could be a company man on his own terms. Hadn't he been a statistician for the state of Ohio for four years? Now his years of late-night writing were well rewarded. His ability to make peace with the commercial realities of fiction was the envy of other writers. He could do more than write novels. He could visualize action scenes that became magical when they were adapted to film. The work he did for pay gave him the opportunity to follow his own instincts when it came to his novels. He was rewarded substantially. In 1943 he would receive an Academy Award nomination for best screenplay for *Wake Island* (1943, Warner Brothers).

With the money he was making from his books and the sales to films, Burnett was also able to fund and enjoy an intensive hobby, enterprise, or sin, depending upon how one rates things. He bought into the industry of greyhound racing.

Except when the Burnetts were apartment hopping, living in Chicago and New York, there had always been dogs around but nothing like this. Burnett was an owner of racing greyhounds. In fact, at one time Burnett had kennels for eighty greyhounds, including the National Champion "War Cry," the fastest dog that had ever been timed on a quarter-mile track.

Marjorie took up the popular Hollywood pastime of pigeon racing.

□ □ □

Marriage with Marjorie continued through the 1940 census, but by February, 1942, in Burnett's WWII draft registration, he listed himself as head of household, his father as next of kin and there is no mention of a wife. Marjorie had returned to Ohio, where she remarried.

In 1943 Burnett married Whitney Forbes Johnston, who was working as a secretary at one of the studios. That same year Burnett's father would die. William Riley and Whitney would move to a new home in the exclusive Bel Air section of Los Angeles while his mother maintained her own residence in Glendale.

The couple named their new home "Longwood," though it was Tudor, and built from old brick. Burnett continued with the simple act of writing, working on a small table with his old black manual typewriter and a stack of yellow paper and an ashtray beside him. He never stopped smoking for long.

Here it must be said that both of Burnett's spouses, Marjorie and Whitney, were supportive of his whims and allowed Burnett the space and time he needed to affect his career. He was able to work at home. In every way possible those women bet on him and they lived both high and low.

Two sons were born, James Addison Burnett, in 1949 and "Butch," William Riley Burnett III, in 1950. By day, when Burnett worked at home he could see the Pacific Ocean from his desk. Habitually he worked at night, from 10 p.m. to 4 a.m. so the kids had quiet mornings.

Bill and Whitney also had two live-in housekeepers and two cars, a black Cadillac Coupe de Ville and an Alfa Romeo convertible—Whitney's car. Burnett did not drive, but Whitney drove fast, with the top down. Apparently she lost her license more than once. Her husband, however, rated her a top driver, good enough to keep up with Horace McCoy, another sporty Hollywood writer who tried to talk her into driving one of his cars in a Palm Springs road race.

The fifties were a decade of screenplays, crime and western novels and two outliers: *It's Always Four O'Clock (Random, 1956)*, a story of a three-piece jazz band and *Captain Lightfoot*, about an Irish revolutionary and outlaw. Burnett also began writing book reviews for the *Saturday Review* magazine.

The sixties, too, had begun as a promising decade.

Burnett's most recent films, *Sergeants 3* (1962) and *The Great Escape (1963)*, had been two of the most pleasant experiences he had ever had within the film industry—and both films became hits. For a period he was a prestige screenwriter and a novelist of both popular and critical success. From the beginning, as Matthew Sorrento has pointed out in his introduction to Stark House's edition of *Little Caesar*, the studios treated Burnett and his novel with uncommon respect and as a salable commodity.

*Sergeants 3* added slapstick to Burnett's own dry humor, a relief perhaps, because Burnett had always fancied himself as a comic writer, in the classical, not necessarily funny but tragic form, the summing up of a weary laugh.

Somehow—even accidentally, as Burnett described it, *Sergeants 3* was shot from Burnett's original screenplay—with no collaborators, save from a nudge from Frank Sinatra, who had the idea of placing Rudyard Kipling's epic poem "Gunga Din" in the Wild West. Everybody was just too busy making money, movies, music and personal appearances to argue over the fine points of the script. Sammy Davis Jr. would play the part of the brave Din. It was a natural. Let's Go!

This was followed by even better luck and greater accomplishment:

*The Great Escape*, a tightly contrived tale of human bonding and organization that mirrored the complexity of the plots, themes and protocols of Burnett's novels. This is all about how people bond together to accomplish their goals, although in this case it is powered by the background of World War II and wide matrix of self-sacrifice. So many people saw this film and it was so well-known that it feels like history, like a documentary instead of fiction. Among readers of a certain age *The Great Escape* will always be Burnett's best-known credit and in 1964, it won the Writers Guild of America's award for the Best Written American Drama.

Burnett was brought in particularly to work on the parts of two Americans prisoners played by James Garner and Steve McQueen. Burnett finished work on the screenplay at the end of October, 1961.

Luck was always part of his life and about a week later Burnett's luck changed. As he entered this last act there were storm clouds ... or, rather, clouds of smoke.

For Burnett the big shock, the wipe-out, came not from an earthquake but from fire. Historically California has always been the burning state, a chaparral desert that has been irrigated with enough water to support golf courses and the flammable, even exploding eucalyptus trees of Australia, shrubs and all kinds of flowers. Southern California summer fires were almost as steady, as seasonal as big waves in August, and the smoke would rain wide-spread ashes for days. During those miserable days the ice rinks would do big business with California's least-skilled skaters.

On November 6, 1961, Burnett was a victim of the Bel Air/Brentwood fire, an event that represented the largest loss of burned-out structures, 484, in Los Angeles County history, until it was passed by the 604 structures burned in the 2008 Sylmar fire almost fifty years later. At the time of this publication the Bel Air/Brentwood Fire still ranked as the third most destructive fire in Los Angeles history. Though there were no fatalities, there were 200 fire fighters injured, mostly from the cinders that rained down from the sky.

The fire chased many California celebrities from their homes, including Zsa Zsa Gabor, Dennis Hopper, Joe E. Brown, Burt Lancaster, Robert Taylor and Richard Nixon. The fire may have acquired a special taste for the writers in the neighborhood, as Aldous Huxley's home, library, books and papers were also devoured by the flames.

The Los Angeles City Fire Department even made a movie about it, *Design for Disaster* (1962). The narrator is the radio actor William Conrad, who was just finishing his ninth and final year as CBS radio's "Matt Dillon," on *Gunsmoke*.

The cause of the fire was never determined but it was not believed to have been purposely set.

For the Burnett family the fire represented a defining moment, a sharp cut between past, present and their unknown future. For Burnett there was no silver lining. It was all loss. When the fire struck, the gas in their home was still circulating and the house exploded. Whitney's Alfa Romeo was charred, flattened and flipped over by the power of the blast.

Another loss: Bill's library with seven bookcases—ten feet tall and eight feet wide and they could be lowered to the basement, if they wanted more room for a party. That represented thousands of books that went up into smoke.

It took the family two years to settle into more modest circumstances.

Aside from losing everything, what, exactly, had Burnett lost? The losses included twenty-nine copies of *Young Casanova*, a short historical novel that had been shopped around without a taker. In the weeks before the fire the manuscripts had been returned pending a new sales strategy. After the fire there may have been one remaining copy that had been sent to a producer who was then living in a mental institution. That last copy has never been found.

Another loss was the outline of a short novel titled *The Lawns Were Green*, a story about the Midwest during Burnett's childhood, about his parents and grandparents, "all carrying the blissful ignorance of the Midwest before World War One, with all its permanent dislocations and violent and bewildering changes," Burnett wrote. "It was almost an ignorant Golden Age, it seems now."

"It should be a short novel, very quietly written, carrying the atmosphere, aura and essence of that long lost time, an America almost unimaginable now, in fact entirely so to those who did not live in it. It was so provincially isolated—especially the Mid-West, that it now seems comical to me. There was war in the Balkans but nobody was quite sure where the Balkans were. Nor did they care much.

"Day followed day without alarms or excursions—it seemed boring at the time, but to this troubled, fearful, fearing generation—half expecting annihilation at any moment—it would seem like heaven.

"Crime books are expected of me and are usually successful—but I'm through with them. I've been far too preoccupied with the wrong-doing and misery of the world and want to dash back into a far more innocent time, a better time, for the American individual.

"It's high time I tried to get out in the sunlight, away from darkness and crime and wicked, unsympathetic people."

□ □ □

There were short stories that were burned, along with poetry and ... well—everything was smoke and rubble!

Some jewelry was salvaged during their flight, along with the boys' school uniforms (like their father, they attended a military school) and Burnett's Underwood typewriter, a heavy black object that would forever seem more industrial than artistic. Typing a manuscript on an Underwood was like domesticating a wild horse. And almost as noisy.

In July, 1963, Burnett made an assessment of his career before and after the fire. He had been knocked down before. Now there was total destruction on one hand ... and a former and perhaps future life of great, almost unimaginable success, both creatively and financially. Could he still catch lightning?

For the moment, he was settled. He had begun assembling a new library, an act most writers would consider both healthful and ambitious, if not inevitable.

"I've got to take stock," Burnett wrote in his journal. "I am at a definite turning point in my long career (34 years) and I haven't got much time left for mistakes—in fact I've outlived practically everybody but John O'Hara—Hemingway (1889-1961), Fitzgerald (1896-1940), Faulkner (1997-1962), Wolfe (1900-1938)—all gone. My work is not rated with theirs at the present time—but *Little Caesar* is still a live book after 34 years and *The Asphalt Jungle* (Knopf, 1949) has a good chance to survive."

Even in the dark, infrequently published days to come *Little Caesar* remained available in paperback and the title became a familiar phrase. New U. S. paperback editions of the novel were released in 1945 (Avon), 1951 (Avon), 1959 (Bantam Books),1972 (Signet), and 1986 (Carroll & Graf Publishers). In 1981 the screenplay was published and in 1996 Otto Penzler, owner of The Mysterious Bookshop and publisher of *The Armchair Detective*, produced a deluxe facsimile edition of the 1929 first edition.

In Britain paperbacks of *Little Caesar* were published by Corgi in 1957, and Hodder Paperbacks in 1968. In 1974 it was published by Kaye and Ward, and in 1984 it was reprinted by Zomba Books and by No Exit Press in 1989. Stark House published its own edition of the novel in 2023

After the fire the count of new published novels dwindled despite Burnett's efforts to remain productive. He finished the decade by publishing seven novels and producing five screenplays. You could characterize Burnett's work during the sixties as eclectic but clearly,

his pace had slowed.
The pile of unfulfilled ideas and unpublished novels would grow.

□ □ □

The seventies were the most difficult decade, a full ten years of obscurity. Always before this Burnett's writing had ensured intermittent prosperity.

Now, besides a few paperback publishers in Europe, Burnett was almost out of print. There were no more of the big hits which had lifted his career. Nor was screenwriting success supporting his career as a novelist. In the studios his generation had retired, or had been respectfully eased out the door. The family downsized. Whitney went to work as a receptionist at a local hospital. Jim Burnett was going to UCLA and working, contributing $200 a month from part-time work and sleeping on a cot. Younger brother Butch slept on the living room sofa.

Burnett's life in the thirties and the forties—life before children and family—must now have seemed almost unbelievable, like a fantastic dream. Despite frustration and depression, Burnett struggled to continue his writing, though sometimes he felt as if he had lost the "feel" for it, for the act itself. He had been so productive for so long that his readers became spoiled. Now he wrote for himself. In his journals he rewrote and revised—as if he was now daydreaming—to finished, professional standards.

What books was Burnett working on? During his period out of the public eye, Burnett had gravitated toward western settings. Since 1950, one year after the classic *The Asphalt Jungle*, six of Burnett's 20 novels had been set in the post-Civil War Southwest. Eight of them could be considered crime novels. He wrote about nineteenth century Irish revolutionaries and Caribbean intrigue in *The Widow Barony* (Macdonald, 1962), published only in Great Britain. In *Whatever Happened to Baseball*, a thin book, he published a collection of his baseball essays from *Rogue* magazine.

It was as if Burnett was writing for a new audience that was not quite ready for him, an altogether different generation that hadn't been around to whip the Axis Powers.

For the reader, if they wanted to read Burnett, they had to make the acquaintance of used bookshops. Today the films based on Burnett's stories are as ubiquitous and available as chat. More of his novels are in print today than ever before. In 2009 Stark House published the first of its Burnett reissues and for fifteen years these reissues have been a steady, optimistic endeavor. This volume presents the publisher's thirteenth and fourteenth new editions of Burnett novels.

□ □ □

The Mystery Writers of America got the ball rolling by honoring Burnett as a Grandmaster in 1980. It was not long after this that I met and interviewed him. I had insisted on including Burnett in an encyclopedia of western fiction prepared for McGraw-Hill in the late 70s, though not published until 1983. I used the announcement of Burnett's last publication, *Goodbye Chicago* (St. Martin's, 1981), as an excuse to leverage an interview with the master, who was then eighty years old.

As much as anyone, Burnett, though aged, was hiding in plain sight. He was still a working writer, alone much of the day at his condo at Marina del Rey. While we spoke his dogs were in a room upstairs and Whitney was at work. It was great to see that a guy as accomplished as Burnett could be so open and cordial. He was pleased to talk about the craft of writing as much or more than to discuss his film associations.

One of the first things I learned from Burnett was that in his opinion he was not and had never been a writer of mysteries. He wanted to make that clear. It's a tricky equilibrium, you see, these categorizations of literature. We weren't going to get bogged down in the distinctions between mystery and crime fiction, not even the distinction between fiction and literature. Burnett had seen both sides of that aisle.

I asked him which among his books he would recommend to readers and he answered quickly and authoritatively: *The Asphalt Jungle*, *Underdog*, *Goodbye to the Past*, *Adobe Walls* (Knopf, 1953), *Pale Moon* (Knopf, 1956) and *King Cole* (Harper, 1936).

I asked him about *Little Caesar*.

"*Little Caesar* I'd have to add, you know?" he said, and shrugged.

The bounce-back continued. There were few living American writers of greater stature, few writers of Burnett's generation to have a new book published at the start of their ninth decade. But Burnett was going to be one of them. That would count as a win, a triumph.

This would also be Burnett's first new novel to appear in 13 years; for me it presented an obvious lead for a magazine or newspaper. Headlines could be switched from disappearance and obscurity to a comeback story. There's always room for a comeback story and this one was sold to *Mystery*, a new magazine that included reviews of crime fiction by the fine novelist Dorothy B. Hughes.

Fifteen hundred words of our conversation, titled "A Literary Exile Comes Home," was published in September, 1981. Later it was reprinted in Italy by the publisher Mondadori.

Finally *Goodbye, Chicago* was published by St. Martin's Press.

Despite this renaissance, some observers stuck with the tried-and-true storyline of disappearance and obscurity, as if Burnett were a cloistered hermit. As late as April 11, 1982, *The Los Angeles Times* celebrated Burnett's comeback with a Ken Mate story titled:
MEMORIES, SUCCESS … AND ANONYMITY:
"As an artistic endeavor, I never took the movies seriously," Burnett admitted.

Two weeks later, April 25, 1982, the author died.
Private grief became public sorrow with a subtle monument that read:
William Riley Burnett II
1899 "Author" 1982
Our dear, sweet Bill
Beloved husband and father

Your precious talents
memories, and love make
our lives forever rich

□ □ □

As we have noted, death did not end the recognition of Burnett's gifts. If you remember the references to piles of unpublished manuscripts there is at least a small pile that remains. Since 1982, through multiple moves, Burnett's son James protected the last two decades of his father's words.
Despite the variety within these unpublished stories, these manuscripts demonstrate purpose more than a flailing about for the marketplace. There is a novel set during the Viet Nam War, another was the story of a pilot who sees a UFO, written with a new pseudonym, James Vance Colwell. As should be expected, this story was more about the people than the technology. There is *The World Is Square*, a story about the relationships among those who perform with a swing band broadcasting on the radio. This one would have been published with the James Updyke pseudonym Burnett had used for *It's Always Four O'Clock* (reprinted by Stark House in 2009).
There are other titles which sound almost irresistible: *Man With A Thousand Enemies, Cafe Nowhere, Children of the Age, The Cabana Crowd* and others.
After *Goodbye, Chicago, The Loop,* came close enough to publication that it was included in at least one bibliography of the writer. This novel, a last Chicago gangster story, offered yet another perspective on

the business of criminality and it included several memorable characters, maybe enough to make this Burnett's last great novel, still unpublished.

Another intriguing manuscript is *Babylon, U.S.A.,* a series of vignettes with fifty-six named characters. Burnett described it as a: "Story Cycle of One Night in the Life of a Great American City From 6:30 P.M. To 6:30 A. M." It contains a rather languorous plot, establishing a mood that Burnett later felt he had difficulty moving away from. This is both the oldest and most recent among Burnett's unpublished manuscripts, since he worked on it both after the fire and then twenty years later under a new title, *City People.* It is not unlike the themes of the city-scape style of books published during the 1920s, with fictional vignettes as in Ben Hecht's *1001 Afternoons in Chicago* (Covici-McGee, 1922) and Don Ryan's *Angels Flight* (Boni and Liveright, 1927), set in Los Angeles.

After this effort Burnett was concerned that his writing had been thrown off course, like he was becoming a reporter or documentarian, rather than a prime mover and choreographer of characters.

Among these novels were also the original manuscripts for *Round the Clock at Volari's* (Gold Medal, 1961) and *Night Without Morning* (published as *The Cool Man,* Gold Medal, 1968). They were published in the sixties ... sort of, and right there, that's our story here.

□ □ □

The greater appreciation of Burnett today, both within and outside the category of crime fiction, offers us a unique opportunity to appreciate his lesser-known work.

*Night Without Morning* and *Around The Clock At Volari's* are a read into uncharted territory, the first true publication of these later works. Somewhere on another Earth these could have appeared in their present form sixty years ago. On this particular Earth, the one we live on, both of these books were scalped.

It's about time, way overdue, in fact, to consider these novels as they were intended. This is a redo and a repair not just for Burnett but for the whole idea of American literature.

In this particular case, Fawcett published these as part of their esteemed Gold Medal series, the third and fourth Burnett novels to be published by the company, which had become financially competitive with the hardback publishers. Unfortunately, these two novels also represent significant stops in Burnett's fall from literary grace. They hit the paperback racks with a dull thud and were infrequently reviewed.

Burnett could adapt to a changing marketplace but he declined to re-write, so the publishers hired others to prepare these novels for their paperback debut. Like the volumes of Gallimard's Series Noir in France, these novels were each cut to fit a tight, standard format and page length.

Both of these novels are also examinations of luck and coincidence. Though these are both crime novels, there is no "hail of bullets" in either manuscript, just a modest four shots in *Night Without Morning*, all finding their mark. These were Burnett's attempts to write a different kind of crime novel.

□  □  □

In *Night Without Morning*, Burnett's protagonist, Willie Maddon, was modeled upon the bank robber Willie Sutton. Sutton was one of the best-known bank robbers in history, taking in between one and two million during his career in the nineteen twenties and thirties, approximately seven million dollars in today's cash. Sutton was known for disguises and his escapes from captivity. He is said to have never entered a bank with a loaded gun. Sutton also co-wrote two autobiographical volumes.

Burnett's Maddon is also a peculiar kind of writer, enraptured by the power of words on paper. He writes messages to himself, questions he is pondering and decisions to be made. After committing these messages to paper, he destroys them with a cigarette lighter. Words, paper and fire; Burnett was still shifting through the consequences of that combination, also referring to small, incidental brushfires in the background of one of his scenes.

In Burnett's original manuscript this peculiar habit—the notes and the burning—is explained. In Fawcett's version, *The Cool Man*, not so much.

In Burnett's *original* manuscript Willie Maddon writes:

"Well, I've had a long run of good luck. Sometimes it runs in cycles. So does bad. Don't ask me why, but any crapshooter or horse player will back me up."

In *The Cool Man* the revision reads:

"You've had a long run. Don't call it luck. Luck can turn. Five years can't be luck. And if you've figured everything right for five years, you can do it for five more. Keep cool."

What next? It sounds like a disagreement. In Fawcett's version of the novel the reader is confronted by both of these incompatible aphorisms. This is almost an argument. In *The Cool Man* these thoughts are too contradictory to hold both ideas in the mind at the same time.

One is that of a "wise" gambler, the second a fool who believes he has supernatural control over chance and circumstance. Can both of these contrary messages come from the same character, the same story, the same book? It does not take much, just a handful of small words to confound. They are not the same observations and the flow is jarring, like hearing two voices when you expect to hear one. As far as the music goes, there's discord. The *Cool Man* becomes more difficult by including both these contrary statements.

So the reader has to make a choice. You've got to pick one of them. Does an individual's skill and instincts protect them from the flip of a coin, or is chance the captain of his fate? Is bad luck inevitable? Does loss come to all gamblers? More broadly, are we all subject to the big fortune cookies of circumstance or can we avoid a downturn by personal skill? Different philosophies, really. Can we always assume that a conclusion will be derived from reason?

To put it simply, one of these thoughts came from the pen of W.R. Burnett and the other did not. The second is counterfeit, a forgery conspired by a publisher that was, naturally, looking out for its own interests.

In *Night Without Morning* Burnett finishes one of his most unusual, his most disturbing novels with a big shrug, an expansion of his life-long tolerance and understanding for life as it is.

It's sweeter and a more memorable "shot" than the Fawcett cut. It seems the film-writing experiences gave Burnett more than a pot of money. This time with just the words, no pictures, it also helped him craft a more memorable, a more "cinematic" novel.

□ □ □

There is more suspense than action in *Round The Clock At Volari's*. Despite thrilling, disturbing scenes, not a single shot is fired.

In *Volari's* Burnett's main character is Jim Chase, who seems to be an attorney/private investigator who unravels an existential mystery while at the same time taking the role of a spectator, sitting on a bench, watching until it is almost too late to make choices.

Jim dreams of crazy puzzles, with pieces that won't fit; he drives to clandestine meetings and camps in a drugstore phone booth waiting for a call.

Crime novels are usually told from the point of view of a doer, not a casual victim or a bystander. But in this novel characters are like suspects who can't resist telling tall tales about their brushes against celebrities.

There is also one of those unnecessary mistakes that are like clotheslining a reader. Earlier in the Fawcett version of the novel, protagonist Jim Chase explains how he travels, for the most part, by taxi.

In the closing pages Jim leaves a meeting, walks out looking for a taxi, then finds himself beside his personal car. He opens the door and drives off as a solitary driver, watching the road instead of musing over the city's shadows.

It's not necessarily a big thing, the difference between a driver and a passenger, more like editorial inattention than a conscious mistake to change Jim's inclination. Nevertheless it makes for a loss of continuity, a slightly different scene and a different mood.

In *Volari's*—originally titled *Suburbanola*—the trim and revision was done with tonsorial skill by Robert Silverberg, a fast and versatile young writer with a lot of upside ahead in his career. Silverberg was a client of the Scott Meredith Literary Agency and Meredith had frequently called upon him to do repair work on manuscripts when writers were suffering through deadline-defying writer's blocks or they had died, leaving their books unfinished. In the fall of 1960 Silverberg was asked to prepare *Round The Clock at Volari's* for publication. In December of that year he was paid $1,000 for his services, an unusually high price for the effort. Silverberg did not consider this a job of rewriting, rather more along the lines of functioning as editor, rearranging scenes and deleting redundancy. "My recollection is that I received a large box containing a very disheveled manuscript and it required a lot of work," he said.

In March of 1962, Silverberg was also asked to work on the Burnett's novel, *The Winning of Mickey Free* (Bantam, 1965), which may have been an unfinished version of a much longer novel with pages that may have been lost. On this occasion Silverberg added 5,000 words, including the last chapter.

In *Volari's*, Silverberg tightened up some of the wording (though tightening up Burnett is a little like taking coals to Newcastle). He sexed it up a little and made it tougher. He removed some of the narrative confusion, adding scenes that were only referred to in the original and scenes that were almost entirely exposition, as when a ringleader announces: "Now here's what we're going do!"—a scene not included in this version.

As Burnett had once written from the point of view of those at the top—from the forces of law and detection to the Chicago gangsters themselves—in *Round the Clock at Volari's* he was now telling his story from the perspective of those at the bottom of the pyramid, those whose lives were affected by the actions and fortunes of the more powerful.

Crime novels are usually told from the point of view of a doer, not a casual victim or a bystander. But in this novel, the second-tier witnesses tell their tall tales about their brushes against criminous celebrities and a corrupt city government.

The perspective is like that of ocean swimmers who are too close to the surface of the water to see details around them, their eyes just far enough above the water to see a splash but not its cause. It is a ground-level perception, as if pawns were trying to intuit their King and Queen's next moves. It is a novel built almost entirely from characters and their reactions to events, and it is probably as close to a mystery story as Burnett would ever come.

□ □ □

There's a lot of sadness and a struggle to survive in both these novels. The grand days are in the past, the big times are over. Money that once flowed uncounted has dwindled or vanished completely. The characters, the "wheels" of yesterday are cautious and insecure, just holding on or considering their escape. Burnett does keep us guessing— he keeps these characters on a slow boil and continues to define them until his last sentences.

Sixty years ago when these novels first appeared they were imposters. Now they are Burnett. Published or not published, revised or rewritten, even in disguise, Burnett never lost his skills. Now it is a pleasure to return to his words and stories. Burnett could really wrap a sentence around an idea. Unlike their first go-round, these resurrected and restored novels bring all the pieces of the earlier bastardized versions to a coherent, unified end, finally drawing the distinction between villains, victims, and scuffed-up anti-heroes.

—August, 2024

.........................................................................................

**David Laurence Wilson** has written for many magazines and newspapers and has written about crime and noir fiction for nearly 50 years, including introductions for Stark House editions of W. R. Burnett, A. S. Fleischman, Gil Brewer, Arnold Hano, Day Keene, Wade Miller, William R. Cox and Harry Whittington. He has also been preparing a history of American stuntmen and daredevils. He lives in Portland, Oregon.

# Night Without Morning
····································
## W. R. BURNETT

In 1968 a shortened version of this novel was published by
Fawcett-Gold Medal Books as THE COOL MAN.

# ONE

For a long time now Willie Madden had been hunted like a wild animal, with a huge national spread in the press. But nearly five years had passed since the first great hue and cry, and now he felt himself to be reasonably secure.

There was an odd thing about Willie that had puzzled him since the time of his adolescence—an almost overpowering desire for self-expression. As a boy it had taken the form of almost meaningless lying. As a high school student it had, in a sense, been channeled into writing—and Willie had become well-known as a purveyor of humorous quips, skits, and bits for the school paper. During young manhood it had been in abeyance, owing to an awakening interest in sex and a two-year stint in the Army of the Republic, European Theatre.

Now, at nearly forty-five, at times this desire for self-expression seemed to be festering, and almost against his will Willie found himself writing down his impressions of his environment, scraps of remembered dialogue, and worst of all letters to himself, beginning: *Dear Joker*. All these meaningless and completely useless effusions were scrupulously burned almost immediately after writing.

"Me," Willie would often tell himself, after reading his scrawls, "I am some kind of nut."

He would write:

> *Big guy at filling station. Pushes his belly along like it was not part of him. Much pious talk, but can't keep his eyes off the high school girls. Some dark night—look out!*

Or:

> *Blond woman—cashier, at the Inn. Told me she was a widow second time I talked to her. Wide open for business. Too wide open. hysterical type. Don't like look in eyes. Trouble.*

Or:

> *Mrs. T., Hotel manager's wife. Cheating, you can bet. I know that look. But you couldn't make him believe it if you took an affidavit.*

*A real idiot.*

Why? Why? Why did he write these things?

Or:

*Four thousand dollar car—piece of junk. Everything
junk now—like the furniture and gadgets in my hotel
room—put together with spit, plastic and God help us.
Might outlast all of us at that. When the Big Explosion
may come at any time, why build for the Future?*

Yes, there were times when Willie had the uneasy feeling that he
was some kind of nut, but nobody who had ever known him well would
have agreed with that. Many had disliked Willie, including his two
brothers. Some had hated him, including a girl he'd married and
abandoned at the age of nineteen; and there were men in both the
police force and the underworld who would take an unholy pleasure in
seeing him stretched out on a slab in his last long sleep. And so far as
is known nobody had ever really loved Willie except perhaps his mother
and even that was conjectural.

But to all of them, high and low, Willie had seemed almost
supernaturally bright and sharp and even highly intelligent in a
philosophic sense. And they had all found something else very unusual
about Willie. His brother, Bernard, phrased it: "Willie is without ordinary
sentiment." Detective Lieutenant Art Kramer spoke of Willie as a cold
fish. His mother was astonished that Willie had not cried a tear since
babyhood, and seemed almost immune to pain and punishment. Carl
Benedict, a criminal acquaintance, once stated: "Willie's mind would
click on like clockwork, even if some bastard was shooting at him."

All this seemed to boil down to the fact that Willie was almost
invariably in control of his emotions and unlike most men and women
did not allow them to hamstring him and make him vulnerable to the
common dangers of life.

This odd trait alone may have caused much of the resentment against
Willie, who had been resented, and even feared, by those close to him—
relatives, police, criminals, business associates—since he was large
enough to make his presence felt.

The fear that he inspired was not physical. Willie was below medium
height and he had always been slender and so narrow in the hips that
his pants were always slipping down. At nearly forty-five he weighed
only a hundred and fifty odd pounds, and his belly was as flat as it had
been when he was in high school. The fear was inspired by a quality.

Willie was no ordinary man and it was apparent even to the dullest. His clear, cold blue eyes seemed to take in everything at once. The fear was largely the fear of ridicule.

Willie was at his meaningless writing again:

> *Church bells woke me. Lots of churches here. Bells*
> *sound good. Reminds me of brothers, going to Mass.*
> *Mom in black dress. Do they really believe? If*
> *so, what children! Can't they look around them?*
> *If the Big Man they talk about is running things,*
> *we need a change of management.*

Or:

> *Old girls on the beach, eye the beach boys and even*
> *each other. Husbands listening to baseball broad-*
> *cast on radio. With women its sex, sex, sex. With*
> *men sport, sport, sport. Makes me laugh.*

Willie was staying at the Pearl of the Orient, a brand new, large and elaborate motor hotel at Tropico Beach, in Southern California. He had a bachelor suite on the second floor of the main building, for which he paid twenty-five dollars a day, cheap, in Willie's opinion, considering some of the prices he'd paid in Miami Beach.

Of course he could have lived much more cheaply but that was not and had never been one of his intentions. Willie had always wanted the best, even as a boy, outraging his careless, insolvent dockworker father, and then later his small businessman brothers. In fact Willie, at the age of about forty, had managed, with the help of six others, to steal a little over a million dollars, so that he could go first cabin and thumb his nose at the sacrifices, hardships and humiliations of the past. Now he was living it up, and had been for nearly five years.

At Tropico he was known as James Shannon, retired, from Chicago—a small, rather dapper black-haired blue-eyed man in expensive and fashionable sports clothes.

From his windows he could see the inner harbor, where the small sailboats and cabin cruisers were moored; and beyond them, over the housetops of the further shore, a faint line of green, from which glanced dazzling diamond points of light on the sea-horizon. It was a bright, hot summer day, and Willie felt lazy.

After writing:

*The Pacific looks different from the Atlantic and smells*
*different. Why? Anyway, they can have them both.*
*I like dry land. Water is for fish. The air, for birds.*

and burning it, Willie changed into shorts, pulled an expensive Italian sweater over his head and went out for a stroll. Since World War II he hadn't been on a boat or in a plane, and had no intention of going on either again. Willie just did not give one good goddamn what other people did or thought. He was next to impossible to influence, persuade or sell. But on the other hand he had no desire whatever to con others into his own way of life.

It was another trait—solitariness—that had caused Willie always to be resented. Even the famous Gimp, Johnny Quait—a loner, if there ever was one—had resented Willie's own loner instincts, which had amused Willie to the point of hilarity.

At the hotel beach there was a big blond young lifeguard and beach boy whose life was a misery to him because of the aggressions of middle-aged lady guests. His name was Waldo—(it figures, Willie had written) and he was bashful and shy to an almost pathological degree. Willie found unwilling Waldo and his potential harem very amusing, and often watched the antics at the beach for hours at a time. The old girls tried everything: from lavish tipping to insistent and frivolous demands for service—and here would come Waldo, his big face boiled red, staggering under backrests, beach umbrellas, beach tables, towels and other paraphernalia, to be greeted by seductive smiles and unambiguous glances.

As a rule Waldo seemed uncomfortable when Willie talked to him and got away as soon as possible. But today there was something new in his manner and Willie detected it at once. Waldo was almost slavishly friendly.

"How's Chicago?" he asked.

"Chicago?" said Willie, eyeing him.

"Yes sir. Mr. Turley says you're from Chicago."

"Haven't been back in some time," said Willie. "I'm retired, following the sun."

"Good deal," said Waldo, "a very good deal. Wish I could afford it."

Willie thought he detected a look of forced shrewdness in Waldo's round blue eyes, as if Waldo was consciously playing a part of some kind.

"You'll never be able to afford it, working at a job like this," said Willie. "That is, unless you tie in with one of the old girls."

Waldo stared in surprise, then seemed to wince. "That's getting it the hard way," he said.

"Maybe," said Willie, calm, reassuring, but studying Waldo from under his lashes. There was something about this he didn't quite like—he felt warning signal buzzing faintly at his nerve ends. "Yes, maybe. But there are harder ways."

Women began to wave to Waldo, to beckon and call to him. He got grudgingly to his big bare feet.

"Excuse me, Mr. Shannon," said Waldo, shifting about uneasily and averting his eyes, "but could I see you after work—say, around six?"

"If it's a touch the answer is no," said Willie, smiling. Trying to get money out of Willie was like trying to get blood out of a stone. Many experts had been foiled. Willie was a freehanded spender when it came to his own wishes, appetites and desires—but as far as others were concerned ... no!

"Well, it's more than that, sir," said Waldo. "I think you might be interested."

Willie laughed, but his mind was clicking on like clockwork. Blackmail! What else? But what could this sorry oaf know?

"All right," said Willie. "I'm going no place tonight. Come up to my room at six."

"Yes, sir. Thank you, sir," said Waldo, like a befuddled school boy, then he gestured rather awkwardly to one of the demanding ladies on the beach, and left.

Willie stayed for a while longer then strolled leisurely back to his room, where he put his clothes in an order that would allow him to pack in a hurry if necessary. Willie was not one to be caught out on a limb, and a stupid young oaf like Waldo might spell trouble just through his ineptitude.

He wrote:

> *A feeling. A hunch. What could it be? But I smell Old*
> *Man Trouble.*

Later, he went down to the little beach town and made many small purchases in various stores, cashing in most of his traveler's checks and putting the change away in his wallet. He held out only enough checks to pay his hotel bill. There was a possibility that he might have to rule out the name James Shannon suddenly and permanently.

He'd made plans for the evening to spend several hours at a small motel a couple of miles down the beach road with one of the girls from the Chez Paree restaurant, but that was no great matter, and would be cancelled or not, as things fell out and he saw fit.

He wrote:

*Well, I've had a long run of good luck. Sometimes
it runs in cycles. So does bad. Don't ask me
why, but any crapshooter or horse player will
back me up. Once a priest cuffed me for saying
as much. He had a hard hand.*

Waldo, in sweatshirt and tight cotton pants, came sliding into Willie's
suite with a sideways movement reminiscent of a beach crab. The
blond stubble on his head looked almost pure white in contrast with
his peeling, sun-boiled red face, and his blue eyes were bloodshot and
squinting. Waldo just did not thrive in the sun.

Though it was well after six o'clock broad daylight still lay spread
out over Tropico Beach. Willie's windows were wide open to the world,
a luxury he couldn't have afforded in the old days, and his curtains
were blowing in a brisk salty sea-breeze. All seemed a picture of peace
and plenty on the Willie front.

Was Waldo the serpent, Willie wondered!

Waldo was carrying something in a large flat manila envelope.

"What's that?" asked Willie.

Waldo flushed and squirmed, then seemed to hesitate, as if he'd had
a second thought about the matter and had decided to back out. Willie
noted this and quickly closed the door. Whatever it was, Willie wanted
it over and done with. There was far too much hanging over his head
as it was.

"You understand, Mr. Shannon," said Willie, "it's only an … well, I
guess it's pretty silly, really. Crazy, I mean. Not crazy like the fellows
say. But … maybe stupid."

Willie regarded him coldly with his blue eyes and Waldo seemed to
shrink almost to Willie's size (he outweighed Willie by nearly seventy
pounds) and then to cough nervously.

"Come on, Waldo," said Willie peremptorily.

And Waldo almost automatically obeyed. He took a gaudy-looking
crime magazine from the envelope and showed it to Willie.

"It's in here. Page ten," said Waldo, offering the magazine to Willie.

Willie masked his surprise and then took the magazine from Waldo
and turned to the dog-eared page. The first thing he saw was a young
picture of himself, staring straight into the camera. The face was leaner
than now but the eyes were unmistakable, at least to Willie. Yet he did
not show a quiver of anything and in a moment looked up at Waldo
blankly.

"What is this, a joke? Or what?" he asked.

Waldo squirmed and looked as if he might dive under the sofa to
hide.

"I told you it was pretty silly, Mr. Shannon."

Willie still continued to look at Waldo blankly.

"What is it?"

"The picture—the criminal, Madden," stammered Waldo. "I thought
… well, don't you think he looks like you, Mr. Shannon?"

Willie held the magazine off and put his head to one side to study it.
After a moment he said: "Yes, maybe he does. Looks smaller. Face more
narrow. Hair doesn't seem to be black, like mine. But … yes. There's a
resemblance."

Waldo took the magazine back hastily. "Well, that's all, Mr. Shannon.
Just thought you'd like to see …" He moved crabwise for the door,
completely fooled and overawed by Willie, who had fooled and overawed
far smarter men than Waldo.

"Seems to me, Waldo," said Willie, "you went to a lot of trouble just to
come up here and show me a picture in a magazine. Seems to me you
had something else in mind, from your tone down on the beach."

"Oh no, sir," said Waldo, hastily.

"Waldo," said Willie, "if I was a different kind of man I'd go to Mr.
Turley about this. But I don't like to cause people trouble, so we'll just
forget it. But, Waldo, let me tell you something. I lived for a long time
in Chicago. We have a lot of criminals there and I used to know several
crime reporters who covered the crime beat. Waldo, all I can say is,
that it's a good thing for you I'm *not* that man…uh, Madden—whatever
his name is. Do you know why?"

"Why, sir?" stammered Waldo.

"Because," said Willie, "if I was him, tomorrow morning you'd wake
up dead."

Waldo's big red face went white.

"But, Mr. Shannon, I didn't …"

"Blackmail, Waldo," said Willie, "is a tough proposition, even for
experts. "Don't ever try it again."

Waldo swallowed hard. Willie stood looking at him.

"Mr. Shannon," said Waldo, finally, "I hope you won't say anything to
Mr. Turley. Please, I've got a fine job here. I'm not getting rich, but
there are the tips and I'm saving up for my degree …"

"Your what?" exclaimed Willie, taken by surprise for once.

"In Phys. Ed.," Waldo explained. "Physical education. I go to college
all winter. I hope to be a coach."

"Well, coach," said Willie, "stick to your job and don't try to stray and
poach."

"You won't say anything, sir?"

"I said I wouldn't."

"Thank you. I told you it was silly. I almost left without saying a word. You see, there's a waiting list for these jobs on account of the tipping. I was one of the lucky ones."

"Well remember that, Waldo, and stay lucky," said Willie.

Finally, with a huge sigh of relief, Waldo vanished crabwise through the door, his face still pale.

Although Willie looked calm enough, even after the door had closed on Waldo and he was alone, he was seething inwardly. He tried to calm himself; he talked good sense to himself in a monotone, but finally hesitations broke loose and he began to rage up and down the room, a desire for violence, for reprisal, tearing at him. For a long time, while the rage was on him, he gloated over the idea of sending the editor of that so-called magazine a time bomb through the mail. Digging it all up again—for what? Just to get a lousy two-bits out of a few thousand tame suckers!

Finally he managed to rein in his emotions and get control, then he sat down to write himself a letter:

> *Dear Joker:*
> *Keep your head. This is nothing. You've had it*
> *soft too long. You're getting slack. This was a*
> *good reminder. Nothing has happened. Nothing will*
> *happen, if you don't blow your stack.*
>
> *To hell with the editor. It's done now. If a*
> *bomb would have stopped it, fine. But why a bomb*
> *now? Stupid. Stupid.*

And at long last Willie finally recovered his equanimity. He'd stay on for another week, and then retreat in good order and put the name, James Shannon, into mothballs. He was pretty sure that Waldo would cause him no further trouble.

## TWO

And he kept his motel date.

Adele, from the Chez Paree, was a large, plump, pale brunette, a little on the languid side, but very pretty, and responsive enough when finally aroused, and Willie spent a pleasant hour and a half, "running the gamut", as he put it.

It was a game he never tired of year by year, but when it had been played he had less interest in the girl—till next time—than in a chair.

While she dressed, Adele began to tell Willie about her two-year-old daughter. Willie didn't even listen. She turned to look at him.

"Don't you have any children?"

"No," said Willie.

"You're married, of course."

"Why 'of course?'"

"They're always married."

"Are they?"

"I mean, it's convenient for them—an arrangement like this. Variety. Single guys can pick and choose; they've got time. Married men, no."

"Very interesting," said Willie, wishing she'd get the hell back to the Chez Paree.

"Vera told me you were an odd one," said Adele, thoughtfully.

"You mean I'm some kind of nut?" Willie demanded.

Adele broke out into giggles, her large still-unrestrained breasts bouncing.

"No, of course not," she said. "Sort of a loner. Vera likes you. I think she's a little put out with me. But it's not my fault."

Willie made no comment. Adele pulled on her dress, then turned her back and said coquettishly: "Zip me, honey."

Willie zipped her, then handed her an envelope. Adele hesitated, then, flushing slightly, turned her back to see if it contained what she'd been promised. Willie was not offended. It was a rough world for girls like Adele and Vera and all the rest; a few short years of reasonable prosperity; and then what … a hash house?

Suddenly Adele turned, flung her arms around him and tried to kiss him. Willie evaded her, and eased her off.

"Why, it's twice what you said," cried Adele.

"You were worth it."

"I'll bet Vera didn't get this much," said Adele.

But Willie made no comment. It was like tipping. Big tip, good service. Normal tip, fair service. Small tip, resentment. Generosity had nothing to do with it. Willie still had a week to go and he'd made up his mind to have another bout with Adele before he left. Elementary!

"Honey," said Adele, at the door, "you call me, anytime, hear? It's a pleasure to meet a gentleman like you."

Willie gestured vaguely and shut the door after her; then, feeling a little sad, a little empty, a little depressed, as he always did after such bouts, he took a long shower, dressed leisurely and strolled back toward the Pearl of the Orient. He liked to walk at night, when he felt safe from attack. In fact Willie loved the night, but was in two minds about the daytime.

It was a night of stars. The sky was swept completely clear of clouds, except for a big bank at the sea-horizon, and the stars winked and vibrated as if agitated by some immense universal force. A cool salty breeze was blowing in from the inner harbor, rustling the tops of the tall Royal palms along the roadway.

Tropico had been a good place. Willie had been happy there. But Willie was a drifter by nature and could move on to other stamping grounds without regrets. Good food, good accommodations, good service could be found everywhere—and the country was full of Adeles and Veras—you could hardly tell one from another after a while. All you needed was money; and Willie had plenty of it, nearly half a million dollars.

# THREE

Back in his suite at the Pearl of the Orient, Willie turned on the TV set and languidly watched a few reels of the Late Show, but little by little he lost interest and began to read the evening paper, which he had neglected except for the sports section. But the miseries of the world did not hold his attention for long, and in a moment he began thinking about the magazine Waldo had brought to his attention, with the scarehead: *MILLION DOLLAR ROBBERY.*

It seemed like ages ago in another world. Leon Bellini dead, shot down by the police, in a running gun battle; Rick Novak dead, from a terrible three-story fall, in the same ruckus; and Willie holding their money for them, which they'd never come to claim, of course, although their relatives were still eagerly hoping that Willie would send them the shares. Fat chance!

Orley Peters, Joe Ricks, and wild Fallon O'Keefe, all in prison—their shares confiscated and returned to the Kenmore Trust making the insurance adjustors very happy.

Carl Benedict? He had escaped with his share of the money, but the police in Willie's hometown had claimed that a body fished out of the river two months later was his. But how could anyone really tell? The police only *hoped* it was Carl Benedict! Carl's share of the money? Nowhere!

And as for Johnny Quait, who had helped Willie manage the operation—well, Johnny had never expected a share but had taken his slice out of the front money, content with that. Johnny had not wanted to be too prominent in the business, realizing the repercussions would be terrible. The Gimp had a reputation to keep up with the police and a license to protect. Old Johnny, the private investigator!

According to the papers you would think that the robbery had been a huge, an unparalleled success, but actually the whole operation had been bungled from the first. And look at the score. Two dead, three in prison; one supposedly dead; and three sevenths of the money recovered.

The police had done well with a difficult case, but they were still smarting from the excoriating they'd received in the press. The fact that Willie Madden had got off scot-free with nearly half a million dollars, or so it was said, was the bone that stuck in everybody's throat. Willie Madden, of all people!—a man with a noncriminal record, except for a stretch in a correctional youth camp at the age of sixteen: a soldier with an honorable discharge, although there'd been some hanky-panky with company funds, finally written off to youthful exuberance; a private investigator for the famous detective, John Q. Quait; a former investigator for the District Attorney's Office; and finally a trusted security officer for the Kenmore Trust.

"He was laying back all along," Detective Lieutenant Art Kramer had told a police reporter. "Can you imagine it? All those years, he was laying back, waiting to pull the big one. Brains, brains. But what a cunning little bastard. Even after the robbery we didn't suspect him for a long time. He disappeared, see, and we thought maybe he'd been kidnapped by the strongarm guys and killed. And even now, he hasn't been named. Those three poor slobs that went to the clink wouldn't name him. He got away clear."

"Amazing!" the reporter had said.

Yes, amazing!

It was very late, nearly two a.m., but Willie sat down to write himself a letter.

> *Dear Joker:*
> *Let's be clear. John Quaint is still alive*
> *and kicking and would kill you for the money if*
> *he could find you and it and a dark empty place—*
> *so he wouldn't lose his license.*
> *Carl Benedict is alive, I'm sure. And if I*
> *know Carl he's been taken for his roll by women*
> *and gambling and big living some place and*
> *would gladly kill you for yours if he could*
> *find you.*
> *So?*
> *They didn't find you. Simple.*
> *But if they do?*
> *It's you or them.*
> *Be clear about it, joker. These things have to be done.*

He burned the letter in an ashtray and then finally got to bed and slept heavily till nearly noon.

# FOUR

The time had come to leave. It was early for the Pearl of the Orient— eight a.m.—and as there was no activity at the private beach at this hour, Waldo, himself, showed up to help Willie with his bags. Willie gave him a ten-dollar tip.

"Get yourself some more magazines," he said.

Waldo was so delighted by this unexpected windfall that he got his big hand on Willie's shoulder. Willie did not like this, but succeeded in masking his desire to shrug it off, and smiled. Willie did not now, and never had, liked easy familiarity. But he wanted to leave a grateful Waldo behind him.

While Waldo packed the bags into the trunk of the car, Willie strolled over to the office to settle up his final bill.

The manager was not around, but his wife was behind the counter. She was wearing a thin, low-cut, summery dress, and automatically leaned forward, in order to display to Willie her chief claim to fame. Willie surveyed the display stoically.

"Sorry you're leaving, Mr. Shannon," she said. "We were hoping you'd stay all summer. Forwarding address?"

"I've got a reservation at the Fairmont, in San Francisco," said Willie, "but since I may only stay there a day or so I'll send you a wire when I find out where I'm going to be for the next month."

"You do that," said the manager's wife. "And please come back. It's a pleasure to serve men like you, Mr. Shannon."

Willie bowed slightly.

Later she even came out of the office and stood with Waldo to watch him drive off. The manager, Mr. Turley, appeared from behind the office and waved hastily to Willie, who waved back.

These three people, Waldo, and Mr. and Mrs. Hurley, were privileged beyond all others: they were watching an unusually strange phenomenon. A man, a human being, was vanishing right in front of their eyes. "James Shannon" was no more. He would never be seen or heard from again.

# FIVE

It was a little after ten p.m. and Waldo had finally finished his chores and was sitting out in front of his little cabin, just beyond the cabanas of the swimming pool, resting his feet, and from time to time stretching luxuriously. His little radio, turned way down so as to not disturb any of the guests, whispered sweet music at his elbow. In spite of everything, life was good. Yes, life was good, and could get better. He was making connections. Mr. Turley liked and trusted him, and Mr. Turley was a big man all over Tropico Beach.

Life probably never would get quite as good for him as it was for Mr. Shannon, for instance; no Cadillacs, no twenty-five-dollars-a-day suites; no expensive girls from Chez Paree (oh, Waldo had heard about that!) at a hundred dollars an hour. But then … such things weren't really Waldo's idea of the good life anyway. Waldo wanted a job as a high school baseball or football coach, for a starter, and a nice big trailer to live in—his own boss, with no giggling, demanding, frightening girls messing up the premises.

But he kept thinking more about Mr. Shannon than he did about his own plans for the future and pretty soon he got out the crime magazine and began to study it, under the dim outside eave's light, for the hundredth time while the radio whispered *Moon River* to him.

"Trying to ruin your eyes?" somebody demanded from the darkness, and Waldo gave a wild jump.

"Jake! You scared me," cried Waldo, accusingly.

Jake, a former Los Angeles police officer, long retired, was the night security man at the Pearl of the Orient. He was sixty-five and portly, and had little or nothing to do. The Pearl of the Orient had never had a major robbery nor a major beef. Occasionally Jake had a small speculation to run down or a harmless drunk to quiet. His job was about as close to a sinecure as a man of his age and attainments could possibly expect.

Waldo considered him a bumbling, boring old fool, and never talked to him at any length if he could help it.

"You read that lousy grimy stuff?" asked Jake, noticing the magazine.
"Now and then."

"You, a college boy!" cried Jake. "Shame on you!"

"They have true crime stuff with pictures of the criminals," said Waldo. "Kind of a public service."

"Yeah," said Jake. "I know. And some guys have been caught through them pictures. All the same its lousy grimy stuff. Lots of naked women in there, too. Right?"

Jake was death on naked women. He was always denouncing them. It was a good thing he was on the night shift and didn't have to witness the antics on the beach and at the pool.

"What's wrong with naked women?" asked Waldo, baiting him. "Just plain ordinary human women with their clothes off."

"Women shouldn't *have* their clothes off," cried Jake, heated. "My mother never let my father see her naked his whole life. No sir. She was a decent woman."

Waldo desisted. It was too easy. "Want to see a picture, Jake?" he asked.

"Of a naked woman?" cried Jake. "Not on your life, young fellow. No. No."

Jake seemed about to retreat as if to ward off temptation.

"No," said Waldo. "You're too old for that stuff."

Jake seemed to tremble with rage but made no comment.

"Just want you to look at a criminal," said Waldo. "Come on in."

Jake, his eyes roving suspiciously as if he anticipated sinister goings-on, followed Waldo into his little cabin where Waldo showed him the picture of the "arch criminal" (as it said in the magazine), Willie Madden.

Jake stared for a moment then took out his glasses, put them on, and studied the picture for a long time.

"Ever see him?" asked Waldo.

Jake turned and stared curiously at Waldo. "What's the game, young man? Of course I never seen him. He's an eastern criminal, and anyway, I'm old enough to be his father. I retired before ... but ..." Jake broke off and took another look at the picture.

"Yes, Jake?"

"But ... well, I sure seen somebody who looked like him."

"Who, Jake?"

"Why, that what's-his-name—the little dandy who drives the Cadillac."

"Mr. Shannon?"

"Yes. Mr. Shannon. Almost a dead ringer."

"You think it might be the same man?" asked Waldo, half serious, half baiting.

"Are you crazy?" cried Jake. "What would he be doing in a place like Tropico Beach—at the Pearl of the Orient, driving a Cadillac and dressed up like that ... a very polite-talking man. Why, he was around here two-three months, wasn't he?"

"Well," said Waldo, "Willie Madden's got five hundred thousand dollars, it says here. I guess he could afford it."

Old Jake sank down on a chair and considered.

"You know, Waldo," he said, "you might have a point. Yes sir. And there's big rewards out."

"Yeah?" said Waldo, his eyes beginning to bug. "Yeah, you're right. Says so right here in the magazine. Says to phone or wire in collect if … or to contact …"

"Wait, wait," said Jake. "Let's think a bit. If it should be him and we'd help to catch him we don't want to split the rewards all up till nobody gets much of anything. Tell you what. Hand me that magazine. I'll give Earl Jordan a call and maybe he can find time to drop by."

"Who's he?" asked Waldo, beginning to feel bewildered. What had started out as little more than a joke was beginning to take on a surprisingly serious aspect.

"Why, he's a young Tropico Beach detective, a friend of my son. Sharp. He'll advise us. And he's got contacts. You know. And he'll know what to do."

"Don't you think maybe we're just kidding ourselves?" exclaimed Waldo, beginning to deflate.

"Maybe so," said Old Jake. "Maybe so. But there ain't no harm in trying. Money's money and I could use some and so could you."

"You're right," said Waldo; then, rather hastily, remembering Mr. Shannon's cold blue eyes and his frightening talk of criminals in Chicago, he went on: "Take the magazine, Jake. You handle it. It's all yours."

"Fine, fine, okay," cried old Jake, moving faster than he'd ever moved since coming to work at the Pearl of the Orient.

That night Waldo had nightmares. Something—a terrifying black shape—was pursuing him across a blasted landscape, then through city streets, then through unfamiliar rooms and finally over the rooftops—and just when Waldo was about to fall to the street below, he woke sweating and panting and with a death grip on his pillow. The sun was shining, and a little bird was singing in a bush right outside his window. The morning world looked mighty beautiful and reassuring to Waldo.

But he was very nervous and preoccupied the next day and could hardly wait until old Jake came back on duty.

"Well?" cried Waldo.

"He's interested. Very interested," said Jake, proudly. "The wheels are in motion. Our friend Mr. Shannon is going to be checked out from hell to breakfast."

Of course neither Jake, Waldo, nor young Detective Sergeant Earl Jordan had any idea of the difficulties involved in "checking out" a phantom.

"He called the town where the robbery was and talked to the Chief of

Detectives," said Jake. "He was on the phone for an hour. The FBI's in the picture, too. Gonna be quite a manhunt."

Waldo shivered slightly. Money or no money, why couldn't he have kept his big mouth shut? If Mr. Shannon was really Willie Madden he'd be pretty sure who started all the uproar and maybe he might come back ... but Waldo quickly closed his mind to such a possibility. No. It couldn't be. Nothing like that could ever happen to Waldo Krebs!

## SIX

The big town on the big Midwestern river sweltered in a heat wave. The town smelled like a stuffy airless old attic, people were falling over in the streets, and the sirens of ambulances rent the downtown air all day long.

Johnny Quait, sweating like a bull and worried, sat staring at the top of his battered old desk. In his morning mail he had found a copy of a crime magazine sent to him in a plain envelope, anonymously, and he didn't like it. He didn't like it at all. As far as he knew nobody was aware of his connection with the Kenmore Trust robbery but members of the Madden outfit. Two of them were dead. Three in prison. One dead or missing. That left Willie. But it couldn't be Willie, which meant Carl Benedict was neither missing nor dead. It also meant blackmail.

Johnny got out his short barreled .38 and thoughtfully unloaded it, then checked the mechanism carefully, oiled it and reloaded. Johnny had no intention whatsoever of being blackmailed and if he knocked off Carl Benedict it would be considered in the light of a public service. Carl was a tough loudmouth and the cops hated him.

Johnny was a big gnarled old man with thick curly iron-gray hair and a massive face that resembled a rubber mask. He had small, pig-like hazel eyes so keen that he'd never had to get glasses. Two cases had made him famous: he'd run down and captured Benson, the trunk murderer, for the *Morning Times*, making monkeys of the police, and he'd broken up the biggest narcotics ring in the state by a judicious manipulation of informers. Even now, in his declining years, he was on the payroll of several big industrial outfits, and was an expert in the prevention and/or cure of strike violence.

Nobody knew how much money he had. To judge him by the way he lived you would have considered him on the edge of bankruptcy. His clothes looked seedy; his office was in an old rundown building and didn't even have air-conditioning; he drove a cheap five-year-old car and ate in hash houses and diners, and he never let go of a cent that wasn't gouged out of him. But in the underworld, where he was hated

# 42 W. R. BURNETT

and feared, it was said that he had money in every bank in town and
had been cheating the government, taxwise, for twenty years.

Johnny was what is known as a "character," a familiar sight in certain
sections of the town. A big stoop-shouldered weird looking old man,
who dragged his right leg slightly and walked with a cane. The cane
was more than a prop, though; at times it was a lethal weapon. Thick
and heavy and swung with Johnny's still-immense strength, it could
dent the thickest skull. When men argued with Johnny they kept their
distance, afraid that the famous cane might rise and descend.

There had been many attempts to kill him, and the one that shattered
his leg—a little matter of felonious hit-and-run—had almost succeeded.
But the tough old man seemed to bear a charmed life, partly due, as he
often stated, to eternal vigilance.

"Yes sir," old Johnny would say, "eternal vigilance, the price of safety,
the price of freedom. All those slobs in prison—they went to sleep. So
they got caught. It's a hard row to hoe and most men are just not equal
to it. The world," old Johnny always added, "is full of slobs."

The truth was that the famous John Q. Quait looked down on
everybody. In all his long life he'd only met one man who had his
complete but grudging, respect—Willie Madden; and the respect had
been justified. In spite of the fact that Willie's masterful plan for the
robbery of the Kenmore Trust had been hamstrung and bungled by
his foolish associates, who couldn't keep their big mouths shut, who
couldn't "hoe the hard row," Willie had managed to get away scot-free
with three shares out of the seven, totaling at least half a million
sound negotiable dollars.

Willie was all right: a quiet, able, dangerous, tough man.

As for the rest of that sorry crew ... well! Old Johnny ticked them off
one by one:

Leon Bellini, a small-time sneak thief—partly a Square John, too
absorbed, like most Italians, in his family. Now dead.

Rick Novak, a former longshoreman, a big bully and street fighter
from the docks. A lunkhead, who thought it was smart to shoot it out
with the police. Dead.

Orley Peters, a former used-car dealer and handler of hot
merchandise, cars, accessories, clothing, jewelry—you name it. Very
tough in his own league. Very tame in Willie's. In stir.

Joe Wicks, a former police officer, fired from the force for undue
violence and roughness toward prisoners. A no-goodnik, who beat
women up, and was always on the docket for some asinine charge like
disturbing the peace, or using unduly profane language in a public
place, etc., etc. A born loser.

Fallon O'Keefe, a big red-haired Irishman who would fight a buzzsaw and give it odds. But too free with the whiskey. Former club fighter, taxi driver and truck driver. For a time, a protected political hoodlum. In stir.

What a crew! And yet for one reason or another it was the best, given the circumstances, that old Johnny and Willie could put together. They had not wanted or really needed big-time outside professionals, who would have insisted on putting their lip in and trying to run the show and making impossible demands for money. Willie, the "noncriminal," was all the pro they needed—or so they thought.

Oh, well. Water over the damn. Old Johnny had salted away nearly twenty thousand dollars, extracting it here and there, in small amounts, from the front money, with Willie's unspoken connivance—a good operator deserves good pay, Willie always said—and after five years the old man had considered himself more or less done with the whole matter.

Now, here came this magazine, and the whole can of peas was opened again. Johnny rose, sighing, took off his coat, strapped on a shoulder holster and carefully settled the compact little .38. If it was war again, so be it. Old Johnny intended, as always, to ride it out and survive.

The phone rang. Mrs. Peet, old Johnny's secretary of twenty years' service, answered it. He heard her protesting and opened the door.

"He won't give a name," she explained. "What's that?" she said into the phone. "I don't quite … Oh." She turned back to old Johnny with a puzzled expression. "He says to tell you it's the 'editor.'"

With a grunt of anger Johnny took the phone away from Mrs. Peet. "What do you want, you dog?"

"One word," said a thick, low-pitched voice that Johnny remembered only too well. "It's not what you think. I might be doing you a big favor."

"Oh, sure," said old Johnny, sarcastically

"Wait," said the voice, hastily. "I got a line on Willie and Willie's got half a million dollars. Could we talk?"

Carl Benedict, a real swinger! He'd probably spent his own share and now wanted Willie's. However, half a million dollars was an awful lot of money, and for a moment greed made old Johnny's hand tremble on the phone.

"All right," said Johnny. "We'll talk. Know the old car barns?"

"Yeah."

"Be there. I'll be around sometime between eight and ten tonight."

"But that's a two-hour spread," protested the voice.

Johnny hung up, then he turned to Mrs. Peet. "Go home, Bertha. Look after your grandchildren. I'm closing for business for the day, though I may stick around."

Mrs. Peet laughed. To her ancient Johnny was no monster, but just an eccentric old codger almost twenty years older than herself, who was hard to get along with and crotchety but paid her well enough and demanded very little of her. In fact there was hardly anything to do anymore around the office.

"Put on your silly hat and go," said Johnny. "I think better alone."

"Did you take your medicine?" asked Mrs. Peet.

"No, I did not take my goddamned medicine," screamed old Johnny.

"Well, take it," said Mrs. Peet, unperturbed.

Old Johnny went back in his private office and slammed the door in protest—but he took his medicine.

Later Johnny sat at his desk and pondered. If he knew Carl Benedict, he had the crazy fool set up. The car barns were no longer used and the whole area was deserted at night. He could do one of three things: he could inform the police, he could kill Benedict himself, or he could parley with him and try to pump him. It still might be only a knot-headed scheme to get money out of Johnny. Carl was obviously broke or he would never have been heard from at all.

Outside, the big town steamed and sweltered. The sun declined and spread gold and reddish spangles across the oily water of the huge river. A lukewarm breeze began to fan the old man's curtains and lift the papers on his desk, but Johnny sat on, deep in thought, pondering every possibility and ramification of the three courses of action.

# SEVEN

The tall doors of the old car barn were open to the elements, and inside, in sorry, derelict row, were the shells of the abandoned surface cars. They had been stripped for junk, wheels and all, and little remained except the skeleton frame and the worn old wooden seats.

Old Johnny, wearing rubber-sole shoes and with a rubber tip on his cane, slipped quietly in through the far back door at a little before seven forty-five. Faint traces of summer twilight lingered over the old brick buildings of the district but the streetlights were on, casting a faint bluish ghostly glow into the otherwise pitch-black interior of the car barn.

Johnny, fighting against it, felt a piercing sense of loneliness and melancholy, as he silently slipped in between the cars and finally took his place in a position that enabled him to keep both entrances under surveillance. The wooden seat beneath him brought back the past with a rush and in spite of a strong will old Johnny could not brush it aside. Summer nights. The trolleys trundling past his own home. 1914. World

War I. *Good God, had it been that long ago?* Young Johnny, eighteen years old, and wearing a stiff straw hat, jumping over the picket fence and running after a trolley that had failed to make the usual stop at his corner. Then … young Johnny standing on the back platform chinning with the conductor and ogling the girls walking along the pavement, during the slow slow journey into the downtown area. The motorman clanging the foot bell and cursing the traffic. Traffic? *What* traffic? A few high rickety Fords and a few carriages and buggies and maybe kids on bicycles; or perhaps a Herrnstein beer wagon, pulled by huge powerful gray horses.

Later, a thick ugly brown uniform and a gun. France? Rain, rain, rain; mud, mud, mud. Cherbourg—as dismal a place as you'd want to see. Then back to the trolley and the stiff straw hat and the same old world; only it wasn't the same old world anymore. And he wasn't the same. And his father was dead. And there were no jobs.

But young Johnny made out. He made out very well in this changed world, and for a very simple reason. Johnny was better suited to the changed world than to the old leisurely innocent one. Johnny was many things but neither leisurely nor innocent. He was driven by a simple form of greed: get the buck. Get it no matter how and get it fast. Some of Johnny's companions-in-arms made the breadlines and sat around diners and poolrooms complaining about conditions and wallowing in self-pity (How can they do this to us? We're returned soldiers, ain't we? Heroes?).

Johnny had put in with a sharp character named Al Davis. Al was a private investigator, shady but licensed, who specialized in getting evidence for divorces. Occasionally, getting more evidence than he had counted on, he politely engaged in a little reasonable blackmail. Al warned Johnny never to strip a sucker. Never drive him to the wall. Never make him desperate. Just bleed him slowly and as painlessly as possible. And Johnny, the former ornament—big and tough—of the Provost Marshal's office, sergeant of the Military Police, was a fast study, and in a short time he left his limited teacher far behind.

Al was heard to lament around town: "I took that big oaf in and taught him to be a gentleman. Now he's my stiffest competition."

Ten years later Al Davis, nearly sixty and on his uppers, came to Johnny for help. Johnny offered him a job sweeping out the office. Al left a sadder and wiser man, and finally wound up in the Knights of Pythias home for the aged and indigent. Al's chief topic of conversation at the home was John Q. Quait, now a national figure. Happy in the home, Al had lost all animosity toward Johnny. In fact, he bragged about Johnny from morning till night as his star pupil. "I made that boy," Al would brag to anyone who would listen. "I taught him everything he knows."

And in a way Al was right at that. But all the knowledge in the world won't help a fool. Knowledge is how you use it.

Old Johnny struggled hard to bring himself back from the past. It was this goddamned ugly old car barn, with its skeletons of earlier days! It was the worn wooden seat that reminded him of riding out to Luna Park and going on the chute-the-chutes, with the girls screaming and water splashing up into the garish lights in a silvery spray.

He looked at his watch, which showed a small circle of ghostly blue in the darkness. Three after eight. Carl would be along any minute now. Johnny had learned the value of the two-hour spread from Al Davis. It made your opponent nervous. If he came too early he might have a two-hour wait; if he came too late he might miss you.

It was very efficacious with men who wanted something badly from you and were considering a trade. It made them stew, and review the bidding. It put them on the defensive.

And then old Johnny, with his keen eyes, saw Carl. He had eeled in from the front, with the street lights behind him, of course—the fool! A dead target if Johnny had intended to eliminate him from the scene—and why hadn't Carl taken that into consideration? So it wasn't blackmail after all. But how had Carl had the nerve to assume that Johnny would believe it? Johnny shook his head over such ineptitude. No wonder the prisons were full of such men. No vigilance.

Carl stopped just inside and stood in the darkness with his back to the front wall, waiting. Had he thought to trap old Johnny as he came in? Oh, God! Johnny laughed to himself. But no … Carl had no such idea, because in a moment he lit a cigarette, the match showing a surprisingly large red flare in the darkness.

"Carl," called Johnny.

And he saw the strongarm guy give a jump.

"Where the hell are you, you old lizard?" cried Carl, irritated by being taken by surprise and startled.

"Walk straight down the row right in front of you to the third car—slow. I've got a gun on you, Carl."

"Oh, for Christ sake, pops," said Carl, in disgust. "I told you I'm not trying to put the arm on you."

"And I'm supposed to take your word," Johnny chuckled to himself. "And don't move your hands fast. I can see fine. You got the light behind you."

Carl stamped out his cigarette in disgust, then raised both hands above his head.

"How's this, pops?" he called.

"Fine. Now keep coming. That's it. Now stop. Right there. Can you see me?"

"I can see kind of an elephant shape. But I know it's you, pops. I know it's you."

"Good. All right, talk. I haven't got all night."

Carl slowly and cautiously lowered his arms before he spoke. "I got a friend at the 7th Precinct."

"So you did a little informing on the side."

"What's that to you, you crooked old bastard!" cried Carl heatedly.

"I just made a remark."

"Okay. So I used to give him tips, like. Not on guys I knew or was running with; that would be murder! But with stuff I heard. Once he got a big beat out of it and got promoted. I also gave him a small cut of my Kenmore dough; and he's been protecting me, like. I'm supposed to be dead, you know."

"I know," said Johnny. "But here you are, as stupid and conniving as ever."

Carl spoke with sudden heat. "I've broken guys' necks for less than that, pops."

"I know you have," said Johnny. "Stupid! That's why I'm holding this gun on your belly, Carl."

"All right, pops," said Carl, changing his tune. "Just listen. Okay? So we got a kind of set of signals, me and the dick. So he wants to see me. So we meet. Old man, things are really hot. Willie was staying in a big fine hotel in a place called Tropico Beach in Southern California, under the name of James Shannon. He just got away in time. It was that crime magazine I give you. A kid at the hotel saw Willie's picture in it. So now the heat's on again, FBI and all. But if I know Willie he'll disguise himself now, change his name, and keep roaming around as if nothing had happened. And if I know Willie he'll stay in California. I mean he won't take no long jumps. Them guys will be looking for James Shannon. See what I mean?"

"I see," said Johnny.

"Well, if I'm looking I won't be looking for no James Shannon and no guy with black hair neither," said Carl.

"H'm," said Johnny.

"What do you mean 'h'm'—aint you got no enthusiasm, old man?"

"You surprise me by talking sense," said Johnny.

"Oh, thanks. Here's the way I figure it. If I see Willie I'll know him, disguise and all. They won't."

"You going to go looking?"

"With half a million laying around? Are you kidding? And I figure you'll want part of the action."

"You mean you want me to finance you."

"That's right."

"You had nearly a hundred and fifty thousand dollars. What did you do with it?"

"I spent it. What else?"

"So you cook up this crazy idea just to get money out of me. I give it to you and that's that. Then pretty soon maybe you're back for more."

"You're forgetting one thing, pops. I'm dead, remember? They stopped looking for me. Now you know better. Turn me in. There's a reward."

Old Johnny fell silent, but greed was nagging at him like a toothache. Half a million! A fortune—more money than most men ever saw in a lifetime ... in three lifetimes!

"Where do you figure he's got the money?" asked old Johnny, more to make conversation than anything else. "Not on him, that's for sure."

"In banks. Safety-deposit boxes, you can bet."

"Right. So how do you get it, even if you find him?"

"All right, pops. I'll level with you. This dick I mentioned. He's gonna take leave of absence from the force. If we can get financed he's gonna help me look, and he's a pretty smart boy."

Johnny began to perk up. Now things were starting to take on a vaguely possible tinge.

"Tell you what, Carl," he said, "I'll have to talk to him. We'll have to get together—maybe out here—the three of us. Or maybe some place else where I can get a look at him."

"You kidding?" cried Carl, "You know him."

"So you say. But either I talk to him—with you—or I won't even consider this proposition."

A long silence.

"He's a pretty cagey guy," said Carl. "I don't know if ..."

"Then forget it."

"Oh, I'll talk to him about it."

"Good," said Johnny.

"I'd like to tell you his name but I can't."

"His name coming from you does me no good. I got to see him, talk to him, hear his ideas. Is he thinking about turning Willie in?"

"Are you crazy, old man? All we want is the loot. To hell with Willie."

Johnny gave a long sigh. Half a million dollars! He didn't want the hope of it gone a-glimmering. "All right. Talk to him. If it works out my way, call me at the office. You're the 'editor.' If it doesn't, I don't want to see or hear from you again."

"You damned old fool," cried Carl. "I put myself right in your hands, didn't I?—trying to set this up."

"True."

"All right then. Remember that!"

"Are you threatening me, Carl?"

"I'm saying that's what I think of the proposition."

"So push it through," said Johnny.

Carl finally left, growling to himself. At the doorway he struck a match on the wall and lit a cigarette. Old Johnny sat shaking his head in disgusted disbelief. A real fool, Carl.

Johnny moved down to another car nearer the rear door and leaned against it. You could never be sure what a strongarm guy, who had been frustrated, if even only temporarily, would do.

In the pitch-dark outside now, with the streetlights of this deserted warehouse district looking dim and lonely in the night. Johnny kept remembering the past, as his big old rear end pressed against the worn wooden seat. The lawn fetes: they suddenly came back to him. He'd see them as he passed along the street on the back platform of the trolley. Girls in long white dresses and long hair; strings of candlelit Japanese paper lanterns; pleasant laughter, and maybe a mandolin playing—and the strong rank-sweet smell of trampled lawn grass.

A peaceful, happy vision of a time long past, dead as ancient Rome.

# EIGHT

A loud gruff old female voice shouted from the doorway: "There's a young man to see you, Mrs. Madden."

Willie's mother turned from the morning chore of looking after her canary and peered through her glasses at Mrs. Fatts, her landlady.

"A young man? Policeman or reporter?"

A big-shouldered detective sergeant—Jim Glinka—appeared behind Mrs. Fatts in the doorway, took off his hat, and grinned at Mrs. Madden, then explained who he was.

"Well, come in," said Mrs. Madden. "I hope you haven't been bothering Bernie and Leo. What is it now?"

Mrs. Fatts went back to her work, grumbling to herself: "A jailbird for a son. Disgraceful! And her such a nice old lady!"

For over five years Mrs. Madden had lived on the first floor, front, at Mrs. Cornelia Fatts' rooming house on Tecumseh Slope. From her windows she could see the river and all the shipping. Buses rumbled past at intervals; and there was a continual coming and going of trucks of all sizes, making for the docks. It was busy, noisy and sometimes dirty. But Mrs. Madden liked it. "I'll get all the quiet I need soon enough," she'd state to her protesting businessmen sons, who considered the district a disgraceful place for their mother to be living.

Being the kind of men they were they felt that if they paid the fiddler they should be able to call the tune. But Mrs. Madden accepted their largesse as a matter of course and felt no obligation whatever to listen to their advice and comply with their wishes. She'd slaved for them when they were boys; they could slave for her now. Not that there was any slaving involved for Bernie and Leo. They were sharpies and saw to it that the other fellow did the work.

Mrs. Madden at times was not quite sure that she approved of either of them, so tightfisted and business-proud, nothing like their dockworker dad, who spent his money as it came and laughed at poverty, a fine open good-natured man—but an unlucky man, who had died young.

As for Willie ... well, he was a changeling. He'd come from a cuckoo's egg that had somehow got into the robin's nest. As least this was Mrs. Madden's version of her infamous son, Willie. But there were some who saw more than a little physical resemblance between Willie and his mother. The same blue eyes, the same black hair, the same unchanging slenderness of body.

And Sergeant Jim Glinka was one of those who noted the resemblance, as he stood eyeing this small, slight, erect old lady with her gray-streaked black hair and her keen blue eyes behind the glasses.

"I don't believe I know you," she said, tidying up the canary's cage.

"No, ma'am," said Glinka. "We haven't talked before."

"What do you want? What is it now? Have they found Willie?"

"Should they have?"

She turned and looked at the big detective sergeant. "I should think so, with all the policemen all over the country looking for him."

"You haven't heard from him by any chance?"

"Young man, please," said Mrs. Madden. "I've been through this for years. No. I have not heard from him. Haven't heard from him since he was accused of that robbery. But if I had, I wouldn't tell you, so why are you wasting my time and yours?"

Glinka smiled inwardly. He admired this old girl, and if her son was anything like her he could understand Willie's acknowledged influence over practically everybody he'd ever met.

"Well, I got a job to do, ma'am," he said. "You know. The old routine." Now he looked about him at the spacious room, with the big daybed converted into a sofa and ornamented with pretty, big pillows. Everything was in spic and span order. No dust; nothing out of place. And Jim Glinka wished that he could hire Mrs. Madden to teach his own wife this kind of housekeeping. Of course Myrt had two small kids to contend with, but even so there was no excuse for the place always looking like a mess when he got home weary from duty.

"If you don't mind my saying so, young man," said Mrs. Madden, "with all your work and routine and so on, seems to me the lot of you could catch one lone man."

"It would seem so," said Glinka. "But your son's a mighty smart and slippery customer."

"Never seemed so to me."

"Oh? How *did* he seem?"

"Like a quiet hardworking boy. Minded his own business. Never tried to give me advice. Practically kept the family going till Leo and Bernie made good, if you can call it making good. At least till they got prosperous. Willie was my oldest."

"He lived at home, I understand."

"That's right. For years. Leo and Bernie were both married by the time they were twenty. By the time they were twenty-five their clotheslines were loaded with diapers and they were up to their ears in debt. Willie never helped them. But he helped me. First I lived with Bernie then with Leo. All I was, was a babysitter. I couldn't call my life my own. You understand, it was my own doing. I was trying to help. But Willie put a stop to it. He made me get a room of my own, a long ways from the families. And he was right. I was killing myself over the children, just like I'd done over my own. Now I'm sound as a dollar and enjoying life, thanks to Willie."

It was obvious to Glinka—and he was a little surprised—that old respectable Mrs. Madden seemed to be very partial to her infamous son.

"But didn't Willie marry very young? Says so in the record."

Mrs. Madden shrugged. "That silly girl. She used to stand out in front of the house waiting for him to come home. I'd often chase her away. Willie was only nineteen. She was in her twenties. No pride. Just kept after him. Then her *father* got after him. To tell you the truth Willie *had* to marry her. I know it's not right. But when a boy is only nineteen and he's got a big voluptuous twenty-three-year-old girl after him ..."

"I see," said Glinka.

"Oh, I'm not defending him, only explaining how it happened. It was a mortal sin according to the Church. But people are human, young man; people are human."

"What happened with the marriage?"

"Willie left her and came home. Her family looked after the baby."

"What happened to the baby?"

"I don't know. They moved away about a year later. Some place out west."

Glinka took out his notebook and wrote something down. Then he flipped back through it and consulted a thumbnail dossier of Willie.

"The family's name was Derucki, I believe," said Glinka.

"Yes."

"Do you remember their house number? They lived on Clayburn Avenue."

"My goodness, young man," said Mrs. Madden, sitting down at last and getting out a sewing basket, "that was around twenty-five years ago. I didn't even remember they lived on Clayburn. This is silly."

"Yes, ma'am," said Glinka.

"Oh, I see," said Mrs. Madden, after a moment. "You think maybe Willie might look them up, and ..." Mrs. Madden laughed. "Not likely. No, not very likely."

"We're trying to trace this family," said Glinka. "After all, the woman is still Mrs. Willie Madden as far as I know, and the baby would be about twenty-five years old. It was a girl, wasn't it?"

"As I recall," said Mrs. Madden, indifferently.

Glinka shifted about, then walked over to one of the windows and looked out at the river. Towboats were pushing strings of barges upstream against the heavy currents, laboring.

"Nice place you got here, ma'am," said Glinka. "Might move over in this neighborhood myself. Rents are awful high where I live."

"All day long the boats come and go," said Mrs. Madden. "And at night it's mighty pretty with all the lights along the shore. Would you like a cup of tea?"

"No, thank you, ma'am," said Glinka.

At last he left, feeling a little baffled, a little frustrated and unaccountably depressed. Mrs. Madden—a really good old girl. How could she be the mother of Willie Madden? It seemed incredible and disturbing.

That afternoon he talked to both Leo and Bernard Madden, meeting them separately at out of the way rendezvous so they wouldn't be embarrassed either at home or at their places of business. This was by their request, as Glinka had shown them the courtesy of calling them on the phone first.

Both detested Willie, it was obvious. Both resented him almost hysterically. Leo owned and operated a big cut-price automobile accessory store. Bernard was in the commission house business. Both looked prosperous, and neither bore the slightest resemblance to Willie. They could offer no help, but both agreed that if they heard from Willie they would contact the police.

"He ought to be put away where he can't do any more harm," Bernard had said.

Although it was no part of his job and none of his business, Jim Glinka returned to the station thoroughly disliking Willie's two brothers.

# NINE

Glinka reported to Lieutenant Art Kramer and added his tiny mite to Willie's mountainous dossier.

"That Derucki lead's not so bad at that," said the Lieutenant. "We better get on that. Any port in the storm, you know, if it would get real hot for Willie! Maybe he kept in touch with that girl he married. Who knows? Anyway, let's try to run that family down. That's your assignment, Glinka. I'll give you all the help you need."

Art Kramer had spent the morning with two insurance adjusters. They were interested in getting their hands on what was left of Willie's money; Kramer was interested in getting his hands on Willie. They talked mostly but unintentionally at cross purposes. Kramer knew that if these guys found Willie first, they would make a deal with him for the return of the money and then Willie would probably be off to Mexico and out of reach. But Kramer, a conscientious man, gave them all the help he could, which, at the moment, was not much.

But the net was spreading, far and near, for Willie. In California Sheriff's offices had been alerted and were "cooperating" with the State Police, whatever that meant; and the FBI had never been out of the picture and were now redoubling their efforts. Eventually, Kramer knew, Willie would be nabbed. How soon was another question! Already five long years had passed.

Art got a buzz from the Captain's office and dismissing Glinka, went down the hallway wondering what was up now. The Captain was a great one for promiscuously buzzing for someone. It seemed to be his chief occupation.

Captain Len Bescher was a big wide man with a baldish head and large horn-rimmed glasses. He chewed an unlighted stogie from morning till night, and small flakes of tobacco were always sticking to his rather thick lips.

"What's this about Detective Sergeant Nick Fay?"

"About his leave? It will be granted."

"Why for Christ's sake? He's one of our Willie Madden experts."

"Bad lung. He had flu, then a recurrence. I've seen the doctor's report. He needs a different climate. He's going to try Denver, Colorado."

"Damn it, Art; this is a bad break."

"Oh, he's not indispensable. We've had him briefing the boys."

"I don't know," said the Captain, wearily. "When it comes to Willie Madden everything seems to go haywire and get loused up. I'd give a year off my life to be looking that little bastard straight in the eyes at this moment."

"Oh well, we didn't do so bad," said Art. "He's the only one left, out of seven."

"Are you so sure of Carl Benedict?"

"I'm not exactly sure," said Art. "It was a tough job, that identification. But he hasn't been heard from since."

"If he's alive, which God forbid," said the Captain, "you'll hear from him as soon as his money runs out. He's a real rip-and-tear operator and those guys are always heard from when they need money—and always caught. So let's put it this way. Carl Benedict is either dead or hasn't run out of money yet. Anyway, as far as I'm concerned, he's a secondary issue. I want Willie, Art," said the Captain, and after a pause, "Did you know I was the sucker who recommended Willie for his job with the D.A.'s office?"

"I heard so."

"And that shifty little rat made the most of my recommendation when he took the job from Kenmore Trust. I'd been promoted to Captain by that time."

"How did you get to know him?"

"Same restaurant. Foley's. You know it. Wonderful food. Willie ate there every night. I got to admit I took kind of a shine to him. Very amusing. Got kind of an Irish wit, you might call it. And him planning ... planning all along, for years. It's hardly human. Could have cost me my job—or at least my promotion—if we hadn't had a sensible Chief. I'm telling you they were really yelling for my blood, and you can bet Willie was laughing himself sick. It's not every day a heister has a Captain of Police recommending him."

Bescher chewed sadly on his stogie and mopped his bald head with a big handkerchief.

"I don't like losing Nick Fay at a time like this," he said finally. "Send him in to see me this evening."

"Okay," said Art, wondering what good it would do. At times the Captain just seemed to like to talk and talk and talk, with no visible results whatever.

## TEN

Detective Sergeant Nick Fay climbed the vertical iron ladder slowly, making a bit of unnecessary noise now and then. Carl was a jumpy, unpredictable guy who might suddenly get the idea he'd been double-crossed and then start shooting, and argue later: a kook; a big rough woolly-headed kook, with the stare of a bull in his dark eyes and with that lock of kinky hair always hanging forward over his forehead. Nick Fay, a great "make" guy, always remembered Carl as he'd seen him in the Bertillon pictures: square, seamed face, pushed-out upper lip, deep-set eyes, and an air of cold implacability. A classic hooligan type, born to violence of some kind.

And Nick did not like this climb, up the side of the abandoned oil-storage tank. Just the kind of rendezvous a kook like Carl would pick. Carl was not interested in anything unless there was a big element of danger in it: with a little different schooling, a little steadier temper, a different boiling point, Carl might have been a mountain climber, or a test pilot, or a human fly, or a professional parachute jumper instead of what he was.

Besides, Nick's left lung was bothering him (he hadn't been forced to fake disability) and he grew shorter and shorter of breath as the climb continued. He tried to keep his eyes on the side of the tank, a few inches in front of him, but occasionally they would stray, as if of their own accord, and he'd get a quick picture of street lights and fanned-out boulevards and lighted buildings, all far away, diminished by distance, but frightening because of their juxtaposition in regard to himself. He was high up, very high up, especially so as the oil-storage tank itself was perched on the crest of a low hill.

Nick began to pant and curse at the same time. This was the end. No more climbing this ladder because of Carl's stupid idea of a safe place. Safe place for eagles! And going down was worse. Nick always had the feeling he might just let himself loose, and fall. You associate with a kook you wind up with kooky ideas!

He was near the top gangway now. There wasn't a sound, and Nick began to wonder uneasily if something had happened to Carl. Then he heard him. He was snoring. This upset Nick so that his foot slipped a little on the rough iron step and he almost let go.

Carl asleep was even more dangerous than Carl awake. And Nick remembered the story he'd heard about Carl and one of his many almost miraculous escapes. He'd been found asleep in bed with one of his girlfriends. Duck soup, the lucky dick thought. Then before the dick knew what happened, the girl was half on top of him, screaming; Carl shot his hat off, giving him a new part in his hair—and then was out the window and down the fire escape before the dick could untangle himself from the hysterical girl. Wouldn't you think a man in shorts and an undershirt would be easy to find? Well, the dick never found Carl, although he had squad cars combing the neighborhood.

Nick eased himself little by little onto the gangway, taking minutes over it. A sharp noise at this moment might cost him his life. Now he could see Carl, who was lying on his side, wrapped in a blanket.

Nick began to whisper: "Carl, Carl, Carl."

But Carl never stirred. Nick's lung was paining him and he was sweating heavily as rage, fear and a kind of dismay fought for emotional supremacy inside him. What a spot to be in! What a damned silly humiliating spot!

"Carl!"

The blanket moved and Nick heard a faint sound as of metal on metal.

"Carl, it's me," he cried, much louder than he had intended.

He waited. The blanket moved again and Nick found himself looking into the barrel of a revolver.

"Give the countersign," said Carl, then he began to snicker.

"You dirty ... You silly son-of-a-bitch," yelled Nick, frantic with rage. "I climb all the way up here, my lung hurting like hell, and you gotta play kid games. I ought to throw you off this gangway."

"Ah, come on, Nick," said Carl, sitting up and putting his gun away. "A guy's got to look for laughs in this lousy world. How'd it go with the Captain?"

But Nick wouldn't reply. He sat down, put his back up against the huge rounded side of the tank and stared gloomily at the city lights all spread out before them.

"If I had any sense at all I'd turn you in," he said at last.

"And lose a fortune?" said Carl, mildly. "You ain't that dumb."

"If it was anybody else ..."

"Yeah?"

"Well, I figure you're the kind of crazy fool who might have a real chance against Willie. Willie figures everything out to the last digit. But how can he figure out a kook like you? This place for instance. I can't think of a sillier place for a meeting."

"Right. Who'd look here? And if they did I'd blow their heads off and they'd never even get a look at me. I got a hundred places to hide on this rig."

Little by little Nick was mollified.

"That Bescher," he said. "Tried to talk me out of my leave of absence. I told him to look at my X-rays. You think he cared? He's drooling to catch Willie, and he thinks I'm the expert."

"I hope you are," said Carl. "You better be or Old Man Quait ain't going to like it ... supposing he puts in with us."

"Will he?"

"I think so, if you'll talk to him personal."

"I can't do that. Did you name me?"

"Of course not."

"Look, Carl ..."

"This old carrion buzzard can finance us. You got anybody else in mind?"

"No. All the same ..."

However, Nick finally agreed to talk with Johnny Quait. He'd known him for years and there was nothing about the dangerous old man he liked except his money.

"Willie's outfoxing them in California," said Nick. "First, the car. The motor guy had the license number. Wonderful, except for one thing. It was a leased car and our Willie turned it back and didn't take out another. Traveler's checks; made out to James Shannon. Good? Well, Mr. Shannon, a stranger in the bank, had purchased them with cash. No other record."

Carl snickered sadly, but made no comment.

"Forwarding address? Of course. He had a reservation at the Fairmont in San Francisco, but he would wire when he was settled. The police checked. Yes, he'd made a reservation at the Fairmont. But it had been cancelled."

Carl snickered again.

"No more James Shannon, Nick. That guy is dead, buried—and you might as well forget him."

"Right."

"And the next alias won't be anything like it, if I know my Willie boy."

"He's a toughie," sighed Nick. "Been out five years in spite of all the noise."

Then Nick went on to tell Carl about the Derucki family lead and Carl snickered.

"They can forget that one," he said. "So they find the family. So what? Why would Willie ever go near them and what would they know of Willie? If I dig Willie he's forgot he ever had a kid and couldn't care less anyway."

Silence fell. They sat looking off at the lights and listening to the boat whistles blasting on the river.

"I'll set it up for tomorrow night," said Carl, finally, referring to John Q. Quait. "If you think this is a funny joint, how about the old car barns? Even gives me the creeps—like a cemetery, kind of. All them dead cars just kinda sitting there."

Nick glanced at Carl. Such an observation coming from such a man surprised him. So then Carl wasn't quite insensible after all!

"He's a tough dealer," said Nick.

"Yeah," said Carl. "He held a gun on my belly all the time I talked to him. And he'll do the same again, so don't make no wrong motions, Nick, or there'll be shooting."

Time passed. They talked on desultorily. Nick had no idea where

Carl really lived. Several times he'd tailed him, just to have an ace in the hole, but somehow, although Nick was an adept at the work, Carl had managed to lose him. Finally, feeling he'd pushed his luck hard enough, Nick quit tailing him. Carl would kill you without a blink of the eye. And tailing him would be excuse enough.

"What a break you got, Carl," said Nick, "when they identified that city morgue stiff as you."

"Yeah," said Carl. "I was on Easy Street. But I met too many chicks with big ideas and too many horses that didn't run where they should."

"A real suckers' game—horses."

"How about chicks?" Carl demanded, snickering.

Nick had little to say about women. He'd been married and divorced and that about summed it up, apparently, as far as he was concerned.

"Yeah," he said, vaguely.

"Funny thing," said Carl. "I got my taste for expensive women from Willie. He took me out one night—first class. We were setting up the Big One then. Willie was promoting me because he figured he might need some muscle. You should have seen them babies. They smelled so good they scared me. Me, I was used to these waterfront bums. You know … real pigs. That Willie!"

Nick finally left with reluctance, but it wasn't because he was so fond of Carl's company. It was the thought of that dizzy journey back down to solid earth. Suppose a guy would suddenly come up with vertigo once he got out on that blasted ladder!

Carl listened to Fay's snaillike progress downward. It was a good night, warm and pleasant. Carl decided to sleep on the gangway till daybreak, as he did from time to time. One morning the boat whistles had awakened him suddenly and he'd found himself at the edge of the railing with one leg hanging over. It had seemed funny to him. Nick would have been panic stricken.

Carl stood looking out at the city. Once he had owned it, in a sense. A body from the river had been identified as his and he had got away clean with nearly a hundred and fifty thousand dollars. Now he was on the make again—the Carl Benedict of B.W. *Before Willie*. But he had no regrets. He'd done what he'd done. For nearly five years he'd lived on the fat of the land. Millions of Square Johns the world over could not make that statement!

# ELEVEN

Olga Bellini, now-dead Leon's good-looking teenage daughter, came home very excited, with her dark hair flying, carrying a magazine one of her boyfriends had given her. In it there was much about "Pop," even a rather vague small picture.

On Tecumsen Slope the Bellinis were not looked down on because the deceased head of the house had been a "famous criminal." In fact, the Bellinis were the nearest thing to "celebrities" to be found in the neighborhood, and they were in a sense truckled to, squired, and cultivated.

Young Leon, nineteen, was a well-known sandlot baseball player and had never thought to change his name. Olga worked an occasional shift at a drive-in where she was proudly pointed out by the manager as that "big-timer's" daughter. The two younger boys, twelve and fourteen, were not exactly sure as yet just what it was all about, but they were definitely aware of the fact that to be a "Bellini" on Tecumsen Slope carried certain privileges, honorariums and even duties. They were expected to be tough, for one thing; and they gladly complied. Leon Jr. was also tough, but quiet about it. Even Olga seemed strong-willed and with a mind of her own. The strangest thing was that not a single one of them had ever been in any kind of real trouble. It was said that the Old Lady "kept them straight."

"Mom, Mom," screamed Olga. "Look what I've got."

Mrs. Bellini, in an apron, came in from the kitchen to see, took the magazine from Olga, then sat down and studied it with a kind of wonder.

"See Pop?" cried Olga.

"Yes," said Mrs. Bellini. "But it's a very bad old picture. Your father was a fine-looking man. Thick, curly, black hair; smooth olive complexion; beautiful teeth ..."

For years now Mrs. Bellini, and her friend Serie Novak, Rick's wife, had been living in hope. Both families were bone poor and from month to month were just barely able to stave off disaster in the form of endless credit payments. Actually they owned nothing, not even their homes. Second mortgages and installment buying to the hilt was their lot. They lived in a welter of "must" payments.

But really all this was nothing, because Mr. Madden had nearly three hundred thousand dollars that belonged to them, and they were certain that when it was possible Mr. Madden would see that they got it. Both Mrs. Bellini and Serie Novak had been deeply impressed by Mr.

Madden, who had been several times to their homes in company with their husbands.

Mr. Madden, they were certain, was not the type of man to do poor people out of their money.

Mrs. Bellini went down to the filling station at the corner to use the pay phone—a "personal" phone being too expensive for the Bellinis. She caught Serie just on her way in from marketing and told her about the magazine, then she made arrangements for the two families to get together that evening.

When Mrs. Bellini got back she said to her daughter: "Olga, you read me the whole story in that magazine and I'll just sit here in comfort and enjoy it."

"Even the part where Pop gets killed? I already read it to myself."

"Even that," said Mrs. Bellini. "I've lived with it for years. Now it's almost like a TV show, as if Leon never really got killed and will come back to us some day."

Mrs. Bellini began to cry and Olga joined her, in sympathy. But finally Mrs. Bellini dried her tears and said: "Go on. Read. Slow and nice, like your high school lessons."

## TWELVE

Before he saw the prisoner, Lieutenant Art Kramer, feeling more than a little nervous and excited, was briefed in the warden's office by the prison psychiatrist, Dr. Traven.

"I don't know what he wants to see you about, Lieutenant," said Traven, "but we all felt, in view of the size of this Kenmore business, that we ought to comply. Now about Wicks—as a prisoner he's hopeless. Fights, knifings, uproar. It's constant. No matter who we put him with, in two days or less, they're at it. Even the most peaceable men. He's been in solitary so much I had to put a stop to it. Now he's in maximum security where he can at least see some of his fellow prisoners and have certain necessary privileges. His intelligence is good enough. He even had one year of college. But he has a terribly high degree of irritability for which there seems to be no physical cause. And he is one of the most emotionally unstable men I've ever seen among men who are still functional. I tell you all this to let you know the kind of man you will have to deal with."

"Thanks, Doctor," said Kramer. "This might be very important. Now about the others?"

"Both are doing well. Peters is managing the machine shop and is classified as minimum security. Seems to be well liked. Fallon O'Keefe is doing even better, also minimum security. Liquor was his problem. He can't get it here, no matter what you hear outside. He's a fine athlete and the best baseball player in the prison. Also, I might add, an undercover pet of the warden's, who is very careful in such things. He gives Fallon no special favors but he likes him. The other day Fallon hit a ball clear out of here, a distance of close to four hundred feet, then he asked the warden if he could go look for it, as he wanted to keep it for a souvenir. This broke everybody up, including the warden. It's a shame a man like that should get himself into all this trouble. However, when he's paroled—and he will be—the liquor may send him back."

Traven sat shaking his head. As a psychiatrist he tried to be patient, very patient, with the men under his care, but he found them so exasperating, so unreasonable, so childish and impossible at times that it was almost more than he could stand, and he could check himself from yelling and cursing at them only by a strong and taxing effort of the will.

They were alone together in the warden's office now. Faint sunshine flooded in from the yard, and Joe Wick's narrow face looked wan and ugly. He was a burly young man—under forty—of medium height, with a thick short neck and a wary, wandering unsympathetic look in his pale gray eyes.

Art Kramer had not known Wicks as a police officer. He'd been stationed in a faraway precinct, and hadn't been around very long even there.

"Well, Wicks."

"I've tried it both ways," snarled Wicks, "cops and robbers, and they both stink. But the cops stink less. What a collection of crumbs I've never seen before. I feel dirty just being here. I can't stand the lying, bragging, thieving, self-pitying, no-good sonsabitches. Every guy in here was framed. It's never their fault. They never got a break. The world was against them. Crap like that, from morning till night. It reminds me of an old prison movie I once saw. One of the cons had killed his mother but a pretty good guy was always buddying around with him. One day another con asked the good guy how he could be pals with a creep who'd killed his own mother. And the good guy said: 'Well, he's sorry, ain't he?' That sums up this joint. That's what you might call our philosophy. What slobs!"

Kramer just let him talk—and talk he did for over half an hour by the clock: gripe, gripe, gripe, but not the usual con griping. Wicks was a man of some intelligence and had come from an economically higher social class than most of the other prisoners. His experience of such men had been strictly limited until this stretch in the Walls. It was obvious that he was just on the verge of running amuck.

"Well, Wicks?" Kramer said again, during a lull.

"I'm ready to talk," said Wicks.

Kramer's heart gave a jump, but he kept his face calm and rigid. "Yes? About what?"

"Come on, Lieutenant. Don't try to kid the troops. You want a certain guy named, don't you? You want him tied in so tight no million-dollar lawyer can get him loose. And maybe there's a few other things you don't know about this blast. Maybe there was eight instead of seven."

"And maybe you're kidding me."

"Come on, Lieutenant. Let's not waste each other's time, even if I have got nothing else but. Make me a deal. I'll make you a big man."

"What kind of deal?"

"I want out of here. Maybe a nice cell all to myself in the county jail—I might settle for the prison farm. Then … a parole."

"With your record here? I talked to Dr. Traven."

"It's why I'm trying to make a deal. No parole, no nothing, the way I'm going. Look, let's put it this way. I've had a change of heart. I'm a cop again. I'm civic minded."

"Are you?"

"No, for Christ's sake," yelled Wicks, violently. "That's a pitch. The high-ups will swallow it—or not, as they please."

Kramer, still excited, considered. Just the naming of Willie would be a great stroke. But what about an eighth member? What did Wicks mean? If true, it was sensational and would make the papers from Coast to Coast, and put further heat on cagey Willie.

"All right, Wicks," said Kramer. "I'll put it in Captain Bescher's lap as soon as I get back to town. Okay?"

"Don't delay," said Wicks. "I might change my mind."

Worried about Wicks' obvious unpredictability, Kramer hesitated, then said: "Let's put it this way. Right now you've got a tentative deal. But I can't take full responsibility for it. When do you talk?"

"As soon as you come and get me out of here."

## THIRTEEN

But in a prison, as elsewhere, things never stand still. Action brings reaction; one event leads to another and to further ramifications and repercussions.

Old Johnny was about to go home for the day when his phone rang in the outer office and he waited, as Mrs. Peet answered it. In a moment she buzzed him.

"It's Y," she said, in the same tone as if she was announcing that Mr. Smith was on the wire. She'd lived so long in an atmosphere of dark intrigue that it seemed like a commonplace thing to her now.

Y was one of Old Johnny's underworld operatives, and the news he brought was very disturbing.

"He's got to go," said Old Johnny.

"Maximum security. It's a tough one. But I might get it done for five G's."

Johnny groaned in bull-like anguish. The thought of parting with five thousand dollars caused him actual physical pain. But a must is a must no matter how much it hurts. Johnny was no miser, gripping pennies and letting the pounds go.

"See if you can do better, but not if you have to bargain too hard," he said. "Pick up the money at the drop, in, say, two hours."

Johnny hung up with another groan and sat looking out at the city, the worn old brick buildings of the district taking on a pleasant, kindly dull-orange patina in the fading rays of the clouded red sun.

Always problems! Always problems! And the Benedict business still hanging fire.

Would Benedict's tame police officer chicken out? (He was pretty sure it was Nick Fay, a very smart operator, who'd been skirting disaster in the police department for years.) Old Johnny hoped not, as hour by hour he was looking forward more eagerly to a cut of Willie's five hundred thousand dollars.

# FOURTEEN

Joe Wicks opened his eyes slowly, feeling that he'd come back from a long, long ways off, a strange alien place full of unknown sinister dark shapes with slim lengthy powerful arms, like those of octopi, that had tried to catch and strangle him.

He seemed to be lying flat on a rather hard surface in a dimly-lit place. Above him a face swam slowly into view, looking short and squat through foreshortening. The glasses …! Doc Parrish!

"He's coming around," said somebody. "You pulled him through, Doc. I thought he was a goner."

Fallon O'Keefe!

Now Dr. Parrish's face came into view.

"How do you feel, Wicks?" he asked.

Wicks tried to speak but could only gasp and rattle.

"All right, all right," said Dr. Parish, hastily. "Never mind. Just try to relax. We'll talk later."

Wicks coughed guardedly, then reached up to feel his throat. Then with eyes and hands he pantomimed: "What happened?"

"Don't you know?" asked Dr. Parrish, amazed.

Wicks shook his head.

"Somebody on the exercise unit in max. sec. tried to strangle you. You were standing apparently with your back to the bars and this man reached through and held you back against them. You saw nothing?"

Wicks shook his head again.

"Almost incredible," said the doctor; then: "There were twenty in the unit and they are all in solitary and will stay there till we get some answers. Who would want to kill you, Wicks?"

By now Wicks had a good idea, a Willie emissary perhaps, or maybe even one sent by the gray-haired Old Gimp himself. A close one; real close; with more to come, if …

O'Keefe, a grade-A trusty, finally managed to get a word alone with the now reviving Wicks.

"You crazy, Joe?" he whispered. "As soon as I heard you'd talked to Kramer I knew you were in for it."

"I didn't talk," gasped Wicks. "I was trying to make a deal."

"I been spreading it around you're okay," said O'Keefe. "That you were only asking about backing on a parole. But, Joe, if you talk to the fuzz again or even look like it, you'll go out of here in a box."

Wicks nodded wearily. He'd been a fool, and knew it now.

Dr. Parrish came quickly over to the operating table and brushed O'Keefe aside.

"What are you two talking about? It's not permitted, you know that—when we've got a matter like this under investigation."

"Sorry, Doc," said O'Keefe, grinning. "Joe's a pal of mine. I was asking him how he felt and if I could get him a drink. Things like that."

"Sure," said the doctor.

"God's truth," said O'Keefe.

He started away, but Dr. Parrish called him back.

"Do you know anything about this, O'Keefe?"

"Me? What would I know about what goes on in max. sec.? I'm minimum, Doc, remember? I never see them guys except at a distance."

Dr. Parrish reluctantly let him go.

Outside in the corridor two other trusties were waiting for O'Keefe: Blackly and Wertz. They regarded him curiously.

"Just like I said," said O'Keefe. "He was talking parole. Spread it around or this man is going to be sent over. If at first you don't succeed … you know *them* guys. Spread it."

Looking dubious, Blackly and Wertz left, in two minds about doing the Irishman's bidding. True, O'Keefe was a big man around the joint and could do you a lot of good, but with O'Keefe it wasn't a matter of life or death—with Willie it was. Everybody in the Walls was persuaded that Willie had reached in out of the shadows to have Wicks erased. Willie was a man to be feared.

At a turn in the infirmary corridor a big dark con, known as Tony the Moloney, was waiting for O'Keefe. Tony was one of the ball players, but he was torn by other loyalties and his face looked hard. O'Keefe glanced at him imperturbably.

"I'm trying to tell you, Fallon," said Tony. "Drop it. Keep your nose clear. Or you'll have a visitor."

"If I do," said O'Keefe, "he'll leave my presence feet first."

"The shiv'll be in before you know."

"Tony," said O'Keefe, "go tell your friends not to mess with me."

"*My* friends?" cried Tony, innocently.

"You heard me."

The morning papers carried a story about the attempted assassination of Joe Wicks, headed: "Did the long arm of Willie Madden reach into the Walls?"

And the 7th Precinct was clouded with gloom. Kramer had immediately driven to the prison. But his mission was futile. Wicks refused to see him. Kramer complained to the warden to no avail. If Wicks did not want to talk, the warden said, there was no way they could make him.

"Well, at least," Kramer said to Captain Bescher, "we know there was an eighth man."

"Do we?" Bescher demanded. "You mean you're taking that yellow louse's word?"

Kramer remained silent.

And that night, after a successful interview with Nick Fay and Carl Benedict, old Johnny Quaint, the man behind the scenes, the serpent in the bullrushes, had a long talk with his operative Y, who spoke as follows: "You can relax. The word is out. Wicks won't talk. Scaring him half to death was as good as killing him and it will only cost you fifteen hundred dollars."

Old Johnny wanted to protest but the return of that huge sheaf of lovely money mollified him. He astonished Y by handing him a hundred-dollar bill.

Y's upper lip kept twitching. The Old Man—was he getting senile at last, handing out hundred-dollar bills? Y felt shaken. To him Old Johnny was like a rock. He did not want to see him change into something else, even at the expense of himself. In a world of flux and chaos Old Johnny was something to cling to.

"O'Keefe went to bat for Wicks," said Y. "Johnny, you wouldn't know the Irishman. He's a big man around the prison. A real big man. With him it was only the booze."

"Drunken Irishmen, the worst," grumbled Old Johnny. "I've seen 'em for forty years lousing things up."

"You can relax, Johnny. Believe me," said Y. "O'Keefe and Orley Peters will never talk. And Wicks has had a lesson."

That night Old Johnny, feeling relieved and temporarily at ease, indulged himself in a bottle of imported beer and a Limburger cheese sandwich. So he would toss and turn later! It was worth it.

## FIFTEEN

The desk clerk looked up with a sudden show of interest, which he masked immediately, then smiled politely at the slim, beautifully-dressed Chinese girl confronting him.

She was San Francisco-smart in a plain black dress, black hat and white accessories, and she was carrying a large wrapped package, like a suit box. The clerk noted the Chinese lettering on the wrappings and the trademark *WU'S*.

"Yes Miss?" said the clerk.

"I'm to deliver this to Mr. Allen personally," she said. "I'm from Wu's."

"Yes, Miss. Shall I call for you? Or would you prefer to use the house phone?"

"Call, please. He's expecting the package."

The clerk nodded, his face composed, and made the call. Ordinarily, at The Carioca, the new big elegant San Francisco motor hotel, such things were discouraged. And perhaps Mr. Sergeant, the manager, might have handled it differently, but the clerk simply was not going to make difficulties for an apparent employee of Wu's—the finest and most expensive store in Chinatown—nor for Mr. Lawrence Allen, of Detroit, a prosperous, polite, quiet gentleman, who had been with them for over a month now and was well-liked by everybody about the place.

The clerk made the call, then said, smiling: "You may go ahead. Out through the lobby to your right. The Red Building. Suite A. First floor. You can't miss it."

But Miss Geraldine Fang, salesgirl and model from Wu's, was feeling very nervous, though keeping a mask-like look, and she wandered down ornamented pavements, past clipped shrubbery and fountains, and through vast congeries of spread out, two-story buildings before she found the place she was looking for. The "Red" Building to begin with was not red, but Mediterranean pink, and Miss Fang had been trained to be exact in regard to colors; it was part of her job.

Her nervousness grew out of the fact that she doubted Mr. Allen's intentions. True, he seemed very gentlemanly. True, young Charles Wu had been much taken with him. But there had been a look in his steady blue eyes that bothered Geraldine. Why must she deliver and model the kimono? True, it was very expensive—nearly three hundred dollars. Perhaps, as Mr. Wu explained, Mr. Allen merely wanted to be sure before he paid for it, as it was for his fiancé. All the same, something had been warning Miss Fang from the beginning that Mr. Allen's intentions weren't exactly as stated.

Mr. Lawrence Allen—or rather Willie Madden—opened the door at once to Miss Fang's knock, and stood smiling at her. He was wearing a roughly-woven polo shirt, with short sleeves. Miss Fang noticed the shirt, very expensive; also the forearms, much thicker than you would expect from Mr. Allen's general appearance.

"Well," said Willie, "did you get lost? Everybody does. They call this place the Little Pentagon around here."

"Yes," said Miss Fang. "Lost. Shall I try on the kimono for you now?"

"Are you in a big hurry?" asked Willie. "How about a drink? I've got rum, gin, and scotch."

"No, thank you. We are very busy at the store. I'm very sorry."

She turned away, took off her hat, then unwrapped the package and lifted out the almost startlingly beautiful black kimono, figured in red, orange and gold, and made of rich, heavy silk. Miss Fang displayed it with professional gestures for Willie's approval.

"Lovely, isn't it?" she asked.

"Great, great," said Willie.

With Willie looking on ironically Miss Fang carefully draped the kimono over her slender figure in various ways, then finally put it on and meticulously unwound and tied the sash.

Willie said nothing. A little out of countenance, Miss Fang took several turns in front of him, model style.

"It will make a lovely gift for your lady," said Miss Fang, professionally. "All women love exquisite garments like this."

"Do you love it?"

"Of course, Mr. Allen."

"Then it's yours," said Willie.

"But, Mr. Allen," said Miss Fang, "no, really. I couldn't possibly accept this. What about your fiancée?"

"Are you kidding?" asked Willie.

"Kidding? I don't know what you mean by that remark. Of course I'm serious."

"I believe you are," said Willie, studying her. "But this kimono, honey—

it's just a starter. A ... well, largesse, you might say. I like expensive women if they are as beautiful as you. Money's just no object with me."

"I'm sure it's not, Mr. Allen" said Miss Fang, draping the kimono over the back of a chair and turning, to put her hat back on.

Willie heaved a long sigh, then lit a cigarette, and began to pace back and forth.

"Sorry, Miss Fang," he said. "I thought you understood. I'm not used to Asian women. When we were talking in the store, I thought ..."

"Then possibly it's my fault," said Miss Fang. "What shall we do about the kimono?"

Willie struggled against feelings of frustration and the desire to be mean about the whole thing, now that Miss Fang had coolly rejected what he considered to be a very intriguing proposition.

"Oh, leave it. I'll find some use for it," he said. "What's the exact amount? Let's get it over with."

"It comes to two hundred and ninety-eight dollars and fifty-three cents, counting tax."

Willie countersigned three one-hundred-dollar traveler's checks and handed them to her, and to his amazement she counted him out a dollar and forty-seven cents change from her purse.

"Thank you, Mr. Allen," she said, rather primly.

"That was a real mixed-up trip I made to Wu's, said Willie. "I was only sightseeing. Too bad you weren't out to lunch."

"Sorry, Mr. Allen. But I didn't ..."

"Okay," said Willie. "Nobody was killed."

Willie held the door open for her, smiling.

"It's a shame," he said, "that's what it is. Maybe I should apologize. The approach. Did I insult you, Miss Fang?"

"Let's just call it a misunderstanding," said Miss Fang, in haste to get away.

He let her go. The door closed. Miss Fang hurried out of the Red Building as if she was afraid Mr. Allen might have a change of heart and pursue her. But really she was running from herself.

In a few short minutes an unknown man had put her through an emotional gamut that was completely outside her experience. Her father, her brothers, all the men she knew were painfully correct businessmen. Nothing in her short life had prepared her for this encounter with the blondish, blue-eyed stranger, who had seemed to be looking straight into her soul. She had wanted to take the kimono. Had he known that? She had wanted to have a drink with him. She had—Father and all her ancestors forgive her—wanted to remain. At the moment she felt warm and alive and torn by unusual emotions. With Roger Sing, the boy who wanted to marry her, it had never been like this, even when he timidly kissed her.

"I must be a bad woman," Miss Fang told herself, as she hurried through the lobby and smiled at the clerk who nodded and gestured politely.

In the taxi on the way back to Chinatown Miss Fang tried to compose herself. Why was she worrying? She'd done nothing wrong. Nothing had happened. And she'd made the sale and Mr. Wu, the younger, would be very pleased, and vindicated in his judgment of that fine gentleman, Mr. Lawrence Allen.

Willie wrote:

> *How about that! The brush by a heathen*
> *Chinese. Joker, you must be slipping!*
> *An offer like that to most girls and you'd*
> *have to leave town to get rid of them.*
> *What a doll! Like porcelain. Too fragile*
> *to handle, maybe. The first Asian woman*
> *I ever took a second look at.*
> *Stick to the kind you know!*

Then he burned this effusion and sent in a call for the bell captain. As he waited, he put on his glasses—and studied himself in the mirror. The glasses made a terrific, an unbelievable difference. He looked more elegant, more refined, more like a scholar or maybe a CPA. And the blondish hair added a further note of difference to the disguise and went very well with his fair complexion and blue eyes. The hair he'd done himself. The glasses were the real thing; no window-pane stuff for Willie. They were prescription. And Willie had been startled to discover that he suffered from mild astigmatism in one eye and mild nearsightedness in both. He found that although he didn't really need the glasses, he could see a hell of a lot better with them.

The bell captain finally arrived. He was a tall blond young man, with a wise guy look.

"As far as I'm concerned, the Sisters are played out," said Willie. "Any new ideas?"

"Of course, Mr. Allen," said the bell captain. "But if the Sisters pulled anything I'd like to know. I'm responsible."

"No, no," said Willie. "They're okay. All three of them. But I like to move on."

The bell captain smiled with a sort of admiration and shook his head.

"Yes sir, Mr. Allen," he said. "Let me make a couple of phone calls. I know a beautiful Portuguese girl—a real knockout; but don't know if she's free now. I been operating mostly with the Sisters. Those big girls take care of this place, you might say."

Willie gave the bell captain a large tip, dismissed him, then decided he'd take a long soak in the tub. He began to wonder why suddenly he'd decided to abandon the Ware Sisters, three big good-natured uninhibited blonds, and why the thought of the beautiful Portuguese girl—undiscovered country, therefore mysterious and intriguing—did not interest him more. Suddenly a vision of Miss Fang rose before his eyes, calm, elegant, aloof.

"Oh, no," cried Willie. "No dame's gonna spoil my fun." Then he soaked in the tub for twenty minutes, whistling scraps of tunes and trying to distract his mind.

He heard nothing from the bell captain, and finally in irritation put in a call for him.

"Sorry," said the bell captain. "I haven't been able to reach her. May be in Vegas. I'm working on it. Couldn't you make do tonight with …?"

"No!" cried Willie, then hung up.

Five minutes later he found himself calling Wu's, and Mr. Wu, the younger, came on full of businessman amiability.

"So glad you called, Mr. Allen. Want to tell you how pleased I am you took the kimono. It's the only one in stock in that class. We simply can't get them anymore."

"I just wanted to say that Miss Fang is a good salesman and a fine model," said Willie. "She's a credit to the establishment. A fine girl and a lady. It's a pleasure to do business with her."

"Oh, thank you. You must come in again. Always happy to serve you."

"Now why did I do that?" Willie asked himself, but in his heart, he—crafty Willie—knew.

Young Mr. Wu, beaming, called Miss Fang in and told her what Mr. Allen had said on the phone. Miss Fang seemed in a kind of fog.

"Was that all he said?"

"All!" cried young Mr. Wu, astonished. "I'd think it would be enough."

Miss Fang made no comment, and young Mr. Wu looked at her curiously as she wandered back to the counter as if in a dream.

## SIXTEEN

The Portuguese girl's name was Bella. She was short, shapely, dark and very pretty, but she had a cold eye and a seductive manner so obviously false that Willie's interest in her was slight from the first. But he forced himself, reading himself a lecture meanwhile.

It wasn't that he expected sentiment. Nor did he expect a girl like this to have any particular interest in him as a man rather than a customer. But Bella beat anything he'd ever seen for obtuseness. It was obvious that she considered Willie some kind of Square John sucker and she kept leading the conversation around to her friend, Ted, in Las Vegas, who knew all the "guys at the tables," as she put it, and might be able to rig up a "big win" for the right kind of man, a man with real money and class. If this didn't work, the badger game would probably be next. Her little head was full of cheap little conventional schemes to rook a sucker.

Willie let her run on. They were in a motel, near the ocean. Willie could hear the fog horns blowing in the distance.

Bella dressed leisurely displaying at some length what hadn't interested Willie very much in the first place.

"Could I contact you about Ted," she asked, slipping into her dress.

"Well," said Willie, "I don't know. I'm not much interested in gambling."

"Who's talking about gambling?" cried Bella. You only pretend to gamble, you understand. *They* see that you win. Then we split up the money."

"But that's dishonest," said Willie, with a straight face.

"Oh, I suppose you might call it that," said Bella. "But those big joints—they've got millions anyway. Who cares about a few thousand or so?"

"A very interesting philosophy," said Willie.

"It's like Robin Hood," said Bella.

"Why, I believe you're right," said Willie. "Like Robin Hood. Robbing the rich to pay the poor. We, I take it, are the poor?"

"Well, I am, anyway," said Bella. "I don't know about you. You look rich and classy to me. Ted's poor. I mean he has to scramble for everything he gets."

Willie had a mental picture of Ted, a sorry M'Gimp, always just one jump ahead of the bailiff or the police. Any guy who would use a silly girl like Bella for a come-on was either not very bright himself or suffering from hard times.

"I'm sorry," said Willie, "but I don't really believe I'm interested in your proposition."

"Oh, think it over," said Bella. "I'll see you again, I'm sure. Chris will know where to contact me."

"Chris?"

"The bell captain."

She was fully dressed now. Willie handed her an envelope. Unlike Adele, of pleasant memory, Bella at once brazenly ripped it open to study the contents.

"But, daddy," she said, pouting, "no tip?"

"Tip?" said Willie, faking bewilderment. "It's what we agreed."

Bella studied his face for a moment, then composed herself. Thinking about the future, Willie was certain.

Hoping for a big take later with the inestimable help of "Ted." "Oh, well," she said. "This is fine. And thank you."

"Thank *you*," said Willie.

As soon as he got back to the Carioca he called for the bell captain to come to his room.

"A dish, eh?" said the bell captain, grinning.

"Get rid of her," said Willie. "She'll get you in nothing but trouble. She's got a cheap hood on the string and she was trying to con me."

The wise guy look disappeared from the bell captain's face as if a slate had been wiped clean; his eyes showed worry, anxiety.

"But I just sent one of our best tenants over to the Shore Motel."

"How smart is he?"

"He's business smart," said the bell captain. "But ga-ga over girls. He's in his fifties and they can tell him anything."

"You sure he's left?"

The bell captain gave a start, then used Willie's phone to check. Mr. X had not left but he gave the bell captain a lengthy argument on the phone and in spite of the warning he could not be dissuaded from keeping his date.

"I gave her quite a build-up to this guy," said the bell captain. "He was drooling. Still is."

"Well, at least you warned him," said Willie. "Dump that girl."

"Yes sir," said the bell captain, definite respect showing in his eyes. "I hope you don't think ..."

"If I did, would I bring it up?" said Willie. "The Ware Sisters are just perfect for you. Stick to them."

"I'm awful sorry."

"No harm done."

"Mr. Allen," said the bell captain, "I pegged you as smart from the first. Maybe you saved my neck."

Willie gestured indifferently and the bell captain left.

Willie took off his clothes, got into his pajamas, and turned on the TV set. It was still fairly early—with a long dull night ahead.

He began to doodle on a hotel memo pad and finally wrote:

> *Dear Joker*
> *Time to move on. Bella was a good reminder.*
> *You may not be a sucker for a trollop like that,*
> *but you are a sucker for a little Chinese girl,*
> *named Geraldine. What is there to keep you here?*

He woke from a long unpleasant vague partially nightmarish dream. He was sitting up in bed sweating heavily and weaving uncontrollably from side to side. In a panic, he jumped out of bed, switched on the lights, and poured himself a drink.

For a while, as he drank, he managed to close his mind to the problem he must eventually face. *He was weaving again.* As a buoyant young man he'd been known as Willie the Weaver, and the name had stuck to him for a long time even after he'd stopped doing it. The cause? Unknown. Diagnosed by several doctors as a "nervous tic," it would come on him suddenly and unexplainably; in school, in a movie theatre, on the street.

In his twenty-eighth year it mysteriously went away. This was its first appearance in nearly seventeen years.

Willie felt very scared and he hadn't felt this emotion—this small boy fear—since he'd grown out of his teens. Terror he'd felt once—during the looting of the Kenmore Trust. Tenseness and nervousness were no strangers to him. And dread had shown its ugly face from time to time. But this small-boy scaredness—no!

He studied his image in the mirror. It was as usual except for the blond hair. Was this weaving kind of a nemesis? Had he been too lucky? Willie knocked wood quickly and frantically, then laughed at himself.

Time to leave. Yes, time to leave. Maybe the Carioca was bugging him—something about the atmosphere of rich, rank, mass-living newness. Maybe his encounter with that cheap pathetic little hustler, Bella, had stirred something deep inside him, something perhaps, connected with the long-forgotten past.

Or—the Chinese girl. Could it be her?

He wrote:

> *Dear Joker:*
> *East is East, and West is West. The inscrutable*
> *Oriental … and so forth. But that's all bosh. A woman*
> *is just a woman. Bella—Geraldine, where is the big*
> *difference.*
> *So roll on, little man. Go. Go. Get lost.*

He felt better as he returned to bed. The weaving did not recur.

# SEVENTEEN

Miss Fang was helping young Mr. Wu put away a new shipment of silk dresses from Hong Kong and Shanghai. It was a mild, gray afternoon, with high fog veiling the sun. Outside, tourists, with children and cameras, plodded endlessly past, staring at the garish sights of Chinatown.

Miss Fang seemed both nervous and preoccupied and was silent for so long that Charles Wu began to glance at her. Lovely girl, Miss Fang. She would make his friend, Roger Sing, an excellent wife. At best she talked little. Seemed to live in a world of her own. But taciturnity in a wife could hardly be classed as a drawback, nor living in a world of her own, if it kept her from meddling in her husband's business. In short, in Charles Wu's opinion, Miss Fang was a gem.

"Look at this," said Wu, holding up a beautifully tailored dress of raw beige silk, from Shanghai. "This is a beauty. Choice. My wife must see this."

"Yes," said Miss Fang, breaking her long silence. "I've been thinking …"

"Yes, Miss Fang?"

"Mr. Allen," said Miss Fang. "He's to be married soon, I imagine. His fiancée … wouldn't she be interested in garments like these?"

Miss Fang tried to keep her eyes lowered to the dresses, but she couldn't quite succeed. She glanced up, but Wu was smiling rather benevolently, innocent of any suspicion of her motives.

"Now why didn't I think of Mr. Allen?" he asked. "Will you call him?"

"Oh, no," said Miss Fang, hastily. "He might misunderstand."

Wu laughed, showing his perfect white teeth.

"You are a cautious one. Didn't I have to sell you on the idea of taking the kimono to Mr. Allen's hotel and modeling it for him? A perfect gentleman, Mr. Allen. But … all right. Maybe it's best I call him. More official."

Wu went to use the phone. Feeling very nervous, and not wanting to hear the conversation, Miss Fang hurried off to the ladies' room, where she stayed for nearly a quarter of an hour, redoing her eye makeup. When she returned Wu was busy with his inventory lists and so absorbed he didn't look up. Miss Fang said nothing.

Finally he glanced at her. "Will you help me check this second Shanghai list. Somehow it doesn't come out quite even."

"Yes, Mr. Wu."

They worked in silence for nearly half an hour until they found what was wrong with the list and finally checked it out.

Miss Fang's hands were cold, the rest of her body warm. It seemed to her that she kept flushing. But of course Wu noticed nothing. What had happened? Had Wu completed his phone call? If so, why did he say nothing?

Suddenly he looked up. "Oh! Mr. Allen. He's gone. Checked out."

Miss Fang couldn't resist a start and a stare.

"What's the matter, Miss Fang?" asked Wu. "Are you so surprised?"

"Yes," said Miss Fang. "From what he said I thought he intended to stay for a while."

"Maybe something came up," said Wu, returning to his work. "Too bad. He was a good customer."

"Did they say where he went?"

"I didn't ask. But I gathered he left town. I didn't inquire about a forwarding address. Mr. Allen is not the kind of man who buys by mail. Too particular. Perhaps he went back to Detroit."

Detroit! In the cold north of the United States, thousands of miles from the Golden Gate. Miss Fang had been born and raised in San Francisco and she'd never been out of the State of California. The Midwest, the East, seemed as remote to her as Europe or India.

"Miss Fang," said Wu. "Why don't you take a break? Get some tea. Walk about. It's slow today and you've been working hard since nine o'clock."

"Thank you, Mr. Wu," she said. "I'll go to Ching's for tea and cakes. If you need me ..."

"But I won't. Take your time."

It was like a reprieve. Now she could be alone in the semi-darkness of Ching's, where the tourists seldom came, and think and dream. All over like that? It seemed incredible, impossible to Miss Fang. What had her intentions been? Vague, very vague. Why'd she had any intentions at all? Mr. Allen obviously was not the kind of man anybody she knew would refer to as "nice." He was, when you came right down to it, just like many other older occidental men who had come into Wu's and ogled her—only perhaps smarter and certainly bolder.

Miss Fang sipped her tea. Molly Ching came in to talk to her but Miss Fang was not very communicative and finally Molly left, eyeing her rather oddly.

Detroit! Thousands of miles away. It seemed impossible. And finally Miss Fang decided that she just wouldn't believe it.

# EIGHTEEN

Carl was getting more and more fed up with Detective Sergeant Nick Fay. Nick was either turning into a hypochondriac or he was a very sick man who spent more time consulting doctors and thinking and talking about his illness than he did worrying about the real object of their quest: the finding of slippery Willie Madden and his loot.

They were driving down a hilly San Francisco street, with Carl at the wheel of Nick's car. Carl had his thick coarse wooly dark hair dyed a carroty red in emulation of what he was sure one of Willie's gambits would be. Nick thought he looked awful, and he was very tired of hearing the story of Carl's adventures in a beauty parlor where he'd gone to get the job done.

"This chick?" Carl would say. "A half blond big-eyed chick—should've seen the way she went for my story. I told her my wife was driving me crazy because she'd gone fruity for a red-haired guy, so I wanted my hair dyed the same color to give him a little competition ..."

"That's the most goddamn, silliest ..." Nick would cut in.

"But she went for it, hook, line and sinker," said Carl. "Man, was she sympathetic. Think I could have laid her right there in the shop if it hadn't been for all the others there. Yeah, she did the job up great for me, and wished me luck, and all that jazz. What bugs me is, I gotta go for a tint now and then as it grows out. You getting worried about me, Nick?"

And to Nick's disgust, Carl would roar.

"You'll go for no tints, you silly bastard," Nick would say. "You'll get some stuff in a drugstore and do it yourself. What are you trying to do, get caught?"

"But I'm dead," Carl would whoop. "Haven't you heard? I'm a stiff. And who goes looking for a stiff?"

There was a long silence in the car, then Nick said: "There it is."

"Wow! What a joint!" said Carl. "Damned if I'd be comfortable in a place like that. But it's Willie's kind. Why didn't we try it before?"

"It's brand new this year," said Nick. "I never heard of it."

Carl drove into the outer edge of the huge Carioca parking lot and parked. Nick got out, and said: "Now stay in the car and keep your head down. If Willie's here, he'll make you with one look, red hair and all."

"I'm listening to the ballgame on the radio," said Carl. "Don't worry about me."

Nick left. Carl sat watching him go, old skinny Nick Fay, with his stooped shoulders and his dejected air, a tough enough guy when you came right down to it, but fading, fading. The truth of the matter was that Carl and Nick had just about had it in regard to each other. A few more weeks of shoulder rubbing and somebody might get hurt. Togetherness was not their dish.

They'd sit down to eat and Nick would begin to shift about uneasily, then he'd rub his left chest gingerly with his right hand, and then shortly he'd begin the tale about his calcified lesion and the ambiguous finds of the electrocardiograph and his shooting pains and his weakness in the morning, etc., etc., etc. Meal after meal had been spoiled for Carl by this constant whining and complaining.

On the other hand Carl's coarseness grated on the far more sensitive Nick. Carl's jokes often made him wince and now and then Carl would do something—like goosing a waitress—that would put Nick into such a rage that it would take him a long time to calm himself.

"A slob, a dirty, stinking slob is what you are," he'd yell. "Suppose the girl makes a complaint."

"She won't," Carl would explain. "I pick my spots."

And Carl was right. His antics seldom caused any difficulties beyond a few outraged looks.

While Carl stayed in the background, Nick had cased the Pearl of the Orient at Tropico, and, using his badge, he'd even had a long talk with the young detective, Earl Jordan. No leads except a no-show reservation at the Fairmont. So they'd driven up the Coast Highway, stopping at all the swank spots for a look-see and inquiries, and then on to San Francisco, where Nick, a fine "make" guy and good at giving descriptions, including peculiarities, combed the expensive hotels, including the Fairmont.

The Carioca was their last stop, as they had already cased all of the richer motor hotels on the Peninsula.

Carl draped himself over the front seat, lit a cigarette, and listened to the Giants baseball broadcast. The season was almost over, and there was a very hot pennant race in the National League.

Meanwhile Cadillacs, Thunderbirds, Mercedes-Benzes and sports cars of all varieties came and went, with Carl ironically watching them. Where, oh, where, he wondered, did all these guys and gals with heavy moola come from? Maybe a million dollars' worth of cars going and coming as he sat there. Terrific! Maybe these Square Johns had a point, after all. The only trouble was, that the point involved knuckling under to something or somebody, and that Carl found impossible to do. Sink or swim, like Willie, he had to be his own man.

He couldn't take it in halves, or try to have it both ways, as mixed-up Nick Fay endeavored to do. And look at Nick. For years he hadn't known whether he was a swinger or a cop. So what happens? He turns out to be a swinging cop, which really, in Carl's opinion, meant turned out to be less than nothing at all.

It's true that he himself had done a little informing, but it wasn't because he was trying to have it both ways; he'd been merely trying to set up a usable connection within the police force—and he had succeeded: Nick Fay.

A sea breeze stirred his wooly red hair. The baseball game droned on. Carl sank lower in the seat so he would be in a better position to see the girls getting in and out of the cars. Life was good, Willie or no Willie. Life was good, if Nick would just shut up about his ailments!

Pretty soon Carl saw Nick coming toward him in the distance, in among the sparkling ornamented walks, the fountains and the shrubbery, skinny, stoop-shouldered, dejected-looking. But Carl knew it would be wrong to make any deductions from Nick's posture and attitude. He was always like that. Nothing seemed to shake him out of his depression, his constant griping, his self-pity. Carl had the strong healthy man's instinctive lack of understanding and even contempt for physical weakness and illness. And he was far too obtuse and thickheaded to try and put himself in Nick's place, to look at things from Nick's viewpoint. To a sick man the world looks sick, stale and unprofitable, and exterior circumstances have little effect on this attitude. Carl merely considered Nick a weak bore, exasperatingly impossible to please.

Nick came over and leaned on the car. "I made him," he said. "We just missed. He was living here under the name of Lawrence Allen of Detroit."

"How long has he been gone?"

"Three days."

Carl cursed under his breath and slapped at the car seat.

"All right, what do we do now?" asked Carl, in disgust.

"He left the same kind of forwarding address," said Nick, wearily, taking off his hat and mopping his forehead.

"Don't know what's making me sweat so much. It's not hot. It's coolish and there's fog in the air and ..."

Carl's big square face showed exaggerated irritation. "Never mind the sweating," he yelled. "What do we do?"

"You're a sympathetic bastard," cried Nick. "Can I help it if I feel lousy?"

Carl just sat looking at him, his lips compressed.

Nick sighed, put his hat back on and continued: "He's got a reservation at the Biltmore in L.A. Says he'll only be there a day or so and then will wire the hotel about a permanent forwarding address. Same gimmick. But as there was no rumble here he might—he just might—keep on using the same alias ..."

"Yeah," said Carl, his face clearing. "Good thinking. So what do we do?"

"I think he'll stay in California. Fall's coming on, and why go back to snow and sleet? I think he'll probably hang around the L.A. area some place. And, Carl—he's got blond hair and he's wearing glasses."

Carl giggled loudly. "Good idea. Think I'll get myself a pair, like Willie."

"When we get to Southern California you can wear sunglasses. Everybody does."

"Yeah," said Carl, grinning. "How about that? Old Carl Benedict, a movie poisonality. So what do we do?"

"We drive back, along the Coast Highway toward L.A. Soon as we get beyond San Luis Obispo, we'll begin to look around. I figured Willie will probably hole up in a Coast motel or hotel—the best, and there aren't too many of them."

"Let's go," said Carl.

"No," said Nick, wearily. "I want a good night's sleep first. This is wearing me down."

"You'll sleep in the car, goddamn it," yelled Carl. "I do all the driving. What the hell are you so worn down about? I'm not going to waste practically a whole day. Get in."

Nick obeyed in silence, sank back against the seat and closed his eyes. There was a lengthy pause as Carl drove up a long hill from the top of which they could see downtown San Francisco spread out before them, the big buildings towering up into the mild, grayish sky, the smaller buildings and houses looking like a cluster of dirty white blocks, set promiscuously on various levels. There was a gray line of water beyond and the mammoth curve of one arm of a bridge. Carl noted that gulls were flying overhead, right in the city, and that seemed odd to him.

"All right," said Nick. "Let's go get your bags. You're probably right, Carl."

"Sure I'm right," said Carl. "Strike while the iron is hot. That's what my old man always said."

Nick turned and looked at Carl in surprise, as if he couldn't quite imagine that once Carl had actually been a boy with anything as usual as a father. "What did your old man do, Carl?"

"Do? Well, you want a list? He fought club fights. He drank. He was a strike breaker. He played the horses. He was scared of my mother, and he belted the hell out of me and I deserved it. He wasn't a bad guy, as guys go—which ain't far! Want to know how he died? This will kill you. It was Christmas Eve. I was fifteen or thereabouts. The old man got loaded and bought a Christmas tree, which he put in the back of the car. The only trouble is, he run into a pig in some bar and took her to a motel. It was cold as hell, around zero. So they turned on the gas full in the heater in the hotel room. Well ... they never woke up. Fumes. And when the cops came, there was still that damned Christmas tree in the back of the old man's car." Carl snickered to himself.

Nick was shocked, remembering the austere North of Ireland face of his own father. Was Carl kidding? But, no—it was not the kind of story anybody would make up. It had the sad, frightening ring of truth. In the midst of life we are in death. Who knows who will be next? Nick shuddered involuntarily and gingerly touched the left side of his chest with his right hand.

But this time Carl did not notice. He was too busy remembering various disreputable and comic episodes in the life of his father, Big Tom Benedict—a real loser.

# NINETEEN

Chris, the bell captain, was a special favorite of Addison, one of the assistant managers of the Carioca, and in the privacy of his small office he often unburdened himself to the tall blond kid. This day was no exception. Addison had suffered a rather severe shock. The Carioca had been invaded by a police officer from the Midwest—badge and all—who had made many odd inquiries, taking up almost forty-five minutes of Addison's valuable time, and at last coming to the very odd conclusion that Mr. Lawrence Allen, of Detroit, one of the Carioca's choice guests for almost a month, was the man he was looking for.

"But that's preposterous," Addison exclaimed.

Chris said nothing. Being on the shady side himself, he had recognized something—a quality, a tone—in Mr. Allen that hadn't quite jibed with his being a retired businessman from Detroit. He had also recognized sharpness and ability of some kind. In fact, Curtis was pretty much taken with Mr. Allen and wanted to do him a favor.

"What did you do?" asked Chris.

"Well, I called the Biltmore in Los Angeles where Mr. Allen had a reservation. But it had been cancelled. I wanted to warn him. This is a terrible thing. But luckily he won't be at the Biltmore when the officer goes to look for him. There's been a terrible mistake of some kind."

"Yes sir," said Chris.

Chris went back to the locker room and thoughtfully smoked a cigarette. Finally he went to a pay phone and called the Ware Sisters, hoping that maybe Mr. Allen might have dropped a hint of some kind to them. But it was no use and Chris had known in his heart that it wouldn't be. A man like Mr. Allen doesn't unburden himself to whores.

But he didn't want to give up. Mr. Allen had treated him well, tipping him far beyond what was usual or necessary. And yet it wasn't just the money. Admiration played its part and the desire to emulate. Mr. Allen, whatever he was—and Chris had little doubt now that it was shady, probably a big con operator—was more or less what in the future Chris hoped to be. He was a lowly hustler now with a stable of girls; all the same he had money in the bank and a good job, and he was only in his twenty-fourth year—and looked younger.

Chris wracked his brain. "He gave me the tipoff on that gruesome little bum, Bella—maybe saved me police trouble."

Finally he remembered the talk around the hotel about Miss Geraldine Fang, of Wu's. The exquisite dish that had come to see Mr. Allen, carrying a package as a blind, or so everybody thought, although her stay had been brief. Yes, Miss Fang.

San Francisco-born, Chris hadn't been in Chinatown in years. Faded yellow sunlight, glancing down through the haze, streaked the garish shop fronts, and glimmered from the cameras of weary tourists plodding their way from shop to shop.

Mr. Wu looked at this tall young man, in tight cotton pants and a tweed sports coat patched with leather at the elbows, with rather polite suspicion.

"Miss Fang? She's right here."

At a gesture from Wu, Miss Fang came over. Chris smiled politely and put on his best Carioca manner, but he was thinking: "Oh, how I'd like to add this baby to my list. I'd make a fortune."

"Yes?" said Miss Fang, veiling her surprise.

"You don't remember me of course," said Chris. "I just saw you at a distance. But I'm the bell captain from the Carioca."

"Yes?" said Miss Fang, growing tense.

"One of our guests—Mr. Allen. I am trying to locate him. There's a letter. He had a reservation at the Biltmore in L.A.—but it was cancelled. And we've heard nothing from him. I remembered that he had business here when he was in town and ..."

Miss Fang seemed incapable of speech and Chris wondered what the hell was the matter with her. Wu joined them.

"Mr. Allen? No, sorry. I tried to contact him myself. I have no idea where he is. Perhaps he's gone back to Detroit.

Chris nodded politely and thanked Wu, but he was certain now that wherever "Mr. Allen" was from, it wasn't Detroit, and trying to locate him there would be the acme of the futile.

"You may be right," said Chris. "And maybe we'll hear from him from there, but if he calls or contacts you, will you please give him a message?"

"Of course. Certainly. Miss Fang, please take this down."

Miss Fang stood with pen and pad poised in her delicate ivory hands, her eyes lowered.

"Mr. Allen is to contact me—the bell captain, Chris—at the Carioca. Very important."

Chris thanked them again and left. Miss Fang carefully tore the note from her pad and handed it to Wu who slipped it into the cash register.

"This Mr. Allen," he said, "you'd think he'd be more careful about leaving forwarding address. He must get many important letters."

"Yes," said Miss Fang.

# TWENTY

The weaving had come back on him with such force and persistence that he'd driven into Los Angeles to see a "nerve" specialist, Dr. Horton Mahon, who had been recommended to him by the manager of the big new resort motor hotel, the Golden West, about two hundred miles or so, down the Coast from San Francisco, where he'd been staying since leaving the Carioca.

Willie could see that the doctor, a kindly-looking gray-haired man with shrewd gray eyes, was both puzzled and interested, after having given Willie a quick superficial physical examination, with the aid of a young nurse, who was deeply upsetting to Willie's equanimity in spite of her thick glasses and her cool silent efficiency ... He felt something in her he couldn't quite name, perhaps a strongly repressed sensuality.

Later Willie and the doctor talked in the doctor's small inner sanctum.

"You seem to be a very—I might almost say—an excessively healthy man, Mr. Allen," said the doctor, "and I hardly know what to tell you. A casual examination seems to indicate that, physically speaking, you are a far younger man than your years, as they say, and should feel the glow and tone of true health. The 'weaving,' as you call it, is very puzzling, and I've got to admit, a new one on me. You have two choices. I mean I will make two more recommendations, and you can choose the one more convenient to you. The first one is to enter a hospital and submit to exhaustive tests under my supervision. This might turn up something. The second one is to try a course of mild sedation that I will lay out for you. Obviously there is no immediate danger, Mr. Allen. If the examination shows nothing or on the other hand if the sedation doesn't work, we'll try something else."

Willie sat apparently thinking it over, as if really considering the alternatives. But actually he had already decided to forget the whole thing. To tie himself up in a hospital was out of the question. As for the sedation, he was a man who had to keep his wits about him at all times and could not risk grogginess, especially at night.

"Well," he said, "I think I'll just mull it over for a few days. Apparently I'm sound physically so it can't be very serious."

"On the contrary," said the doctor, "such a manifestation if unchecked might lead to something *very* serious. In my opinion this 'weaving' is only a symptom, of something much deeper. If you have time, we might delve back into your family history to look for a lead. But I'll leave all that up to you, Mr. Allen."

Then the doctor offered Willie a cigarette and they lit up and sat smoking. The nurse came in with some reports and Willie once more had a strong reaction to her. He glanced up. The doctor was looking at him curiously.

"Thank you, Dorothy," said the doctor, as the nurse seemed inclined to dawdle over her duties.

She went out.

"Polish?" asked Willie.

"Yes," said the doctor. "Dorothy Velinsky. Why?"

"I thought so," said Willie. "I'm of Irish descent. I used to live in a neighborhood that was half Irish, half Polish. I recognized something in that girl."

"What?" asked the doctor.

"Strong sex," said Willie. "Very common to Polish girls."

But Willie was really not certain what he *had* recognized and was a little surprised and even annoyed when the doctor laughed.

"You must have recognized something else," said the doctor. "Around the building Miss Velinsky is known as the 'Nun.' The men like her, she doesn't like the men. She is an interesting case. She studied to be a dancer—even ballet—but the looseness of morals of show business offended her so that she took up nursing."

"Something is wrong some place," said Willie.

"No," said the doctor. "Miss Velinsky is a highly intelligent girl and is only trying to find her niche. She would like to study medicine but she is already twenty-five and the pull would be long and rough, not to mention the expense."

The doctor seemed inclined to detain Willie for talk but Willie finally managed to take his leave. Miss Velinsky was standing in the outer office, talking to the girl receptionist behind the wicket.

"Goodbye, Mr. Allen," she said.

Willie turned and studied her. Even the starchiness and pure whiteness of her uniform did not disguise the lines of her voluptuous body. Behind the thick glasses, her eyes were a bright blue, and the hair under her cap was a glossy, blue-black. There was something about the soft curve of her firmly compressed lips ... Willie didn't know just what ...!

"Goodbye, Miss Velinsky," he said, then he went out rather hurriedly. The doctor buzzed and Miss Velinsky went into his office.

"What did you make of our new patient, Dorothy?" he asked.

"I'm not quite sure," she said.

"But something."

"Oh, yes. Something."

"I find him very interesting," said the doctor, "and I hope he comes back. But I have the feeling he will not."

"He looks so healthy. What could it be?"

"I don't know. There may be epilepsy in his family background. It's a delicate matter. But I would say he is a very troubled man."

And the doctor, though not perhaps in the way he intended, was right. All the long way back up the Coast Highway Willie felt vaguely shaken and deeply worried. What was it about Miss Velinsky ...? Only that she had reminded him of a time of his life he had almost completely forgotten? What else? And what did it matter? But in spite of his resistance, time rolled back over twenty-five years. He was a young spark again, with a wonderful way with a pool cue and a very sure hand with the Polish girls of his district ... Maia, Doll, Rosicka—how many more.

That was it—Miss Velinsky! She was very like—*too much like*—the Polish girls of that era.

And then suddenly a name struck at him out of the dark—Derucki! Lena Derucki—his shotgun bride. He remembered with a groan the fierce implacable looks of the Derucki tribe—her male relatives—with their blond mustaches and their fanatical blue eyes—and their threats that could not be ignored. For the first—and last—time, Willie had been forced to do something violently against his will ... marry Lena Derucki, a rather silly large voluptuous blond girl, with a body reminiscent of Miss Velinsky's.

Yes. That was it. Memories of the past crowding back pell-mell into his unwilling mind! And yet ... Velinsky ...? He'd heard the name before. In fact it rang a distant bell. But what was so strange about that? It was a common enough Polish name. Doubtless there had been quite a few Velinskys or Belinskys or names with a similar sound. Willie was not satisfied, but finally at long last he managed to shut off the thronging memories and escape back into the present.

He stopped off at a motor hotel that had a bar and grill, bought himself a sandwich and a glass of beer and sat looking off through the huge view windows at the Pacific Ocean spread out enormously before him, blue and calm to the farthest horizons. But he found that the sandwich seemed tasteless, the beer flat.

Later, when he'd got back to the Golden West, he wrote:

> *What is it with me, when nothing seems*
> *right, and everything is so mixed-up and*
> *confused? What am I worrying about?*
> *Why do I weave? Why does the sight of a*
> *Polish girl send me flying back into the past?*
>
> *Is there anything deader than the past?*
> *Joker, you are in a bad way.*

That night Willie took a solitary walk around the immensely spread out hotel grounds, with its hundreds of lights glimmering in the darkness, the music of a stringed orchestra flowing out from the dining room, and the old Pacific slapping peacefully on the sandy beach.

"Willie," said Willie, "I don't understand you at all. You've got it made! Can't you get that through your thick Irish head? You've got it made! So stop with the worrying."

But things did not improve with Willie. The weaving was now an almost nightly thing. It seemed to lie in wait for him. All day long it was out of the picture, so much so that at times Willie managed to forget about it entirely; in the morning he'd walk down the huge white beach, toward an old barnacle-covered breakwater, with the fresh, salty sea-breeze cooling and calming him; he'd dawdle at the pool, studying the women during the long sunny afternoons, and in the evening, after a walk through the grounds of the hotel, he'd have an excellent dinner in the grill, where there was a large white brick fireplace, and an air of opulent comfort—through all this his Enemy was apparently nowhere. Later, he'd read the papers and maybe a weekly magazine or two; then he'd mix himself a drink (Willie was and had always been very moderate with his drinking, having learned a lesson from the excesses of his father), settle himself comfortably, and watch TV. Where was his Enemy?

At last he'd go to bed, feeling calm and but mildly tired, and in a few minutes he'd be asleep. A blank hour or two would pass—and then suddenly the Enemy was there in the quiet deep of the night, in full force. Willie would awake with a wild start and find himself sitting upright in bed bathed in cold sweat and weaving uncontrollably from side to side.

His first emotion was always the petrifying little-boy scaredness, followed by wild annoyance, then rage. He'd jump out of bed and pace about the darkened bedroom, swearing and raving. And then little by little he'd calm himself, take a shower, change his pajamas and sit down in front of the TV set and stare for a while at whatever he could find on the dial at that late hour. Soon his eyelids would grow heavy and he'd go back to bed and fall into a deep dreamless sleep. The Enemy, too, slept, having apparently been worn out by the single attack.

In his youth, it hadn't been like this. The Enemy had been both more active and weaker, attacking him unexpectedly in and out of season, but with nothing like the strength of the present nocturnal assaults.

One night Willie wrote:

> *It must be as I thought. I've been too lucky.*
> *I pulled off the biggest coup and got away with*
> *it. It's like something is offended and wants to*
> *punish me. Nemesis—what else?*
> *If I hadn't lost my Faith, I might have some*
> *different ideas, but I leave all that jazz to*
> *the Old Lady and to Leo and Bernie. I had a*
> *bellyful of priests and cant in Parochial School*

After one very rough bout, he made up his mind he'd drive in and see Dr. Mahon again, but in the reassuring sunshine of the next morning things seemed to have a different look to them and he decided against it.

A night or so later, when he was getting out a box of new shirts from his closet, he noticed a large cardboard suit box pushed far back on the shelf. He didn't remember it. What could it be? After he'd shaved and dressed and got himself ready for his pleasant nightly visit to the grill, he took the box down and opened it. His first impression of the contents was of rich, glowing beauty. Black, gold, yellow, orange—a profusion of shining, shimmering silk. The *kimono*. Miss Fang's rejected present. He took it out, stared at it, then hung it over the back of a chair in his neat white-and-beige bedroom, where it made an opulent pool of Rococo beauty and almost completely changed the character of the room. In fact it looked so wonderful to Willie—a real feast for the eyes—that he left it there.

And it greeted him on his return, shimmering beautifully in the bare, austere, fluorescent-lit modern room, a protest against the deliberate ugliness, a promise that there was more to the world and to living than mass efficiency and good plumbing.

He left it on the chair. Even in the darkness dim reflections from the ground lights of the hotel touched it here and there, causing a faint rich glimmering in the bedroom. Willie fell asleep almost at once. The next thing he knew it was morning, with cars starting up outside, people talking and laughing, and little birds singing in the bushes beneath his bedroom windows.

Willie felt like a new man. Miss Fang! That was the answer. Miss Fang!

## TWENTY-ONE

Carl Benedict walked down to the pier for the hundredth time to watch the patient fishermen. These guys—wow! All morning, all afternoon, every day, they had their lines in the water and sat staring at the horizon. They cut bait. They untangled lines. They fixed reels. But they seldom talked. Among them were a few middle-aged women in shapeless clothes and old hats. Only their sex distinguished them from the men. They were just as silent, just as preoccupied. These people drove Carl daffy. He couldn't understand them at all. What did they think they were doing? Half the time they threw the fish back or gave them away. What clods!

Carl would sit on one of the benches, drinking beer from a can, and watching the fishermen sardonically. Did they all think they were going to live forever? Hour after hour after hour, fishing and cutting bait and staring at the horizon, while life roared past them on the Coast Highway and the sun moved slowly across the sky and then shortly another day of their lives had passed irretrievably into limbo, and what did they have to show for it? A few poor stinking fish.

Carl was in a bad mood. He wanted action. The fact that he had plenty of money in his pocket was no solace. What good was money if you couldn't trade it for pleasure? But day after day passed and Nick Fay still lay on his motel bed, groaning, and looking forward to the next visit of the doctor, a little near-sighted guy who seemed to have a cockeyed sense of humor and a genius for laughing in the wrong places.

Stranded: In a place like this—a diner, a filling station, a battered motel, a few scattered cottages up among the wooded hillside above the beach; and close by a pumping station and off-shore oil wells. Guys in oil-stained jumpers would crowd into the little diner in the evening laughing and talking up a storm and Carl would look at them and wonder what the hell they had to be so cheerful about. Carl was a big city boy, had never really known anything else. To him anywhere beyond the city was the Sticks—to be avoided. And this little Southern California beach village was the Sticks—all right—in spades!

That night after dinner Carl barged into Nick's room. Nick gave a jump on his bed, and then stared up at Carl in irritation.

"I was just falling into a nice doze," he complained.

Carl swore with feeling, then said: "You're always falling into a nice doze, and that little croaker is getting rich off you. You're a stinking goldbrick, that's what you are, taking old Johnny's money just to get a vacation …!"

Nick protested weakly, gesturing, and suddenly Carl, who was almost completely insulated from the troubles of others and obtusely unobservant, got a good look at Nick's hands. They were unbelievably skinny, like claws almost, and seemed transparent. The sight shocked him into silence. Then Nick really *was* a sick man; damned sick! The hands looked to Carl like those of a dead man.

"What took you?" asked Nick, raising his head, with a painful effort.

"I been thinking," said Carl. "I don't want to push you, Nick. I know you're pretty sick … so …"

Nick dragged himself to a sitting position and stared at Carl. It was one thing for him to insist that he was very sick indeed, but it was another thing altogether for Carl suddenly to be agreeing with him. He felt worried and frightened.

"Oh, I'm getting better. Feel stronger today."

"Sure, sure," said Carl. "I can see that. But you ain't going no place for a few days, and all I'm doing is sitting here on my can. Why don't I take the car and scout down the Coast, maybe a hundred miles or so, and then come back. See? At least I'd be doing something. Pretty soon I'm gonna flip, Nick. I can't take much more of this."

"I don't know," said Nick, suspiciously.

"Why not?"

"You're such a crazy bastard, Carl—you might get yourself in some kind of trouble and get picked up. You'd have my car, wouldn't you? It might be one hell of a mess."

"Nick," said Carl. "I may be a crazy bastard and likely to do crazy things, but not now. I'm thinking about that five hundred G's. I'm thinking how close we got to that little bastard, Willie. I'm thinking maybe luck's running with us. Come on, Nick. What can it hurt?"

With deep misgivings, Nick finally and weakly gave in. The truth of the matter was that he felt too ill to care very much.

The next morning early Carl got into Nick's car, adjusted his new sunglasses with a flourish, waved ironic goodbye to the patient fishermen on the pier, threw an irritated glance at the pumping station where a huge oiled piston worked day and night, and drove off southward along the winding Coast Highway, feeling free for the first time since leaving Chicago.

"That Nick," he muttered. "What a millstone!"

It was a beautiful late-summer day, with a tremendous bank of sculpted pure-white clouds at the sea-horizon. The sky was a clear azure, the sea a darker blue with streaks of green where riptides were running and brownish-red where there were marine fields of seaweed. Gulls were everywhere, flying overhead, thronging the beaches, creaking like rusty gates. The air was almost as pure and clear as in a desert and distances seemed impossibly vast.

Grinning to himself, Carl took a driving cap from the glove compartment and jammed it on his head. Sunglasses, a snazzy driving cap ... who would recognize old crazy Carl Benedict tricked out like this? Maybe not even keen-eyed Willie. No, not even Willie.

"A movie poisonality," said Carl. "That's me."

At noon he stopped for a sandwich at a roadside restaurant that overlooked the beach. There was a heavily made, sad-eyed blond woman behind the counter and Carl got talking with her.

"Any big beach hotel around here?" he asked, finally.

"Not close," said the woman, eyeing big rough-looking Carl with interest. "But there's a little motel right down the road, maybe a quarter of a mile. In them big places they charge awful."

Carl considered, in two or three minds about everything. Singleness of purpose had never been his long suit. He was no Willie. Why not lay over? The woman was ready for a tumble, that was obvious. Probably got bored in this out-of-the-way spot. But Nick would throw a fit—that was for sure—if he didn't turn up sometime that night. And anyway, would laying over be worth it?

He eyed the woman speculatively. She seemed to grow uncomfortable and finally said: "There's a real big expensive motor hotel about thirty miles down the highway—the Golden West. They tell me they get forty dollars a day for some of their rooms. Imagine!"

"Yeah," said Carl. "Jesse James without a horse. It's funny what the suckers will stand for."

He decided to move on and case the Golden West. Sounded like a place Willie might like. He could always come back. The woman would still be here, and besides, she wasn't really anything to write home about—just lonesome and willing.

"May be back this way," he said. "You usually around?"

"Yes," said the woman. "Till around six. Live just across the highway."

Carl winked at her. "See you," he said.

Carl gave a start and then sat rigid. As yet he couldn't quite believe his eyes.

He had just turned into the wide, tree-lined drive that led to the main building of the Golden West Motor Hotel ... when there it was—straight in front of Carl—in all his glory, the great Willie Madden, in a white Cadillac, parked, and nonchalantly talking to a bellboy in white jacket and plum-colored trousers with a gold stripe. Willie was also wearing sunglasses, like that movie personality, Carl Benedict, and his hair was blondish—but it was Willie all right. Little, shrewd and dangerous Willie, smart as a cobra and twice as deadly.

Carl began to sweat. He didn't know just what to do, how to handle this unexpected confrontation. Willie had the money stashed. He had to be patiently and carefully followed and dogged. But Carl was neither patient nor careful.

All Carl's instincts were for action and because he knew it would be folly to act now and he couldn't make up his mind how to proceed, he just sat there, sweating, in a daze of unaccustomed indecision.

While Carl hesitated, Willie gestured briefly and drove out along the road that led away from the Golden West to the Coast Highway, then he started North, driving leisurely, Carl noted, as if he didn't have a care in the world.

Suddenly making up his mind, Carl drove up the private road and headed off the bellboy.

"Yes sir?" said the boy, turning.

"Excuse me, son," said Carl, trying very hard to sound like his idea of a tame citizen or Square John, "could you tell me if you have a Mr. Lawrence Allen staying here?"

"Yes," said the boy; then he gestured. "He just pulled out."

"Oh, I didn't notice him," said Carl, with such unnatural casualness that the boy studied him, wondering what struck him as so odd about this big guy with the crazy-looking red hair. "Checking out?"

"No," said the boy. "He's just taking a drive up the coast, to see the sights, I guess. He'll be back."

"Did he say when? You see, I'm a friend of his, from his hometown. I'd kinda like to surprise him, for old time's sake."

"No," said the boy. "But I figure he may go on to San Francisco and eat dinner there."

"Then you expect him back tonight?"

"Oh, yes. I'm sure he'll be back tonight. Anyway, he'll be back. All his luggage is here. I just moved him to a new bungalow. A better one, away from the pool area. Gets pretty noisy there."

Carl grunted to himself with satisfaction. They had Willie now. Luck was with them. If Willie had "made" Carl there would have been an altogether different kettle of fish. They had him! The thing to do now was to drive back and give the good word to Nick—and it would probably pull him straight out of his sickbed—and then that night they would lay for Willie and start following him. Spending money didn't last forever; the stock would have to be replenished. Eventually they'd get a line on where Willie had stashed his loot—and then they'd figure some way to force his hand, scare him, make him run for his loot and then nail him once he'd got his hands on it.

Willie was just too smart to have very much of it with him at any one time. Of course his source of supply might be San Francisco—but Carl doubted that very much. Willie had just come from there. He wouldn't go back for money so soon.

"I gotta be living right," Carl told himself; then he said to the boy: "Is Mr. Allen's bungalow around this end of the place?"

"Yes," said the boy. "It's the one over there with the shake roof. Nicest one we got."

Carl grinned and handed the boy a dollar. "I may drop in on him tonight. We're old buddies. Will he be surprised! Kid, don't say nothing to him if you see him. Okay?"

"Okay," said the boy, still studying Carl, wondering about him. He looked tough, very tough. But that wasn't it entirely. There was something odd about him; the boy was not sure just what. Hardly the kind of man you would expect to be buddies with the gentlemanly Mr. Allen. "Were you in the Army together?" he asked.

"How'd you guess that!" said Carl, laughing to himself. "You're a smart kid."

Now the bellboy was satisfied. The Army. That explained it.

Carl drove back up the highway, chortling. For a dead man he was doing pretty good. He kept repeating the "joke" to himself and laughing.

He was so preoccupied and so pleased with himself that he passed the little eating place up the highway without giving the lonesome woman behind the counter a thought. He drove on, trying to imagine what it would be like to get his mitts on five hundred thousand dollars. And he remembered how wild and crazy he'd felt when he'd seen that over-a-million dollars dumped on the floor in that crummy little apartment ... and all had been well until the cops flushed Novak and Bellini—crazy bastards—they blew their stacks—they could have got away clear, but they wanted to play tough and fight it out with the cops. That blew the whistle! Carl sat hating those two men. All right, so they were dead. They just weren't dead enough to suit Carl. And he didn't blame Willie one bit for clouting those two extra shares. Why should he pay off the Novak and Bellini families when Novak and

Bellini had blown up the carefully planned job?

Willie had been livid. As for himself, he'd taken it on the lam with his share, while those three squares, O'Keefe, Wicks and Peters, were fooling around and hiding when they should have lammed out of town—and had got themselves grabbed by the furious coppers who caught them with their shares in their pockets.

Now thinking it all over, Carl began to feel little unusual stabs of worry. That magazine story—well, it had sure started the snowball rolling again. For a long time now the business had been cooled. But you could bet that the insurance men were heavy-handedly back in the picture, and the FBI, and the local fuzz and any other bastard who had any reason at all to get back into the act—aside from himself and Nick and the Old Gimp, John Q. Quait.

"It's going to get crowded, like," Carl told himself. "Pretty crowded."

But they had the inside track now. They'd "made" the big boy. There was just one thing: Nick. Was he equal to it? One man—even an iron man like himself—couldn't handle it alone.

As Carl drove into the little beat-up motor court, he looked about him with distaste. In contrast with Willie's Golden West, this was a real pigsty, and while Carl was not exactly choosy, being confronted graphically with the contrast made him extremely conscious of the disparity. Well ... maybe he could put Willie in a pigsty while he—Carl Benedict—pushed it up at forty dollars a day if he felt so inclined!

The door was ajar, the curtains drawn and there was an unpleasant smell of staleness in the room. Nick was lying on the bed, with his face to the wall. With a grimace of irritation, Carl let the blind fly up. Nick didn't stir. So Carl grabbed him roughly by the shoulder—but started back, shocked ... there was something ... something ... a chill breeze seemed suddenly to blow through the room ...

"This guy is dead," said Carl to himself, slowly, then he sank down into a chair and sat staring at Nick Fay's dead back. "So Nick had been *that* sick all along, and complaining about the pain in his left side, and all the rest, hadn't even been partly a gold bricking act ...?"

Carl felt no pity for Nick. He was just amazed how wrong a guy could be about another guy. Nick had been dying ever since they'd left the big Midwestern town on the river—and Carl hadn't even had an inkling of the state of things till that every morning when he'd noticed Nick's hands!

Luck—a weird thing! How it goes by fits and starts! A few minutes ago luck had given Carl a golden smile—he'd made Willie; now luck had turned its back on him. What a mess!

A dead guy on his hands. And if he held still for it, cops, questions, trouble, trouble, trouble.

Carl leaned his elbows on his knees, took his big head in his hands and started to think it all through. What was the best thing to do? But pondering alternate courses was new to him—and in a short while his head began to ache.

A couple of flies started to buzz around Nick, and cursing—feeling strange about the flies—Carl chased them away with a grimace of disgust.

"Nick, you bastard," he said aloud: "Why did you have to do this to me?"

Later that afternoon he went to the office and paid their bill. He was carrying not only his own money now but Nick's, and with it Nick's police department credentials and driving license—which might come in handy. Who knew?

"How's your partner, Mr. Carl?" asked the owner, a dreary-looking old geezer wearing a green eyeshade. "Struck me he was a pretty sick man."

"Yeah," said Carl. "I got to get him into L.A. to a special doctor, so we'll be checking out tonight."

The owner stamped the bill and counted out the change to Carl. "Yeah, he's a sick man, all right," he said. "I could tell. Been sick a lot myself."

Carl had the owner fill up the tank of the car and look it over generally—then he paid for the gas and oil and returned to the cabin.

A cheerful prospect was ahead of him. He intended to sit in the cabin with the remains of the crazy-mixed-up-cop, Nick Fay, till dark. He wanted to go and loaf on the pier or into the diner and listen to the jukebox, but he was afraid somebody might blunder into the cabin and find Nick dead. He'd just have to sit it out as the California sun climbed down the sky. Some vigil!

## TWENTY-TWO

Willie parked in a side street in Chinatown, and then set off in the direction of Mr. Wu's with the big cardboard box under his arm. The thought of seeing Miss Fang again had given him quite a lift, and maybe if things went well with them he might move back closer to San Francisco: he had noticed some nice spots on the Peninsula.

The streets were wreathed in thin grayish fog, through which the tourists trudged doggedly, looking about them at the sights of Chinatown, and although it was still afternoon, lights were lit in Mr. Wu's.

When Willie entered the store it was deserted, but Miss Fang came in immediately from the back, and then froze.

"Hello," said Willie, smiling at her, very pleased to see her—and she was just as he had been imagining her—a delicate unusual beauty, very very different from all others. It wasn't just something he had dreamed up out of loneliness.

"Don't you know me?"

"Of course I know you, Mr. Allen," she said. "But I am so surprised to see you."

Now she recognized the cardboard box. "Do you wish to return the kimono after all?" she asked, after a pause. "I'm sure Mr. Wu would ..."

"Well," said Willie, eyeing her ironically, "I don't have any use for it anymore. I've called off my marriage."

Mr. Wu appeared suddenly from a side office, peered at Willie through his glasses.

"It's Mr. Allen," said Miss Fang.

"Of course it is," said Mr. Wu, coming forward to shake hands. "And did you tell him there was an important letter for him at the Carioca?

Willie froze, then recovered. But Miss Fang seemed to be in a trance.

"Miss Fang," said Mr. Wu, peremptorily, leaning forward to study her.

"A letter?" said Willie.

"Miss Fang," said Mr. Wu, impatiently, "please get that message out of the cash register for Mr. Allen."

Willie began to feel very uneasy. Something was wrong, very wrong. Letter? Message? Willie put the cardboard box down on the counter and moved inconspicuously away from the windows. Out in the foggy streets somebody might be laying for him with lethal intent. For five years he had given them all the slip. Now that damned story had revived it all again. Were his enemies swarming once more as they had done during the first months?

Miss Fang punched the no-sale key and withdrew a small slip of paper from the till which she handed to Willie, who took in the message at a glance.

"The young man from the hotel said there was an important letter," said Mr. Wu, helpfully.

Willie pondered. The blond guy, Chris. Willie had done him a favor, maybe saved him from a police rap. Was he maybe trying to repay the gesture in kind? Willie knew the letter business was bosh, and instinct warned him there was danger—and here he was putting his silly neck out because of a heathen Chinese girl. It was hard to believe.

"I must look into this at once," he said. "I'll leave the kimono here, Miss Fang."

"I'm sure Mr. Wu will take it back, if that is what you wish," said

Miss Fang.

"Oh, yes," said Mr. Wu. "But we have some new materials from the Far East that might be of interest to you."

Miss Fang looked at nice but obtuse Mr. Wu with veiled irritation. Couldn't he see that something very important had come up for Mr. Allen?

"Yes, well, thanks," said Willie. "If I should happen to get hung up and not get back to you, I would like Miss Fang to have that kimono."

Mr. Wu merely stared uncomprehendingly. But Miss Fang felt weak. Something warned her Mr. Allen was in serious trouble, some emanation that passed between them.

Willie stood looking at her, then turned and went out. So the old weaving had come back on him with added strength! All right. He could take it. It was better than putting his neck in a noose over a girl. That was for suckers like Carl Benedict!

"I simply do not understand this at all," said Mr. Wu, staring at Miss Fang. "That kimono cost Mr. Allen three hundred dollars."

With an effort Miss Fang forced herself to speak. "I think it is his way of joking," she said. "Of course he will be back."

But she felt certain in her heart that she would never see him again.

Willie called the Carioca from a public pay phone, after he had put the foggy streets of Chinatown behind him—he was high up now, with San Francisco spread out below him, only visible here and there, as the fog blew and drifted slowly away, nudged by lazy wind.

After some delay, Chris came on and after a blank pause, due to surprise, he explained to Willie what had happened. Willie asked for further details but Chris said: "I didn't see the guy. Mr. Addison talked with him. But he was a detective from the Midwest. Mr. Addison was very upset and anxious to contact you because he was sure it was a mistake and didn't want you embarrassed."

Willie pondered. A detective? Anybody could carry a badge. It might be some smart-alecky hoodlum, looking for half a million dollars. He asked to speak with Mr. Addison and after a long delay, Chris put him on.

Willie had a hard time getting Mr. Addison to stop apologizing but finally he got him down to business and in a few minutes he had "made" his man: Nick Fay, the crooked copper.

And this was bad, as Nick was a very shrewd operator, patient, thorough—and he himself was registered at the Golden West under the same name he had used at the Carioca.

Willie thanked Mr. Addison, assured him it was all a mistake, then Chris got back on and Willie told the bell captain to expect something in the mail. Addison was a fool but Chris was not, and the kid had tabbed Willie as an "operator" and so had done him a favor, and a big one!

And so without further delay, and putting San Francisco behind him, Willie drove off toward the Golden West, turning over in his mind just how he intended to proceed. Checking out now was out of the question, with Nick Fay roaming the West. He'd have to slip in after dark and break into his own bungalow—which offered no difficulties; the big French windows could be opened with a knife blade and were in a sheltered spot at the back. Entering the front with a key was too dangerous. The place might even be watched by now. But Willie refused to simply walk away from it. One of his bags had a cunningly hidden false side; and in this false side was a lot of necessary equipment, a handgun, a book of traveler's checks (now useless) and a wad of emergency getaway money—three thousand dollars.

As Willie drove south along the Coast Highway, with the day already beginning to fail, he kept working out step by step the way he intended to proceed. It was the first really bad rumble he'd had in years. The magazine rumble at the Pearl of The Orient had been minor compared to this.

Nick Fay was a bad one—and you never knew which side of the fence he was operating on. He might even be playing both ends against the middle—and then there was that crooked old devil, John Q. Quait. Had they teamed up?

Carl Benedict, of course, never crossed his mind.

## TWENTY-THREE

Night had finally fallen and the lights had come on along the pier and at the pumping station. Carl heaved a sigh of relief—it was time to move. He opened the door and looked out. Nobody in view. The jukebox was playing in the diner. The owner was nowhere to be seen. Carl slid past on the Coast Highway.

Carl drove the car up as close to the door of the motel cabin as possible, then he put the bags in the back and locked the trunk.

"Nick," he said, "you're next."

It was a gruesome task, even for Carl, who grimaced with distaste as he hefted the body of the featherweight Nick in his arms, carried him across the room to the door, and laid him in the back seat after an irritating struggle in which various parts of Nick's anatomy kept finding obstructions and impeding him. Finally Carl covered Nick with a blanket.

Then he got in the car and was just driving out when the owner appeared from the diner, and waved farewell.

"So long."

Carl grinned and waved back then he jerked his thumb at the backseat. "He's laying down. Me—I'm the chauffeur."

The owner laughed, then started toward the filling station. Carl shook his head as he moved off onto the Coast Highway and turned south. Man, what life—dull, dismal, with that damned big piston going day and night and the slobs out on the pier fishing and the jukebox playing kid-music in the diner and the crummy-looking filling station, with the owner pumping gas from morning till night—day after day after day—how did guys stand it? Carl had rebelled from just such a life. Which was better—a long and dismal life, or a short and merry one? With Carl it was no contest! But the trouble with his friend, Willie, was, he had, in a way, wanted it both ways—and a man just couldn't have it both ways; at least in Carl's opinion.

Carl had already picked the spot to dump Nick. On his way south that morning he'd noticed an old rickety wooden breakwater or former pier extending well out from the beach, and it was located in an empty stretch of the road, with nothing about—the palisades on one side and the ocean on the other and then what looked like an endless curving stretch of sand, loaded with reddish seaweed and driftwood. The only inhabitants, gulls, hundreds of them.

But night changes the look of things, and Carl drove several miles past the breakwater without realizing it and then had to go back and search for it. But there it finally was—a long splotch of blackness in the starlight, with the waves rolling in past it and breaking, with a soft slap and murmuring, on the sand.

Carl drove off onto the shoulder, as close to the water as possible, then he got out, lifted Nick in his arms and carried him to the end of the breakwater, stumbling and cursing, and with the piles swaying under him as if the whole thing might go at any minute.

He put Nick down, then returned for Nick's bags and a couple of lengths of rope he'd prepared during the afternoon vigil in the motel room. He tied the bags—and one of them was very heavy—to Nick's feet. Then he rose and looked about him. Nothing. Emptiness, as if he was at the end of the world. Then a car went past at a high rate of speed, and another. And then finally, emptiness again. Stars, palisades, beach—and a soft California night.

Carl looked down at the supine figure of Nick for a moment. "Well, Nick," he said, "here goes." He rolled Nick over and heaved him off the end of the breakwater. Nick hit with a splash. The heavy bags went down first, pulling Nick with them.

"So long, Nick," said Carl.

But there was just one trouble. Nick's hat floated. Cursing, Carl knelt down on the rickety breakwater and leaned far over to retrieve it. Then he just squatted there looking at it. They'd find Nick eventually perhaps, but why leave a marker, like a buoy, to guide them?

Carl crumpled up the wet hat and thrust it into his pocket. Further along, he'd toss it out.

A dozen miles south Carl pulled into a rather large complex of filling station, restaurant, and motor court and looked for and found a public telephone booth. He was alone now and that was no good. It was a round-the-clock job. And it was worth five hundred grand. And he just wasn't going to blow it out of heedlessness, his usual heedlessness!

He stood in the booth with the door open, trying to figure out the time differential. Finally it came to him; three hours. That would make it about right. But it took him quite a while to get Quait on the phone, and the old boy was wary and sore as hell.

But when he heard the beginning of the "tale," as the boys called it, he calmed down and listened as the "editor" gave it to him.

"I'll get the first plane out if possible," said old John Q., and Carl could hear his heavy breathing all the way from the hometown—the old boy smelled money, big money, and he was excited, very excited!

John Q. had been to the Coast several times in the course of his life and he knew a small hotel in downtown Los Angeles that was "private" and with no questions asked. Carl was to contact him there by phone the next day. If he wasn't there, Carl was to keep calling. He'd be there eventually. He had to round himself up a helper.

"You see," John Q. explained, "I ain't as young as I used to be."

"You're breaking my heart," said Carl, as he hung up.

Soon the Golden West loomed up before Carl, a huge string of lights among the trees—what a joint it looked like at night!

Carl drove out on the shoulder and parked, with the entrance road just ahead. Willie would not be able to make the place without Carl seeing him—and Willie was expecting nothing, nothing. He was beautifully set up.

Carl, shifting about in his seat, smoked one cigarette after another and finally he grew impatient. Why not prowl Willie's bungalow, just to see what he could see—maybe a wad of loose money, with Willie blaming the theft on the help, maybe on the kid bellboy who had moved his bags and knew he was away!

The idea pleased Carl and chortling to himself, he left his car and followed along beside the tall hedge at the end of the Golden West and moved past the elegant backs of several bungalows. In one of them a woman was walking about in a very short sleeping coat and apparently nothing else, probably getting dressed to go out. Carl, a born prowler, watched her for a moment. Should he look in the window and scare hell out of her?

"Carl, you idiot," he told himself, "what are you looking for—a rumble?"

All the same his new role was growing very irksome to Carl. To be patient, to be careful—that was not his line. He acted on impulse. So it got him into trouble. So what?

"Be smart, be smart," he pleaded.

And finally he managed to make himself move on.

It was dark in Willie's bungalow. Carl crossed a kind of small garden and reached the back, where there were floor-length glass doors—nothing, flimsy, duck soup. Carl sprung the catch with a penknife, opened one of the windows and walked in—just like that.

Had Willie gone soft? Anybody could slip in on him in the middle of the night. But then … of course … Willie thought he had it made, and was living now just like any other Square John with money!

Now Carl was on the flat roof of a two-story complex of small apartments, a part of the Golden West's vast spread of dwelling units, directly across from Willie's bungalow, and he was getting very impatient with Willie. The prowl had netted him only three dollars and seventy-five cents in silver and a pair of star sapphire cuff links. He'd prowled Willie's bags and found nothing. That Willie—what a cagey character! Of course in other days Carl would have taken the two electric razors, the television set, the radio, the bags, the clothes and practically anything else that wasn't nailed down—but that was then and now was now!

Carl overcame his irritation long enough to chortle. Willie would probably raise hell with the help about those star sapphire cuff links, worth maybe from five hundred to a thousand dollars, and also about his tipping-silver that Carl had found in a drawer. Oh, Willie would be livid!

Carl raised his head and looked about him. He was in a perfect spot. On his right he could see the entrance road where Willie would have to drive in. And at the side of the bungalow was a carport for Willie's car. Carl intended to "put Willie to bed", and then grab a little shuteye himself on the rooftop. As it began to get light he'd return to his car. Keep an eye on Willie and later maybe get a chance to put in a call to old John Q.'s hotel. He needed that helper bad. A guy could go nuts on around-the-clock stakeout.

Time passed. Carl yawned, then shook himself awake. This rooftop stakeout kept reminding him of something; what was it? And finally it came to him. The old oil-storage tank, where he'd fallen asleep waiting for his meeting with Nick Fay.

Yeah, the old oil-storage tank, that had served him so well as a hideaway when he'd been on the lam. The last place anybody would ever look—high above the city, with the lights stretching away in the darkness in all directions ...

Cars kept driving into the Golden West. Music came to his ears. The Square Johns were holding a dance someplace on the grounds, and people were coming in droves. A dinner dance, must be, as it was still pretty early.

Time drowsed on. Carl got down behind the parapet, lit a match and looked at his watch. At first he thought it had stopped. How could time go so slow?

Cursing, Carl thought: "This just ain't for me. Not for me at all. I wish I'd told the Gimp to bring *two* helpers."

Beyond the swank confines of the Golden West to the north was what had once been a picnic grounds. It was now being readied for use as a housing development; beach houses, for upper income groups. But little had been done as yet beyond clearing the area of rustic picnic tables and benches.

The ground was solid and well packed and Willie, with his lights out, drove across it with no trouble at all, in among widely spaced tall trees.

Willie drove up fairly close to the high Golden West boundary hedge, then turned the car around, so he would be heading for the road, and getting out of the car, he left the motor running.

After a quick look around, he moved in behind the bungalows through a small gap in the hedge he had noticed earlier, a gap so narrow that he had to take it very easy as he squeezed through, otherwise he might rip his shirt or coat—and he didn't want to leave in a hurry tattered and torn.

In total darkness he moved in behind his bungalow—it was the only dark one in the row—crossed the little backyard or garden, where he had expected to sun himself the next day, and he was just reaching for the big pocketknife he always carried when he noticed that one French window was unlocked and slightly ajar.

Willie froze and stood listening. Did he have a visitor? Was somebody laying for him and expecting him to enter normally by the front door? Willie let the minutes pass.

His hearing was excessively acute and he was very patient in an emergency and could outwait anybody. A faint slide of a foot would give a man away; even heavy breathing.

Dead silence. Slowly and silently Willie opened the French window and then stood with his back to the wall beside it and listened. Nothing.

Maybe he was making a Federal case out of an accident. Maybe he himself had left the window ajar. After all, he'd been busy supervising the transfer of the luggage and all the rest, and not expecting a rumble of any kind.

All the same there was only one way to proceed: as if his life was at stake.

He took the big clasp-knife out of his pocket and sprung the longest blade—it was quite a shiv—enough to give a guy his finish if applied correctly. Holding the knife low in his right hand, he swung around the wall into the room, and with his back once more against the wall, inside the bungalow now, waited.

He could hear a clock ticking someplace. But he had no clock. So it must be in the bungalow next door and he was hearing it through an open window, that's how quiet it was.

Still Willie waited, but there wasn't a stir, a sound; it was like a tomb except for the distant ticking.

Now he moved, inching along with his back to the wall, till he reached the bedroom. Its door was wide open. He listened. All quiet. He slipped quickly into the bedroom, knife held low, ready, but only blank darkness greeted him.

After a long wait, Willie silently shut the bedroom door behind him, then taking a pinpoint flashlight from his inner pocket he began to get ready to pack.

On the roof opposite, Carl yawned widely, then roused himself, cursing. This was too much of a good thing, far too much!

Willie saw at once that the joint had been prowled all right, but probably by a sneak thief, or somebody that worked in the place—maybe that bright, cheerful bellboy!

What would Nick Fay be doing clouting a handful of silver or even star sapphire cufflinks?

Willie opened the false side of one of the bags, examined the contents—all secure—then he took out the snub-nosed handgun and slipped it into his coat pocket.

Sneak thief or no sneak thief—he was taking no chances, with Nick Fay on his trail.

Carl stiffened. He felt almost sure he had caught a glimpse of a very faint beam of light in Willie's bungalow. Or was it only a reflection from some place? Maybe on the windows—a car turning in or ...

But there it was again ...

Carl climbed down hurriedly, making quite a lot of noise, but nobody seemed to notice in the big dwelling unit, with television sets and radios, and talking and laughing—people living it up.

Carl approached the bungalow with very little caution, watching intently. A beam of light—a tiny little beam—moved through the living room, then went out. Carl thought he heard a door shut or a window slam. His heart gave a leap—and wild anger tugged at him. Willie— that son-of-a-bitch was outfoxing him!

He tore down the row of bungalows and then around the last one in time to see a dark moving object disappearing into the hedge—as if the high vegetation had swallowed it up.

Carl ran heedlessly down the hedge row, and after quite a struggle forced his huge heavy body through the gap, tearing his shirt and scratching his face, and emerging just in time to see a slight figure, carrying two bags, moving staggeringly toward a big white car.

Willie!

Carl blew his top and jerked his gun. "Willie! Willie!" he yelled. "I gotta talk to you."

Willie started, but ignored him. Carl Benedict! Good God!

Just as Willie climbed into the car Carl fired and Willie felt a sharp painful sting, like a rip from barbed wire in the lower calf of his left leg, then he slammed the door and drove out, headed for the Coast Highway.

South now, toward the strung-out complexities of Los Angeles over two hundred miles away. No more small towns now. No more Highway luxury motels. It was time to bury himself among the millions.

But he hadn't gone three miles when he realized that Carl was after him—and that big gorilla was nobody to have on your trail. He simply did not know the meaning of caution or fear once he was aroused, the most crazily dangerous guy Willie had ever met. And where in the name of God had he come from? Was he teamed up with Nick?

A cold chill went down Willie's spine. Had crazy Carl prowled his bungalow? It was more than likely.

There was a stretch of empty road. In the rearview mirror Willie saw Carl's car swaying from side to side as it gathered speed. Willie was never one to overestimate himself. He knew Carl could outdrive him simply because Carl would not count the costs. So there was a crash. So he got killed. So what the hell!

Willie gave a start. Up ahead he saw a string of lights, a filling station, stores, and a traffic signal. No good if he got it on the red light; Carl would be right on him. Off to his left was a paved road that seemed to lead into the mountains. Willie took it, tires screeching.

It climbed up and up, winding around the shoulder of a hill. Willie could see nothing in the rearview mirror, too many curves, but he was pretty sure that Carl was right behind him. Suppose this road led to a dead end, to nothingness? No good!

Just as he took another curve he saw on his right a wide flat space beyond the shoulder of the road and hidden by a mountain spur—maybe a little picnic spot or a place to look at the scenery. He pulled off into it quickly, cutting his lights.

In a moment Carl roared heedlessly past, on his way up the hilly road. But just as Willie was starting to turn his car around, here came Carl hurtling back. He'd got the idea quickly.

Now things got suddenly very mixed-up for Willie. Carl was yelling at him, cursing. There was a wild screeching and screaming of brakes. But acting automatically Willie coldly fired three times. With a loud despairing curse and cry, Carl fell back on the seat and disappeared. But just as Willie was pulling out, Carl raised up again trying to get in a shot. Willie ducked down and went on up the mountain, just barely skirting disaster.

But no shot was fired by Carl, who staggered out of the car, stood calling curses after Willie, then fell flat on his face beside the road.

Lights whirled before Carl's eyes, round and round. He was up on the oil-storage tank, waiting for Nick Fay. Something happened, something dark and terrible—he didn't know what. Then all at once he jumped off the platform—sailing head over heels down toward the black asphalt below that seemed to fly up to meet him.

The road appeared to wind over hill and dale, up and down and going no place fast, but finally it flattened out. Willie crossed kind of a deserted plateau, then saw lights up ahead. A town.

He pulled into a filling station and asked the way to Los Angeles and was told; and then for two hours Willie wound on across open country till finally up ahead he saw in the sky the wide red glow of the great metropolitan area of Los Angeles.

His leg was throbbing like a toothache, but Willie knew enough about wounds to realize that this one was superficial.

He kept thinking about crazy Carl and his stupidity. What did he have to gain by shooting at Willie? It didn't make sense. Did he think Willie carried five hundred thousand dollars around in his pocket? "If that big gorilla's not dead this time, I give up," thought Willie.

Moving through dimly-lighted, immensely strung-out suburban areas, Willie finally got completely turned around, took a wrong turn and instead of winding up in downtown Los Angeles, he found himself once more in a beach community—but this was a big town—Santa Monica— and well enough suited to his purposes, at least for the night.

He was soon settled in a very nice room—nothing like the Golden West or the Carioca of course—but new and clean and with all appointments, and now dressed in nothing but the top of his pajamas, he was taking care of first things first: the wound in his leg, which was worse than he had thought. He bathed off the coagulated blood, revealing a cut—or snag—about an inch long and fairly deep, if the bullet had been a little to the right he might have been in real trouble, with possibly a broken bone. No, the bullet had merely nicked the flesh in passing, ripping through and going on.

Willie used aftershave lotion as an antiseptic, then he danced around on one foot, grimacing and cursing as the pain shot all the way up through his leg. Kill or cure? Finally he tightly bandaged it with strips torn from the tail of a white shirt. But Willie didn't like the looks of the wound, and all he needed now was to get an infection!

A plan began to run through his mind in regard to the wound; and the plan brought a quick momentary smile to his lips—it would be a test of his instincts; but it would have to wait till early the next day. Meanwhile, there was work to be done and plans to be made.

He put in a call to the Golden West and finally got the assistant manager on the phone; explained to him that he had been forced to check out in a hurry, due to the extreme illness of a relative, asked the amount of his bill and told the manager it would be in the mail, first thing in the morning. The assistant manager had been very taken with gentlemanly Mr. Allen and was all concern and cooperation. Willie could hardly get him off the phone.

Willie had no desire to leave a rumble behind him that might lead to inquiries; besides, he intended to pay the bill in countersigned traveler's checks that were of no use to him now—Lawrence Allen would soon join James Shannon in limbo. And a new phantom would appear on the morrow—John Ward. With out-of-state driver's license and other credentials all complete—they were resting at that moment in the false side of his traveling bag.

And there were other matters.

He intended to reward Chris at the Carioca with a large hunk of countersigned traveler's checks in the name, of course, of Lawrence Allen. Chris was a bright boy and out of acumen had saved Willie from a bad beef. Carl Benedict, for God's sake. Besides, Willie might return to San Francisco and Chris could prove useful.

Then there was the matter of the rented car. It was from a downtown L.A. rental office. Willie would return it in the name of Lawrence Allen, then go to another rental office and get an entirely different kind of car, in the name of John Ward. If anybody was looking for a white Cadillac involving Lawrence Allen they would be looking in vain.

And finally, in a few days, when the heat was off, Willie would have to make a trip to his source of supply. In the name of Lawrence Allen he was taking quite a loss—better than two thousand dollars—but safety at times is worth far more than money, a lesson that Carl Benedict, of ferocious memory, could never learn.

It was getting late. Willie turned out the lights, switched on the TV, and got into bed. Cars whipped past on the Coast Highway, not thirty feet from his door; there was laughter and talking in the street. A cool ocean breeze was blowing in through one of his windows.

Nervously tired from the strain, Willie fell into a deep sleep—then started out of it, shaking. A voice seemed to be murmuring in his ear. Cold sweat rolled down Willie's back until he realized that he'd fallen asleep with the TV on, and now a "drama" was in progress in which a young lady seemed to be in one hell of a mess.

Willie got out of bed and switched off the TV; then he glanced at his wristwatch. He was amazed to discover he'd been asleep for nearly two hours.

He poured himself a glass of water and sat on the lounge to drink it. Then he got out his pen and wrote:

> *Dear Joker:*
> *Did you expect it to be all peaches and cream?*
> *Willie, when a guy gets away with five hundred*
> *thousand dollars of somebody else's money, he's in trouble.*
> *The vultures will gather.*
> *The hounds will smell the money.*
> *But what makes a man a big man? Money.*
> *What gets a man respect? Money.*
> *What get a man contempt? Being out of money.*
> *So Willie, sit tight, hold your horses, keep your shirt on.*
> *You got the wherewithal. The problem: keeping it.*
> *This, joker, you will do, come hell or high water.*
>
> *At least you didn't wake up weaving.*

Feeling better now, as he always did after giving written expression to his feelings, Willie sat sipping his glass of water and watching the little letter burn up in the ashtray.

# TWENTY-FOUR

The jet roared on and John Q. Quait, of course, was in economy class. He sat with his eyes closed, feigning sleep, but actually worrying— black worries. Reports from the Walls were that Wicks was at it again, had been flung into solitary, in spite of the protests of Dr. Traven, and was finally and completely cracking up. Y had told old John that they might have to take care of him as soon as he was released from the hole—at an additional cost to old Johnny of thirty-five hundred dollars.

Did the fools think money grew on trees?

But if Wicks finally talked and the coppers made it stick old Johnny would lose his license and maybe, in spite of his advanced age, do a jolt in the very same prison.

Why was the world so full of incompetent fools? Why were there so few Willie Maddens?

The jet roared forward through the starry night sky and Quait sat with his eyes closed, worrying.

Several seats back was his helper, a character by the name of Cheever, who was known variously as the Cheev and the Cat and also, by a few, as the Skunk. He was a former private investigator who had specialized in divorce cases, and blackmail—had been caught at it, had lost his license, and the huge iron doors of the Walls had closed behind him, but only for a short jolt that the Cheev bragged he had done "on his head."

Although he often worked for Quait, he was not on any scannable payroll and was completely unacknowledged. Quait was a "respectable" licensed practitioner and could not associate himself officially with such as the Cheev.

The Cheev spent half his time catnapping, making up for sleep he'd lost on stakeouts and night prowls. At the drop of a pin his yellowish, catlike eyes would open. He could leap from complete immobility to furious action. At times he seemed to have no bones in his body and to be made of rubber. He was an adept at escaping from impossible situations. And he had very little to say about anything.

He was, to Quait, a weirdie—but a valuable one, because he was always broke, and had to take what the old man gave him and shut up about it. Beggars can never be choosers.

He and Quait were traveling separately, and it was the play to ignore each other. They would register at Quait's little "private" hotel separately and from different towns. They would get together only surreptitiously ...

Old Johnny opened his eyes. A pretty blonde stewardess was regarding him indulgently.

"Have a nice nap, sir?"

"Yeah, thanks," said Quait, then he quickly closed his eyes again. Women were no longer of any particular interest to him. Money was his one and only love.

The jet roared on. The Cheev napped, occasionally eyeing the stewardess's shapely rear as she passed on her various errands. The Cheev was wondering if he'd get a chance to bang a few Southern California girls—he'd heard they were choice. Or would that crippled gray-headed old monster take up all of his time?

John Q. sat worrying. Could he trust Y to have Wicks sent over, even when the thirty-five hundred wasn't at the drop? God, what a complicated world it was! How had he managed to stay alive and prosper in such a tangle of monkeys? Not a guy you could trust across the street if a dollar was involved!

Meanwhile, the sweet-faced stewardess prowled the aisle on errands of mercy.

## TWENTY-FIVE

Willie appeared at Dr. Mahon's office shortly after eight o'clock in the morning. He eased a new black Oldsmobile into the parking lot: it had been rented to John Ward, of course, and Willie had made quite a hit at the rental office with his fine clothes, his manner and his bankroll. This John Ward was quite a fine little gentleman, the girl behind the counter had thought, and she had got quite kittenish as Willie ogled her through his sunglasses.

He was now officially John Ward of St. Louis, retired; though he was still Lawrence Allen, of course in Dr. Mahon's office.

An air of desertion hung over the anteroom. But the receptionist, still fussing with her hair, came in hurriedly from the back.

"Oh, Mr. Allen," she said. "Do you have an appointment? I don't recall ..."

"No," said Willie. "It was on the spur of the moment. I'm leaving town early so I just took a chance."

"But Mr. Mahon never comes in before ten or sometimes eleven. I'm very sorry. He's at the hospital with his patients in the morning. Sometimes he's not here till after lunch ... so sorry. But I could try to reach him."

"Oh no," said Willie. "Don't bother. But maybe Miss Velinsky could help me."

The receptionist spoke on the intercom and in a moment Miss Velinsky appeared. She was not wearing her nurse's uniform as yet, but was clad in a pale pink sheath that clung to the voluptuous body Willie had noted even in spite of the starchy whiteness of her official dress.

Her hair was cut shorter than he remembered and was black as coal. Only the thick-lensed glares seemed the same.

"Mr. Allen!" she said in surprise, then the girls exchanged a look and Willie felt pretty sure they had discussed him since his last visit.

"Can I help you?" asked Dorothy.

"Well," said Willie, "I'm leaving town this morning and I thought maybe you could give me that sedation the doctor talked about. To take with me, I mean. I've been having trouble lately."

"Oh, but I couldn't," said Dorothy. "It was a graduated system the doctor had in mind, I believe. Really I'm sorry, but ..." She seemed very concerned.

Willie smiled indulgently. "Oh, that's all right. I'll live. But actually I came here to kill two birds with one stone. I had a slight accident to my leg—the edge of a car door ripped it. I just wanted it looked at and bandaged. It's really nothing."

"But one must never take chances," said Dorothy. "If you'll wait till I change perhaps I can handle that for you."

They were in a backroom now and Dorothy in her nurse's uniform and all business. She had given Willie an anti-tetanus shot and was now bandaging his leg. Twice he had repeated his version of how he had received the injury; and neither time did Dorothy reply. Willie could see, or sense, that she did not believe him.

Finally she was finished and Willie rolled down his pant leg. He felt very much aroused by Dorothy's ministrations—there was something about this girl, this odd silent girl ... that got to him. Was it just the Polish bit? The thronging memories of the past when he was a lad of nineteen and there had been Doll and Rosicka and Maria ... and yes: Lena Derucki, his so-called wife.

He lit a cigarette to steady himself, then said: "How much will that be? You see, I'm leaving, so I'd better pay."

"Twenty dollars," said Dorothy, and Willie handed her a twenty-dollar bill.

"You're pretty clever," said Willie, eyeing her. "The doctor told me you wanted to study medicine."

"I have studied," said Dorothy. "But I ran out of money."

"Couldn't your folks help you?"

Dorothy's lips tightened noticeably, then finally she said: "My folks wouldn't help me across the street if I was crippled. My folks do not approve of me. When I was working as a waitress at sixteen they were happy."

"Poor people?"

"Drawing welfare now," said Dorothy, contemptuously. "My stepfather has a backache every time a job turns up."

Willie smiled slightly. This girl not only fractured him physically, he liked her. Which was not usually the case—in fact, it very seldom happened.

"And the ballet?" asked Willie.

The girl threw him an odd look.

"Oh, Dr. Mahon told me. He said you gave it up because you didn't approve of the morals or something."

"That's what I told *him*," said Dorothy.

Willie laughed. It was obvious what was going on. This kid was promoting the doctor.

"I ran out of money again," said Dorothy. "I'm pretty good."

"I believe it," said Willie. "I believe you are pretty good at a lot of things."

They eyed each other.

"He also said they called you 'the Nun' around the building."

"It's true," said Dorothy. "We have got the usual contingent of wolves—most of them married. You know … dinner, dancing and a motel."

Willie laughed outright.

"And you have other goals in mind."

"You might say that," said Dorothy, then she took one of Willie's cigarettes and he lit it for her.

"You see," she went on, "Dr. Mahon is a wonderful man. He's been married for perhaps thirty years. He never gets out any place. He just doesn't seem to know what's going on. I couldn't bear to disillusion him."

"So you play the part you think he likes."

Dorothy studied Willie for a moment, then nodded. "That's it."

Willie stood smoking and looking out the window for a while. The California sun was blazing down on the buildings of this rather suburban area on the edge of Beverly Hills—Los Angeles to Willie.

"You know," he said, "I think the two of us could have some very interesting talks."

"I'm sure of it," said Dorothy. "Too bad you are going away."

"Oh, I'll be back," said Willie. "And I'll contact you, if that is all right with you."

"Call me here before ten in the morning," said Dorothy.

Willie paused, thinking. This might really develop into something. He hadn't seen a girl in twenty years, aside from Miss Fang, who interested him as much as Dorothy Velinsky—and he had known it at once. The thing for him to do was to go to his source and load up with spending money, then come back and they would see what they would see.

He turned and studied her. "Do you have to wear those glasses?" he asked.

"If I want to see," said Dorothy, unconcernedly.

Willie laughed.

"I've acted in a few plays," Dorothy went on. "I had a hard time not falling over the furniture—and the audience was just a blur. I'm very nearsighted. When I was a little girl in Polishtown they called me 'Four Eyes.'"

"Well," said Willie, eyeing her up and down, "you can't have everything. I hate to think what would be happening in this building if you *didn't* wear glasses."

"It's bad enough as it is," said Dorothy. "Most of them I pass along to Julie. She's the girl out front and she goes to dinner, dancing and motels."

"Most of them?"

"Some of them I wouldn't pass on to my aunt," said Dorothy. "And if you knew my aunt …"

The kid was all right, Willie decided. In fact she reminded Willie of his own youth. Things were tough for her, she had no money and big ambitions, and she was playing a game with the Square Johns. Willie to the life, only in a feminine form, and maybe not so tough. Except he wasn't sure even about that.

A pause.

"Well," said Willie. "I'd better be on my way. You think that rip in my leg will give me any trouble?"

"I doubt it," said Dorothy.

They stood eying each other. "You will explain to the doctor?"

"Yes," said Dorothy, eyeing him steadily. "I will explain that it is superficial and that you injured it on your car door."

"Good girl," said Willie, then he suddenly put his arm around her and hugged her; her body, firm and strong, felt wonderful.

She neither withdrew nor responded.

"And don't try to pass me along to Julie," he said, taking his arm away.

"Mr. Allen," said Dorothy, "I have no such intentions, I assure you."

After he had gone, Dorothy went behind the glassed-in enclosure to smoke a cigarette with Julie.

"Well …?" Julie demanded, excitedly.

"Oh," said Dorothy, "he's all business. Even if he is retired. All business."

Julie's face fell. "It took you so long back there I thought you might have something interesting to tell me." She sounded as if her whole morning had been spoiled.

"Very nice man," said Dorothy, yawning. "Polite. A gentleman."

"Kid," said Julie, "you're slipping."

"Yes," said Dorothy. "Could it be the glasses?"

They both laughed.

Willie felt fine as he drove eastward through the streets of Beverly Hills toward his new place of residence, a conservative old hotel in a park district, near downtown Los Angeles.

Had the ghost of Miss Fang been exorcized? After all, Miss Fang, with her delicate beauty, had made her impact before he'd ever seen Dorothy. Time would tell.

If his old Enemy kept its distance, he would know. But if Nemesis returned once more in the form of night weaving, it would be the tip-off that he'd been right about Miss Fang. Had she accepted the beautiful kimono? Was she wearing it?

The answer was yes. She had accepted it and was displaying it to her fiancé, Roger Sing, who listened in blank incomprehension as Geraldine, usually so silent, told him the story of the strange gentleman who …

But Roger was worrying about a loan he had okayed that day. Roger worked in a bank in Chinatown and was expert on real estate loans. Now, as Geraldine told the fantastic tale, he was wondering if he hadn't been *had* by that plausible operator, old Mr. Chu.

## TWENTY-SIX

In his Los Angeles hotel room Quait sipped his beer and tried hard to relax while the Cheev slept on a nearby couch. The Cheev was about as much company as a department store dummy, his eyes nearly always closed. It was said he could see in the dark, which perhaps accounted for some of his more famous escapades and escapes.

"What the hell do you suppose has happened to that crazy bastard?" Quait finally broke out, slamming his beer glass down on the table. "He should have called me by now."

"Maybe he's shacked up with a broad," said the Cheev, without opening his eyes. "You know him."

"With all this at stake?" The old man was aghast.

"He's a nut," said the Cheev.

The old man sat nodding his head slowly. The Cheev was right. Carl was a nut, and here he had allowed a nut to drag him into this crazy business. Expenses. Expenses. Money going out. Nothing happening.

Had Carl lost Willie and gone looking high and low for him?

"Cheevers," he said, "we can't just sit here. Rent a car and drive up to the Golden West, on the Coast Highway. It's a couple hundred miles or so. See what you can find out about Lawrence Allen. I'll stay in this room."

"Roger and out," said the Cheev. He seemed to disappear on cat feet.

Quait sipped his beer and tried to make himself enjoy it. Expenses, expenses; good dollars rolling out.

He put his glass down again and gave a long elephantine sigh. "I'm getting too old for all this," he told himself, feeling a wave of self-pity. "Too old."

Behind the glass enclosure Julie regarded the unknown arrival with distrust. He was a sandyish young man—mid-thirties, perhaps—in a neat black suit, black tie and white shirt. Sartorially he looked like one of the young men from a big Beverly Hills theatrical agency who occasionally came to consult Dr. Mahon about their nerves, their ulcers and other occupational disabilities—but the resemblance ended with the clothes. This young man seemed to move on silent feet over the uncarpeted parquet, where women in high heels clattered maddeningly.

"Yes sir?"

The young man came to her wicket. "I am trying to locate a friend," he said. "And I'm informed he consulted Dr. Mahon—oh, maybe a week ago. Just his address would be a big help. I'm from his hometown."

Julie tried to keep her composure, but there was something about the young man's yellowish eyes that upset her. Without replying, she called Dorothy Velinsky on the intercom. The doctor had gone for the day.

In a moment Dorothy appeared and Julie explained. Dorothy studied the Cheev for a moment, then asked: "What is your friend's name?"

"Lawrence Allen."

Dorothy and Julie exchanged a look that was not missed by the Cheev, whose antennae—or cat whiskers—began to tremble slightly.

"Did you go to his hotel?" asked Dorothy.

"Where is that?" asked the Cheev.

"I mean," said Dorothy, "how did you know he came to consult Dr. Mahon?"

Smart girl, very smart, thought the Cheev, studying her, and what a hunk of stuff, in spite of the thick glasses and the stiff white dress.

"Yes," said Cheev, "I went to his hotel. But he had checked out. The manager informed me about Dr. Mahon."

"What hotel was that?" asked Dorothy.

"The Golden West. Up the coast."

"I believe," said Dorothy, "that is the only address we have on him. He was only here once, you see."

Julie, fumbling with her box of cards, kept her eyes lowered. What was going on here? Why all the fencing—the secrecy? That Dorothy was an odd, cagey one!

"Yes," said Julie, lifting out a card, "that is the only address we have—the Golden West Motor Hotel."

"I think he left town," said Dorothy. "I believe I heard him say he was leaving, though I didn't pay much attention."

The hell you didn't, thought the Cheev. A blank wall. It was obvious—and a very smart girl behind those glasses. Could she be one of Willie's? It was possible. The Cheev, who did not know Willie personally, had always heard that the big boy (biggest thief in town it was said: stole over a million bucks) ... yes, the big boy had quite a way with the ladies.

The Cheev realized that further inquiry was useless, but he felt that it might not be a bad idea to put an occasional prowl on this girl—Dorothy. No problem. She was a working girl. Regular hours. She could be followed to and from work whenever necessary.

"Well," said the Cheev, "thank you very much, girls. I have another lead that may give the information I want."

He smiled and started out.

Dorothy called to him. "Would you like to leave your name and address in case Mr. Allen might phone in to ask the doctor's advice?"

"Why don't you quit, honey?" Cheev wanted to say. But what he did say was: "Tell you what: if the other lead doesn't pan out, I may give you a call. Thanks again, girls."

He went out as soundlessly as he had come in.

"He doesn't make any noise when he walks," said Julie, feeling slightly shaken for reasons unknown to her—nevertheless, she had felt a kind of odd tension between the young man and Dorothy.

"He's a creep," said Dorothy. "That's why I tried to find out who he was. Mr. Allen is a rich man, I think. And rich men are always in danger of men like that."

"And that's why you said he only came here once?"

"Yes," said Dorothy, "none of his business anyway."

"Gosh, kid," said Julie. "I'm sure glad you were here with me. He made me so nervous I could hardly get that card out."

They smoked a cigarette together and then the calls began to come in; Julie got very busy, and Dorothy retired to a back room, where she sat staring out at the sunshine, lost in thought.

Mr. Allen was in trouble; that was obvious. And she knew a gunshot wound when she saw one. But what kind of trouble could a man like

Mr. Allen be in? And would he come back? Would she ever see him again?

In all her life, Dorothy had never met anyone who interested her as much as Mr. Allen. She felt for him a kind of odd respect, a sort of subterranean admiration. Most men she merely dismissed with contempt. Since she was twelve or thirteen years old they had been running after her, with only one purpose—single minded clods: pleading, coaxing, wheedling, sometimes rough and resentful and hard to get rid of—especially two that she'd had rather boring affairs with: once she'd had to leave town; several times she'd had to hide, until the heat blew over.

Stupid egotists who simply could not get it through their armor of vanity that they bored and irritated her.

Lately, she had fought shy of entanglements—thus living a somewhat unnatural and frustrating life. But in her rather extensive experience of the male the game had never yet been worth the candle. And she was simply weary of all the silly uproar.

Mr. Allen was something altogether different. She liked to hear him talk. And she knew that he would be a responsive listener; she could tell him anything—anything—and he would understand and not disapprove. She was sick and tired of hypocrisy and cant. She was sick of pretending to be the "Nun." She was sick of being Rebecca of Sunnybrook Farm for the benefit of Dr. Mahon.

Above all she wanted to be Dorothy Velinsky—herself—just as she was. And she felt that with Mr. Allen this was entirely possible.

So he was in trouble. So somebody shot him. So what?

Quait sat slumped down in his chair but half listening to the Cheev's "tale." All was not well: no word from Carl and as yet no word on the long distance from Y. Old Johnny sat worrying about that idiot, Joe Wicks. Would he talk? Would one of Y's men get to him before he could manage it?

"I'm too old to go to the clink," John Q. kept thinking, as if pleading for clemency to some unseen power. "I'm too old. I'd die."

He was paying no attention to the Cheev now, and breaking in he said: "When Nick died, the operation went out the window. If I was smart, I'd head back for home and forget the whole thing. Trouble, trouble."

"Will you listen?" cried the Cheev, irritated. "This girl—listen, Mr. Quait. I'm going on instinct, but it's a great lead. I think maybe she's Willie's girlfriend—or at least he's banged her and may come back for more. I would …"

"Yeah," said the old man, irritably, "I'll bet you would. Now don't try

that on me. We didn't come out here so you could run after the girls—
you mink! Wait till you get home. I'll tell you once, and I'll tell you
again, Willie don't get himself in trouble over women. Not once that I
ever heard of except when he was nineteen. That cured him. Some
dumb Polish broad—it was a shotgun ..." The old man droned on.

"Please, Mr. Quait," the Cheev begged, "listen. We got nothing but
this lead, and it's a good one. Believe me. I hit some of my biggest
'making' women. I mean, reading 'em. See what I mean?"

"I don't know," said the old man, pessimistically.

And at that moment the phone rang and John Q. reached for it, his
hand shaking. He felt his stomach turn over. He just knew this was *it*.
Wicks had talked and he might have to stay on the lam, a tired old
man like him.

It was Y, long distance, and John Q was quickly given a pay phone
number to call in the hometown. And that concluded the conversation,
with the old man still shaking as he pulled himself hurriedly to his
feet.

John Q. chose a pay phone on a downtown street corner, and the
Cheev stood on the street nearby, watching the women walk past. Oh,
those short skirts!

"First," said Y, "about Joe Wicks ..."

The old man held his breath.

"You can forget it, Mr. Q. He's completely flipped. "They got him
strapped down in the nut suit. Nobody's gonna pay any attention to
anything he says. Right now he's just raving. This cools it."

"You're sure?" asked John Q., wiping the cold sweat from his brow.

"I'm sure. And how about this—Fallon O'Keefe's up for parole and
he'll make it; and maybe Orley Peters, too."

The old man couldn't care less; he said nothing; just let it pass.

"And now brace yourself, Mr. Q.," said Y. "They found Nick Fay all
shot up outside a little California town, called—you wanna take it
down?—San Ygnacio; up in the mountains. Last I heard he was still
alive in a hospital there. And get this: Lieutenant Kramer's on his way
out to see what it's all about ..."

John Q. stared in bewilderment. Nick, up in the mountains? Shot?
Nick was in the Pacific Ocean, according to Carl ... but wait; could it
be Carl, with Nick's ID...?

If so, no wonder he hadn't heard from him!

Y went on: "The town's not up in the mountains. In case I got you
mixed-up. The town's on the beach. Nick was found up in the mountains.
How do you figure this?"

"I don't," said John Q., nor did he enlighten Y in regard to his suspicions—and in a little while he ended the conversation, which in his opinion had cost him far too much as it was, in spite of the good— but rather inconclusive—news about Wicks. It still wasn't settled in old John's opinion. Dead men don't talk. Live ones do, even when crazy.

John Q. was in a quandary. At first he decided to send the Cheev to San Ignacio to see what he could see. That way he himself wouldn't be involved in any way with the red-hot Carl Benedict—oh, what an uproar this would cause back in the hometown, once he was identified!

But after long pondering, John Q. worked out a plan that would cover him, so he put in a call for Y; the pay phone bit was repeated and the "deal" was set. Now old John would have nothing to say for himself if it came to police questioning.

They drove up the Coast Highway, which was now becoming a wide thoroughfare for "Willie hunters," as it had formerly been for Willie himself.

The old man sat lost in thought as the miles sped by. He noticed neither the deep-blue sky as evening fell, nor the lonely glimmer of lights on the water, nor the froth-fringed waves breaking on the beach, nor the ocean breeze with its clean tang of salt. He was wandering back among the days of five years ago.

He began to tick them off for the Cheev's benefit: "Bellini dead, Novak dead, Wicks crazy, Willie free, O'Keefe and Peters still in the Walls— and now Nick dead and maybe Carl dying. How's that for a score on one stand—even if it was for over a million?"

But the Cheev wasn't interested in ancient history. He was interested in selling this obtuse old bastard on tailing the girl in the doctor's office. Why couldn't he see it?

He took up the business once more, very persistent about it. John Q. listened in silence, shifting his cane from hand to hand now and then. Maybe, maybe. Also maybe he'd just take the first plane out. Finally he said as much.

"Okay," said the Cheev. "If you do, I'll go it on my own."

"On what?"

"I'll dig up some scratch someplace."

John Q. glanced at the Cheev in surprise, but said nothing. However, the Cheev had won his point. The old man was convinced now that he was serious and not just goldbricking so he could hang after a skirt.

They could talk it over later.

They found the little one-story hospital on a street to the north of the Coast Highway and paralleling it, and a rectangle of canted yellow light from its entrance lay across the dark roadway—not a streetlight in sight.

But this peaceful, not to say backwoods, street, had been invaded. There was a State Highway patrol car out in front, and just beyond it a local squad car, and through the glass front door old Johnny could see a tall policeman in a dark blue uniform and white crash helmet, moving about, as if guarding the place.

Why all these precautions over a brother officer? Or had they made the "dead" Carl? How—through fingerprints? Carl's were certainly on file with the FBI and also back home.

Something was up.

"Cheev," said Johnny, "stay in the car and keep out of sight. I don't understand this."

"Roger and out."

Then the Cheev sat with a pitying smirk on his face, watching the old Gimp half limping across the pavement and up the three steps, using his cane. What an old bastard! Tough as a boot; tight as the bark on a tree and loaded with loot. The Cheev had often tried to puzzle out just how to relieve the old boy of some of it. But it would be a chancy thing. Old Johnny had vicious friends who would shoot you in the back on order. And there was always that little rat—Colin—hanging about, one place or another, looking after the old boy's interests. But there must be some way to take old Johnny. He was human. And any human could be taken—with the right angle.

Maybe, if things went as planned, he could grab all of Willie's loot for himself, not cut the old man in at all—just disappear with all that lovely money, maybe to Mexico. What did the old man need with more money?

"God, what a score that would be!" the Cheev told himself, dreaming pleasant dreams of affluence and power. The guy with the dough called the turn. It was the way of the world. "And I didn't make the world that way," the Cheev reminded himself, "but I have to live in it."

Old Johnny crossed the white tile of the hospital lobby and approached the tall young officer. There was an emblem on his dark blue shirt that proclaimed him to be of the local police.

"Excuse me," said Quait. "Would it be possible for me to see Detective Sergeant Nick Fay? I understand he is here."

"Oh?" said the young cop, looking him over.

Johnny took out his wallet and showed the cop his credentials. "I've been hired by his family to see how it is with him and what can be done."

"Oh, you're from clear back in the Midwest."

"That's right. Came out by jet."

"Wait here a minute. I'll be right back."

Johnny lit a cigarette and paced, exaggerating his limp and his dragging foot for the benefit of the starched young lady behind the counter, who kept eyeing him. Poor old man—she must be saying. Such things always pleased Johnny. Old man, yes, but poor? No. And in no sense of the word.

The young cop returned followed by Lieutenant Art Kramer and a tall young man in civilian clothes who was introduced to Quait as Mr. Alford of the FBI.

Old Johnny had struggled to suppress a start at the appearance of the police lieutenant from his hometown—and yet he'd been warned of his coming by Y.

"I've got a big disappointment for you," said Lieutenant Kramer. "Nick's not here."

"What do you mean he's not here?" cried Johnny, acting it out very well. "I'm being paid to talk to him and see what he needs. Where is he?"

Lieutenant Kramer, with a mocking smile, beckoned, and Johnny followed him back through a corridor to the open door of a small hospital room. And there was Carl Benedict, lying in bed, a ghost of himself, and with his crazy-looking dyed red hair going all directions and standing up in fuzzy wisps. His sunken eyes rolled toward the doorway, but he didn't crack at the sight of old Johnny—not a blink or flicker.

"Carl Benedict!" cried Johnny, feigning great surprise.

"Yes," said Lieutenant Kramer. "He had Nick's credentials and his car. Probably killed Nick and dumped the body."

"Then who shot him?" asked Johnny.

"It's a good question."

A doctor stopped by to talk to them, as Mr. Alford kept in the background, across the hall from them, smoking a cigarette thoughtfully.

"He's certainly a rugged man," said the doctor. "Yesterday I wouldn't have given you a nickel for his life when I was operating. Now—barring complications—he may make it."

"They can't kill me," said Carl, hoarsely.

"Well," said Johnny to Kramer, "now you've got them all but Willie."

"Correction," said Kramer. "There's an eighth man."

"Who says? Some crazy con?" asked Johnny, mildly.

"It's a theory," said Kramer.

Old Johnny puffed thoughtfully on his cigarette, then asked: "What's Carl's story? It's my job to find Nick."

Kramer said: "Carl tells us he borrowed Nick's car and he was miles away before he found Nick's wallet on the seat. He left Nick back at a motel; he won't tell us which one. Don't remember, he says. Then he drove up this mountain road and three guys stuck him up and shot him, but they got scared off by a car going past and didn't grab the money."

"I'm gonna fight extradition," cried Carl. "I got money to get a good lawyer."

"And he has," said Kramer. "About four thousand dollars. He and Nick had quite a bankroll between them."

"Where'd they get all that money?"

"Your guess is as good as mine. But apparently they'd teamed up for some reason. Maybe to look for Willie, after that magazine article broke things open again."

"That's crazy," said Johnny. "Nick?"

"It's theory," said Kramer, mildly.

"What does Mr. Alford think?"

"He's not saying."

Carl called: "I know who you are you crippled old bastard. John Quait. And you're so crooked you could sleep on a corkscrew."

Kramer laughed. But the old man winced faintly, hoping crazy Carl wouldn't overdo it. Though he was certain the coppers would get nothing out of him—nothing at all, and they probably knew it. What a wild guy!

"Want to see his effects?" asked Kramer.

Johnny nodded, but as they started away, Carl called:

"Hey, Kramer. Get me a good-looking nurse, will you? That one I got frightens me."

Kramer laughed again and shook his head, then Johnny followed him out into the lobby where there were now three tall young cops in crash helmets. Mr. Alford seemed to have faded out of the picture.

They went into a little side office, where Kramer took a big manila envelope out of a drawer; first, he displayed the wallets and the money, a huge wad of it, in two piles held by rubber bands, then he displayed Nick's driver's license and other identification cards, including his departmental ID, then he showed Johnny the star sapphire cuff links.

"Look at these."

"Must be worth a thousand dollars. Carl must have stolen them someplace. Nick would never have cuff links like that."

"Carl insists some woman gave them to him for spending the night with her." Kramer chuckled to himself. "Did you ever see such an idiot? They'll throw the book at him and all he does is make jokes."

"He's a nut," said old John. "What's being done about Nick?"

"We're checking all the cheap motels along the Coast."

"How long you going to be out here, Lieutenant? It's my job to find out what happened to Nick."

"I don't know yet. If Carl fights extradition I may go back and then let Captain Bescher handle it. If not, I may stay and take Carl back, as soon as he can be moved."

"Where can I reach you?"

"Call the station here—San Ygnacio. They'll know where I am."

Kramer kept compressing his lips. He knew he was engaged in an elaborate game of pretense. The Fays didn't have the kind of money they'd have to put up to pay Johnny for a trip like this. It was a mere subterfuge. But well taken care of back home; you could bet on that. One of the Fays would certainly swear he'd hired Johnny, if it came to the point.

Johnny was a cagey old buzzard.

Finally they shook hands and Johnny left, and Kramer stood watching him limp across the lobby on his cane, dragging his foot. A big formidable-looking wicked old man. By the time they got to Johnny's age most men—even some of the worst—had been tamed into harmlessness by the years. Not so Quait. The years seemed to have left him unmarked in that respect.

Later, Alford joined him in the office. Johnny Quait was fire-new to him and he wanted to know all about him. Kramer gave him a rundown, then said: "This is just theory—but if there really is an eighth man, and Wicks wasn't just signing in order to get out, it's a good bet Quait is that man."

"I'll have him watched."

"I wouldn't. You'll scare him off. Anyway I think it would be useless now. Here's my theory; we'll never prove it, maybe, but here it is: Nick Fay and Carl Benedict teamed up to find Willie and run down his money. The old Gimp—Quait—financed them. Something happened. Now it's all off."

"You think so? You're the local expert."

"Nick's dead, I'm sure. Maybe he quarreled with Carl, and that's suicide. Carl will never open his mouth. Neither will Quait. End of the line. Anyway, what we want is Willie Madden and the money."

And about one thing Kramer had been so right. It was useless to follow Johnny Quait, but not for the reasons Kramer had given. Johnny had a change of heart. He was too old for the game. Too old, too conspicuous, and of little or no use, except as a purveyor of front money.

What he was considering was risky, very risky, but at least he wouldn't be putting his neck in a noose—he would be safely at home, letting others take the risks—and he felt pretty sure he could count on Colin—Y. Colin was well-known in the underworld of the big city on the big river and he had a kind of pride about being what the boys called "right." If Johnny gave him a cut at the big dough and they scored, it was odds-on Johnny would get his share. With the Cheev it was a different matter entirely. You couldn't trust him across the street. But the Cheev was afraid of Colin. Everybody was. And that would keep him straight.

After they were settled once more in the old man's room, Johnny proceeded to break the Cheev's bubble. The Cheev had been dreaming dreams about running off with all the money ever since the old man had limped across the roadway to the hospital.

The mention of Colin's name brought the Cheev sharply back to reality.

Colin and the Cheev would handle things from here on in; Johnny would allow them reasonable front money (oh, all that money—most of it his, over half of it, anyway—lying on the table in that hospital office; the sight of it had almost brought tears to Johnny's old eyes) yes … reasonable front, or expense money—but paid in installments this time—and he himself would return to the big town, to solicitous Mrs. Peet and his own comfortable office.

The Cheev felt deflated. He said nothing. Colin would have you killed as quick as look at you.

"What's the matter with you?" cried the old man. "I thought you were so eager."

"I am, I am," said the Cheev, rousing himself.

The next morning Kramer received a call from Johnny at the San Ygnacio police station. Johnny explained he was going home by train that evening and would appreciate it if the lieutenant would keep him posted regarding Nick Fay. He didn't feel equal to traipsing all over Southern California. He was too old.

Kramer assured Johnny he'd wire him, collect, the first news he had.

And that was that. Kramer smiled to himself. The Gimp had backed out.

## TWENTY-SEVEN

It was very late. Kramer, after a long snooze in a nearby hotel, dressed and went back to the hospital to see if all was well in regard to Carl Benedict. No matter how many times you cautioned these young California officers, you just couldn't be sure they'd take the proper precautions with a man who had almost died not too many hours ago.

They had had no experience with the likes of Carl Benedict. With him anything was possible.

The town was sound asleep. Not a light showing anywhere, except in the foyer of the hospital and even there the dimmers were on. And it was as Kramer had expected. A young officer was dozing on a couch; and behind the counter an old gray-haired man, a watchman, or something, was also dozing. Just as Kramer entered, a middle-aged, weary-looking nurse came in from the back, carrying a clipboard.

Kramer stopped her. "Is our man okay?"

"He's under sedation, sleeping, Lieutenant."

Kramer nodded, then went over to the young officer, who got to his feet, rather embarrassed.

"I been losing a lot of sleep," he said before Kramer could speak.

"Then you should ask to be relieved," said Kramer, trying to hide his annoyance.

"But that man's half dead."

"Don't count on it," said Kramer. "What are you trying to do—get yourself killed?"

The young officer swallowed but made no reply. Kramer walked down the corridor and glanced into Carl's room—the door was always kept open; in fact, it was latched back. Kramer gave a start. Carl was sitting on the edge of his bed.

"Lie down, you fool," snapped Kramer. "What's the matter with you?"

"I'm kinda groggy, with all that junk," said Carl. "I was dreaming, I guess." With a groan Carl fell down on the bed sideways, then slowly and painfully drew his legs up.

Kramer kept studying him, sure he was lying. But in his condition was the big fuzzy-headed hoodlum actually considering anything as crazy as a lam?

"You keep this up," said Kramer, "and I'm going to chain you to the bed. Carl—use your head. If you don't take care of yourself you got a good chance of dying. The Doc said he might give you another transfusion tomorrow. Get wise."

"All right, all right," said Carl, irritably.

"You read to them yet what you were doing out here with Nick Fay?"

"You figure it out. You're the detective."

"I think I know."

"Goodie for you. How do you prove it?"

A pause.

"You want to get Nick off the hook?" asked Carl, finally.

"Why should I want to do that?"

"You're a cop; he's a cop. Nick nabbed me, see. He was taking me home for trial."

"Great. So then he loaned you his car so you could take a joy ride."

"Yeah," said Carl. "Think it would stand up in court?"

Carl laughed, then he began to cough and finally rolled painfully over on his back and lay looking up at the ceiling.

"Hey—I'm pretty sick, I think. I almost passed out just then."

"That's what I'm trying to tell you, you damned idiot," said Kramer.

"All right, all right," said Carl, drowsily.

Long pause.

"Did you kill Nick, Carl?" asked Kramer. "Off the record."

"Off the record," said Carl, yawning, "No."

"Okay, sleep," said Kramer. "But any more funny actions—I mean it—and I chain you to the bed."

"Quit worrying," said Carl. "That big young jerk out there—the local fuzz—is always looking in here. I was just groggy, I tell you."

And Kramer finally decided that maybe Carl, obviously very weak, was telling the truth.

## TWENTY-EIGHT

Parry, the young FBI man, even with the address plainly in his book, had a hard time finding the district. He was fairly new to the Los Angeles area and it was so spread out and endless and confusing, with dead ends and duplication of street names and with the people themselves not knowing about a street two blocks away from them, that it was like a labyrinth or an experimental maze, even in the daytime—at night it was impossible.

Now it was day, and Parry was getting close to his objective. It was late September. A Santa Ana was blowing; and up in the hills not too far away—in fact, too close for Parry's comfort—he could see men fighting a roaring brush fire. It was an area of open spaces, riding schools, and little old white-painted, neglected-looking frame houses, a kind of country slum, but still within the city limits—or so his guidebook said.

Finally he found the address, opened a rickety gate and went in. Just as a man came out on the porch, a medium-sized brown dog hurtled round the corner of the house growling and snarling.

"Brownie! No!" yelled the man, and the dog stopped, cowered, but kept staring balefully at Parry.

"You shouldn't walk in a gate like that," said the man, reproachfully. "If I hadn't been here you'da got bit. We been having trouble round here with prowlers and creeps and peeping toms and we've got some tough dogs in the neighborhood."

Brownie kept growling.

"Excuse me," said the correctly dressed and correctly mannered Parry, "are you Mr. Velinsky?"

"Me?" cried the man, annoyed. "Hell, no. They live in the back. Follow the fence."

The man now gave Parry a contemptuous look, yelled to the dog and then both man and dog disappeared into the house.

Parry, watching warily behind him in case the dog got loose, followed the fence, and beyond a tall, scraggly-looking hedge, he found the Velinsky abode. It was a small ramshackle frame house, formerly the tack room of an antiquated riding stable. A large fat baldish man in work pants and an undershirt was sitting in a beat-up canvas chair reading a newspaper and sunning himself. Just beyond, a fat blonde woman—in her late forties—with a round, pretty face and large, black-rimmed blue eyes, was hanging out a washing.

"Excuse me," said Parry, "are you Mr. and Mrs. Velinsky?"

The couple exchanged a long look.

"You collecting for something?" asked the man. "We got no money."

"You one of them political fellows who asks how we're going to vote? They already been here," said the woman.

Parry stepped forward and showed the man his credentials.

"FBI," the man said to his wife, then they exchanged another long look, this time with deep meaning.

"Yes," said Parry. "But only a routine inquiry. Nothing to worry about. Are you the Velinskys?"

The man nodded. The woman pulled up a couple of canvas chairs and offered one to Parry. Now they were all seated in what from the outside must look like an intimate little circle.

Parry took out his notebook and turned to Mrs. Velinsky. "You are the former Lena Derucki? Am I right?"

"Yes sir. You don't need to be so cautious, young man. We know what this is about. But it's the first time they run us down."

"Oh, it's not matter of running you down," said Parry. "Just a few routine questions. We have no desire to embarrass you."

"That bastard?" said Velinsky, with feeling. "What kind of a world is it when a man like that gets away with a million dollars five years ago—and nobody can catch him. Other poor guys, working their backs off for low wages!"

Mrs. Velinsky eyed her husband ironically but made no comment.

"He'll be caught," said Parry. "We're all working hard at it." He turned to Mrs. Velinsky again. "I believe a daughter was born to you twenty-five years ago."

"Dorothy, yes," said Mrs. Velinsky.

"And are you in contact with her?"

Velinsky gave a derisive snort. "She's too good for us. She wouldn't wipe her shoes on us, after all I did for her. Like she was my own daughter. In fact, everybody thought she was."

"And she was," cried Mrs. Velinsky, heatedly, "and you know it, Thad.

So stop lying."

"Cut it out," cried Velinsky. "Let's tell the truth. Why lie to the FBI? Maybe it's important ..."

"It might be," said Parry.

"Well, she's Willie Madden's daughter—and that's the truth of it, and I married Lena anyway, in spite of it."

Parry looked at Mrs. Velinsky, then looked away. She was flushing and seemed very embarrassed.

"Is this true, Mrs. Velinsky?"

"Yes sir," she said, then she began to sob and dab at her eyes.

"Oh, Lena, cut it out," said her husband. "What does it matter? You were only a kid."

Parry cleared his throat and paused, waiting for the emotions to die down.

"When was the last time you heard from her?" he asked.

"Maybe a year ago," said Mrs. Velinsky. "We haven't seen her in two years. She came one day and told us she was going to Chicago to be in a show; then about a year ago we got a letter from Detroit. She said she might go on to New York and try her luck there. She's very pretty and she was very smart in school—and she had three or four semesters of college, working in between. She's a very ambitious girl."

"She was fine till she was about sixteen," said Velinsky. "Then she began to get ideas. Wanted to be somebody. Was ashamed of us, after all I'd done for her. Treated her like my own."

"She lived out here for a while."

"Yes," said Mrs. Velinsky. "But now she never lives any place long—since she was about seventeen. She is a very restless girl. Not like me at all. I was never restless, was I, Thad?"

"No," said Thad, "never." He fixed Parry with his pouched blue eyes. "She's been a fine wife to me, a good woman. A fine woman. It was all that damned Willie Madden's fault."

Mrs. Velinsky began to sob again and wipe her eyes.

"Cut it out, Lena, please," begged Mr. Velinsky.

"You've never heard from Willie Madden? No letters? Phone calls? Nothing?" asked Parry, feeling this was all futile, but doing his job to the hilt.

Up above them and not too far away they could hear the brush fire roaring and crackling and Parry kept glancing up at it nervously, but the Velinskys ignored it.

"I haven't seen Willie Madden nor heard from him in twenty-five years," said Mrs. Velinsky.

"If he ever turned up here, God forbid," cried Velinsky, "I'd sit on him till the police came and I'm big enough to do it."

"And he knows nothing about his daughter?"

"He knows she was born—or that a baby was born," said Mrs. Velinsky. "But I doubt if he even remembers it. I know he don't care. He was very cold-hearted. He just walked out of the house and left. Never said a word."

"And then her brothers had it annulled," Velinsky came in, taking up the story, "and I agreed to marry Lena. Lena was always my girl till that Willie got after her, a kid four years younger than Lena. Can you imagine? So then Lena and me left town and went to Cincinnati where everybody thought Dorothy was my daughter. Then we come out here."

Mrs. Velinsky was sobbing and wiping her eyes again, but this time Velinsky didn't remonstrate with her. He merely patted her shoulder.

"I'm sorry to upset you people," said Parry. "I'll be through in a minute. How about the daughter? Does she know Madden is her father?"

"She never heard of Willie Madden," cried Velinsky, as if annoyed. "We saw to that. But we made a mistake, I think. It was Lena's brother's idea. He came to live with us for a while. He's a very strict Catholic and he didn't want to lie to Dorothy, so when she was about eleven years old her uncle told her that her father had been killed in the war and that I was her stepfather. That wasn't really lying, you see, according to Joseph, because Willie really was dead—to all decent people, that is—and I was really her stepfather."

Parry sat thinking this over. Who could imagine it? People—and all of their unexpected twists and turns!

"It was a mistake, I still say," Velinsky insisted. "If she had thought I was her real father, she'd have given me more respect and she wouldn't have run away from home like a juvenile delinquent."

"She didn't really run away," Mrs. Velinsky protested. "She just left. Told us she was going. I don't call that running away."

"She was just as gone," said Velinsky. "And too young to be running around."

"Do you have any pictures of her?" asked Parry.

"No," said Mrs. Velinsky. "Not since she was about eleven. We had some but she took them all. I don't know what she did with them."

Parry finally, with a sigh of relief, got away. The brush fire was roaring loudly and he was very glad he didn't have to spend the rest of the day in that neighborhood.

In his opinion it had been a futile and useless interview. And then he sat thinking of all the work, all the man hours, that had been devoted to running these people down—just one minor facet of the stepped-up hunt for Willie Madden—from officer Glinka in Willie's hometown through much complicated processing and finally to him, one Ed Parry, and all for what? Willie wouldn't go near those people if the bloodhounds were after him. And it appeared, regarding his child, that he might not even be aware of its sex.

All the same, a report would have to be filed.

# TWENTY-NINE

Willie was back in L. A. and had slept well in his big bedroom at the St. Nicholas—an old, very fine smallish conservative hotel that had been repainted and redecorated, but had preserved its former charm, with no attempt to "go modern": the ceilings were high, the windows big and deep set; and its air was one of spaciousness, as of the past when there was room for people and life moved at a slower tempo.

Its cornerstone had been laid far back in time, before the rush of the masses, at a period when people were not eager to live shoulder to shoulder and to tramp on each other's feet in the name of togetherness. It was a time before the mob scenes; before mass demonstrations, before the thronging thousands with their banners of protest. It had been in short, a leisurely time, with a full allotment of space to each individual.

There had been no huddling. Willie had at times felt the sensation of being crowded at the Pearl of the Orient and especially at the Carioca, and even at the Golden West. What were these places after all but rhinestone hives, as were the huge high-rise apartment buildings now going up all over the Los Angeles area!

The St. Nicholas had a soothing effect on Willie ever since he'd entered its doors. And this was a mere side effect, or bonus; because Willie had chosen it for other reasons. He was well aware of the police's reliance on a "criminal's" modus operandi: as a rule lawbreakers were very unoriginal people: what they had done before, they would do again. Willie had now been definitely typed as a man who frequented swank beach resort motor hotels—with prices ranging from twenty-five to fifty dollars and up per day. And he knew that now every hostelry of this kind on the Pacific Coast was being combed, possibly by FBI operatives, as well as others.

Also, the so-called "commercial" big hotels, like the Biltmore in Los Angeles or the Palace or Fairmont in San Francisco. In fact, Willie had given them the lead, without appearing at any of them, by way of cancelled reservations. The officers of the law now figured luxury beach hotels for Willie's long stays and big "commercial" hotels for spells of transiency.

Unless the law officers got very lucky, one way or another, such a place as the St. Nicholas would be far off their itineraries. It was a gambit he had used successfully before, during the first year when things had been at about the present heat.

It was shortly after eight o'clock in the morning. Willie went to the window and looked out. He was on the second floor. Across the street from him towered a big expensive department store, and to the east of that, through the trees, a wooded park with a lake that lay among the greenery like a huge mirror, reflecting the shore and the trees and an old-fashioned-looking boathouse. It was a bright sunshiny day and people were already in the park. A rowboat, moving slowly, was crossing the lake.

A good spot, thought Willie, contented enough, and yet more than a little worried, too. Always a fly in the ointment. He had withdrawn additional funds from his source and he was now well-enough heeled for a good long stay, but in the town where he kept his money, he had noticed a familiar face on the street in the company of an unfamiliar face, but one that looked like that of a plainclothes copper. FBI?

The familiar face belonged to Tom Corby, a former security officer with Kenmore Trust, and once upon a time Willie's superior. What was he doing thousands of miles from home? And what was he doing in that particular town?

There was an easy explanation of course. It was a resort town—from Fall to Spring, and maybe Tom was taking a vacation. And if so, there was no reason why he couldn't have a friend with him, a brother dick of one kind or another. Police officers buddied together as did musicians or actors or truck drivers.

And yet Willie was no one to dismiss things the easy way. He'd got out of town fast. Luckily, Tom had not "made" him, though they had come fairly close to each other in the street several years before. Willie had established identity in the town as James Williard, of Cincinnati, Ohio—the identity was very precious and necessary to him and he did not want to jeopardize it. In fact it was a must. He'd got away clear and free, but he was not happy about it. Could it be possible that Tom Corby, retired, had taken up residence there? The way he had been dressed might indicate it. He certainly hadn't looked like a tourist.

Willie stood at the window, staring out into the sunshine, worrying. It was possible that it was time to look for a new place to hide his money, no matter how he winced away from the thought. Transporting nearly half million dollars in cash to a new location was not something you did lightly. One slip and goodbye.

Willie decided to make no decision on this major matter for a while, but to mull it over; then he tried to dismiss the whole thing from his mind, and concentrate on Dorothy Velinsky. She had been in his thoughts constantly while he was away.

He called the doctor's office. If Dorothy answered, fine. But if it was the other girl he'd hang up and try again.

It was Dorothy who answered. She sounded surprised and excited.

"What about tonight," said Willie, "dinner, dancing, and a motel?"

Blank silence at the other end, then a laugh. "I suppose I'll never hear the last of that," said Dorothy. "But I'll settle for the dinner and dancing."

It was set. "And shall we keep it dark?" Willie suggested and it was so agreed. He was to meet her in the lobby of a nearby hotel at eight o'clock that evening.

There was a difficulty, of course, that eventually might have to be ironed out. To Dorothy he was Lawrence Allen. But "Lawrence Allen" was no more; he had joined James Shannon in limbo. Willie was now John Ward and already favorable comment was being passed at the St. Nicholas on Mr. Ward in Suite 2B.

Willie had asked Dorothy for her address, explaining that he might send her a "corsage" for the evening. He had a surprise for her and wondered how she would take it.

Dorothy hung up feeling both excited and elated, and with an almost irresistible urge to tell Julie all about it. But she did not.

## THIRTY

Quait had gone back to the hometown, but the Cheev was still at the little "private" hotel in downtown Los Angeles and now Colin had joined him. Colin was small, wiry and tough, and of indeterminate nationality. His eyes were very dark, almost black, and his heavy black eyebrows went straight across with hardly the suspicion of a break. His clothes were good enough, but he took no care of them, seldom had them pressed and would just as lief sleep in them as not; and although he always wore a tie, it was generally to one side, with an unbuttoned collar.

Back home, Colin was considered to be a very dangerous man, and the Cheev was afraid of him.

They were eating together in the Cheev's room. It was getting dark outside and they could hear the hum and rumble of the never-ending stream of traffic in the streets below. A jam-packed city, Los Angeles, the Cheev had found. As for the freeways … he was explaining about them to Colin, who stuffed his mouth full of food and chewed loudly, smacking his lips.

"You worry about that," said Colin. "You're the driver. Say, about that chick. Lay off. It's a dead end. Willie don't hardly even go back twice. I know. If we trip him it won't be with no broad."

"But Colin ... look," the Cheev pleaded, "I got a feeling. I ... well, I've always done pretty good "reading" women ..."

"All right, you read her. Maybe Willie climbed her. That means he won't be back. Don't you get it?"

"But listen, Colin ..."

"You listen. The Old Man warned me about you and chicks. Now you lay off 'em till this job's over. You do what I say. The Old Man put me in charge. We can't be wasting no time tailing chicks. We comb the resorts. We go south. All the way to San Diego, maybe into Mexico. I know Willie by sight. You don't, so you can do the inquiries while I keep my eyes open."

The Cheev gave a long sigh and began to turn a plan over in his mind. Once he got his mitts on some front money he might just disappear and work on his own. It was dangerous to cross Colin and the Old Man, but if he turned up Willie for them they'd forgive him. Did he have the nerve to try? Time would tell. But in his opinion Colin was a hundred percent wrong and was getting ready to set out on a wild goose chase.

"Okay, Colin," said the Cheev. "You're the boss. Whatever you say."

Now Colin ate without speaking, chewing loudly; finally he pushed his plate away from him and lit a cigarette.

"The Old Man won't listen to me," said Colin. "But if I had my way, this is what I'd do: find Willie and take him to a backroom, if you know what I mean. I got the money to buy muscle out here. They'd soften Willie up and he'd lead us to the money. The Old Man says he'd spit in our face. But I've seen some pretty tough guys softened up."

The Cheev lowered his fork and put the food back on his plate. Suddenly he wasn't hungry anymore.

And how about that plan of his?

## THIRTY-ONE

It was after six o'clock when Dorothy got to her apartment. A large package was waiting for her at the entry desk—large as a suit box, and she couldn't imagine what was in it. A corsage? Was it a joke?

She had felt highly nervous and excited ever since she had got Willie's phone call shortly after eight o'clock that morning, so much so that Julie had noticed and the doctor had insisted that she take an extra coffee break.

Now, with the package under her arm, it was worse; she felt herself shaking, and she stumbled climbing the stairs to her little one-room apartment on the second deck.

Night was falling. The lights were coming on, and below her, just as she put her key in the door, the swimming pool was suddenly illuminated and a trembling pale-bluish glow spread throughout the patio and the courtyard.

The place had just recently been built, and had filled up with tenants immediately. It consisted of a warren of tiny box-like ultra-modern apartments, clustered, in two stories, around the courtyard, the patio, and the swimming pool. The walls were paper thin. Music was playing half the night. And the pool lights were not turned off till two in the morning, sometimes not then. It was terrifically noisy, crowded—and all young people, but no children. It was what was called in the news, a "swing joint," and sometimes there was trouble, and squad cars.

But to Dorothy, tired of the austerity of the doctor's office, it was kind of a haven. She liked the noise—the constant activity. And it was accessible, and far from expensive as things went in Los Angeles. And people minded their own business. If you wanted to join in, fine. If you didn't, nobody twisted your arm.

She hurried into her apartment, the whole front wall of which, overlooking the pool, was glass. She quickly drew the curtain, but the box on the lounge and opened it—and out poured the most beautiful kimono she had ever seen in her life: of a subtle and glowing richness, red, gold and yellow on a ground of black. (It had been the closest thing Willie could find to the magnificent specimen from Wu's. And it had cost two hundred dollars.)

Dorothy took off her dress and then put on the kimono and modeled it in front of the bathroom mirror, in spite of the fact that she could just barely turn around in that little box-like enclosure.

It looked unbelievably beautiful and very expensive, and Dorothy had a hard time forcing herself to take it off—but as she had only about an hour, or a little over, in which to get ready to meet Willie, and as she wanted first to take a long soak in the tub …

She found the water warm and soothing. And she lounged in a kind of bliss, thinking: "Well, something has happened in my life after all. Something has finally happened."

## THIRTY-TWO

Kramer came back from the telephone with a kind of smug look, a triumphant look on his rugged face, and Carl, lying on his side, and smoking a cigarette, kept eyeing him.

In the corridor outside, a tall officer in a crash helmet was standing at ease, reading a newspaper.

"Kramer," said Carl, "you look like maybe your worst enemy had just got run over by a garbage wagon."

Kramer smiled, sat down on a straight chair, and leisurely lit a stogie. "Carl," he said, finally, "I'm going to do you a favor."

"Gee, thanks," said Carl, sarcastically.

"Yes sir," said Kramer. "I'm going to give you a chance to get in on the ground floor and turn state's evidence."

"About what? Guys have already been tried and convicted on the same charge."

"About that eighth man."

"What eighth man?"

"Okay, be stupid. Might get you sent to the honor farm."

"Me? The escape artist? You're crazy, Kramer."

"And it'd help if you told me all about Nick."

"No way. I want to sleep," said Carl. Then: "Hey, you," Carl called to the tall officer in the corridor, "stop pretending you can read; you don't fool me; and get this dick out of my room. He's propositioning me."

Kramer gestured for the young officer to pay no attention.

"You're going up anyway, Carl," said Kramer. "Prove to me you didn't kill Nick and I'll really go to the front for you."

"I know," said Carl. "You'll walk the last mile with me and hold my little pinkie."

"I'm serious."

"Cops are always serious. I'm going to complain to the Bar Association or somebody. You are putting undue pressure on me. You are not respecting my constitutional rights. I read the papers."

"Okay, Carl," said Kramer. "Don't say I didn't give you a chance."

Long pause. Carl turned over on his back, stubbed out his cigarette, and lay looking at the patterns of light on the ceiling.

Finally Carl asked: "What happened, Art?"

"You will read it all in the papers shortly."

"Is a little birdie about to sing?"

"You're saying it."

"Well," said Carl, after a pause, "it can't hurt me, that's for sure."

"Suppose it's somebody who knows how you killed Nick?"

"Off the record, I didn't kill Nick. So quit with the pressure yet. That one's no good. And everybody knows I helped cloud the Kenmore Trust."

The worst of it was, somehow Kramer believed him in regards to Nick.

# THIRTY-THREE

It was ten after eight when Willie entered the lobby of the hotel where he was to meet Dorothy. He had noticed it several times at this hour, dimly lit and full of activity—a good place to meet, where the lobby of his own hotel was brightly lit and at all hours practically deserted.

She was waiting and rose to greet him—a different Dorothy, in a simple short black dress, woven stockings and low, buckled shoes, and the glasses she was wearing tonight were ornamental, with oddly shaped black rims, that gave her a strange distinctive look as of a mysterious person, perhaps from another country.

They both froze and stood looking at each other, almost as if they were meeting for the first time. Willie's hair seemed darker to Dorothy—or was it just the lights? (In fact he'd toned it down a little to go with his new identity). And he too now was wearing glasses, with thick black frames. And he was shorter than she had remembered him, shorter than herself, perhaps no more than five feet, eight, and slimmer, with a kind of high school boy slenderness, that went rather oddly with his somewhat worn face.

"Well," said Dorothy.

"Well," said Willie.

"I almost didn't recognize you with the glasses," said Dorothy. "I didn't know you wore glasses."

"It's a new thing," said Willie. "While I was away I had my eyes examined. Astigmatism and nearsightedness. How do you like that?"

"They're very becoming," said Dorothy. "You look like a diplomat or a doctor."

"How about a drink?" said Willie. "I understand the bar here is the thing."

"So I've heard."

They passed back side by side to the big dimly lit bar, where a small combo—piano, clarinet and guitar—was playing in a raised corner niche. The place was packed and people were milling back and forth, and screaming conversation at one another as at a cocktail party. With the aid of a little "oil" Willie got them a small corner booth and they ordered: a whiskey sour for Willie and a daiquiri for Dorothy.

People moved past the booth, back and forth, heedlessly greeting friends, passing drinks, bumping, apologizing …

"I didn't know it was like this," said Willie. "Do you mind?"

"No," said Dorothy. "I like it."

She kept looking around her, her pale-blue eyes brilliant, taking in everything, behind her glasses.

The waiter brought their drinks.

"Did the "corsage" arrive?" asked Willie.

Dorothy's face showed a mind of dismay. "I'm sorry. How could I forget to mention it. Yes. It's the most beautiful thing I ever owned in my life. I left it on the lounge. It lights up the room."

Willie repressed a start. His experience of the kimono from Wu's had been similar. It had definitely lighted up the room at the Golden West and gained him a good night's sleep.

"Why did you select it?" asked Dorothy. "I mean … well, I guess I shouldn't ask … but I'm so curious."

"I wanted something beautiful for you," said Willie, not knowing what else to say.

"Well, thanks," said Dorothy. "It's quite a contrast with my work uniform."

They had another drink. The tension, the initial awkwardness between them had eased. Both relaxed.

"Do you like dancing?" asked Dorothy.

"To watch?"

"No. To do."

"No," said Willie. "I never was much of a dancer."

"I love to dance. And I so seldom do anymore."

"The way they dance now," said Willie, "you don't need a partner."

"Could we go on to a place I know later?"

"Whatever you say," said Willie, enjoying himself so much that he permitted himself a third drink, one beyond his usual before-dinner quota.

They ate at an English restaurant not too far away from Willie's hotel. In fact they had walked to it through the soft Southern California night, both a little high, both infected to some extent by the mass uproar and chatter of the bar they had just left.

"The manager of my hotel recommended this place," said Willie, after they had ordered. "If it's no good I'll refuse to pay my hotel bill."

But it was excellent, the best roast beef Willie had eaten in years.

"I hope you like this food," said Willie. "Maybe it's little too masculine for your taste. If you don't like it, the next time I'll let you pick the place."

Dorothy smiled at him, feeling high and happy and rather confused, not really knowing exactly how she did feel—next time! That sounded fine, very fine, to her. And then suddenly she remembered something— the sandyish young man who walked on silent feet. But she decided that this was no time to bring it up. Why break the spell? Why drag up mundane matters in the midst of this pleasant fantasy of pleasure?

It was nearly eleven o'clock when the doorman called a taxi for them in front of the little restaurant. Dorothy gave the driver an address, and off they went through the excessively heavy traffic of Wilshire Boulevard.

Dorothy's rather large firm hand gripped Willie's in the darkness of the taxi cab.

"Good dinner?" asked Willie, warm and shaken with desire for this big, and to him violently, attractive Polish girl. He was so anxious to have her that he almost suggested that they pass up the dancing place for this night. But she seemed so eager to go there, so anxious to show him the place, that he kept still about it.

"Beautiful! Wonderful! But I shouldn't have had that after-dinner drink ... that ..."

*"Grand Marnier."*

"Yes. It was like fire. Whew!" Dorothy fanned herself and laughed, and Willie gripped her hand and tried to subdue his sudden impulse to take her right there in the taxi. What folly! Willie sat staring out at the passing lights, reading himself a lecture. He was acting like a fool, chasing all over town in taxis, like some tourist just in from the Midwest. What the hell was the matter with him—with the hounds closing in from all directions ...?

You had to see it to believe it. The place was packed with dancers, who wiggled and jerked, and squirmed, like African medicine men, in the midst of revolving colored lights and the blare of heavy-beat music from piped in hi-fi, with outlets, high up, all about the room.

Bearded guys. Girls with long straight yellow hair. All jerking and squirming with rapt, faraway looks in their eyes.

It was new to Willie, who had considered the jitterbug of his young years ridiculous, a comic dance. But there was nothing comical about all this. To Willie it was like getting down to bare essentials, all wraps off and no holds barred, metaphorically speaking, of course—because the couples—if you could refer to couples in this mad scramble—never really approached each other at all.

It was like a dancing madness—the old St. Vitus, or the crazy dancing of the Middle Ages that Willie had read about in parochial school at a time when, of all things, he had been an altar boy.

Willie didn't like it. It bothered him; he wasn't sure just why. Maybe because it struck him as being nature in the raw. But Dorothy's eyes were shining as they sat, crammed into an airless corner, watching.

Finally she got up and joined in. It didn't matter to anyone—every soul for himself. She was hardly noticed by the dancers in the flickeringly-lit bedlam. But she was noticed by Willie—the sinuosity of that voluptuous body made him forget Tom Corby and big Carl (was he dead? He hadn't seen anything in the papers), and crafty Nick— and the net spreading out from the Midwest that was trying to catch that big fish, Willie ... all that he saw was Dorothy ...!

Dorothy Velinsky! Suddenly he gave a wild start. *Thad* Velinsky— the big muscular Pole—Thad Velinsky ... hadn't he ... but Willie quickly put the thought from his mind. A coincidence. What else could it be? A wild coincidence. Velinsky was a common Polish name.

Nevertheless, Willie was gripped by a kind of dread.

... Dorothy was patting him on the shoulder. "What's the matter, Mr. Allen?" she said, towering over him. "You're not watching."

She studied his face for a moment, then sat down beside him. "I'm sorry I got so wound up," she said. "But you see, I never have any fun. This is like a vacation for me. I guess you are bored to death. Would you like to go?"

"Yes," said Willie, "let's go."

In the taxi Dorothy said: "I'm sorry. It was pretty silly of me to take you to a place like that. I should have known better."

She was really worried. Had she spoiled everything?

"It's all right," said Willie.

But she noticed that he did not grip her hand in the taxi. In fact he sat rather away from her, looking out at the lights.

And then once more she remembered the disturbing young man with the sandy hair and the black suit.

Willie decided to go in with her—it was not good for him to be on foot and at the mercy of taxis—but this, in a sense, was an emergency.

They went in through the entrance arch. Beyond them was the lighted pool, casting a pale-blue unearthly glow all over the courtyard, and it was full of cavorting, yelling people.

They climbed to the second deck in silence, Dorothy now definitely subdued, and Dorothy opened the door with her key and switched on the lights. And there on the lounge was the kimono, brilliant even in the fluorescent light.

But Willie hardly noticed it.

Dorothy touched it lovingly. "It was so thoughtful of you," she said, but Willie merely nodded and motioned for her to sit down.

She sat on the couch. Willie pulled up a chair and leaning forward kept staring at her, his eyes running over her as if trying to puzzle out her innermost thoughts from her posture, her attitude.

"What's the matter, Mr. Allen?" she asked, very upset. "If you're angry at me just say so."

Willie rubbed his cheek distractedly, then took out his cigarettes and they lit up.

"There's something I must tell you," said Dorothy. "Maybe I should have told you before, but we were having so much fun." And then at a look of marked attention from Willie, she recounted in full detail the visit of the young man to Dr. Mahon's office.

Willie said nothing, and the feeling of dread he had noticed in the dancing place began to grip him again. But in spite of the very good description, Willie did not recognize the young man: yet there was no doubt he was one of the hounds on the scent, from the insurance company, the law, or the underworld.

"Look, Mr. Allen," said Dorothy, as the silence lengthened, "You don't have to pretend with me. I know you are in some kind of trouble—and I don't care what kind it is."

Willie studied her, then forced himself to smile. He believed her. She didn't care. Why? Because she had all the makings of a promoter. He had come along like a breath of air in that uncongenial setup she had got herself into. He was her way out. But what a way she was choosing, if she only knew the facts!

Willie considered. His connection with her was bad, not smart. She had already been questioned by one of the hounds. Would they watch the doctor's office in case he came back? Would they have her followed? But that seemed unlikely. Nevertheless, it was just not a good situation.

Besides, something ever more important was knocking around at the back of his mind, though maybe this was just the result of his overheated imagination in that preview of hell he had just been witnessing, with the wild lights, the loud thumping music, and the jerking, spasmodic, rapt dancers.

It had to be!

Willie sat back, puffed on his cigarette and tried to appear unconcerned.

"I flew all the way back to the Midwest, by jet," he said. "Had business back there, in my hometown."

"Oh?" said Dorothy, feeling a little easier with him now. Maybe things were all right after all. "I was born in the Midwest."

"I was too," said Willie, "if you call Cincinnati the Midwest."

Dorothy smiled. "I was born not too far away. What do you think of that?" And she named the big town on the river that Willie had not wanted her to name.

"That so?" said Willie, deadpan. "I know that town pretty well. What part of the town were you born in?"

"And shall I tell you something funnier?" said Dorothy, rushing right on. "I grew up in Cincinnati. How's that for a coincidence?"

"Yes," he said, "how about that?"

"Oh," said Dorothy, "you asked me a question, didn't you? I'm dopey tonight. Well, I was taken away to Cincinnati when I was a baby. But I was born in Polishtown. And I know the street and address. Do you know how? My mother had snapshot of her old home—she hated to leave it, and it used to hang on the wall in Cincinnati. There was a frame house and a big fence and on the fence it said: 231 Clayburn ... "

Willie was seeing that fence as if through a mist of disbelief. But then a sudden thought struck him. Hadn't there been a lot of the Velinskys and Deruckis—cousins, aunts, brothers, sisters, god knows what all. A tribe that he had never been able to keep straight.

"I used to know a lot of people in that town; I was in and out, you see," said Willie. "And I knew some Polish people. What was your mother's name?"

Dorothy studied him, then laughed. "Oh, you wouldn't know my people, a man like you, Mr. Allen. Polishtown was no more than a slum."

"Do you think I always had money?" asked Willie. "I worked for it myself. I had nothing."

"Well, my mother's name was Lena Derucki."

That settled it. Willie rubbed his hands across his face, then sat looking about him rather vaguely. Dorothy didn't know what to make of him at all. Was he drunk? He had been drinking quite a lot.

"I told you that you wouldn't know my people," said Dorothy.

"That's right," said Willie, then he got up and looked at his wristwatch. He felt stunned, as if he'd been hit with a club.

How had this happened? How had he managed to walk into it, in a nation of 200,000,000 people? Was it just an accident? Or was there something ... something ... with intent behind it. He tried to shake such preposterous thoughts out of his mind.

At least something had saved him from what even Willie regarded as heinous, if not a mortal sin

"Mortal sin, for God's sake," thought Willie. "What in the hell is happening to me?"

He had left all that behind him years ago. Confessing to the priest: "Father, I have lied to my mother." Father this and Father that—and all for what? Sometimes he had made up lies about his sins in order to get a rise out of the old priest.

Just a lot of silliness. But did you ever quite shake it out of your system? He could remember back to a time when hellfire represented a real fear.

"It's late," said Willie. "I'd better go."

Dorothy rose. What had happened? She felt terribly let down. And she decided that it was that crummy dancing place she had taken him to; was he disappointed in her?

"I'll come down with you," said Dorothy, "and call you a taxi at the front desk."

"All right," said Willie.

This big girl was his daughter? The word entered his mind for the first time and seemed shocking and unbelievable! And then he thought back to his urgent desires in the taxi and was shocked again. He had not known his own any more than a tom cat would have! So much for such nonsense!

Dorothy waited with him till the taxi came. She didn't know what to say, but she had the feeling she'd seen the last of Mr. Allen—and now all of her dreams of a different, an exciting, full life were going glimmering.

"I'll phone you," said Willie. "You will hear from me."

She stood watching as the taxi drove off. Did he mean it, or was he only being polite?"

## THIRTY-FOUR

The Cheev was napping on the couch, with the portable TV going but turned way down. Colin had gone out to a pay phone due to a warning call from the hometown. What was up?

The Cheev lay half wondering and half sleeping. Occasionally his mind, as in a dream, would turn to vague, rather mixed-up thoughts of that black-haired girl in the doctor's office. What was it? A hunch? More than that. He had read her concern. He had smelled a cover-up. Could it possibly be only her manner? Was it the office routine at the doctor's office to guard the patients to that extent—a patient, who, according to the girl, had only consulted the doctor once?

The Cheev came out of his nap. Why was it he never had any money of his own? Why was it he could never call the turn for himself anymore but had to be a nice little yes-boy for the likes of that old crippled gray-haired monster? And now for a slug like Colin?

He had a lead. He was certain of it. A real hot lead, and here he was getting ready to take off along the Coast Highway, south, to comb the luxury hotels.

"My God, I'll get me a stake if I have to stick a gun in somebody's belly," the Cheev told himself.

But would he have the nerve to make a break from the supervision of Colin? Only time would tell.

A few minutes later Colin banged noisily on the door and the Cheev let him in.

"Pack," said Colin, looking grim and unapproachable.

"But I thought we were starting tomorrow."

"We're not starting at all," said Colin. "We're going back. There was a squeal. The Old Man's gonna be questioned by the police, maybe arrested."

"Who squealed?"

"Joe Wicks. It was all an act, his flipping and getting thrown in the nut ward. They got him out of the Walls, so he wouldn't be knocked off. They got him hid someplace—the cops, and I gotta go back and try to find out where. With Joe Wicks as a witness they may send the old Gimp up."

"You mean this is going to come out in the papers?"

"It's already out."

"Colin," said Cheev, "don't you see what that will mean? More heat on Willie."

"To hell with Willie. We got other fish to fry now. What good would all that dough be to the Old Man if he gets thrown in the clink? So pack. I'll be with you in ten minutes."

Hopeless. Cheev merely nodded. Colin went out, talking to himself.

Hopeless. And yet the Cheev rebelled. He did not give one goddamn for Quait—let him go to the clink. He was just not going to allow them to rob him of his lead and his chance to run down Willie.

He packed hurriedly; went down the stairway, instead of using the elevator, gave a bellboy five dollars and the keys to the rented car. Then he said: "Will you hand those keys to Mr. Brown? He'll settle up our bill. Then I'll meet him where I told him I would."

"Yes sir!" said the bellboy. Five bucks! Nice tip!

The Cheev hurried out the front door and was immediately swallowed up by the millions of Los Angeles. He kept giggling hysterically to himself. He was scared to death, and yet what else could he do? He kept seeing the face of "Mr. Brown."

"Mr. Brown" would throw a fit—and the Cheev could never again go back to his hometown, or at least not for a good long time, unless he had with him a wad of money with which to appease "Eyebrows," which was his new secret name for "Mr. Brown," better known as Colin.

# THIRTY-FIVE

It was very late. Kramer had taken a good long sleep as usual and had then returned to the hospital. Carl was awake and looking at the ceiling.

"I didn't know you cared, Art," he said, as the police Lieutenant looked into his room.

Kramer went in and sat down by the bed. "I've decided to give you one more chance, Carl."

"Oh, you're too good to me."

"You better start taking things seriously. You may be up for murder, along with everything else."

"Have they got a corpus delicatessen?"

"No, but we caught you with his car, his money, and his credentials."

"Art," said Carl, "will you quit? I been around for years. Stop with the policeman bit. I can't be had."

"You'll get five to twenty for sure, maybe a steeper jolt, Carl. How does that strike you?"

"I won't commit suicide."

"But if you would just give us a little help with Willie."

Carl raised his head and looked at Kramer. "Willie? How'd he get in on the act?"

"Carl, we all read the magazine and the newspapers just as you did. We figure you were out here looking for him. How about a lead, just between us? I'll go to the front for you. Captain Bescher will go to the front for you."

"For a murderer?" Carl asked, as if in immense surprise.

Kramer felt very discouraged. Why did he persist? Maybe with Carl now fighting extradition, he might be relieved at any minute. Was he just putting in the time?

Carl turned over and lit a cigarette. "Art," he said, "I'm not in the clink yet. Just remember that. And if I get put in, it ain't no cinch I'll stay there. Meanwhile the State has to keep me."

There was trampling in the corridor outside and in a moment Kramer was called away. He was gone for a long time. Carl lay smoking and half dozing. Just as he was stubbing out his cigarette, Kramer came back. There was an odd look on his face, Carl thought.

"Well, Carl," said Kramer, "maybe you can forget the extradition business. I don't think you're going back."

Carl turned over on his side to study Kramer.

"How's that?"

"They found Nick's body."

Carl made no comment.

"Too bad, Carl."

There was a further long pause, then Carl said: "Don't count your chickens yet, Art. Wait till you get the coroner's report. After that I may talk to you."

# THIRTY-SIX

Dorothy couldn't sleep. For a long time she'd turned and tossed and she had even taken a sleeping pill, something she very seldom did. It had made her slightly groggy but hadn't brought sleep.

Now she was watching a late show on TV—a show that dated back to the Forties and seemed preposterous to her not only in regard to the cars and the clothes but also in regard to the sentiment. To her it seemed like very Old Hat, indeed, ancient history. The picture had been filmed the year she was born.

She kept thinking about Mr. Allen and occasionally she flushed with embarrassment. How could she have taken him to a place like that? She had just drunk too much, that was all. Three Daiquiris. Wine. And that liquid fire with the delicious taste that Mr. Allen called *Grand Marnier*. That was it—she'd been boozed up; something that seldom happened to her; and there she'd been in the middle of the floor with all the rest of that weird crew, shaking it around, as they said, and poor Mr. Allen sitting in his corner, looking as if he'd like to shrink away from the whole thing.

And yet had that really been the trouble? Mr. Allen had been around, that was plain. It was ridiculous to think he'd been shocked by the "go-go" joint. And it was also plain that he was in some kind of serious trouble that even involved shooting. And who was the sandyish young man? What did he want? Why had he given her the creeps?

She felt a kind of despair and a cry coming on but resisted it. Tears, futile tears. As a little girl she had been a great one for tears, as also had her mother. And yet was there anything more useless?

But there'd been such a turnabout, such a reversal, in one short evening that it was very hard for her to adjust to it. She'd had such hopes. Now what was there to look forward to? Dr. Mahon, the office, the patients, Julie and the building's population of heavy-handed married wolves. All as before. And practically nothing in the bank.

She was wearing the kimono, and it had a marvelous heavy rich feel to it—luxury, elegance, a far cry from the antiseptic aroma and atmosphere of her daily work. Why had he bought it for her? Well, at worst it was something to remember him by.

She felt very depressed, because she was certain that somehow she had disappointed him, had turned out to be so much less than he had expected. And little by little the depression turned to restlessness. The walls of the boxy apartment seemed to be pressing in on her. She rose, turned off the TV, took off the kimono, put on a raincoat and sandals, and went out for some air. It was very late, after 4 a.m. Music was still going faintly someplace along the row.

At first she just walked along the deck, past silent, darkened windows, then finally she went down the stairs to the courtyard and strolled about. The pool lights were out; the water moved restlessly, agitated by unknown forces and occasionally gave little slaps at the sides. Only the dim night lights were on.

It was pleasantly cool and dampish, after a long hot day.

She wandered out to the entrance arch. The counter was dark; the steel shutter down. Silence throbbed all around. Far beyond, there was the vague indistinguishable rumbling and murmuring of the great city of three million souls.

Mr. Allen had suddenly come up out of that welter, like a new hope. Now he had gone back into it. She didn't even know where he lived.

Suddenly she leaned against the wall and began to cry. It just couldn't end like this, it just couldn't.

A small truck drove up with a wild squeal of brakes. Something sailed through the air and landed with a loud smack on the pavement under the arch; then the truck drove off. The morning papers, heralds of a new day.

Dorothy controlled herself and stopped crying. It was silly and useless. Tomorrow was another day; and she would just have to face it, as she had faced so many before.

In a couple of hours or so she would have to be making coffee and toast and getting ready to leave for the office. Time didn't stop. The world didn't stop, just because of a personal disappointment.

## THIRTY-SEVEN

It was nearly eight-thirty in the morning. The sky was overcast, and Willie's big room at the St. Nicholas was grayish without the lights on. He sat trying to eat his breakfast and read his morning paper. But he felt restless, nervous, shaken, uninterested.

He had dozed fitfully all night long. He hadn't managed to sleep one consecutive hour. And all those hours he had been conscious of the great city spread all about him, with its traffic going and its mysterious murmuring and rumbling, and its unexpected and unpredictable hazards for one Willie Madden. The sandy-haired young guy for instance. Who was he? Where had he come from?

And how many more were tramping the streets of the city and driving along its roadways, looking for him?

And just by the veriest accident one of them might stumble on him.

You could figure things out to the final digit and yet in spite of all your trouble, all your patience and vigilance, all your ordered thought, one stupid coincidence could wreck your plans.

But Willie's distress was only partly due to fear of apprehension; in fact that was only incidental, although he hadn't quite realized it as yet. Willie had come to a crossroads without sign posts. The past was behind him. He was no longer the completely irresponsible Willie of the Pearl of the Orient—and eventually this realization would have to be faced and dealt with.

Now Willie was mentally circling it, trying to keep it out of his conscious mind, trying not to let it influence him …

He poured himself a fresh cup of coffee and read the headlines in the paper: war, war, trouble, trouble: then he turned the pages languidly, trying to find something to interest him—and finally he did. A dispatch from the hometown, nearly half a page of rehash of the Million Dollar Robbery story, and a garbled account of its aftermath—obviously badly cut by the editor: there it all was again and with an added bonus, the questioning of John Q. Quait, "Nationally known private investigator" (and the Gimp's history was quickly recapped)—Was he the Eighth Man? And where was Willie?

But no pictures.

Yet Willie knew that now that the whole business had been revived because of a major squeal by either Wicks, O'Keefe or Peters—or all of them—the pictures would soon be reappearing, and once more the "crime" magazines would take it up.

The Big Heat was back on.

And yet Willie couldn't keep thoughts of Dorothy Velinsky out of his mind. He had wanted her as he hadn't wanted a woman for twenty years. Her face, her body, kept getting between him and the plans he should be making because of the new heat. And he kept wincing away from the thought that she was his "daughter." A preposterous idea. Ridiculous.

But there it was. Reality kept jumping and hitting him the face.

He tried to calm himself and reread the account of the robbery and its repercussions, to see if he had missed anything, but the print kept blurring before his eyes and his thoughts kept drifting away …

Grabbing up his pen he wrote:

*Dear Joker:*
*You have turned out to be as big a fool as*
*Carl Benedict.*
*Think. Think.*
*Take care of the kid if you like, but back*
*away and never see her again.*
*You have problems. You've got to move that*
*money.*
*That town is too small. L.A.'s the place.*
*Get busy, Willie.*

Willie's final method of handling his money had come about by accident, a happy accident this time: a bolt out of the blue, a gift of the Gods.

Two years back Willie had wound up in Mexico, only a jump or two ahead of the FBI, or so he had thought—with all of the money in a steamer trunk, overlaid with books and magazines. It was like carrying a bombshell around with him and called for twenty-four-hour vigilance.

He'd settled down in the good-sized town of San Tomas in a cheap little adobe he'd rented on the edge of town—James Williard, of Cincinnati, free-lance newspaper writer and novelist. He was supposed to be far from well-fixed and he tried at all times to live up to that picture. The steamer trunk was locked in a closet and Willie visited it daily, just to check. But it became a kind of bugbear and Willie realized he'd have to find a place to plant it. But where?

He had made friends with a rather shady character by the name of Hernandez who seemed to know all about what went on along the border, and it was plenty.

Hernandez would talk and Willie would "take notes" for his stories. He had Hernandez completely fooled.

Willie drove a beat-up ten-year-old Chevrolet that Hernandez would sometimes contemplate with heavily-acted derision. "An American with a car like that," Hernandez would say. "I know a lot of Mexicans who would sell it to a junkman."

One day Hernandez drove up in a black '57 Mercedes-Benz two-door sedan. "Here's a real car," he said. "You want to buy?"

"What with?" asked Willie.

"I sell very cheap."

"Why?" said Willie. "Drive it to Mexico City and you can get a top price for it."

Hernandez was silent. A week or so later he returned with the Mercedes-Benz. Willie was out in front changing a tire on his Chevrolet.

"You will kill yourself with that car one day," said Hernandez. "Look how slick the tires are. You got more money than that, with all your stories! Why don't you buy this car?"

And finally Hernandez broke down. The car had originally belonged to two brothers who had been running narcotics of all kinds into the States. One brother had been badly shot up by a rival bunch; the other brother had been arrested by the Mexican authorities and was now in prison. A younger brother had begged Hernandez, who was a kind of local "horse trader," to take the useless car off his hands.

"I traded a lease on a house for it," said Hernandez, triumphantly. "A year's lease and the kid's whole family moved in. It cost me nothing."

"Then keep it."

"In San Tomas? People will think I am a millionaire with a Mercedes-Benz and overcharge me for everything. Look, my friend. I show you something that will interest you, you who are a writer of stories."

And Hernandez showed Willie the secret compartment under the back seat. A kind of small safe had been carefully welded to the body of the car. You lifted out the seat, then you lifted out a kind of false top, and under it was a thin sheet of steel with a combination lock in one corner: two turns to the right, one to the left, then you opened it with a key, revealing a rather shallow rectangular compartment that would hold quite a lot of goods of most any kind.

"You see?" cried Hernandez, laughing.

"Fine," said Willie, his mind already working on the plan. "Great, if I was a junk runner."

"But don't you find it interesting, you a writer?" cried Hernandez.

And Willie found it very interesting indeed.

For days after that, the bargaining went on and finally Willie—in order to get rid of Hernandez as he said—agreed to buy the Mercedes-Benz for a thousand dollars and throw in his old Chevrolet, which Hernandez seemed to covet.

"The only trouble is," said Willie, "I haven't got a thousand dollars. You'll have to take it as I get it."

Hernandez agreed. Later Hernandez drove the rebel Chevrolet through the streets of San Tomas in triumph, delighted that he'd "stuck" the American with a car that ate gas and wasn't really a practical proposition at all.

Willie took over a month to pay for the Mercedes-Benz, doling out a hundred here, two hundred there.

Meanwhile, in the secret compartment of the Mercedes-Benz was all of Willie's lovely money, in about as safe a place as it could be.

And that was where it still reposed, with the Mercedes-Benz in a huge fireproof storage garage in Phoenix. Willie paid his storage bills six months in advance, and had established with the owners his identity as James Williard, itinerant writer, who might be in Europe, or California, or the South Seas—but would occasionally appear to look over his prize possession, the 57 Mercedes-Benz, and take it out for a spin.

Although this plan had worked successfully for a long time now, the sight of Tom Corby on the streets of the Arizona town had brought Willie up short and got him thinking that the town simply wasn't big enough: and L.A. was the place.

Willie sat reading himself a lecture. He shouldn't have lammed out of the town as he had; he should have made arrangements for the transfer right there and then. But he had been so anxious to get back to L.A. Why? Dorothy Velinsky.

The signs on the crossroads were growing clearer now. He would have to make a choice. No more Dorothy Velinsky. No more. He pledged to himself that he would not see her again.

First, it was a completely impossible situation, futile and frustrating; and besides, she had been "made" by the sandy-haired young man, who might be from any place or any organization, and might at the present time be following her or at least keeping the doctor's office under surveillance.

After all his care and patience, why put his neck in a noose now?

Fighting off a sudden feeling of depression, a feeling new to him, he sat down at the little writing desk in his room and made his plan; he would keep his room at the St. Nicholas—Dorothy did not know his new name nor where he was living. He would scout for a big fireproof storage garage in the Hollywood area—and then he would make the transfer at once, Tom Corby or no Tom Corby.

He studied the plan—he had even worked out a time schedule—then he burned it in the ashtray, and went in to shave. The face that stared back at him from the bathroom mirror, though tanned, looked haggard, with heavy creases between his eyebrows and around his mouth.

Though he felt a certain amount of self-approval because he had forced himself to act now as he should have acted before—and in the face of one of the worst shocks he'd ever had in his life—yet his stomach kept turning over in a very disturbing way and the world looked not grayish in the misty morning, but black.

# THIRTY-EIGHT

It was twenty after six, and already nearly dark, when Dorothy got home from the office, feeling tired and bored and as if she just wanted to lie down and turn off the world till the next day.

There was a large sealed manila envelope waiting for her on the desk. It had been delivered by messenger, the girl behind the counter said. It seemed, Dorothy thought, to contain a slick-paper magazine.

Hope, excitement, began to mount with her. Could it be from ...?

She hurried up to her apartment, drew the curtain, blotting out the courtyard and the swimming pool, and nervously ripped open the envelope.

It seemed to contain nothing but the current *Harper's Bazaar*. She began to leaf through and in a moment found a large flat envelope: in it were ten one-hundred-dollar bills and a note which read:

> *I am going away. Put this money in the bank*
> *and keep it for an emergency. Or maybe it*
> *will help you take up some course of*
> *study. Tell no one.*

That was all. Dorothy stood stunned in the middle of the room, then she sat down and read the note over and over. Did it mean he was going away for good? Had he been forced to, because of the trouble? If so, why had he been so generous with one he hardly knew? And what had happened to spoil things the night before?

She sat there, holding the bills in her hand, looking at them as if she had never seen money before. Her feelings alternated between hope and despair.

This meant—it might mean—that she would never see Mr. Allen again. And yet on the other hand, why ...?

It was nearly eight o'clock before she roused herself and went to the little Pullman kitchen to make coffee and a sandwich. She had no desire to go anyplace. She'd watch TV, go to bed early.

It was just possible that she might hear from him ... at least she kept assuring herself that it was possible ...

# THIRTY-NINE

Carl had made "friends" with the local fuzz and now one of them would occasionally join him in his hospital room for a talk. Carl amused them all very much. In San Ignacio he was rara avis indeed, a big-time hoodlum who didn't seem to give a damn about anything—lying there, wounded, nearly dead once, with major raps hanging over his head— grand larceny and murder—telling jokes and laughing it up and outraging the patient nurse by some of his remarks.

But tonight it was different. Officer Snell noticed that Carl seemed moody and withdrawn.

"You sure he ain't left?" he kept asking in regard to Kramer.

And Snell kept reassuring him. "No, he's still here. Had a very busy day. He might be sleeping now."

Carl turned over to look at his wristwatch on the night table. "It's after midnight. Some day he's had! I guess he must've run into a new broad. I tried to put him onto one—just up the road but he wouldn't listen to me."

"You mean Sally at Mike's Fish Shack?" asked Snell.

"Naw," said Carl. "This one's back up the highway almost thirty miles or so."

"That's out of our jurisdiction then," said Snell.

"You banging Sally, kiddo?" asked Carl.

"No," said Snell. "I'm a married man with two kids."

"So what does that prove?" asked Carl.

And Snell laughed. Things were picking up. The hoodlum was beginning to be more like himself. But he still kept harping on Lieutenant Kramer.

"I'll bet that bum's took a runout on me," said Carl. "No matter what you say."

"He'll be here," said Snell. "Say—how does it feel to get all shot up like that?"

"It don't feel good. First I fell backwards, then I fell forward. You ever been shot?"

"I never even been shot at."

"Well," said Carl, "someday I'll break out of here and then I'll accommodate you."

First Snell laughed, then he sobered; if all that Lieutenant Kramer said about Carl Benedict was true this might not prove so funny after all. He was just about to make a comment, then Kramer appeared in the doorway.

"You got to quit running after them hoods," said Carl. "You've got circles under your eyes."

Snell left, and Kramer pulled up a chair. "Carl," he said, "I've been talking to the coroner. He says Nick died of natural causes, then was weighted down and thrown in the ocean."

"You see?" said Carl.

"They're trying to rig up some charge to hold you on. Do you want to wind up a California prison, far from home?"

Carl studied Kramer's face for a long time. "What have you got in mind?"

"What did Willie Madden ever do for you?"

"Well," said Carl, "he put three bullets in me for one thing."

"You ready to tell us that story and give us a little help?"

"For what?"

"We've only got one squeal on John Q. Quait. One more would do it. And Joe Wicks has named Willie as the leader. It is now official. Your evidence would help cinch the whole business. You can still turn state's. And we'll look after you, Carl."

"How?"

"Suspended sentence. It's possible."

"H'm," said Carl.

"And if you would just break down and tell us what went on out here with you and Nick and Willie … it might give Mr. Alford a lead. Wouldn't you like to see that smart aleck Willie behind bars? All the rest of you guys have taken it on the chin. Why should you protect him?"

"Kramer," said Carl, "my father used to tell me, never trust a copper's word."

"All right. Tell you what I'll do. You waive extradition and I'll get you out of here. But if you don't cooperate, I'm gonna leave you here and the California authorities can do what they want with you. Then when you've served your time I'll be waiting out in front with a warrant."

"You're a real bastard, ain't you?"

"Yes," said Kramer.

"Let me think it over."

"And if you help us nail Willie, Captain Bescher will be your friend for life. He hates Willie's guts. Did you know the Captain recommended Willie to the District Attorney's office?"

This was too much for Carl. He started to giggle, then to laugh. In a moment, Kramer joined him. Carl lay roaring and wiping the tears from his eyes. Finally he got himself in hand and subsided.

"Some ways you got to like that little Irish bastard," he said. "Can you imagine such crust?"

Long pause. Kramer sat down, lit a stogie and puffed thoughtfully for a while. "Well," he said finally, "what do you say, Carl?"

"I got a feeling I ought to go for it. So they call me a fink—they'll be inside and maybe I'll be out. As for the set over, that don't scare me. I been shot at by experts."

Kramer said nothing. He didn't want to press his luck, but he felt a strong surge of triumph. This might even mean a promotion.

# FORTY

The Cheev had been watching the man for nearly two hours, a big drunken fool with a wallet loaded with money. Now a little blonde had him in tow and would no doubt take him some place and roll him. Somebody would roll him before the night was over, that was for sure.

The place resembled a smoky cave, with baby spots gleaming down here and there through the obscurity. The bar was packed, with people standing three deep and it was so jammed otherwise that the unlucky people in the booths kept yelling vainly for service. On a platform at the back of the bar a striptease was in progress, to howls of delight and even cheers.

The crowd swayed this way and that; there was hardly a square foot of space. The Cheev slowly worked his way through the press in front of the bar till he was standing next to the big prosperous drunk and the little hard-faced blonde, who was half falling out of her dress.

"But it's so crowded here, daddy," she was saying.

"I love it, baby."

"I got a nice cozy room right down the street."

"Later, baby, later." Then the big oaf cheered as the stripper peeled off another garment, and raised his left arm in a gesture of exultation.

The perfect gesture, from the Cheev's point of view. Turning sideways as if propelled by the crowd. The Cheev collided with the big man, quickly lifted his wallet from a left inside coat pocket, then backed off, apologizing profusely.

"That's all right, pal, that's all right," said the big drunk.

The Cheev got out of there as fast as possible, though impeded almost every step of the way and expecting any moment a hue and cry behind him. But luck was with him—or rather the stripper had fascinated the big drunk, who was still yelling and gesturing to her as the Cheev hurried out into the night.

He went down a dark side street. The Cheev knew that the wise thief got rid of the incriminating wallet or "poke" immediately. Stripping the wallet of a reassuringly thick wad of bills he turned and heaved it up onto the flat roof of a darkened garage. Now if he was caught, it was *his* money in his pocket, and let them prove otherwise.

But the Cheev wasn't caught. He returned safely to his dismal little hotel room in Hollywood and sitting on a beat-up, crummy couch counted his take: six hundred and thirty-five dollars. Now he was in business. If he handled it carefully, this represented a free hand for at least two months.

"I don't need you, Old Man," he cried, in triumph. "Nor you, Eyebrows."

Why hadn't he taken the bull by the horns before? Very simple. In the hometown it was impossible for him to operate in this fashion. In L.A. he was in the midst of three million strangers.

Now he could play his hunch to the hilt. The girl in the doctor's office had a definite connection with Willie Madden and he was going to prove it.

# FORTY-ONE

Mrs. Peet was worried about her eccentric old boss and found it almost impossible to sit at her typewriter and pound out the reports he had asked her to copy, after he'd dug far back in the files for items she remembered, if at all, but vaguely. They had something to do with the trouble he was in at present, serious trouble, according to the papers.

His license had been suspended, and several big clients, who paid large monthly retainer fees, had dropped him. His limp had grown worse, and he seemed to have aged ten years during the last month. Mrs. Peet felt very sorry for him in spite of all of the criticism. After all, he was just an old, old man, and should have retired to a park bench and sunshine long before this.

She kept making mistakes, then swearing to herself as she erased them. What did all these musty reminders of the past mean, anyway? How could they help Old John in his fight with the authorities?

Finally she glanced at her wristwatch, then rose and got John's medicine. Now she almost had to force it down his throat, couldn't trust him to take it on his own, as he had done, with a little nagging, before that fatal trip to Southern California. Oh, if he just hadn't taken it. Everything had gone wrong ever since.

She tapped at his door, got no response, tapped again then grew worried, almost panicky, and barged right on in, bottle and spoon in hand. Old John was asleep in his swivel chair, his chin on his chest, his hands lying flat on the desk, as if he was bracing himself. At intervals he snored faintly.

On his right was a telegram. Mrs. Peet quickly picked it up and read it:

*Nick's body found. He died of natural causes
according to coroner. Carl Benedict has waived
extradition!*
*Kramer*

Mrs. Peet put the telegram back and started to tiptoe out. What did it mean? And why had an officer of the law, Lieutenant Kramer, sent old John such a telegram? Behind her, the old man stirred. She turned. He had raised his head and was looking at her, his eyes weary and sad.

"Take your medicine," said Mrs. Peet, severely, pouring it for him.

And to Mrs. Peet's surprise he took it without a murmur, though no one realized the futility of medicine more than did old John at this moment. To work on his minor ailments now was like treating a dying man for a common cold.

There was no medicine in the world that could help him now. Only too plainly Old John could hear the steps of doom approaching.

"I'm working hard on those reports, Mr. Quait," said Mrs. Peet, trying to give him news that might cheer him.

He nodded slowly. "Thanks."

She went out, feeling very depressed, then put the medicine away, sat down at her machine, and began to type at a high rate of speed as if these reports could stave off disaster and she had a time limit.

An hour later Y called and Mrs. Peet put him on.

"Can't locate where they got Wicks," said Y. "But I'll keep trying. Grapevine: from the Department; Carl Benedict will turn states."

"Oh, no!" groaned Old John.

"Could be wrong. Have you heard anything from that crazy Cheev?"

"No," said Old John. He'd even forgotten all about him. When the sharks are running who remembers tadpoles?

"We're not through yet," said Y. "I'll get to Wicks. Carl's another matter. Anyway we're not sure yet. But you better have that money at the drop just in case."

"All right," said Old John, wearily, and hung up.

Business as usual for Colin, but for himself, definitely not. He'd see that the money got to the drop, he'd go through the motions, but it was all useless now and in his heart he knew it only too well.

He was done. Old John, after all these crooked years, was finally done.

## FORTY-TWO

Julie had noticed Dorothy's nervousness since early that morning, but as there could be a normal feminine reason for it, she kept ignoring it; but by mid-afternoon she was worried. Dorothy was usually the soul of efficiency; everything she did, she did well; today she had already made two very surprising mistakes.

The doctor hadn't been in all day as he'd been held up at the hospital because of two very serious cases and three regular appointments had already been cancelled. About three o'clock the doctor phoned to say he'd be in close to four. At that moment Dorothy was lighting a cigarette. The matchbook exploded in her hands; she gave wild jump and Julie saw tears in her eyes.

"Kid," said Julie, "he won't be back for an hour. Go get a cup of coffee, read a magazine, relax. I don't need you."

"Thanks, I will," said Dorothy. "It's just not my day."

After a brief hesitation, Julie asked: "Anything wrong?"

"Oh, no," said Dorothy, hurriedly. "You know how it is."

"I know," said Julie, relieved.

Dorothy had a strong impulse to unburden herself to Julie, so strong that she quickly hurried out to the elevators. Not once had she mentioned anything about Mr. Allen to her, except after that time when she'd bandaged his leg. No one knew she'd ever heard from him, let alone seen him. And that was the way she wanted, and intended to keep it. But it was very trying for her to have it all bottled up inside her day after day.

And then, after last night ...

The little prescription clerk smiled at her eagerly and wiggled his fingers as she went past him, chose a far corner, and ordered a cup of coffee and a tuna fish sandwich. She'd had nothing but a coke since breakfast, and even now didn't feel hungry.

... last night. Julie had dropped her off at her apartment at close to six o'clock. Julie had a beat up little compact, a "family" car that was driven by both Julie and her sister. Sometimes Julie would have it for days and would swear about the bus she had to ride. Dorothy lived much closer to her job, transportation was not much of a problem, and she could even walk if necessary, though it was a long pull.

(To meet Mr. Allen she had taken a taxi and it had put quite a hole in her weekly budget.)

Yes, Julie had let her off. After work they'd gone "shopping" in a big sell-all drugstore and Dorothy had picked up some small items and a couple of magazines.

Just as she was half way through the arch, she realized she'd left her magazines on the back seat of the car, and as she had been looking forward to reading them that evening, she turned abruptly and hurried back to try to catch Julie …

A man had come in through the arch. At her sudden turn, he quickly retreated and disappeared around the corner. But Dorothy had got a very good look at him in the light from the courtyard. It was the sandyish young man.

She froze. Fright gripped her. He'd disappeared like a phantom. For a moment she even wondered if she'd actually seen him and if maybe it wasn't just a hallucination. But she'd see him all right: black suit, black tie, white shirt and all, just as before.

Forgetting her magazines and Julie, she had run up the stairs to her apartment, let herself in quickly, and then bolted the door after her.

She had spent a very uneasy night alone in the locked apartment and had very little sleep …

"Hello there … how's my big beautiful girl today …?"

She looked up vaguely. The prescription clerk; a married man with two children who just wouldn't give up.

"It's not my day," said Dorothy, forcing a smile.

He leaned on the table to talk to her, very neat and antiseptic in his spotless white jacket, and black-rimmed spectacles.

"Problems?"

"Not enough sleep."

"Oh, you girls. You will run around. Why not with old Doc Duval?"

His name was Ernie Duval and he was quite a swinger, or so he thought.

"My idea is you were spoken for," said Dorothy, wishing he would go away.

"If that's all that's worrying you, forget it. I've got a very understanding wife."

"That's nice."

"Old Doc Duval" eyed her for a moment. "You know what I think? I think I'm just too short for you. You're ashamed to be three or four inches taller—I mean in public."

"How did you guess?"

"But in private …?" He fixed her with a libidinous eye behind his glasses.

Luckily he was called away.

Dorothy finished her coffee hurriedly and got out. Was there anything in this world more irritating than having a completely impossible man on the make for you, especially at a time when the best-looking man in the world would have been an annoyance?

Next time she'd take her coffee break down the street at the dark little diner-like place. Girls waited on you at the counter and there was no prescription clerk or any men at all—except a cook, who occasionally glanced in and grinned.

She went out into the sunshine and walked down the street, looking into shop windows, just to have something to do. Time passed. She began to feel a little less nervous. She came to the corner and started back. At the corner was a scale with a glass front. She decided to weigh herself, as weight had always been a problem with the women of her family, especially her mother, and she tried to keep herself at a reasonable level.

She looked at the dial. Its center was of glass, and in the circle of glass, going in the opposite direction, and crossing with the light, she got a quick glimpse of the sandyish young man, who immediately disappeared into the crowd.

All of her nervousness came back. And she decided that she'd return to the office and tell Julie she felt so unwell that she'd have to go home. What did he think he was doing? Why was he following her? Oh, if only Mr. Allen would come back. He'd know how to handle this.

She had stayed longer than she intended. It was five of four when she returned and Julie said to her: "Kid, the doctor's looking for you. He's in his office with some man. He wants you right away."

Apprehension stabbed at Dorothy and she had to resist an impulse to get out of there fast.

"Who is the man?"

"I don't know, kid. But he's cute. Very well dressed. Polite. You'll like him."

After this description Dorothy felt a certain amount of relief. Composing herself, she tapped at the door of the doctor's inner sanctum and was told to come in.

The doctor introduced her to a rather tall young man, with dark-brown hair and a pleasant smile, who rose and shook hands with her.

"This is Mr. Alford," said the doctor, "of the FBI."

"You look alarmed, Miss Velinsky," said Alford, smiling. "I assure you there is nothing to be alarmed about. This is merely a routine matter. Please sit down."

Dorothy sat down and tried hard to compose herself. But she felt confused, worried, scared. The sandyish young man, now this! Could it be possible that the sandyish young man was also with the FBI?

"He's making inquiries about Lawrence Allen," said the doctor, patting Dorothy on the shoulder. "I understand from Julie you are not feeling well today and after this is over you can go home. In fact I'll take you home as I have an emergency—so they say—out your way. What a day! The most mixed-up day I've had in ten years!"

"I'm sorry if I've added to it, Doctor," said Alford, "and I will be as brief as possible. Miss Velinsky, I understand that Mr. Allen was here in the doctor's absence and that you treated him for a cut and gave him an anti-tetanus shot."

Little by little Dorothy was getting a grip on herself, and Mr. Alford's manner was helping; he seemed so polite, so considerate.

"Yes sir. That's right."

"Why didn't you wait for the doctor to handle it?"

"The doctor wouldn't be in for two hours or more, and Mr. Allen was leaving town."

"I see. Did he say where he was going?"

"No, sir. You see, we hardly knew him. He'd only been in once before. He didn't talk much."

"That's right," said the doctor. "I found him very interesting and I would have talked longer with him, but he left."

"What was the nature of his injury?"

"It was like a cut," said Dorothy. "He told me he ripped it on the edge of the car door. I could understand this, because I ripped my coat once in the same way."

"Describe it."

"It was about an inch long, not very wide, and deep."

"Parallel to his foot?"

"Yes, sir."

Alford studied her for a moment and when she returned the look he smiled at her pleasantly.

"Now you aren't finding this alarming, are you?" he said.

"No, sir."

"And you haven't heard from him since? He hasn't called in to report the progress of his injury, or anything like that?"

"No, sir."

"I think that'll be all, Miss Velinsky. And thank you very much."

It was a little after five when the doctor drove up in front of the arch.

"What in the world do you suppose the FBI wants with Mr. Allen?" asked Dorothy, as she was getting out of the car.

"He told me it was merely a routine inquiry," Dr. Mahon said. "Maybe there was a business scandal or something, and Mr. Allen is wanted as a witness. Dorothy, tell me, are you sure that wasn't a gunshot wound? I think that was what Mr. Alford was getting at."

"I'm sure it wasn't, Doctor. But I am really not an expert."

"Well, child, you must be more careful. Gunshot wounds should be reported. We might get into trouble."

"Oh, I'm sorry, Doctor. It never occurred to me. Who would be shooting at Mr. Allen?"

"I know what you mean. Now get a good sleep. See you tomorrow."

It was broad day and Dorothy did not feel so nervous about going through the arch where the night before she had seen the sandyish young man. But she bolted her door quickly, then sank down onto the couch.

It was going to be another long night.

## FORTY-THREE

All had gone according to plan with Willie and he was now back once more in his big comfortable room at the St. Nicholas, with the pleasant park visible from his front windows, with its lake, its boathouse and its carefree loungers.

It was night now, early evening, and Willie stood at the window looking out at the rush of traffic on Wilshire; it hummed past endlessly, day and night. In this big city everybody seemed to spend most of their waking hours on wheels.

Mechanically all was well. The Mercedes-Benz was on the second floor of a huge fireproof storage garage in Hollywood; Willie had established his identity as James Williard, a writer who might be gone for months at a time—or might not; and he had made friends with the boss of the garage, who was much taken with the dapper little "writer" and questioned him about Hollywood. Did he write scripts? Did he know any movie stars?

Willie explained he was not that kind of writer, but specialized largely in articles, though occasionally he wrote a novel. Mostly he traveled around the world.

He'd had a hard time getting away from the garage boss, who said later to one of his men *"that Williard is quite a guy."*

There hadn't been a single hitch of any kind, from first to last. He'd turned in his rented Oldsmobile at the rental chain's regional office in the Arizona town, paying his bill with traveler's checks, countersigned John Ward, and then he'd driven the Mercedes-Benz straight through to Los Angeles in one long jump, having already made arrangements at the Hollywood storage garage.

Not one moment of anxiety, in spite of the fact that there was over four hundred thousand dollars under the back seat!

He was now driving another rental car, from still another rental office: a light-blue Plymouth. Willie had decided, things being as they were, to scale down to a more common type of car, not so easily spotted. It was rented in the name of John Ward.

Yes, a perfect, a very smooth operation, the kind of operation that had kept Willie out of the hands of the law for nearly five years.

And the hounds of disaster were baying loudly, no doubt about it.

Willie, after his return, had bought some hometown newspapers at a stand in Hollywood: and there it was, spread all over the pages, the Million Dollar Robbery and its Aftermath.

The Score:

> Novak, dead.
> Bellini, dead.
> O'Keefe, in prison.
> Peters, in prison.
> Wicks, in a private mental hospital.
> Benedict, in custody.
> Quait, facing indictment.
> Fay (now connected with Benedict) dead.
> William H. Madden, the leader, still at large.

Willie couldn't get over the fact that Carl Benedict had survived. Willie thought it over for a long time, then he said: "As soon as he gets his health back, he'll be long gone. It's odds on he'll escape. And I hit him three times, at close range."

It was like he had a charmed life.

But Willie could look forward to no such miracles personally. If he continued to stay free it would have to be through his own efforts, constant wariness, constant vigilance, constant stratagems and shifts and turns.

But lately he had been asking himself some disturbing questions. What was he fighting to stay free *for*? And what had he stolen all that money *for*?

Not long ago these would have seemed like stupid questions to him. Now they were the most important questions in his life.

He was not happy. He didn't know what to do with himself. A guy could only wear one suit at a time, eat one meal, drive one car—all the rest was unnecessary excess unless there was some reason behind it. Now there seemed to be none. Money in itself was nothing: just green paper with politicians' pictures on it. Its worth was that you could trade it for something valuable, like pleasure.

But Willie couldn't find any pleasure. Once it had been a matter of Cadillacs, and forty dollar a day suites, and hundred dollar a jump girls, and star sapphire cuff links, and the respect of all those who only respect people who have more money than they have. He had lived it up, just as he'd intended to before he looted, with the help of a lot of poor clowns, the Kenmore Trust, and now he'd *had* it!

In Arizona he'd even spent part of the night with the hostess from one of the swank restaurants. She'd bored him, and he'd been so indifferent to her charms, though trying hard, that he'd hurt her feelings.

He could still see her weeping exasperation, a big redheaded woman, her mascara running.

He had been introduced to her by Jim Paisley of the Acme Storage Garage as "*James Williard, the well-known writer.*"

And Paisley had told him that Greta would "play" for big money. Well, at least she'd got her big money.

What an irritating fiasco!

The next morning, he'd started for L.A. just as the sun was rising over the flat-topped Arizona buttes, and the dew was really sparkling on the sage, like in the movies.

The one thing Willie wanted he couldn't have: Dorothy Velinsky.

And he was weaving at night. Not too bad as yet; not as he had at the Golden West. But there was something about it now that worried or disturbed him much more than before. Once in a while in a public place, he'd feel a tendency to weave suddenly come on him—and he would have to brace himself and fight against it. It was as if he was regressing slowly toward a time earlier than his twenty-eighth year.

Where would it all end?

He was eating at the little English restaurant—with the excellent roast beef—where he had taken Dorothy that night.

Suddenly he shrank back in the corner of his booth. The place was very busy and bursting with activity and not too well lighted, but over the heads of all he could see a party up at the front waiting for the headwaiter to seat them. Three girls and two men. One of the girls was Dorothy; looking beautiful in a white dress that shimmered slightly under the lights.

Willie waited. He couldn't just jump up and run out. And finally to his relief the party was seated far across the room from him in a very large booth that almost hid them from view and he noted that Dorothy was sitting at one end with her back toward him. Then he recognized another of the girls: the one who worked behind the glass enclosure at Dr. Mahon's office.

Willie continued his meal as before, passed up the dessert and the brandy he'd intended to drink, paid his bill and left.

Just as he was passing out through the front door, Dorothy turned and looked in his direction, half rose out of her seat, then sank back.

This was getting ridiculous!

She'd have to fight hard against it. Several times now she'd thought she'd seen Mr. Allen, at one place or another, but each time she'd been wrong.

"What's the matter, kid?" asked Julie. "Hot foot?"

"I lost my shoe," said Dorothy, which was the truth.

They all laughed.

"I like this place, I like it, I like it," said one of them. "It even smells good. Oh, that meaty aroma. Glad you steered us here, Miss Velinsky."

"Call her Dorothy, for heaven's sake," cried Julie.

"Okay, Dorothy, if I may be so bold."

Julie had persuaded Dorothy to come. At first Dorothy had refused. Julie had finally called on Dr. Mahon for help. "I don't know what's the matter with her," she'd explained to him. "She just sits in that apartment. And she seems awfully nervous."

So the doctor, who liked both girls very much and thought of them in a way as his "daughters," had insisted.

It was Julie's sister's birthday. One of the men would shortly marry her; the other was his friend, who was now having occasional dates with Julie. Julie had surprised him. Marie was prim. But God knows Julie wasn't—and as for this big girl in the white dress—wow, man, wow!

He whooped it up.

Willie sat in his hotel room grimly trying to watch TV. God, Dorothy had looked wonderful to him!

The TV show droned on monotonously, and finally, with an exclamation of exasperation, Willie switched it off, went to the front window and stood looking out. Just over the housetops was the English restaurant and in it was Dorothy in a beautiful shimmering white dress. But who were the guys?

"To hell with the guys," Willie lectured himself. "That's none of your business. Or are you like the doctor and want her to be a Nun?"

And then he remembered the embarrassing tableau with big red-haired Greta—it could be pretty ugly and sordid at times …!

Swearing, Willie turned away and began to pace the floor.

Couldn't he at least talk to her on the telephone?

At eight-fifteen the next morning he called Dr. Mahon's office. Dorothy answered the phone to his relief. If the other girl had answered he had intended to hang up.

"This is a wrong number," said Willie—and she recognized his voice immediately. "Can you be at the Callan drugstore one block down at one o'clock?'"

"Yes," said Dorothy, "but I'm afraid you have a wrong number."

"I'll call you on the pay phone just inside the door."

"I understand, but you are calling the wrong number."

Julie came in from the back, fussing with her hair, and heard the tail end of the conversation. Dorothy shrugged.

"Some foreigner," she said.

"My, you look pretty this morning," said Julie, studying her. "I wish I had a complexion like that. When I was fifteen I had acne; God, did it embarrass me! So what happened? So I end up running around with a boy who had acne. We consoled each other. Oh, you certainly flipped Quentin last night. He thinks you are the living end. He says you dance like a professional. He's got a friend of his he wants you to meet. Quentin's a nice guy. Maybe his friend is, too ..."

Julie chattered on. But Dorothy stood as if in a trance, then finally she said: "I've got to change"—and disappeared. Her hands were shaking, but she felt warm all over. So he wasn't just being polite that night. He had meant to call.

It was just one o'clock when Dorothy hurried into the big cut-rate drugstore, Callan's, and looked around for the pay phone, and there it was, but a middle-aged woman was already in the booth. Dorothy gave a gasp of exasperation, and waited, tapping a foot.

She had thought of nothing all morning but arranging things so she could get away in time to take the call. As she walked through the streets, the sandyish young man had hardly crossed her mind; she hadn't scanned the crowds, watching for him.

But the Cheev had just entered at the far end of the store and was now at the magazine rack, glancing at a newspaper, screened from Dorothy by a tall turntable of paperback books.

He noted the agitation. He noted her eyes traveling irritatedly toward the woman in the booth. Was this the call place?

But the woman talked on, and soon it was five after one and the woman was putting more coins in the slot for further conversation.

Dorothy could hardly stand it, and began to pace back and forth. Finally the conversation concluded at seven after one, and Dorothy gave a long sigh of relief.

The woman had a lot of packages and kept dropping them. Dorothy, who really wanted to give her a shove, helped her pick them up and get them resettled in her arms.

"Thanks, dear," said the woman. "I never get a chance to talk on the phone at home with all the kids yelling."

Dorothy smiled, got quickly into the booth, closed the door and pretended to be looking up a number.

Finally the phone rang. It was nearly ten after now. Dorothy answered it eagerly. It was Mr. Allen. She quickly explained the delay but he did not laugh or make a funny remark as she had expected.

"Is everything all right?" he asked in a very serious tone.

It was just what she needed. Things definitely were not right and she had been longing to unburden herself. "No, Mr. Allen," she said, "I'm being followed."

He asked for particulars and she gave them to him at length.

In the booth of another pay phone two miles away, Willie doodled on the phone book as he listened. Anger was rising in him. This bastard, scaring Dorothy half to death!

"What is your impression of this man?" asked Willie.

"He's a creep," said Dorothy. "Some kind of creep."

Should she also tell him about Mr. Alford? But she decided that could wait. Mr. Alford was a nice young man who wouldn't really worry her very much if he also took to following her. No—it was this creep she couldn't bear the thought of; this weirdie who just seemed to disappear that evening at the archway, like a phantom!

"A creep," mused Willie; and any day he would take a woman's judgment about such a thing. It was obvious to him that this was not a matter of the law, but maybe something even more dangerous— either an underworld spotter from the hometown or a freelance hood, with reward money on his mind or blackmail.

And this guy, whoever he was, was no amateur. He'd been clever enough to get information from the manager of the Golden West about Willie's visit to Dr. Mahon. But actually Willie was furious at him because he was terrorizing Dorothy. He could take his own plight coldly and objectively.

He quickly made up his mind what to do.

"Dorothy, listen," he said. "At nine o'clock tonight you go out for a walk …"

"A walk? Oh, Mr. Allen, I couldn't … the streets are all so dark around there."

"Just listen. And don't worry. I'll be there. You won't see me. But don't worry about that. At nine o'clock you go out through the arch and turn to your right. Then just walk around the block and come back. But don't stroll. Walk as if you are going someplace. Do you know what I mean?"

"Yes," said Dorothy, feeling very nervous and excited but relieved, too. Mr. Allen was going to take care of things and rid her of this constant fear.

They went over it again, then hesitating slightly, Dorothy asked:

"And will I see you afterwards?"

"No," said Willie. "For a while I think we'd just better talk on the phone."

"But how will I know if ...?"

"Don't worry," said Willie. "It will be taken care of. Tomorrow nobody will be following you. And you can relax."

He said goodbye and hung up, rather abruptly, she thought.

Far across the drugstore, the Cheev was smiling to himself, his yellow eyes giving off sparks. Something was definitely up. He could tell from her attitude it hadn't been any ordinary phone conservation.

Was he getting close to pay dirt? Maybe, and he'd have to watch more closely than ever now.

## FORTY-FOUR

Even though it was night and the sun had been down for hours it was still hot in downtown L.A. and the smog had been heavy all day, adding to the burden of the heat.

Alford was sitting at his desk, in his shirtsleeves, his chair tipped back, a glass of water from the cooler in his hand, and a faraway look in his eyes.

He had been going over the coordinated reports on the Willie Madden case with young Ed Parry all afternoon. Parry was slightly in awe of the handsome Alford, his superior, and was inclined at all times to defer to his judgement, though there had been many points in the reports on which they did not see eye to eye.

For instance, Parry thought that Alford was too willing to accept Carl Benedict's story of his relationship with Fay and Willie. It seemed fantastic—the whole thing—to him. It fit no rational pattern, and young Parry was too young to realize that maybe this was one of its virtues. Benedict was just not a rational human being. He was far beyond Parry's imagination

"Well," said Alford, finally. "I now have to add my own little mite to this mountain of paper. And it will deal mostly with a rather pleasant subject—a gorgeous young lady by the name of Dorothy Velinski."

Parry had been sitting lost in clouds of surmise in regard to the big-time hoodlum, Carl Benedict, and he had only half heard.

Suddenly he looked up. "What was that name?"

Alford repeated it, smiling. "Not euphonious exactly—but what's in a name?"

Parry was aghast. "Didn't you read my report about the Velinsky family?" he cried, jumping up. "Where did you see her? Where'd you find her? What has she got do with this?"

"Wait," said Alford, staring, then he took a little black book from his desk and looked through the indices of reports. "It was marked non-relevant, my boy. No, I didn't read it. Should I have? Why is it marked non-relevant?"

"Casey must have done that," said Parry, hurrying to a file cabinet. "I talked with him about it."

Casey was an overworked coordinator of the old school—who only had one thought in mind: run down Willie Madden, never mind all these silly reports that get you nowhere. And for years this system had worked for Casey because it made for a minimum of dead ends. This time it had slipped up.

Parry found the report and put it in front of Alford, who glanced at it and then looked up. "You marked it non-relevant, yourself. Here's your signature."

Parry nodded slowly. "Then Casey backed me up after he read my summary and conclusion. Read it."

Alford read it slowly, digesting every word; finally he laid it aside and sat lost in thought. "There is only one conclusion we can come to," he said, finally. "Either these people fooled you or they know absolutely nothing themselves and in some way Dorothy Velinsky has got in touch with her father or vice versa."

"What do you mean?" cried Parry, all at sea.

And Alford told him all about Dr. Mahon's office and Dorothy Velinsky and the possible gunshot wound. "And there is no doubt whatever that Lawrence Allen is Willie Madden, and Carl Benedict claims he shot at him and maybe hit him. And it's too fantastic—a ten million to one shot—that Willie Madden would suddenly appear by accident in the doctor's office where his daughter was employed. Am I right?"

"Of course, of course," said Parry, hurriedly.

So much for rational thought!

"And don't you think it is too much of coincidence if this young lady is not the Dorothy Velinsky we are looking for?"

"It all fits," said Parry.

"She has to be," said Alford. "All right, let's put the machinery in motion. She must be watched, round the clock. Call Strickland. He's home. I want him to take charge of this. By the way, what time is it?"

"Twenty of nine."

Parry got on the phone and tried to reach Strickland, but there was no answer.

"Keep trying," said Alford. "Sometimes he drives his wife to the supermarket in the evening. She can't drive. Broke her arm."

Parry glanced at Alford, then shook his head. Roy seemed to know everything about everybody.

He kept trying. Time passed.

In spite of this sensational lead, Alfred was calmly reading or rereading the coordinated reports. Parry, at the phone, kept watching him.

"In all my experience," said Alford, "this is the cagiest man I ever tried to run down. We still haven't got the faintest kind of lead or even a theory on where he is keeping all that money—and he's been on the run for nearly five years. It's unheard of. He's a kind of genius."

"All that experience as an investigator…"

"It helped," said Alford. "But you have to know how to put it together." A pause. "No answer," said Parry.

"Keep trying."

# FORTY-FIVE

At nine o'clock Dorothy came down the steps from the second deck and started across the courtyard. She felt a kind of cold panic, verging on terror, that she fought hard to overcome. She had to do this; she just had to. Not only for her own later peace of mind, but also because she didn't want Mr. Allen to be disappointed in her again.

The pool area was thronged with people, talking, laughing it up, wading, swimming and diving, and Dorothy crossed to the archway envying these carefree souls who had nothing more serious in their heads than beating the heat and having a little fun.

There was so substitute in this world for peace of mind and for the first time in her life Dorothy Velinsky was learning that lesson. Fear colored everything in dark hues; it was like an insidious creeping plant that thrusts its tendrils everywhere and finally overruns everything. Nothing could be enjoyed when you were afraid.

Not that she had been hilariously happy. Far from it. But in the midst of this chilling fear she looked back on an earlier time—when she was at intervals merely irritated, or annoyed, or bored—as halcyon.

It was a still, breathless night, with a faint smell of smog in the air. The street beyond the archway looked very dark and ominous to her and she hesitated and drew back before she could force herself to leave the safety of the known for the dangers of the unknown.

Finally, gritting her teeth, she left the archway, turned to the right and started down a street that consisted of old two-story duplexes and apartment houses and an occasional little one-story frame house, of the California past. The corner was a long distance off, with a dim streetlight burning there. In between was nothing but darkness and trees, bushes and hedges, and beyond the vegetation, a few dimly-lighted windows, generally with the shades drawn. Cars were parked almost bumper to bumper, all along the curb, and the Creep might be hiding in any one of them.

She hurried purposely, as Mr. Allen had told her to do. She did not look around. She heard nothing but faint music coming from radios or TV sets. Someplace a car door slammed suddenly and she gave a start and almost broke into a run, but managed to control herself. Would she never get to the safety of the streetlight?

But she finally made it, and turned the corner into a similar little street—with the same makeup of habitations and with cars parked all along the curb, enough that it seemed to be darker here, lonelier.

Up ahead beaconed another dim streetlight and she tried to concentrate on it, hurrying, not looking back.

The Cheev turned the corner and watched, smiling to himself. She was hurrying all right, as to a rendezvous. This was no stroll, that was for sure. Had it all been arranged by pay telephone that morning? He kept smiling to himself, very proud of his operation.

But all at once he froze. Somebody had suddenly, out of nowhere, stepped in behind him. A gun was jammed into his back.

A harsh voice said: "If you follow that girl again I'll kill you."

Then the gun was removed from his back and the barrel came down on his head, once, twice—and there was a great splattering as of an exploded sun—with huge bursts of brilliant golden light ... Groaning, he fell to his knees, then gradually slid forward and lay face down on the pavement.

Dorothy had neither heard nor seen anything. She was on her way to a new beacon now, with the boulevard up ahead and a reassuring number of cars passing. The last leg of the journey wouldn't be too bad.

She was almost back to her starting point. She'd turned into the boulevard and there were people about and cars passing, and she paused for a moment to catch her breath. Had anything happened? Had it all been in vain? That is what she feared now. And maybe tomorrow, once more, she'd catch a glimpse of the Creep following her in the street. But it just couldn't be. Mr. Allen was to be depended on. She was sure of it.

Would he call her early the next morning to let her know that all was well?

But when she reached the archway, just round the corner from the boulevard, she gave a start. A man was leaning against the inner wall, smoking a cigarette, as if waiting. It was Mr. Allen. Her heart gave a kind of leap and she hurried over to him.

"Is everything all right?"

"Yes," said Willie.

"What happened?"

"I persuaded him not to follow you anymore. You have nothing to worry about now."

A terrible weight seemed to lift from her shoulders.

"Oh, I'm glad you waited," she said. "On the phone I thought I understood ..."

"I changed my mind," said Willie.

"Well, then," said Dorothy, "why not come in and let me make you a cup of coffee? And what about a sandwich? Oh, all of a sudden I'm starved. I haven't been eating much lately."

Willie let her run on. The thing to do was get out of there, maybe out of town, maybe far, far away. He was acting like a fool and knew it. He'd had no intention of seeing her. Up to the last second his plan had been to get quickly back to the hotel and call Dorothy in the morning. And yet here he was, as if he'd lost conscious volition. But something about Dorothy wandering around in the dark streets of this dangerous city had got to him. He had wanted to be certain that she got back. That was all. Why make a Federal case of it.

Yes, that was all. Willie kept reassuring himself.

"Won't you come in?" Dorothy insisted.

And in a moment he was following her across the courtyard, where the denizens of Dorothy's pad were whooping it up in loud but light-hearted gaiety, with the agitated water of the lighted pool casting flickering bluish light all up the stairways and across the windows.

They climbed to the second deck, Dorothy unlocked the door, and they went in. In the dark—before she switched on the lights—weird-looking bluish reflections ran up and down the walls, in zig-zag patterns, giving Willie the odd feeling of being in a goldfish bowl. And wasn't that really where he was? A public place like this could be a trap. He was not even sure there was a back way out.

The lights were on now, the curtains drawn. Dorothy disappeared into the back. Willie paced nervously for a moment, then sat down and lit a cigarette. In a few minutes Dorothy returned. She was wearing the Chinese kimono and to Willie she looked like a dream.

But her eyes showed surprise. Mr. Allen seemed very different to her now that she got a good look at him under the lights. He did not have his glasses on and he was wearing a black suit and a black turtleneck sweater.

"What's the matter?" he asked.

"It's the sweater, I think," she said. "You look so much younger."

"Oh," said Willie, "that's my night consultation costume. The commandos blacken their faces. While you make the sandwiches, I'll get out of it."

Dorothy did not quite understand but she had an inkling and decided to say no more about it.

When she came back, Willie had removed the sweater and now seemed to her like his true conventional self in a white shirt and tie, and the black-rimmed glasses.

They sat on the lounge with the food in front of them on a coffee table.

"This is nice. I like this," said Dorothy, smiling at Willie and eating with gusto.

"Who were your friends at the restaurant?" asked Willie.

Dorothy stared. "Then I *did* see you?"

Willie nodded. "I was there."

Laughing, Dorothy went into Marie's birthday party at length, explaining how Dr. Mahon had insisted that she go. "It was that Creep," she went on. "I was afraid to go out of my apartment at night and Julie noticed I was very nervous. Oh, it was quite a party. We went to the go-go joint. Somewhere Quentin—Julie's boyfriend—found some candles and lit them and put them on his head, in honor of Marie's birthday. He danced around like that; fractured everybody. Some other fellows put candles on their heads, too."

Dorothy laughed.

But Willie was not laughing. She studied him, wondering what was the matter.

They ate in silence for a while and then she poured them some fresh coffee.

"Well, you can run around all you like now," said Willie. "I've got to go away on business. I don't know when I'll be back."

"I wish I could go," said Dorothy.

Willie turned and stared at her. "What do you mean?"

"I mean I wish I could go, that's what I mean. Oh, I know you wouldn't take me, but I'm so sick and tired of that office and old Doctor Mahon and the patients and the smell of antiseptics ... and, well, I'm just sick and tired of it, that's all. When you're here it's fine. But then you go away and it's just like it all was before. I can't stand it much longer. Someday I'll just get fed to the teeth and start for Chicago or New York or Detroit. I'm sick of sick people, and I'm sick of acting like Florence Nightingale ..."

"Well!" said Willie.

Why not? Mexico. That was it. San Tomas ... but all of a sudden he put on the brakes. No. Stupid. How could he explain to her ...?

"Maybe I'll stay around for a while," he said.

Dorothy brightened noticeably.

"And then maybe we can go out to dinner and maybe to a show," she said. "Do you like plays? There are some very good ones running right now."

Willie just sat looking at her. This was worse. He couldn't go running around like the insurance man next-door, to restaurants and plays and all that nonsense … with the pack closing in as it hadn't closed in for years.

But he wanted Dorothy with him now. All the time. He did not want any more of this hopscotch. He didn't give a damn whether she was his daughter or not. Some way it had to be worked out.

"Let's go to Mexico," he said.

Dorothy sat up straight and stared at him. "You mean it? When?"

"In about half an hour," said Willie.

Dorothy's face fell. "I thought you were serious."

"I am serious," said Willie. "We can be at the border in an hour and a half, two hours."

"But this is crazy."

"Of course it is."

"I don't care if it is," said Dorothy. "But how do we arrange things?"

"That's the easy part," said Willie. "Pack a small bag. Maybe we'll be back in a week. Who knows? I'll be downstairs with the car in half an hour."

Willie got to his feet and started for the door, but Dorothy rose quickly and came after him.

"I don't believe you," she said. "I think this is a joke."

"Some joke. I'll be down in front in half an hour. Be ready."

He went out and down the steps and across the flickering blue light of the courtyard, with Dorothy standing in the open doorway watching him go.

She felt stunned.

Dorothy was at the archway ahead of time, feeling hopeful, confused and skeptical, not exactly sure how she felt. This was crazy, crazy! Impossible! You just didn't pick up and rush off like this!

Or so it seemed at the moment—and yet she had done it once before—and alone—to get away from a man—Jay Joyce—who had been pestering the life out of here with his jealousy and then had taken to drinking and threatening her and phoning her at all hours.

Had that been so different? She'd walked away from her job, her apartment, her friends.

And into a new life, such as it had been.

Actually, in one way or another, through either compulsion or boredom she had been rootlessly drifting for nearly eight years: from Chicago to Detroit, from Detroit to New York and from New York to Los Angeles—then back and forth once more.

From time to time she walked to the edge of the curb, trying to catch a glimpse of the car she was waiting for—not really, in her heart, expecting to see it, but nervously hopeful. Maybe Mr. Allen, for reasons of his own, had wanted merely to get out of the apartment quickly. He was an odd man, at best. And yet there was the thousand dollars—no trivial gift. It was not like handing a girl a small present as a come-on. There must be something deeper behind it than that. And even the kimono was an extravagant item ...

Suddenly Dorothy realized she hadn't mentioned the money to Mr. Allen; not so much as even a quick thank you. Had this angered him? He couldn't help being a little annoyed ...

As she moved back and forth from the archway to the curb, her mind kept ticking on purposelessly, full of fears, dreams, and surmises ...

And then there suddenly—as if out of the blue—was the car and Mr. Allen leaning forward to look at her.

"All right," he called. "Come on."

Dorothy felt almost hysterically relieved. He swung the car door open for her. She put her small bag in the back and got in.

Just as they drove off, a siren began to wind its way toward them, an insistent ribbon of sound growing louder and louder. And as they reached the next cross street the vehicle—an ambulance—passed in front of them, the siren grinding slowly now, and came to a stop halfway up the street—one of the streets Dorothy had traversed—where a squad car was partially blocking the way and a crowd had gathered.

Willie slowed down to allow two men to cross in front of him and then as he went on Dorothy saw one of the men turn and glance at her quickly and intently—or so she thought, but the glow from the street light was very dim, and almost at once she dismissed the impression from her mind.

"What do you think, doc?" asked the cop, as the Cheev was carried past them on a stretcher.

"Blunt instrument—and he was really whacked. Call us for a report later."

The young intern was in a hurry to get away and work his man.

"Think he'll pull through?"

"I don't see why not, barring the unforeseen. At the moment he doesn't know his right hand from his left, or if he has hands."

He got away from the slow-talking cop and in a moment the

ambulance drove off, siren going.

The cop moved along to the couple—teenagers—who had stumbled over the Cheev, lying half in the girl's driveway.

He patiently took down their very garbled, and even contradictory, statements; snapped his book shut and said to his partner: "The guy had nearly five hundred bucks on him. How do you figure it?"

"Somebody was laying for him for personal reasons. Or the mugger got scared off."

"Hell, this guy's been lying here God knows how long, the doc said. Maybe half an hour or so."

"I don't get it," said his partner.

"And what are those FBI guys doing here?"

"Where?" cried his partner, his head jerking round.

"They showed me their credentials, or one of 'em did."

He looked about him for a moment, then said: "I guess they've gone."

The partner stood shaking his head. "This is a funny one. Everybody claims they never saw this guy before. Not from the neighborhood."

Now he climbed into the squad car and began to talk on the two-way radio.

They were far down the Coast now, almost to Del Mar. Without a word, showing no intent whatever, and very suddenly, Willie swung off to the left and up a dark, two-lane road that led across flat empty country, away from the sea.

"What's the matter?" asked Dorothy.

"A car's been dogging us, I think," said Willie. "I want to find out."

He drove for a long time in silence. There was no moon. It was very dark, and across the flat land behind them, no headlights showed.

Willie glanced at his wristwatch. "It's nearly midnight," he said. "I haven't been south of the border for some time. I forgot about them closing it. I mean, I don't know if it's open twenty-four hours now or not."

He was already regretting this wild—this next to insane—folly. But he'd had only one idea in mind and it had dominated him: to get Dorothy to himself and away from all others. And he realized with a feeling of shame and chagrin that it was the kind of idea that would have occurred to Carl Benedict and would have been acted on in somewhat the same manner.

With Carl it wouldn't last very long, but it would be an obsession as long as it did.

Willie had a vague feeling that he was beginning to crack up. How could he have done such thing?

"You mean we're not going to Mexico?" said Dorothy.

"Tomorrow," said Willie. "Then I'll be sure what I'm doing. I know a wonderful little town down there. It's in the foothills, pretty high up, and cool at night. In the flatlands it's hot as the hinges of hell. There's an old adobe hotel, spread all over the place, with the biggest verandah—I guess they call it a terrace—that I ever saw ..."

Why was he running on so? Was he trying to sell himself?

"Sounds wonderful," said Dorothy.

"You'll like it."

The road began to rise, still through empty but now rolling country, and at shortly after one o'clock they came to a prosperous looking medium-sized town, very new and modern, with bluish boulevard lights and new shops and hotels and residences—a part of the Southern California population explosion. As the natives said: It wasn't here yesterday!

They drove through the town, then at the far edge of it, where the road they had been following widened out into four lanes, they saw a very large and spread out motor hotel, set well back among well-kept trees and shrubbery that were lit by ground spotlights.

A big stylized pink neon sign read: *Flamingo*.

"We'd better spend the night here," said Willie.

And Dorothy merely nodded. As far as she was concerned, he was calling the turn.

They were registered as Mr. John Ward and Miss Dorothy Kramer, secretary, Willie having suggested Dorothy's alias, as a wry secret joke in commemoration of the Lieutenant, the Department's "Willie" specialist. And they were now in a double bedroom suite with a small living room in between. Dorothy was wearing her kimono, a garment obviously for special occasions; Willie pajamas and a dressing gown. It was after two a.m. and they were eating a snack (all-night service) in the living room and paying little or no attention to a late show murmuring monotonously on the TV.

Finally Willie turned it off and said: "We'd better get some sleep. I want to start early."

"Just as you say," said Dorothy, eyeing him.

Willie rose and yawned: "This was pretty crazy, you know," he said.

"Take me back if you like," said Dorothy. "I don't seem to interest you at all. Might just as well *be* the secretary. I simply don't understand you, Mr. Allen."

Willie studied Dorothy's face for a moment, then he resumed his seat. It was like a grotesque replay of the embarrassing scene with the red-haired Greta.

And it was all his fault—not Dorothy's. Here was this beautiful girl

willing and even eager, and expecting him to show some sign of
recognition that she was her own girl and could not ordinarily be had
for the asking ... in short, she was offering him the precious gift of
herself and he was refusing her.

He leaned forward and took her hand. "Dorothy, listen to me," he
said. "There is a lot more to this than you know. You must be patient
with me. Maybe later I'll explain. I don't know. If I was smart I'd take
you right back to your apartment and let you go on living as if I did not
exist ..."

"No," cried Dorothy. "I don't know what this is all about. I don't know
why you've been so kind to me. But whatever this is, I like it better
than before I met you."

"Then get some sleep," said Willie, relieved. "Tomorrow we'll be in
Mexico and maybe the world will look different to both of us."

As Willie lay back in his bed and tried to sleep, he said to himself:
"You don't even know what you are talking about, Willie, the devils are
really after you this time."

He'd considered retribution in all its forms and phases but who in
God's name could have thought this one up!

He had a strong impulse to set his chaotic thoughts down on paper,
but resisted it.

Was she sleeping? He lay worrying about her and about himself and
about the coming new day.

Strickland and Alford on the phone:

"Richardson ran off the road following the car without lights, bent a
fender, but managed to get going again. The girl is at the Flamingo
Motor Hotel with a man by the name of John Ward. Now what?"

"Continue surveillance."

"Will do," said Strickland. "Richardson thinks the man picked us up
following him and swung off the highway. If that's true he might have
something to hide."

"Or he might fear robbery. Or maybe that's the way he drives. Let's
not jump to conclusions. Just keep the girl under surveillance."

"What if they keep going south tomorrow and cross into Mexico?"

"That's a thought. I'll make some arrangements with the Mexican
police as soon as you hang up. If that's where they're going we can't
stop them. Maybe Willie's in Mexico. This might be the blowoff."

"That'll be the day," said Strickland, wearily. His private opinion was
that this was just "another one of them things." God, was he sick and
tired of the very name of that elusive thief, Willie Madden.

Willie woke with a start. Gray was showing at the window blinds. He was bathed in cold sweat and weaving from side to side. For a moment, half groggy, he sat terrified—then he jumped out of bed and began to pace.

What a stupid thing he'd done! It was as if he's been trying to put his neck in a noose. And the weaving—he'd been stupid about that, too, with all that rot about the Miss Fang kimono, and then looking to Dorothy for help—there was no help: the weaving was part of himself; it was a Willie manifestation: how could he have thought otherwise? It had been part of him as a boy and as a young man. Maybe he'd been right to go to a doctor. Maybe it was a kind of physical sickness, Willie's kind; where another man, like Nick, would have a tendency to weak lungs; and still another diabetes or heart trouble.

The truth of the matter probably was that he'd been on the lam and under severe tension and strain for nearly five years and maybe the return of the weaving was the price he had to pay.

Well ... there was no help for it. Probably no cure. No quick way out. He'd just have to live with it. Sedation might help, as the doctor had suggested. But sedation was very dangerous for him. Even relaxing, even sleep might prove dangerous.

Willie lit a cigarette, and tried to think clearly. He had the sensation of not being at his best—not too sharp, as he'd earlier had the sensation of cracking up, comparing his actions to Carl Benedict's.

No. Something had happened to him. It couldn't all be laid to the strong hold Dorothy had over him—his irrational moves—the slugging of the Creep, as if he was some hooligan working for Colin, his silly idea of a flight to Mexico ... the last place he should go; especially to San Tomas where there was a shady character, Hernandez, who already knew all about Willie's—James Williard's—purchase of a special Mercedes-Benz with a built-in safe ...

There was a tap at his door, then it was slowly pushed open and Dorothy peeked in. "I thought I heard you," she said. "I've been sitting in the living room; I woke up, then couldn't sleep. I don't know what's the matter with me."

"We're going back," said Willie. "Right now. This was a mistake."

"I'm beginning to think it was," said Dorothy. "I couldn't live like this."

"All right," said Willie. "Get ready. You can get to your job on time and nobody will know the difference."

"I will," said Dorothy, then she shut the door.

Willie paced back and forth, swearing at himself. "You flipped, Willie. You flipped," he kept saying.

Alford was sleeping in the office, dressed except for his shoes. The phone woke him and he looked about groggily; the windows were showing the rosiness of dawn.

It was Strickland.

"They're on their way back. And, Roy, hang on to your hat. It could be … I say, it *could* be … Willie Madden, in the car with the girl …"

Alford sat bolt upright. But how could that be? Why would Willie be taking his own daughter to a motel and staying a few hours with her?

"All right," he said. "I doubt it very much, but I'll proceed as if it was. Coast Highway?"

"Yes. So far."

"There'll be a checkpoint. Watch for it. I'll be there. We've got to be careful. If you're wrong we might scare the girl off for good. How's Richardson's car?"

"We straightened the fender while the lovebirds were sleeping, or whatever they were doing. It don't look pretty, but it's okay."

## FORTY-SIX

It was around eight o'clock of a bright sunshiny morning. The sun was well up over the ocean now; and strong sea-wind blew hard, propelling the high greenish-blue waves toward the beach where they broke in a wild white froth. Gulls were everywhere.

Willie drove, eyes straight ahead, as if he was hardly aware of Dorothy's presence. But she was looking all about her at the waves, the beach, the brilliant sunshine—wishing that they could just stop and take a walk in the sand, and dreading her return to the boring routine of the doctor's office.

She should have known it was too good to last. She had been disappointed before, but never was it quite as sharp and unexpected as this.

Now she began to watch Willie out of the corner of her eye. What was it with him? What was he thinking? What did he want of her? Why were they chasing around in this crazy purposeless way? The whole business was a complete and unsettling mystery to her.

"We got further off the main drag than I thought last night," said Willie. "You're going to be late."

"All right, so I overslept," said Dorothy. "No problem."

"I'm sorry about all this," said Willie, after a long pause. "I got thinking to do. I'll call one day and give you the wrong number bit and we can talk on the pay phone."

"All right," said Dorothy, but from now on she'd expect nothing of him, nothing at all.

They made a wide turn now and came into the outskirts of a big beach community. Traffic began to pick up, with cars moving into the Coast Highway from all the side streets, and as they drove toward the center of the town the congestion increased, till they were finally moving almost bumper to bumper.

Then the traffic slowed down to such an extent that Willie leaned out to see what was the matter. A motorcycle cop was in the middle of the street directing traffic around some kind of obstruction, a work truck it looked like, maybe water, power and light, or telephone.

Now the traffic stopped altogether. Willie took out his cigarettes and they lit up. Then the traffic began to inch along and Willie noted that it was moving around the construction in two streams, and when finally Willie drew up to be the first car in line the cop waved him to the inside. Willie complied.

And at once a car came up beside him, in which were three men in civilian clothes, and one of them leaned out and said quickly to Willie: "Pull over to the curb. Let's not have any trouble about this."

Willie showed no reaction at all. It was as if he hadn't heard. But he noticed that the big cop was staring at him with keen interest.

Was this *it?* If so, he had no alternative but to do as he was told and brazen it out.

"Okay," he said, casually, and pulled into the curb and stopped.

Dorothy sat very still, saying nothing. She'd known for a long time that Mr. Allen was in some kind of trouble.

Out of the corner of his eye Willie could see two of the men approaching him from the rear with professional caution, with the big cop backing them up without appearing to, as the streams of traffic rolled on.

"What's the matter?" asked Willie as one of the men appeared at his window, while the other one went round to Dorothy's side.

"Driver's license," said the man, showing his FBI ID.

Willie gave it to him and he took such a long time studying it that Willie began to fidget. "What did I do?" he demanded. "I'm from out of state. You can see it's a rental car. But I thought I knew the California traffic laws."

The man said nothing, continued to study the license. Willie glanced up ahead and noticed that a tall man standing on the curb was looking directly into the car, studying him at length. All of a sudden the man of the curb nodded emphatically.

At a sound at his elbow, Willie turned and was now looking into the muzzle of a handgun.

"Just sit still," the man at Willie's window said.

Willie shook his head disgustedly as if to say, well, this beats everything. Now he saw both the big motorcycle cop and the man who had been observing him from the curb approaching, slowly, from opposite directions.

The civilian opened the car door on the curb side and said: "All right, Miss Madden. Get out."

Willie couldn't repress a start, and as if through a fog of unreality he heard Dorothy say indignantly: "My name is Dorothy Velinsky, Mr. Alford. And you know it."

The man at Willie's window, backed up by the big cop, now reached in and snapped the bracelets on Willie.

On the other side, "Mr. Alford" helped Dorothy out of the car, then looked at Willie.

"Madden," he said, "I've got a warrant here for your arrest as a fugitive from justice. And I warn you that anything that you say may be used against you."

"You're crazy," said Willie. "My name's John Ward. I was driving along minding my own business, so …? So I wind up in handcuffs."

"I think the fingerprints will tell a different story," said Alford. "Get out on the other side."

Willie got out and was brought round the rear of the car by two FBI men and turned over to Alford. Dorothy was already being walked down the side street by a man in civilian clothes, maybe a local dick, and a policewoman in uniform.

The operation had been handled so smoothly that most of the people driving past weren't even aware of it.

And so far the Press had not had an inkling of it.

Willie was turned over to Alford, who said: "I hope you will walk along with me and give me no trouble. The local station's only half a block away."

"Do I look like I'm giving you any trouble?" said Willie. "I've already been frisked; that one boy of yours must be an ex-pickpocket."

They walked along in silence for a moment, then Willie asked: "Why did you call Dorothy Miss Madden? And where did she know you? What was it—a team job?"

"I questioned her in Dr. Mahon's office," said Alford. "It was my impression she was trying to protect you."

Willie smiled to himself.

"But—the Miss Madden …" Willie persisted. "That's a new one on me. I only knew her as Dorothy Velinsky."

"Have it your way, Madden," said Alford. "But we contacted her parents. They live in the L.A. area."

"My name's John Ward," said Willie, "and the first thing I want is a lawyer, though I may have to fly him out."

"Waive extradition and save yourself the trouble."

Long silence. As they neared the station Willie said: "She doesn't know anything one way or another. I suppose you're going to question her under the assumption she's Miss Madden."

"Naturally."

"Well," said Willie, "you first better explain to her who she is. Because she doesn't know, believe it or not."

At the station they found Willie very pleasant and very uncooperative. He was almost cheerful. Why? Because he was in the driver's seat and intended to keep it that way. Where was the five hundred thousand dollars? He knew. And nobody else did.

And there was no way on God's earth, that he could think of, that they could find out. He had carefully destroyed the receipts from the Hollywood Storage Garage, Inc., that had been given him when he paid his six months in advance, and he had gone out of his way to make a good impression on the boss and convince him that he actually was a writer by the name of James Williard who spent most of his time traveling.

Yes. No doubt about it. Willie was still a big man. His bail would be very high; but he'd be able to make it. And he could look forward to the endless delays and legal chicanery and backing and filling and hemming and hawing and maybe even a mistrial, and if the worst finally came to the worst, he would probably get five to twenty, and be out in five if not before.

After all, he was a "first offender," except for a little hanky-panky with company funds during World War II—written off, and a little more hanky-panky at the age of sixteen when he'd been fingerprinted and sent to the Youth Correctional Institute, for hoodlumism, malicious mischief and a few other like charges.

For years Willie had been a model citizen, and even a public servant as an investigator for the District Attorney's Office.

As soon as he was back in the hometown—naturally he'd waive extradition—he'd engage Darrel Rankin III, the best criminal lawyer in the Midwest, who had plenty of political muscle and moxie, and would throw every roadblock possible in the way of Willie's conviction.

What was their case against him? The word of a couple convicted felons, if Carl Benedict had talked, too. The two witnesses were as follows: Wicks, a renegade cop and nut; Carl Benedict, a very dangerous strongarm guy, a recidivist, and also a nut. Darrell Rankin III would tear them to pieces.

Where was all the money Willie was alleged to have stolen?

Among his effects they would find no more than a few thousand dollars, which he would fight them on, if they tried to confiscate it. They'd have to prove that he stole it first.

"And that won't be easy," Willie told himself. "It won't be easy at all."

Willie felt almost like a new man. He hadn't realized before what a terrible strain and tension he'd been under while he was on the run. Being caught, believe it or not, gave him a very uplifting feeling of release.

Now he would sleep well at night, even in a jail cell, and he did not intend to be in jail very long.

Willie settled back into his chair and lit a cigarette. He was alone for the moment. It was late afternoon. He'd even been given lunch on a tray in the big anteroom with the heavily screened windows where he had been questioned.

There was the shooting of Carl Benedict, of course. But in the first place they'd have to prove it. He'd ditched the gun he'd shot Carl with and bought another one. And even if they brought it home to him, he'd claim self-defense and make it stick. Carl's reputation was so bad that killing him might even be considered in the nature of a public service.

The door opened and Dorothy came in. He hadn't seen her since early that morning. She looked pale and uncertain, and she just stood there and stared at him. Alford shut the door behind her.

"Come on in," said Willie. "Sit down."

Dorothy pulled a chair up fairly close to Willie and sat studying him as if she'd never seen him before. Willie smiled at her, then he reached out and patted her on the knee.

"I guess you understand it all now," he said.

"I should have told you about Mr. Alford," she replied, rather intensely. "But I was so wound up about the Creep that I forgot all about it."

Willie nodded slowly. "It might have made quite a difference," he said, mildly, and as if it didn't really matter much.

Dorothy's face brightened. "I thought you'd be furious with me. I wouldn't blame you if you were."

"Well," said Willie, "it was in the cards I'd get caught sooner or later. Now it's sooner. Besides, I was getting kind of crazy, I think."

"What will I do?" asked Dorothy, suddenly. "It will be in all the papers, won't it? I can't go back to the office. Anyway, I don't want to. I hate that place now."

Willie studied her. "What do you want to do?"

"I want to stay with you," said Dorothy.

"And if I don't beat the case ...?"

"Then I'll wait. I'll take care of things for you. I'm a smart girl, Mr. Allen." Suddenly she put her hand over her mouth and they both laughed rather self-consciously.

And while they were laughing, Alford came in, stopped, frowned, and stared at them with rather annoyed incomprehension.

Besides, Dorothy was one of the most desirable girls he'd ever seen and it was a terrible thing, in his opinion, that she had to be the daughter of a dangerous cunning criminal like Willie Madden.

"Alford," said Willie, "I hope nobody's thinking about pressing charges against Dorothy. If they are I'll fight 'em every step of the way in the courts. And I'll start right now."

"No, I don't think so," said Alford. "I gave her a clean bill of health. Technically the local authorities could make trouble for her."

"If they do, I fight extradition."

Long pause.

"Madden," said Alford, "you are beginning to be a kind of public nuisance and I'm going to do everything in my power to see that you are put away for a good long stretch."

Willie stared at Alford angrily for a moment and then said: "Once I get back to the Midwest your power won't amount to that—" and snapped his fingers.

And it was true; and Alford knew it and hated it and hated his job for a moment and the restraining and restricting laws—and getting worse all the time—that kept him from dealing ruthlessly with such men as Willie Madden.

"Miss Madden," said Alford, "I think you're free to go. Check with Miss Pace. She'll find you a room nearby if you like. Or we'll put you on a bus for L.A. They will only warn you not to leave the state without checking here.

Dorothy rose then turned to Alford. "When can I see him again?"

"Not till tomorrow morning."

"Get a good sleep," said Willie. "Have you got money for a room? If not, check with the Sergeant. He's got all my money by this time, I imagine."

"It's impounded," said Alford.

"Oh, we'll see about that," cried Willie.

"I've got enough," said Dorothy, hastily. "I'll see you tomorrow."

After she'd gone there was a long silence. Then Alford started in again about the five hundred thousand dollars and Willie said: "What five hundred thousand dollars?"

But Alford persisted, as he had persisted during the morning.

"Wait till the insurance company hears you've got me," said Willie. "They'll rush in and talk deal. But my lawyer will handle that. Just supposing I might have that five hundred thousand dollars."

"Do you have it?"

"It always says so in the papers."

And so on, with twilight falling outside, and the late-stayers wandering up reluctantly from the beach after a long hot perfect day, for swimming, surfing and sunning.

In the small local hotel room Dorothy lay sleeping like a baby. She was exhausted. Willie was not sleeping, but he felt perfectly relaxed and lay on his back in the jail cell with his hands under his head staring up at the ceiling. Every time a car turned a certain corner, beams of light ran quickly across over Willie's head. It was soothing, nearly hypnotic.

He felt almost like the young Willie now. Two heavy burdens had been lifted from his shoulders. No more fox-like running. And Dorothy knew who she was, and wanted to stay with him, as his daughter of course. But what else could she ever have been in spite of all his folly.

But suppose the thought of Thad Velinsky had not occurred to him— at just the right moment—the night of the wild dancing place?

What then?

But in a short time Willie dismissed such speculation from his mind. "What then" never got anything or made any money for anybody. The past was the past.

Finally, he slept.

And while they slept—father and daughter—the press had got hold of the story and now wire services were crisscrossing the country with it, and radio news media was broadcasting it on the half hour—

And in the hometown Captain Bescher was smacking his lips with satisfaction over a big stein of beer. The police were vindicated. And the Million Dollar Robbery of the Kenmore Trust could now, after five years—and reams of unfavorable publicity—be moved from the active to the inactive file.

## FORTY-SEVEN

Two months had passed and the stalling and the delays went on. Darrell Rankin III's first gambit had been to claim that it was impossible for Willie Madden to get a fair trial in his hometown and he had petitioned for a change of venue; after many delays his petition was finally denied, but the District Attorney's office was not happy about it, and lights burned late in the City Building as a staff worked hard to close every loophole the defense could possibly imagine or dream up or invent. The conviction of Willie Madden was a must.

But the question was, would a change of venue have been smarter?

Now if Willie was convicted, Rankin's first move would be to ask for a new trial, which would mean more delay and maybe at last deep embarrassment for the District Attorney's office and the Administration judge who had denied the change of venue.

Rankin was a viper, no doubt about it. Smooth, shrewd and young: certainly not over forty, and the scion of a very old city family. And with plenty of political pull—and also political ambition, and the Willie Madden case was playing right into his hands by giving him a million dollars' worth of national publicity.

Willie did not like Rankin at all. He considered him a snob, for one thing—besides, Willie thought he was too friendly with Dorothy, and Dorothy too friendly with him. Rankin kept telling Willie what a smart girl his daughter was and how proud of her he should be.

Dorothy was in the Liberal Arts College of the State University now and was majoring in acting and drama. From time to time she appeared on local TV under the name of Dorothy Velin, but everybody knew who she was and while there had been some protests from the viewing public, the favorable reaction had been far stronger.

Otherwise, around the hometown, things were much as before. Leo and Bernard Madden were denouncing their infamous brother to all who would listen, and completely disavowing him. While old Mrs. Madden went her way as before, keeping her own counsel.

Willie and Dorothy had adjoining apartments in an old building on the edge of the very district where Willie—and Dorothy's mother—had been brought up. Money was neither tight nor plentiful—and the rent was not cheap, but cheaper than it would have been if they'd moved into one of the new high-rise buildings.

Dorothy had received ten thousand dollars from a national magazine for her "life story" and there was even talk of a movie—with various shoestring producers turning up now and then with grandiose plans but no money to put on the line—all was to be deferred, of course.

Materially, things were not bad, and Willie was still a big man because he was "sitting on five hundred thousand dollars"—and sharpies all over the nation spent their nights trying to figure out a way to cut in on the gigantic nest egg, and the sharpies were from all walks of life, from lawyers and insurance men to shoestring movie producers and assorted hustlers and con artists. Besides, the money was the talk of the local underworld.

It was, in a way, a kind of carnival of greed.

But Willie ignored it. What he couldn't ignore was the completely changed relationship with Dorothy—she had become his daughter in fact. There was embarrassment and constraint between them. Dorothy had put the symbolical kimono away and it was never seen again. From morning till night she was preoccupied with her own personal affairs; they didn't even meet at meals, except once in a while for dinner.

Occasionally she talked about going to New York; in fact, she had made tentative plans to go at the end of the present university semester, which would be late June of the following year. Willie neither opposed her in this, nor agreed. He kept still. But one night Dorothy had Rankin talk to him about it and Willie had lost his temper.

It hadn't been mentioned since.

Although the weaving had not returned, Willie began to feel at loose ends, confused and purposeless as legal delays dragged on. He'd lost his zest for life. Women seemed to mean very little to him anymore, and sometimes at night he would look back on his stay at the Pearl of the Orient—before the crummy magazine had turned up—as the high point of his life: long before—(in that simply happy time)—the weird complications of Miss Fang, Carl Benedict, and finally Dorothy. It seemed to Willie now and then, especially in depressed moods, that some outside force had little by little put these totally unexpected roadblocks in his way.

Nemesis? A silly thought. But one that had occurred to him time after time. A kind of holdover, it must be, from a consciously buried past that wouldn't stay buried.

It was the unlikely chain of Miss Fang, Carl Benedict and Dorothy that had unsteadied his hand and influenced him to make mistakes that ordinarily he wouldn't have made. For nearly five years he had been immune to such errors of judgement.

And yet, maybe it had to happen, one way or another.

It was nearly seven o'clock in the evening and Willie went down the hall to say goodnight to Dorothy. She was getting ready to go out. Rankin was to pick her up around eight and Willie did not want to be there when the tall young lawyer arrived. He really put Willie's back up now. They were going to some *avant garde* play that the University drama school was putting on—and Dorothy had patiently tried to explain what it was all about to Willie, but Willie just closed his mind. He couldn't care less.

Dorothy was ready except for her dress—that is, she'd soaked in the bath for a long time, and had taken nearly an hour to arrange her hair and do her nails and put on her makeup …

"Hello," she said, letting him in, with a beautiful pink dressing gown draped about her figure—the figure that had been the first thing Willie noticed about her.

"Just wanted to say goodnight," said Willie. "I may sack up early tonight. Have a good time."

"Thanks," said Dorothy.

They stood looking at each other like strangers. Dorothy was sure one good-looking broad, Willie told himself coarsely, feeling perverse and left out; in fact, not even sure he knew what he felt.

"Say hello to the mouthpiece," he said.

"You don't like him much, do you?" asked Dorothy

"No," said Willie. "But he's the smartest lawyer in town. Goodnight."

He went out abruptly, closing the door rather more loudly than was necessary.

Dorothy stood there looking after him. What could she say? Willie had been the most interesting, the ablest man she'd ever met until Darrell came along. Now she had begun to be aware of all of Willie's faults and deficiencies. Besides, he was her father; she owned him, in a sense, and now took him for granted. Darrell—well, Darrell needed a little promotion. For him the situation was very touchy. After all, like it or not, she was the daughter of a man who had stolen a million dollars. Not that it bothered *her* in any way. But Darrell, though Willie's defender, had a certain reputation to keep up in the city; besides, he was politically ambitious.

It was a delicate problem; but Dorothy—a kind of feminine Willie—was working on it; she was working on it!

In an irritated state of mind, Willie barged into his apartment through the door he had left ajar—and found himself confronted by Carl Benedict, who was sitting in Willie's own personal chair, grinning at him.

"How the hell did you get in here, you crazy bastard?" cried Willie.

"The door was open. Willie—don't make any funny moves. I got a gun in my pocket."

Willie studied Carl for a moment, then lit a cigarette and sat down. He'd dominated crazy Carl before and he felt he could do it again.

"What are you doing out, Carl?" he asked.

"I got my reasons," said Carl, grinning. "I was the fair-haired boy, see, so they got so they didn't watch me too close. So I lammed. Know why? The grapevine. The old Gimp has lost his grip; he's a lost cause, home in bed; he's given up. And Colin's running wild. He's got guys trying to get to Joe Wicks—for the knockoff; and he's after me. Now he's after you, Willie."

"That crumb! What do you mean?" cried Willie, angrily.

"I got it straight. Fallon O'Keefe; he's close to Tony the Maloney. Fallon helped Maloney out of a bad beef; and the Maloney got him parole. Colin tried to hire him for muscle. The idea was to grab you and beat it out of you, Willie."

"I'll kill him," said Willie.

"Wait," said Carl. "He couldn't get any takers. So the idea now is to grab your girlfriend that you call your daughter ..."

"Carl," said Willie, breaking in, "you need money, right? This is the old con, like you're always pulling. Well, say so. Don't come up with stories like this."

"Willie," said Carl, "I'm leveling. I don't say he'll get takers—lot of guys are afraid to buck you, Willie—but that's the scheme. Look, we worked together before; why can't we work together again?"

"What do you have in mind?"

"You hold still for a touch now and then, and I'll erase Colin. Look, Willie—I'm not figuring that five hundred thousand. That's ancient history to me; I ain't even sure you got it anymore. You may just be using it as a lever. But I'm on the lam, see? But I got to trust you not to blow the whistle, and you got to trust me to erase Colin and not be too hungry."

"I got no big dough in my possession," said Willie.

"Am I talking big dough? Give me two hundred and an overcoat. I'll get to Madame Annie's, then I'll be okay. Some morning you'll pick up your paper and see a familiar name. Then I'll brace you for maybe a thousand."

"Five hundred."

"All right, Willie—and let's move fast."

When Darrell Rankin arrived to pick up Dorothy, he found Willie waiting to talk to him. Dorothy was sent out of the room, then Willie explained to Rankin that Dorothy's life might possibly be in danger and he'd appreciate it if Rankin would take Dorothy to New York that night by jet, where she would stay under an assumed name until it was safe for her to come back.

Rankin was taken by surprise at first and then he listened with a frown on his face, and finally nodded. "I've been fearing something like this," he said. "I'll take care of it—and all the odds and ends."

Dorothy came in to say goodbye to Willie, while Rankin waited in the hallway.

Willie seemed nervous and irritable. "Don't worry," he said. "It's only a precaution."

But Dorothy was so hopped up and excited she hardly heard him— on a jet to New York and with Darrell; an almost perfect situation for the promotion plans she had in mind.

"Well, go," said Willie.

They stood looking at each other as before, strangers, then Dorothy said: "Well …"

And Willie just stared at her.

Now Willie was alone, as he hadn't been for months. He put a handgun in the drawer of the night table, checked all the doors and windows, then got into bed and propped up on three pillows lay watching TV.

Occasionally he got a fleeting mental picture of a huge jet flying through the night, with Dorothy and Darrell Rankin III aboard. Who could have ever foreseen such a conjunction?

And what a real crazy place the world was, after all!

# FORTY-EIGHT

It was about the same time of night, a week later, and Carl was back on the top gangway of the abandoned oil-storage tank.

Still wearing one of Willie's overcoats that was bursting at the seams, Carl was wondering how long it would be before they found Colin, who was now reposing deep in the big river, with three slugs in his back. And he was also wondering how long he should wait before he braced Willie for the five hundred.

Carl was doing all right. At the moment he had nearly a hundred and fifty dollars in his pocket, and he was up on the oil-storage tank only because there'd been a bad beef in a pad next door to Madame Annie's and he knew the neighborhood would soon be swarming with fuzz.

Just before dawn he'd return; the beef would be over and all would be clear by that time.

He sat with his back against the oil-storage tank, looking down at the city, which spread out before him, its wilderness of lonely lights reaching to the horizon in every direction.

Carl's city.

And in a way it was really Carl's oyster.

THE END

# Round the Clock at Volari's
......................................................
## W. R. BURNETT

# 1: THURSDAY

Jim Chase stood at the window, looking absentmindedly down into the street, while behind him his partner, Larry Packard, nervously read a brief and kept glancing at the clock. It had been an extremely hot day—with the official temperature at 92 degrees—and outside, the city, at eleven o'clock at night, still had the stuffiness of an old attic. Inside, the air conditioner whirred on with mindless efficiency, spraying chilly dead air through the cramped little suite of ultra-modern offices.

Jim could never get used to the new place. He'd preferred their old offices in the ancient Taft Building, with its creaking cage elevator, and the old colored elevator man who had known his grandfather, and the air of leisure it still retained from a vanished past. Here all was *New!* From the air conditioner to the self-operated elevators, hardly larger than coffins, that shot up silently like projectiles. Although the new office building was nearly two years old the offices still smelled of varnish, paint and Naugahyde. Jim wanted to open the windows and let in the Midwestern air, hot and stuffy as it was. At least it was real.

The phone rang and Larry made a nervous grab for it. Jim turned to listen.

"Oh, Gert!" Larry said, with a disappointed grimace. "No, we haven't heard anything. No; no tips as yet. Expecting one. No. You just go to bed and get some sleep. See you tomorrow."

"Good old Gert," said Jim, turning back to the window.

"We'll lose her yet," said Larry. "Bryson down the hall's been trying to … and he's got more money than …"

Larry broke off and went back to his brief.

Jim turned and looked at him. When Larry's nerves began to kick up he always talked in that disjointed manner. After the collapse of the Administration Larry had got to drinking heavily for a while—to soothe his nerves; but his new marriage had saved him, or so Jim thought.

The phone rang again. Larry made a grab, almost knocked it off the desk. "Yes? Oh, honey; thought you'd be getting your beauty sleep."

It was Larry's young wife, Beth. Jim, with a pang of envy, saw Larry's delighted smile, saw him relaxing visibly in his chair.

"No, no word yet, baby," said Larry, smiling at his wife's picture on the desk. "Jury's still out. I can't tell. You never know. Jury's are mighty funny things. Sure, sure. I'll come right home. Sleep tomorrow? How can I? But, look …" He grinned up at Jim now. "But he needs his sleep, too." He covered the receiver and spoke to Jim. "She says you're big and strong and I'm small and weak, so I should sleep till noon tomorrow."

"Okay by me," said Jim, laughing.

"He says it's okay, baby. But I just couldn't do it. Breakfast in bed? Oh, please. I'd feel like a kept woman." He listened, then laughed loudly.

The phone rang, and Larry glanced up at Jim in distress. Jim hurried into Gert's office, threw the switch and took the call on their second line. They had three; but as a rule one was all they needed, although neither of them ever referred to that fact.

"Mr. Packard," said a guarded male voice.

"This is Chase," said Jim.

"Oh, then I can talk to you just as well. The jury's about to come in. I hear they've reached a verdict."

"And?"

"Not good, Mr. Chase, I understand, although of course I could be wrong. Not good for your client."

"Thanks," said Jim.

Larry was still talking to his wife, laughing it up a little too much now. Jim gestured for him to get off the phone, and finally Larry hung up.

"Well?" he demanded, nervously.

"Your tipster thinks we blew another one," said Jim.

Larry stood up and scratched his head in a bewildered manner. "I was afraid ... I had a feeling ... maybe he's wrong, though. It's happened. Well ... that jury... a couple of hard-faced old ladies bothered me ... well ... I'd better..."

He grabbed up his briefcase, took his hat from the closet. They looked at each other in silence. Both felt guilty, as if they'd deliberately let each other down. Jim had prepared the brief; Larry had tried the case. It was the third loss in a row, none of them of anything approaching major proportions, but a matter of record all the same.

Their relationship at best was an uneasy one. They were from different parts of town, different strata, different schools; and actually they had little in common except the law. Jim was the son of a well-known lawyer, Robert Chase, now dead; and the grandson of the civically famous Judge Weldon Chase. Jim had gone to a private military school and a small exclusive Midwestern university. Larry, the son of a mechanic, had worked his way painfully through State. It is doubtful if they ever would have met if they hadn't both worked for the DA. during the last City Administration; Jim as chief investigator and sort of general troubleshooter, Larry as one of the prosecutors.

"Well," said Jim, smiling at Larry, "we tried."

"Yeah," said Larry, depressed. "Well ..." He turned and went out into the hallway, but put his head back in. "See what I can do when I find out what I'm up against. See you tomorrow."

"Better listen to your wife," said Jim. "Sleep till noon. This one was a little rough."

"I'll try. Doubt if I can do it."

He gestured and left. Jim heard the faint whoosh of the self-closing door, then he poured himself a drink and sat down at Larry's desk. His own was in another office across the little anteroom, that Gert presided over all day long and sometimes far into the night. He hated his office. It seemed to him like a plush-lined, air-conditioned cell, with its rustproof furniture and the cockeyed pictures on the wall.

Sipping his whiskey, he studied the picture of Larry's wife. A real doll; and a damned nice kid. It was up to Larry to behave himself and make the marriage work—for good! Jim began to think about his own messed-up life and for the moment couldn't restrain himself from going back over all the old quarrels, the reconciliations, the second and third chances, the bewildered kids—divorce court, humiliation and shame!

Finally he jumped up impatiently. "I've got to get out of here—go someplace," he thought. "We just went haywire—all of us. The DA set the pace and we all followed, like silly sheep. We had too much power. We thought it would never end. We all got swell-headed and arrogant. Too much liquor, too many women—like college boys up for the weekend for God's sake ...!"

And then the shock of defeat. A whole administration flattened, from top to bottom. And none of them had been smart enough to see it coming. From political boss Tom Patton to the youngest recruit in the DA's office, all laughing at the pretensions of Judge Bayard—a hard-bitten reformer, who'd been around for years. Judge Bayard—for *Mayor*? Judge Weybrecht—for *DA*? (Another hard-bitten old reformer.) Preposterous! And yet it had happened. A landslide! And the two old gray-haired judges had cleaned out the City Building and the Hall of Justice—and this time it was not the musty old new broom routine. It was the Augean Stables bit—as it had said in all of the newspapers. Even the political writers had been aghast at the proportions of the debacle.

And now the leaders of the old Administration were scattered about over the country like the remnants of a defeated army. Jake Webb, former DA, known all over town for years as His Highness, was in Florida, and it was rumored that he'd had a stroke and no longer made sense when he talked. Tom Patton was in hiding around on the edge of town someplace, or so it was said, nobody knew where. Various other remnants were spread from Canada to Southern California. Jim remembered his own resignation with shame.

He'd been told that Judge Weybrecht wanted to see him. Having a pretty good idea what this meant, he'd written out a curt resignation.

The old judge had read it in silence, then after a long pause had said: "Very well. I accept it."

Jim had said nothing, but the old Judge had studied him for a long time, making him very uncomfortable, then he'd said: "From Jake Webb I never expected anything, nor from Tom Patton, our esteemed Highway Commissioner—nor from their followers, all predatory politicians of the worst kind. But from Judge Chase's grandson I expected something. I intended to say nothing. I was merely going to ask for your resignation. But I find I can't keep still. I'm baffled. You want to try to justify yourself?"

"No," said Jim.

"Well, that's something," said the judge. "Good day, Mr. Chase."

Now Jim rose from Larry's desk, put the bottle away, grabbed up his hat, and left hurriedly for someplace. But where?

The coffin-like automatic elevator shot him from the fifth to the first floor in a matter of seconds. Outside, the heat hit him like a physical blow after the tomb-like coolness of the Kreidler Building. Halfway down the block he saw the Hall of Justice looming up in the night, with all its seventh-floor windows lighted. Poor Larry!

He walked toward the center of the city till he found a cruising taxi cab.

"Volari's," he said, as he got in.

He'd been staying away from the place lately, embarrassed at the huge tab he owed and was unable to pay. In fact, he had no more than a few hundred dollars to his name. His income was uncertain but the outgo was not. Alimony payments; regular payments on his debts; office rent, apartment rent, food etc., etc., etc.—a hopeless treadmill.

"Is it hot enough for you?" asked the taxi driver. "People are sleeping in the parks tonight. Had some trouble down along the river. Young hoodlums. Downtown sent a cop detail over. Hell of a thing, when a guy can't take his family and sleep in the park without being rousted by hoodlums."

"Yes," said Jim, preoccupied.

Down the street he saw the huge diagonal golden neon sign: VOLARI'S. In the days of the old regime it had been called 'Administration Headquarters,' for laughs. The DA could be found there nearly every night, surrounded by sycophants both male and female.

In fact, Tom Patton's brother, Al, had bought the place from Gino Volari—and, as everybody had said at the time, "Now it's official."

Chauncey, the colored boy who picked up the cars in front of Volari's and parked them for the patrons, opened the cab door, then saluted facetiously when he saw who the passenger was. As he paid the driver, Jim noticed that the gold braid on Chauncey's royal blue "Volari's" jacket was tarnished. It figured.

"Hi," said Chauncey, as the cab drove away. "I'd about given up on you." Chauncey was a bright boy and in spite of the late hours he worked, he was managing to put himself through State University. "The law must be rushing."

"It never stops," said Jim. "Like crime, it's round the clock."

"Maybe I'm in the wrong college," said Chauncey. "I thought about law."

"Stay where you are," said Jim. "Physical education, isn't it?"

"That's right. And it's easier, too. I don't have much time to swat the books."

"How's business?"

"If every night was Saturday night it'd be okay. You can shoot deer in the parking lot tonight. Not like the old days."

Chauncey had been around for nearly five years now. Tom Patton had recommended him for the job. It was one of the many ways Tom had of carrying the colored districts. Word got around. White Man Patton's party was okay. Getting good jobs for colored boys Downtown, where the money was.

Jim started in.

"You really been *this* busy?" asked Chauncey.

"No," said Jim.

Chauncey held the door for him, laughing.

There was a new checkroom girl who did not know Jim and glanced at him indifferently, as he deposited his hat and picked up his check. Silly as it was, this depressed him a little. The sight of Chauncey had raised his spirits. He had a definite longing for the familiar.

Gus Bailey, the young barman, saw him, stared and made a funny face. There were no more than six people on the bar stools and only three wall-booths were occupied. Tully Burke and his boys were playing discreetly under the big archway, and Jim could see the lighted candles in the round supper room beyond. Tully was a fixture, although his boys changed from time to time. He played what he called "digestive" music and sometimes referred to himself as the 'Rolaid Kid.' Jim looked about for Judy but did not see her so he walked over to the bar to shake hands with Gus.

"Hi, stranger," said Gus. "Things are slow, so Judy and Zena took three. They're out back, smoking. How you been?" Gus was a ruddy-faced blond in his late twenties with big shoulders and a pleasant grin.

"Well, well," said a high-pitched masculine voice behind him and Jim turned. Gino Volari! Looking as suave, pleasant and well-dressed as always. Although Gino was fifty or better he didn't have a single gray hair; nor had he put on an ounce of weight in the last twenty years. In the old days Tom Patton had always referred to him as Vasco da Gama, a malapropism for Ponce de Léon. Gino now acted as maître d'hôtel in the place he'd formerly owned.

"How have you been, Mr. Chase?" Gino asked. "We've been wondering about you."

"I'll bet the credit department has," Jim thought, feeling very uncomfortable. He owed the house almost a thousand dollars. Gino of course, made no reference to Judy; but it wasn't because he didn't know all about it. He was just more subtle than Gus.

"Been busy, Gino," said Jim.

"Scotch and soda?" asked Gus.

"What else?" laughed Gino, then he patted Jim's arm and moved up front to corral a bewildered-looking couple who were obviously in strange surroundings.

"Oh, we get 'em," said Gus, putting Jim's drink in front of him, then gesturing with his head toward the couple, "Sightseers, since we hit all the papers as a hangout for you bad boys. But mostly peanut eaters, if you know what I mean. One look at the prices on that supper menu, then out, brother, out! But some of 'em got the nerve to come in here and sit in this bar all evening listening to the music, taking up space, and drinking beer. We're thinking about handling nothing but them imported beers, it's got so rough."

Someone patted his shoulder and Jim turned. It was Cecile, the third bar girl, a French-Canadian with a cute little mouth and manner. There were only three now; Cecile, Zena and Judy. In the old days there had been as many as six. Actually, the jobs had been fought for, as Volari's, then, boasted the lushest tippers in town.

"Bon soir, m'sieu," she said "Have you been away?"

Cecile had never paid the slightest attention to him until he'd started taking Judy out; then she'd made a pitch. But that was all long ago and far away—in another world.

"No," said Jim. "Just busy."

Cecile passed on to the slot and called: "One Manhattan, two Burgies."

Gus winced. Jim signed the tab, then carried his drink to a booth in a far corner, near the supper room into which he glanced. Four tables taken! Mighty discouraging for eleven-thirty on a Thursday night, even if it was still summer. Al Patton must be worried as hell—this, on top of everything else!

The music stopped and Tully Burke came over to speak to him.

"Thought I saw you, dad," he said. "Like here he comes, dig. Dig?"

Jim looked at the curly-haired young Irishman blankly.

"How do you think I handle it?" asked Tully, sitting down opposite Jim.

"Handle what?"

"The lunatic lingo. We been getting a lot of squares lately. Did I say 'lot'? Some. They see the idiots on TV. They expect us to talk like that."

"I see," said Jim, laughing.

"Crazy, man—you know—wild. Boy are we dying here."

"Pretty bad, eh?"

"Murder! You should see it on Tuesday night. Echoes. I'm not kidding. Our bass player gets frightened. He says he just can't stand being alone. You think Al might fold it, God forbid?"

"I doubt it."

"I suggested we get a real classy striptease artist or maybe a comic for the bar. But Al said we already had Zena—and me! Damn near threw me out of his office."

"How is Al?"

"Aging, man, aging."

Jim glanced up. Judy and Zena were at the bar now, looking over at him. They were both wearing the royal blue Volari jackets with gold braid, and short, tight, skimpy white skirts. They were of about the same height and build—but what a difference! Xena, with her dark-red hair butchered into a shaggy-looking boyish cut, her handsome, tense aquiline face and her hard green eyes, seemed at opposite poles from Judy, who, though slender, was all round contours and softness, her black hair soft and luxuriant, in a bun at the back, her face colorless but creamy-looking, her big gray eyes pleasant and friendly. Zena always seemed on guard; ready to strike, like a reptile, while Judy was always relaxed, calm and confident-seeming. And yet they were the closest of friends, and had been roommates for nearly four years.

"I didn't know he was coming here," said Judy.

"Probably wants to borrow some money," said Zena, turning her back.

"You know better than that," said Judy, mildly.

"He'll get around to it. Now is the time to dump him."

"Very funny," said Judy.

"I don't get it," said Zena. "Boy-girl stuff in this day and age? It's a gag. You'll never be able to tell me different."

"A pretty serious gag," said Judy, watching Jim surreptitiously as he talked with the little peacock, Tully Burke. "A pretty sad one."

"So you broke up his home. So what?" said Zena, impatiently.

"I did not break up his home," said Judy. "I've told you a thousand times ..."

"Girls, please," said Gino, gently; but gave each a hard little pinch.

Judy jumped slightly, then hurried off toward the wall booths. But Zena showed no reaction. "You can do better than that, Gino," she said, then she moved her body insolently before she walked away.

"Harpy!" said Gino, under his breath.

Judy's customers were new to the place and sat looking about them with awe and embarrassment at the dimly lit, Continental lushness of Volari's, the most expensive supper club in the state. The man was wearing a wrinkled white coat and a gaudy, Hawaiian shirt; no tie. The woman had on a backless cotton dress and her hands and arms were covered with cheap costume jewelry: outsized rings, bangles, and charm bracelets. She was smoking a cigarette in a long holder and trying to look haughty.

"You got Pabst, sister?" the man asked.

"Yes sir," said Judy.

"Honey," said the woman, putting her hand on the man's arm. "Don't drink beer in here. The drinks are delicious."

"I didn't know you'd been here before, baby. Okay. What?"

"Miss," said the woman, "do they make drinks here like at the Seven Seas?"

The Seven Seas was a phony Hawaiian trap, just off Maquette Square, a tourist haven.

"We don't specialize," said Judy. "But I can get you most any kind of rum drink."

She stood with pencil poised, smiling politely, as the man and woman held a long consultation.

"A tall one," said the man, after deep thought.

"Planter's Punch," said Judy. "Very refreshing on a hot night."

"Will it do something for me?" asked the man, with a sad grin, surreptitiously eyeing Judy who overwhelmed him with her poise, and her model-like shapeliness, set off by the exaggerated tightness of the white skirt.

"Oh, definitely."

The man turned to the woman, but she wasn't quite sure. This was a weighty decision, and she wasn't going to be rushed into anything.

Now a party of four appeared at the entrance, and stood looking about them, bug-eyed. Judy glanced around for Gino, didn't see him, then excused herself and hurried to the front quickly so the two couples wouldn't change their minds and leave. On Saturday nights Judy acted as assistant maître d'hôtel, and her public manner was considered almost perfect, even by Gino.

"Good evening," said Judy, smiling pleasantly. "Will it be drinks? Or are you interested in supper?"

The men said nothing, but eyed their wives for a lead. They were obviously from out of town, and overawed. Gino came hurrying from around the far end of the bar

"Thank you, dear," he said to Judy. "I'll take over."

Judy went back to her other customers. They were now studying the bar menu with the aid of a lighted match.

"Miss," said the man, "you mean to tell me a Planter's Punch is a buck-fifty?"

"Yes sir," said Judy, eyeing him politely.

"Pabst," said the man.

The woman's face showed both rage and embarrassment. "A Planter's Punch please," she said, haughtily.

... and so the night wore on.

Jim had been brought his third drink by Cecile before Judy stopped by for a moment.

"Why didn't you tell me you were coming?" she asked.

"I didn't know."

"You're not going to sit there till two, are you?"

"No," said Jim.

"I might be able to get away a little early if it stays as slack as this."

"Good. I'll make us some sandwiches," said Jim. "You grab a taxi out in front. Okay?"

"Okay. See you."

She turned and left. Zena was eyeing her from the slot where Gus was putting drinks on her tray.

"Touching, isn't it?" she observed.

"Burnt to a crisp," said Gus.

"Who? Me? Listen, you cheap…"

"Never could figure out what was eating you, Zena," said Gus. "No matter who the guy is you don't like it and especially Jim Chase, a real good guy. You girls going steady or something?"

For a moment Gus thought he was going to get the tray over his head, drinks and all. Zena's green eyes seemed to give off electrical sparks. But finally she calmed herself.

"Gus," she said, "in some ways I envy you; you're such a simpleminded character. It's either this or that with you, no in-between."

"Yeah? So?" said Gus, trying to understand.

Zena studied his tough young face for a moment, then shrugged, gave it up, and walked off with the tray, just as Gino came up to hurry her along.

"Tough break," she said under her breath to Gino. "No pinch."

Gino shrugged and grimaced, then turned to Gus.

"Couldn't we maybe cut down the social activity a little, Gus?"

"Anything you say, Gino," said Gus, cheerfully, starting to polish a glass. "What's with her, anyway? Got any idea?"

"She's a no-good tramp who belongs in the gutter," said Gino. "Only thing in the world that holds her up is Judy."

"So that's it," said Gus.

"She hangs on to Judy like an octopus. How Judy stands it, I don't know."

"Sweet kid, Judy," said Gus, then he began to whistle the tune Tully Burke and his boys were playing.

The house phone rang at the bar and Gino answered it. "Yes, Al. Yes, he's here. Sure, sure. I'll tell him."

Gino walked over to Jim's table and stood smiling at him. "That was Al on the phone. Somebody told him you were out here. Would you like to drop back and see him?"

Jim had dreaded talking to Al Patton, not only because of the big tab he owed, but for various other reasons, the chief one being that Al had never recovered from the shock of the political defeat and was still bewildered and resentful.

Al's office in the back of Volari's was big, roomy and odd. It was set at an angle, against the back wall, and had no windows, just two ventilators high up that whirred monotonously. One corner of it was blocked off by a tall black and gold Chinese screen that had cost Al a small fortune. But why the screen? Did it mask a door? But why a door? The room already had three; one that led to the club proper, one that gave into the alley, and another one, always locked and bolted, that perhaps opened onto a storeroom or another office. Jim had never been able to figure out the reason for the huge, ceiling-high screen, that would not have been out of place in the lobby of the biggest hotel in town. Here, it dwarfed the room.

Al, a big man, beginning to go bald, was hunched behind his desk in his shirtsleeves smoking a cigarette, and sipping from a tall glass of lemonade.

"Hot! Jesus, what a night. Their system's gone haywire. Did you notice how hot it was out front? And as for those ventilators—man, it's hot!"

"Listen, Al," Jim began, "about that tab ..."

"What tab, for cryssake!" said Al, irritated. "You think I want to talk to you about a lousy tab?"

"Well, *I* want to talk about it," said Jim, firmly. "It's over nine hundred dollars. Soon as I get straightened around I'm going to pay it, maybe a hundred at a time. I'm no deadbeat."

"Somebody accusing you?" said Al. "And don't stay away on account of a lousy tab. We miss you around here. Hell, everybody's run out on us. Except for the tourists. We're getting *them* now. Brother! Jim, look. Funny thing. I was thinking about calling you, and here you turn up."

"I didn't run out," said Jim, shifting uncomfortably. "I've been up to my neck trying to make a living."

"Like all the rest you didn't save a cent, did you?" said Al. "Man, were we riding high! How could it have stopped all of a sudden like that? I still can't believe it. Go to bed one night on top of the world—get up the next morning, dead-out. It's sure took a lot out of old Tom. And I hear Jake has flipped in Florida—for the birds, now. Tom says we'll come back. What do you say?"

"I say, not a chance," said Jim.

Al sighed and looked down at his lemonade; then he held up the glass. "Doctor's orders. Stop with the liquor. High blood pressure. I'm used to having a glass in front of me all night long—so now it's lemonade. It's not as rough as you'd think."

"I've slacked off," said Jim.

"Maybe it's a good idea. We used to wonder where you were putting it, used to wait for you to fall, but nothing ever seemed to happen. You could really belt it, Jim."

"Yeah," said Jim, wondering to himself: Why? Why? It was hard for him to remember how things had been. The hectic days and nights; the hysterical atmosphere of success and power all about him. His wild, egotistical affair with Judy. What had he been thinking about? Why had it never occurred to him then that he had responsibilities to Alma and the two boys, responsibilities that should have come first? Maybe it was just that they'd all gone a little crazy, from top to bottom. And now look. Chaos.

"I wanted to talk to you about Tom," said Al. "We've been hearing some bad rumors. About the Grand Jury. Somebody is finking, or so we hear. Tom might be subpoenaed—and that could get mighty rough. You hear anything?"

"No," said Jim.

"Jake's gone. The Mayor's in Southern California. Commissioner Ridgely's in Toronto. Tom ... well, he might be holding the sack."

"Why doesn't he get out?"

Al wagged his head impatiently. "He won't. I can't figure what it is with him exactly. Tom's a funny guy. He loves this town. We come up from nothing, you know, Jim. Our grandfather dug ditches and couldn't read or write. Our old man worked as a stevedore for nearly forty years, but he sent us all though high school. I guess Tom kinda thinks he owns the town, says he wouldn't be happy anyplace else."

"He may *have* to get out."

"He may. He may. But, Jim, please—you get around, Hall of Justice, all over the place. Check on it, will you? You lawyers, you've all got tipsters. See what you can find out. I'll put you on the payroll."

"No," said Jim. "I'll do what I can. Glad to."

Al studied Jim, then smiled reminiscently. "Yeah," he said. "You'd say that. Jake always had your number. 'There's a gentleman,'" he'd say. Tom felt that way, too. We were sure glad to have you aboard with your name and all."

Jim tried to keep from wincing, said nothing.

"So … if you won't let me put you on the payroll," said Al, "let's say this—we'll write off the tab. You do what you can. Okay?"

"It's too much," said Jim, but he felt a great sense of relief. At least one burden might be lifted from his shoulders.

"For a guy who can be trusted," said Al, "it is not too much. Okay? A deal? Shake."

They shook hands and Jim accepted a cigarette; they lit up.

"How's it with you and doll-face?" asked Al. "You haven't been around, so I got to wondering. I'd leave home for her, but I'm too fat, I guess."

"Oh, I see her all the time," said Jim, resenting the question but trying not to show it. After all, old Al meant well. He just didn't know any better.

"I'll never forget the way it started," said Al. "Why, hell, that poor girl could hardly do her work. Jake was pretty much annoyed with you at first. Did you know that?"

The DA? What did Al mean? Why? "No, Al."

"Well, Jake liked her. And it was like father and daughter, you know. I mean it. He took her out. Very polite. Oh, I heard all about it, don't worry. Then blooey! Gone!"

"But Judy is no floozy, so Jake was all thumbs, you know." Al laughed, then began to cough. "Didn't know how to begin, him being nearly forty years older. Well … you solved the problem for him. He growled around for a few days; that was all."

"He never said a word to me about it," said Jim.

"Course not," said Al. "Too much pride. That old geezer was full of pride."

Al sighed and they both sat looking off into space, Al remembering how it had been in the old days with Tom and Jake and the Mayor in power and Volari's roaring, while Jim, surprised by Al's revelation, sat wondering how many other things had been happening all around him during that hectic era without his knowing anything about them.

It was not what it had been in the past; in fact, it had got so lately that it was hardly anything at all, merely a habit of long standing; but, after all, it was better than nothing … this, in a sense, was what Judy was thinking as she slipped out of bed and hurried in for a shower. But her actual thoughts, obscured by her emotions—her dreads and her worries, her fears for the future, her regrets about the past—were far vaguer, and so unclear to her that she shrugged them off, and then forgot them entirely as the needlepoints of hot water stabbed at her and brought a glow to her firm young body.

Jim was in the kitchen, wearing pajamas and a dressing gown, and making coffee, when Judy came in from the bathroom, fully dressed. Jim looked her over, showing a slight surprise.

"What's the matter with that kimono I bought you in Chinatown? You make me feel naked."

"It's late, Jim," said Judy. "Nearly four o'clock. It'll be light in a half hour or so."

"Well," said Jim, "sit down and eat your sandwich. Here comes the coffee."

They sat at a cramped little breakfast nook in a corner of the kitchen. Judy could never understand why Jim lived where he did: in a rundown old residential section, two miles from anyplace. As for his apartment— it was a relic, lacking in comfort, with ugly, old-fashioned furniture and rooms so big (except for the kitchen) that you could play hockey in them, as Jim had once said. It was on the second floor of an old stone mansion that had been crudely broken up into a four-family apartment house. The woodwork was dark, the floors creaked, there was no air conditioning, no television, no anything. A fleabag, in Judy's estimation. It just didn't go with what she knew about Jim, or thought she knew.

As for herself, she and Zena had a spic and span bandbox apartment, with a cute bedroom, living room and Pullman kitchen. Everything was built-in: the beds, the television set, a desk, the dining table, and it was all ultra-modern and smart and in pleasant colors, with abstractions on the walls, and a general air of up-to-the-second newness.

Long ago she'd stopped trying to find out why Jim lived in such a place. At first she'd asked, and Jim would laugh and say that he was just a Bohemian at heart, or that he liked to pig it, or that it was cheap, which it was not. Judy happened to know that rents in this part of town were very high. It was a great puzzle to her.

What she did not know, being a relative newcomer to the big town, was that Jim had played all over this neighborhood as a boy. That his grandfather's house, long ago converted into an office building, was only one block away, and that Jim's closest friends, the Ambroses, now scattered all over the country, had lived directly across the street in that old brick place, with the arched stone doorway, that now housed the Jarecki Printing and Lithographing Company.

How could Judy know that Jim was, in a sense, communing with the past? As he walked along the street he'd suddenly remember the jam he and Hugh Ambrose had gotten into one Halloween, or he'd remember how his grandmother used to drive her Packard erratically round the corner, causing people to jump back on the curb. The houses, the streets were still there ... but where were the Chases and the Ambroses? Where was that happier time?

Judy noticed his preoccupation. "You make a nice sandwich sir," she said. "And the coffee's not bad either."

"If I was Greek I'd open a restaurant," said Jim, trying to be funny, but it was labored and Judy glanced at him curiously, wondering how it was that they never seemed easy together anymore. Only in bed was there any closeness now, and even there ... well ... But the trouble was that Jim had spoiled her for other men. He was a gentleman, quiet, undemanding, with none of the thickheadedness, none of the rough edges she'd been used to before she'd met him. Zena thought she was a fool, wasting her time with a man in his middle forties who was so obviously on his way out. But then Zena thought that everything Judy did was foolish. While in Judy's opinion Zena was the fool. Such men! Loudmouthed vulgar braggarts. All right, so they were loaded, as Zena insisted, and could be muscled for presents ranging from good costume jewelry to fur coats. But it wasn't worth it. "I couldn't take it," Judy told herself. "I just couldn't take it."

And that new one! Mr. Mount, with the wary, still face and the closely-clipped black hair. Where had Zena found *him*—with his Alfa-Romeo and his tight-lipped talk? Except for a certain arrogance in his manner and his expensive clothes, you'd take him for a small-time actor ... or ... what? Salesman for a big chemical firm—and loaded, Zena said.

The phone rang in the living room and Judy jumped slightly startled out of her thoughts.

"Now who in the hell ...!" Jim muttered impatiently, as he rose and went to answer it.

Judy sat listening to his voice. "Yeah. Who? Oh, Zena. Yes, she's here. Judy!"

Judy's face showed some embarrassment as she picked up the phone. Jim turned away, irritated. That damned Zena!

You'd think she owned Judy the way she acted.

"Sure I know what time it is," Judy was saying. "Now look, Zena. All right, all right. But I wish you wouldn't do this. Do I call and bother you? Of course you're bothering me!" There was a click at the other end.

Judy hung up the phone in silence.

"Come on," said Jim, wearily. "Finish your sandwich."

They sat down in the breakfast nook again.

"Why do you put up with that?" asked Jim, finally, as he poured out the last of the coffee for them.

"I've told you a dozen times," said Judy. "Besides, she really can't help it. You've never seen anybody so nervous. She can hardly stand to be alone for five minutes. When she comes home and I'm not there she panics."

"My God, she's not a child. Look, Judy, you can only stretch gratitude so far."

"I know, I know," said Judy. "But when I got in here from Memphis ... well, I needed help. I was down to my last dollar. Anything might have happened to me. Well, Zena, she ..."

"All right, all right," said Jim, then he finished the last of his coffee and stood up. "Take your time. I'll get dressed and drive you home."

"I wish you didn't always think you had to do this, Jim. Just call me a cab."

"No," said Jim.

As she finished her sandwich, she heard him moving about in the bedroom, changing his clothes. It had always been like this with Jim. She'd never met a man like him before. So considerate. So ... well, he certainly must have been brought up right! And she sat thinking about her own Old Man who used to sit out on the front porch with his bare feet up on the railing; her brothers—Link and Todd—who used to come home every Saturday night, stinking drunk, and vomit all over the house. Of Mr. Colby, the first man she'd worked for, who just wouldn't take 'no' for an answer, and then fired her for immorality and called her a slut!

"And Zena wonders what I see in him!" she observed to herself, shaking her head.

## 2: FRIDAY

The phone woke Jim. Groaning, he rolled over and looked at his wrist-watch on the night-table: ten minutes of eleven; then he got out of bed and staggered into the living room, yawning and stretching, to answer the phone.

It was Gert. "Well," she said, "nobody works but me. Mrs. Packard called at nine and said she was making Mr. Packard stay in bed till noon. So I wait and wait—and I'm flooded with calls and there's nobody here to …"

"How many calls?" asked Jim.

"Two," said Gert, with a laugh.

"I'll be down as soon as I can get there. What were the calls?"

"A Mr. Wiley. I made an appointment for 2 p.m. … Wants to see Mr. Packard. A client, I think … I hope. The other call was from the DA's office. Something about the Lampson Case. Nothing important. Mr. Packard is to return the call at his leisure."

"Okay, Gert. See you."

Gert was a goodhearted, rather grim old girl in her early fifties, efficient, hardworking, uncomplaining. They both liked her very much and hoped that they could keep her. Really good law secretaries were at a premium and they could afford to pay her only so much. She'd been with them about a year, and had, in a sense, engineered the move into their present suite of offices. She always referred to their old suite as 'that dirty filthy disorganized place.' Gert was a fanatic against dust and carelessness and disorder of any kind.

"I'll bet she drove her husband to his early grave," Larry observed one day after he'd heard Gert giving Jim a piece of her mind because he just wouldn't keep his desk in any kind of order.

Jim took a shower, then made himself some coffee and stood at one of the big front windows holding the warm cup. He felt disgusted with himself. He hadn't even remembered that Larry wasn't coming in till noon.

It was an overcast day, and the air was heavy and humid. Dirty-looking gray clouds hung low and motionless over the big buildings, downtown, and all the lights were lit in the printing company, across the way.

"I better get myself together," Jim thought. "I'll be forty-five this November, got no time to be fooling around." Turning away from the window, he tried to fight off the worries and fears that almost invariably nagged at him in the morning before he washed and dressed and more or less "organized," as Gert would have said.

Suddenly he remembered Al Patton. Hell, he'd even forgotten that! "I must be punchy," he said, studying his face in the bathroom mirror as he got out his electric razor; and as he shaved it occurred to him that Larry was not getting a fair shake in regard to Al Patton's writing off a personal debt in lieu of a retainer. "I'll be goddamned," said Jim. "I'm just not thinking straight."

He had a hard time trying to make Larry listen to him in regard to Al Patton. Fortified by the best sleep he'd had in months, Larry was bouncing around the office like a puppet on wires. Larry was a man of extremes. He was either depressed or cheerful, nothing in between. He was ready to either whip the world, or give in entirely. This was one of his optimistic days.

"It's not fair," said Jim. "We share and share alike. So I owe you a little over four hundred and fifty dollars, and I want it on the books. I'll pay it off as I go."

"You're crazy," said Larry.

But Gert agreed with Jim and they finally wore Larry down.

"All right," said Larry, finally, "but I won't take money for doing nothing. I've got a new tipster—a dandy, if he can just keep going. I'll put it up to him. Okay?"

"Can you trust him?" asked Jim.

"No. Not entirely. You can't trust any of them," said Larry, smiling cheerfully. "But this boy gets the job done." Jim was going to say something and Larry noticed his worried look, so he held up his hand to stop him. "Don't say it. Let's not get into the stubble-field of ethics."

"The stubble-field of ethics!" cried Gert. "My God! He'll be on the Supreme Bench!"

They had a good laugh over this, then Jim went into his office to write some letters.

Gert and Larry were silent for a moment, then Larry said: "All he had to do was keep his mouth shut, and he really needs that money. He's up to here in debt."

Gert stood shaking her head. "I don't see how a man like Chase ever … Oh, never mind."

"I know what you mean," said Larry. "But we all blew our tops, Gert. Beth saved *me*. Trouble with Jim is, he's got no Beth."

"Why doesn't he …?" Gert broke off, feeling that maybe the conversation was getting a little too personal and intimate.

But Larry, of a different stripe, had no such qualms.

"Go back with his wife? I don't think she'll have him."

"She's a fool," said Gert. Then: "I mean … well, life's short, no disrespect intended. I was too rigid with my husband, Larry; I know it now. We broke up. We went back together again, but it was too late. He died a few months later."

Larry saw tears in hard-bitten old Gert's eyes and stared at her in wonder.

"So don't think I'm being too harsh with Mrs. Chase," Gert went on hurriedly. "I know. I know."

"Well," said Larry, "we don't know the inside, Gert, so it's hard to judge. Got two fine boys, too. Used to bring them in the office with him. But that was before your time, Gert."

"I saw their pictures," said Gert. "Here, too. Nice family. Oh, it's really awful. Girls like that … like that … well, they've got no respect for anything. And they put pickpockets in jail! There ought to be a law against girls like …" She broke off, her eyes showing anger now, her lips compressed.

So *that* had been Gert's husband's trouble!

"There *is* a law, Gert. There is indeed. But it's damned hard to enforce. Don't you know you can go to jail for adultery in this state? Trouble is we haven't got enough jails. It's just not possible, Gert."

"How about capital punishment?" asked Gert, sardonically.

"You want to decimate the country?" cried Larry. "Besides," he said seriously, "I don't even think the girl's to blame. I met her once. Seemed like a nice sweet kid. I'm telling you, Gert, we just went hog wild."

"They all seem like nice sweet kids to you men," said Gert, "providing they're young enough."

It was two-thirty when Larry tapped at Jim's door, then looked in.

"We've got a client," said Larry. "But let me tell you about it first. He's guilty as hell and I don't think he's got a chance. He's given up on his other lawyers, who managed to get him a continuance, then asked off the case. He has also got money. Do we take him?"

"What's the charge?"

"Embezzlement. Big."

"We take him," said Jim, and Larry laughed, then sobered and said: "I got my tipster working already on that other matter. He may have some word for us by tomorrow. He's got real fine connections."

"Good," said Jim, then he got up and began to pace about restlessly. "Larry, you think you could do without me for the rest of the afternoon?"

"Sure," said Larry. "Gert and I will be busy the rest of the day getting all the stuff down from Mr. Willey. Tomorrow morning I'm going to have a conference with his former lawyers, sometime tomorrow afternoon. I'll give you all the stuff, then it's up to you."

"Fine," said Jim.

All of a sudden it had hit him. He wanted to see Alma and the kids. The court had given him monthly visitation rights, and for a while, after the divorce, he'd appeared promptly on a stated day. But for reasons unknown even to himself he hadn't been to see them for nearly three months now. Alma never called him and was full of pride.

She'd only called him once since the divorce and that was the day, a year ago, when Bob broke his collarbone playing football. She hadn't even called him when he'd got two months behind on his alimony payments.

Jim drove his three-year-old Ford at a steady sixty miles an hour up along the northern freeway. Although it was only a little after three o'clock there was a heavy stream of traffic, both ways. During the rush hours the freeways were just impossible. Traffic was getting completely out of hand in the big town—with the new freeways already obsolete and no relief in sight—so Jim very seldom used his car, walking to his office in the morning, which was about half a mile from his apartment, and grabbing a cab for short hauls in the city.

Jim looked about him like an alien. He hardly recognized the city at all anymore. Now it sprawled in all directions like an abnormally overgrown giant. Most of the old landmarks were gone, and a steady stream of newcomers poured in from all points of the compass, to man the new industries that were springing up like mushrooms all along the vast outer perimeter of the city.

When Jim was a boy the city, with about three hundred thousand inhabitants, was hardly more than a widely spread-out country town, with many parks and much open space; now over a million people were jammed into the same area, people from everywhere and no place. Jim often wondered where they all came from. Were the smaller towns being denuded? It did not appear so when you drove about the countryside. Even the smallest places seemed to be getting bigger, with traffic lights and shopping centers and most of the other big town amenities.

"She'll just swell up till she busts," Tom Patton had said one day. "It's like this all over the Midwest and the West. You ought to see Southern Cal.; they're coming in droves. Moving away from the East. New York State's already in trouble. Pretty soon the whole thing will point West— and Los Angeles and San Francisco'll be the spots. Not New York. Lost their baseball team already."

Jim did not care one way or another about that. All that he knew was that every year he felt less and less at home in his own hometown.

In many ways the Upper River still bore some resemblance to its former state, in spite of the many new real estate developments and the street after street of little box-like houses, with all the latest appointments, and walls that you could put your fist through with little effort. The river was still there, huge and winding, and at least they'd had sense enough to keep most of the ancient big trees, some of them over a hundred years old.

Alma and the boys lived in one of the little boxes on one of the little streets. There was a carport with a storm door, a television aerial, a picture window from which you had a wonderful view of the house across the street with its picture window glaring back, a square of lawn just like the squares on either side, and a few clumps of low shrubbery. But at least the street was fairly wide and hard and there loomed one of the old trees, dwarfing the flat one-story houses and making them look as impermanent as tents, mitigating the rawness and fresh-paint bleakness of this brand-new suburb of four thousand souls—West River.

A teenage kid in a sweatshirt was delivering the evening papers from the front seat of an open, beat-up jalopy, forward-passing them against the front doors with a thud. He grinned at Jim as they almost tangled fenders at a corner.

"Sorry, dad," he said.

Jim resented his manner, then laughed at himself. "God, I *am* getting to be an old fogy," he thought.

Alma worked at Reed's, Electrical Appliances and Contracting, Inc., a small, but wide-awake and growing outfit controlled and operated by Andy Reed, Alma's boss. She was a combination bookkeeper, accountant, typist, chief clerk and straw boss. Once upon a time, in Antediluvian days, she'd been working as a secretary in his father's law office. A lot of people thought that Alma had made quite a marriage for herself—the boss's son! Now the same people thought differently. The Honorable Robert Chase losing all his money speculating! And his son hardly better than a hoodlum, one of the minor big wheels in the worst administration the city had ever had in its nearly one hundred and fifty years of existence!

Reed's was located in the shopping center at West River. The company had come up out of obscure insolvency by getting all of the electrical contracting of the three latest real estate developments: of course the developers had to be cut in, but it had turned out to be a good deal all around. Andy Reed, a widower, now had one of the finest houses in the section—at cost—and was on his way to his first million.

"Which proves," Jim told himself, "that anybody can do it." He'd gone to military school with Reed, whose father had been a prosperous farmer, south of town. He'd always considered him a big, good-natured goof. Later he'd run into him in Paris, toward the end of World War II. Andy, a captain, had managed to wangle himself onto some general's staff, but had seemed even goofier than before—the kind of guy you couldn't help playing jokes on.

So? Who was the comedian now?

Alma had been seeing quite a bit of Andy, going out to dinner with him, and to bridge parties. But Jim just couldn't take it seriously. Not that goofball!

The boys seemed a little startled to see him. They had just got home from a playground up the street, and dressed in sweatshirts and jeans, were playing catch on the front lawn.

"Hi," said Jim, coming up the walk.

"Hi," said Bob, but Lloyd merely stood regarding him with a puzzled look.

Lloyd, blond like his mother, had always been slower in every way than Bob, who was a Chase all over, as Jim was always reminding himself. Tall, dark hair, light eyes, and with an almost colorless complexion. Lloyd had a sort of Huck Finn look, with his close-cut reddish hair, his freckles, and his white eyelashes.

"Mommy never told us you were coming," said Lloyd, finally. "Where've you been so long?"

"Busy," said Jim. "Making a living."

The boys exchanged a long look, then sort of squirmed before him.

"How was school? Haven't seen you since it closed."

"Okay," said Bob, without enthusiasm. "I made the C baseball team. So did Lloyd. He hits real good. Can't handle a ground ball, though."

"I can so," cried Lloyd. "You heard what Andy said Saturday. He said I was better than you."

"He was just trying to build up your morale."

"He was not," yelled Lloyd.

"You talking about Andy Reed?" asked Jim.

"Yes," said Bob. "He takes us up to the Dam sometimes on Saturday afternoon and we play ball and eat fried chicken. Andy's a pretty good ball player."

"Your mother go along?"

Both boys laughed loudly. "Mommy!" exclaimed Bob. "No. She hates baseball. All she talks about is swimming and tennis."

"She used to be pretty good at both," said Jim.

"Sure," said Lloyd, with disdain. "But that's for girls. Andy played tennis with her one day and she beat his pants off."

The boys howled with glee. "Not that Andy cared," said Bob. "He thinks it's a girls' game, too."

"Swimming is for girls?" asked Jim, beginning to feel notably annoyed, but left out, and almost a stranger.

"Oh, we can swim good," said Bob. "A boy's got to learn. But the pool down the street's always full of girls. It gets pretty tiresome, all that yelling and screaming."

There was a short silence. The boys tossed the ball back and forth, their eyes intent on the game, but finally Lloyd held the ball and turned to his father. "We didn't know you were coming, Dad."

"That's right," said Bob quickly.

"It was on the spur of the moment," said Jim, feeling uncomfortable, wondering what they were trying to say. "I was up this way, anyway."

"Oh," said Lloyd.

"Just drifting past, you mean?" asked Bob.

"Well, yes, I guess so. Why?"

Lloyd burst out now. "We promised, that's all. We didn't know, so we promised."

"You promised what?"

"Andy hired this boat. He's going to pick us up pretty soon and we're going up the river and have supper on an island, and then ride back in the moonlight. A diesel launch. We promised. We didn't know."

"I see," said Jim. Jesus, this guy Andy was really cutting in for sure. "Well, that's okay." He stood looking down into their puzzled faces, then suddenly he realized that he was just lousing things up for them and that they, far from being glad to see him, were wishing that he'd never come at all. "Tell you what," said Jim. "I got to get back anyway. Just tell your mother that I was up this way, and dropped by. Maybe I'll see you next week. I'll call first."

"Okay," said Bob. "Fine."

"We couldn't help it," Lloyd insisted. "We promised."

"Sure, sure," said Jim, then he turned and started for his car with the boys tagging along rather disconsolately behind him. Although they were glad that they weren't going to lose out on that diesel deal— oh, boy! Night on the river in their own boat—they sensed the fact that their father was upset and this disturbed and unsettled them.

Just as Jim was opening the door of his car, a big grey station wagon turned the corner, and pulled up behind him. Andy and Alma. They both stared as they got out. Andy, in jeans and a red-checked shirt, looked as if he'd just come fresh off his father's farm. He'd lost some of his hair since Jim had seen him last and he was now wearing a fashionable short haircut to mask this fact. Also his waistline had expanded a little and the jeans looked as if they might burst.

Alma in a white summer dress, was her usual wholesome-looking self. At thirty-five she showed almost no sign of the passing of the years. Her mouth maybe was a little firmer, and there was perhaps a more mature look in her blue eyes—nothing else.

"Jim!" she cried.

He intercepted a worried look that passed between his sons, knowing that it meant: Good Lord, is our outing going to be loused up after all? Andy rushed forward to shake hands. "Good to see you," he cried, just as in Paris, and added: "Ole Hoss," as before. Jim had an odd feeling that a cockeyed scene was repeating itself in grotesque circumstances, as in a nightmare.

"Hi, Andy," said Jim. "Understand you hired a boat and are going to take the boys up the river."

"That's right," said Andy. "Alma's going, too. I'm trying out the boat, see? If I like it, I buy it. It's a bargain. I can get it for sixty-five hundred. Nothing ... for a boat like that."

"Well," said Jim. "I was out this way talking to a client so I just dropped by. Got to be getting back."

He glanced up. Alma was studying him. "Everything okay otherwise?" he asked her awkwardly.

"Yes," said Alma. "Everything's fine."

"I couldn't run the office without her," said Andy. "One day last week she wasn't feeling so good and stayed home. Boy, were we in trouble. Nobody knew from nothing. We kept calling her. She had a sick headache. Oh, how she hated us."

"Yes, I did," said Alma, laughing.

"She tried to quit," said Andy, looking at Jim in wonder. "We panicked and kept quiet as mice. Right, Alma?"

"Yes," said Alma.

Jim glanced at his wristwatch. "Well, I've got to go. I was just leaving when you drove up. Glad to have seen you, Andy." Then he turned to Alma: "Might be out next week to see the boys. But I'll call first. Bye, boys."

Bob and Lloyd were all smiles now and reached out and hugged their father. "Bye, Dad."

"Say," said Bob, "whatever happened about the fungo bats?"

Jim looked at him blankly. "The what?"

"Jim," said Alma, her eyes showing annoyance, "the last time you were out here you promised to bring them some kind of bat or bats?"

"Fungo bats," cried Lloyd, eyeing his father impatiently. "*You* know!"

"Oh, sure," said Jim, not remembering a thing about it, and feeling very depressed and alone. "Next time, boys. I've been pretty busy."

He got into his car quickly, slammed the door, and drove off, gesturing goodbye. In the rearview mirror he could see the boys standing at the curb, waving, but Alma and Andy had already started up the walk toward the house.

"Well," Jim told himself, "can't say I blame her much. He's passable, he's got money, and he's available. It's a rough world."

Jim felt pretty sure that Alma was figuring on marrying Andy now. But in his heart he didn't like it, he didn't like it at all.

A strong, unreasonable feeling of having been rejected nagged at him persistently. Massed cars were going in both directions now along the northern freeway. Horns honked and hooted; and at intervals there was the wild squealing of brakes. The stench of carbon monoxide made his eyes sting and hurt the inside of his nose. Southward, toward town, the huge hazy hulking buildings of the financial district loomed up toward a threatening overcast grayish-yellow sky.

Granite, concrete and chrome, blurred by exhaust fumes, industrial smoke and river mist, jarred by the throbbing vibrations of senselessly powerful car engines into a sort of mindless, angular dance!

Jim, with a sudden sensation of being completely alone, felt like a man lost and wandering in stony wilderness.

This feeling became so strong, as he neared town, that he took a firm hold on himself. It was almost like a hallucination.

"This is stupid," he thought, at last, and pulled off the street into a little parking lot behind a bar. "I need a drink."

The place was crowded with people he'd never seen before, yet he was hardly more than a block away from his apartment. Everybody seemed to be watching the bar television set where a baseball game was in progress.

"Oh you bum!" yelled a man. "Struck out again. I'll bet he's left six men on base this game; and that big slob gets thirty thousand dollars a year!"

"Double Scotch and soda," said Jim, then he stood trying to force himself to get interested in the baseball game.

Jim was having his dinner alone in a little corner restaurant a few doors down from Jarecki's. It was a few minutes after eight, but the city was still sweltering. On the chair beside him was his briefcase packed with information regarding the dubious Mr. Willey and his tortuous financial dealing. At the office Jim had glanced through Gert's neatly typed sheets, wincing at what he'd gleaned there by only a mere skimming. It was obvious to him already that it was not a question of working out a solid defense, but of working out any defense at all. Mr. Willey, long a respected accountant, was actually a self-righteous, hypocritical thief—and not a very smart one.

"Oh, well," thought Jim, "it's a living—such as it is." A vision of the glories of the past rose before his eyes: His Highness, Old Jake, with his arm around Jim's shoulders, proclaiming at a High Brass meeting in the City Hall: "Here's my successor, boys. Judge Chase's grandson. My God, won't his name look good on the ticket?" At that time Old Jake was certain that he himself would be the next governor of the state. And now his Highness, Jake Webb, a political outcast, had suffered a stroke in Florida, while Jim, the Crown Prince, still in town, was having a solitary dinner in a cheap little table d'hôte restaurant, trying to figure out a plausible-sounding defense for an unsavory malefactor who should have been behind bars years ago.

Jim smiled wryly to himself and sipped the weak coffee. His waitress, whose white uniform was blotched with soup and gravy stains, came and stood beside his chair.

"'Scuse me," she said, "Are you Mr. James Chase?"

"Yes," said Jim, looking up in surprise.

"You're wanted on the phone." She gestured with her thumb toward the back of the place.

Jim went around the counter to answer the phone. Had to be either Larry or Gert; nobody else knew that he sometimes ate at Allie's— Choice Foods and Beverages.

"Jim? Larry. Can you meet me in the Regent bar? Don't want to talk over the phone."

"Yes. Fifteen minutes."

As Jim was hanging up, he noticed that an old man was looking out at him from a passageway that led to the kitchens.

"Excuse me, sir," the old man said, as Jim turned away. "I heard 'em calling you. Mr. James Chase, wasn't it?"

"That's right," said Jim, looking at the old man curiously.

"Don't remember me, do you?"

"No," said Jim. "I'm sorry. I don't."

"Used to work at Smedley's Candy Kitchen when you was just a kid."

Jim stared. Smedley's! The place had been out of business for nearly twenty years. It was where the teenage kids used to hang out and drink sodas and eat Sundaes and make dates on those hot summer nights long ago.

"Yes sir," said the old man. "I says to myself when I heard the name, 'That's Judge Chase's grandson—Jim!' You don't look much different."

"Well, thanks," said Jim, not knowing what else to say. He had no memory at all of this little, scrawny-looking old man.

"Have you been away or something?" asked the old man. "I haven't set eyes on you for, oh, maybe twenty years. I was behind the counter at Smedley's. Nice job. But hell, I'm too old for it now and this pearl diving is killing me."

"This what?"

"Dishwashing, son. That's what we call it, 'pearl diving.' It's hell the way everything's changing ain't it? Look at this street. Nothing left. I don't know. They call it progress. The more people the more progress, I guess. Man can hardly turn around anymore."

"Amos, Amos!" yelled somebody in the back.

"That's me," said the old man. "More dirty dishes. Sure is a pleasure to see the Judge's grandson again. He was a mighty fine man, the Judge. I wonder what he'd make of all this."

"Amos, you old bugger...!" came the voice.

Jim tried to slip the old man some money but he wouldn't take it. "No, no, son; thanks. I'm making pretty good money, if my back will only hold out. Just want to take a look at you. Thanks all the same."

He hurried away. Jim went back to the table, paid his bill, picked up his hat and briefcase and left. He felt depressed and even a little shaken. It worried him to discover that his viewpoint in regard to what was happening in the city was exactly the same as that of this poor, defeated old man.

"What's the matter with you?" asked Larry, studying Jim, after they had sat down in a booth at the Regent and ordered drinks.

"It's hot," said Jim.

"It sure is," said Larry. "And no relief in sight, the paper says. For once I'm looking forward to winter." A pause, then: "Jim, it's your own business, but you've been looking what my old man used to call 'kinda washed out' lately. Do you get enough rest?"

"It's just the heat," said Jim, impatiently, remembering, in spite of a resolution he'd made, on the way over, to stop thinking about the past, how the Chase family used to leave the city every year after July 4th and move into their big, ramshackle summer cottage at Half Moon Bay, on the lake. His grandfather, then later, his father, had commuted by interurban, while he roamed the lake from morning till night, fishing, swimming, sailing, with Hugh Ambrose and various girls. "Heat always gets me," he added, quickly, trying to shut off the crowding memories.

"Yeah," said Larry. "I've even been trying to persuade Beth to go up to the lake for a week and get cool and relax, but she won't do it. Afraid I might run wild, I guess." Larry laughed sadly.

Their drinks were brought and they sipped them in silence for a moment; then Larry looked about him to be sure nobody could hear. "I've got that tip for you," he said. "Our man's almost positive that a subpoena is to be issued for that certain party within a week, maybe sooner."

"Wow," said Jim, sadly.

"I told you he was a live wire," said Larry. "He's also hungry—always got the old hand out. I slipped him fifty. Okay?"

"It's worth a lot more than fifty to that certain party. I'd better drop by as soon as we finish our drinks. This is nothing to phone about."

Larry nodded, and kept glancing surreptitiously at Jim wondering what was bothering him tonight, why he seemed so nervous and so withdrawn. Meanwhile, the nightly uproar of the Regent bar boiled all around them. It was the sporting and theatrical hangout of the big town, and usually packed from six o'clock on. At one time it had also been popular with politicians, but during King Jake's regime Volari's had taken the play away. The new administration did not go in for roistering, so the Regent was now almost entirely devoid of politicians.

"It's going to be rough," said Larry in a low voice, "if they get Tom Patton in front of the Grand Jury."

"Yes." said Jim. "But Martin Cowan'll look after him. Toughest lawyer in this town. If it comes to that. The thing for Tom to do is get out, like all the rest of them. So I'd better finish my drink and go."

"Jim," said Larry, "you don't think they'll drag any of us in, do you? The small guys?"

"I doubt it," said Jim. "Anyway, we didn't set policy. We just went along like sheep. If I know Judge Weybrecht he's only after the big boys."

"I hope you're right," said Larry. "I'd hate to drag Beth through it. She doesn't know anything about it. I was out when I met her."

Jim patted Larry on the shoulder. "Don't worry about it. There's thousands of us. We're reasonably safe. Anyway, what would we tell a Grand Jury? They'd have to bring up the disposition of specific cases, things like that. *You* know. No, Larry. The Judge is after big game."

Larry seemed relieved and Jim patted him again, then got up to go. "See you tomorrow."

"What do you think about our friend Mr. Aldus Willey?"

Jim held his nose. Larry laughed and ordered another drink for himself and a phone.

"Got to check in with the little woman," he explained. "Some guys hate the idea. I like it."

"*Keep* liking it," said Jim, then he turned and left abruptly.

It was a little after nine when a taxi dropped Jim off at Volari's. Chauncey smiled and saluted, as before.

"Say," he said, "you're getting to be a regular again. Good, good."

"Hi, Chauncey," said Jim. "Is Mr. Patton here?"

"Yes, he came about seven-thirty."

The new check-girl gave Jim a blank look as she took his hat. It was a Friday night and the bar stools were all full but only three of the wall booths were taken and there was nobody in the supper room, although it was a little early for that. Gus waved and grimaced, and Zena said, facetiously: "Well … hi! This is beginning to be a habit."

Jim nodded and moved over to the house phone. Gino appeared from around the end of the bar. "Something I can do for you, Mr. Chase?"

"Yes," said Jim. "If Al's not busy I'd like to speak with him." His appearance on successive days after such a long absence was obviously causing curiosity and speculation, so he said: "I promised I'd see what I could do about getting Al some good seats for the San Francisco series. He's a Mays fan, you know."

"Yes, I know," said Gino. "Wait just a minute."

While Gino was on the phone Jim turned and looked unexpectedly into Judy's eyes. She was standing in the slot regarding him steadily. She seemed vaguely puzzled.

"Hi," said Jim.

She gave Gus her order, then came over to him.

"I see Zena's right," she said.

"What do you mean?"

"She says something's going on between you and Al. That's the reason you're showing up here."

"Tell Zena to mind her own business," said Jim.

"I thought you came to see *me* last night," said Judy.

"I did."

"And tonight?"

Jim sighed wearily. "Last night Al asked me to see if I could get him some baseball tickets. Al's an old friend of mine."

"But not lately," said a voice behind him. Zena!

Jim repressed an angry retort and walked over to the house phone, where Gino was standing.

"Al's waiting, Mr. Chase," said Gino.

Jim nodded and started for the back of the place. But Judy intercepted him.

"Don't get mad at me just on account of Zena."

"I'm not mad at you," said Jim.

"Meet me tonight."

Jim glanced at her, puzzled. "I thought we said …"

"I know what we said," said Judy. "But we were both worn-out and it was hot and … well … you know. I've got a surprise for you."

"All right," said Jim. "I'll pick you up at two."

In spite of the fact that Al had been, in a way, expecting it, he seemed thunderstruck.

"God, this is terrible, Jim," he said. "I got to get him out of here right away and that's going to be some job. Wait. I'll get him on the phone. He's living it up at the lake."

It took a long time to contact Tom; meanwhile Al sat tearing a cigar to shreds and Jim paced restlessly.

Finally Tom came on and Al told him about the subpoena. Jim could hear Tom roaring down the phone at his brother and at last Al turned to Jim in despair and said: "He says I'm an old woman. He says I'm crazy. He says I'm a goddamned sissy. He says …" Suddenly he yelled into the phone: "Goddamn it, all right, if you want to get dragged up in front of the Grand Jury and put under oath. Yes, yes, yes ...! Here," yelled Al, handing Jim the phone. "Talk to him."

"What is all this crap, Jimmy boy?" yelled Tom Patton.

"The Grand Jury's going to issue a subpoena, Tom," said Jim. "We've got a damned good tipster."

"Not just another one of those stupid rumors, is it? Al's always shaking like a bone-fed dog. Can't put no trust in him. Listens to all the scaredy cats. Always did."

"No, it's not a rumor," said Jim. "Al asked me to look into it. *He* heard rumors. He retained me, in fact, Tom—just doing a job."

"You really believe it, oh, Jimmy boy?"

"I do. It might not happen. Something might come up to kill it. You know how those things are. But I wouldn't take any chances, Tom. You can always come back."

"Well, at least you talk some kind of sense, goddamn it," yelled Tom, "and don't sound like you're shaking in your boots. Okay. Put that old-maid brother of mine back on."

Al took the phone and spoke into it quickly. "Okay Tom. Hold on a minute." Then he turned and offered Jim his hand. "Thanks, boy. You sure earned your money. I'll be talking to you."

Jim shook hands with Al and left.

As Jim passed from the empty supper room—empty, that is, except for a few hopeful waiters and busboys—into the far end of the bar Tully Burke detained him at the archway.

"It's every night now," he said, "You must like my new arrangements."

"I do, I do," said Jim, smiling; Tully always amused him.

"I say to my arrangers, now, look, boys, nothing raucous or discordant; above all, nothing original," Tully was explaining, "we must never, oh, never, offend anyone. We must not make them think. We must not make their feet tap. The music should go right in one ear and out the other, but soothingly. Dig, dad, dig ...?"

As Tully went on, improvising, as he would have explained, Jim saw Zena talking and laughing with a little pale-faced man with clipped black hair, who was sitting alone in booth number one, the preferred booth at Volari's, usually reserved for prominent customers of long standing or "celebrities". Zena was really laying herself out to charm. A new Zena, to Jim.

"... since you're not listening," he heard Tully say, "I'll fold up my fiddle case and go see the Union."

"I'm listening," said Jim.

But Tully shrugged and walked away. Jim stopped for a moment to pass a few words and say good night to Gino and Gus. Judy accompanied him as far as the checkroom.

"Two?" asked Judy.

"Yeah. I'll be parked down the street. You know."

"Okay," said Judy.

"Zena's really putting on an act," he couldn't help saying.

"Oh, that's her new boyfriend, Mr. Mount. He travels for some big chemical firm. Rich. But what a creep!"

"Odd-looking gent," said Jim.

"You ought to see his clothes," said Judy. "Silk gabardine shirts—all tailored, with monograms yet. Never wears the same suit twice. Got a big Alfa—not a Julietta."

"Wow," said Jim, sardonically.

Judy studied his face. "You think that means anything to me? I wouldn't pass the time of day with that creep. Oh, I got to be going. Here comes Gino. See you."

Jim left. Chauncey saw him coming and went out into the middle of the street to whistle for a cab, and until it came Jim and Chauncey stood at the curb quietly talking baseball. Chauncey was a good ball player and had even had some pro offers but they hadn't been large enough to shake his determination to graduate from State University.

Jim worked at the Willey case hour after hour, sitting in a corner of the breakfast nook, with a pot of coffee beside him, and a huge glass ashtray full of cigarette butts at his elbow. He had all of the windows open and he could hear faintly the clamor of the sweltering city. There wasn't a breath of air; all the curtains hung limp.

Little by little the clamor died away till all he could hear was the occasional hooting of a taxi and the shriek of brakes as cars pulled up at a nearby stoplight. At long intervals a towboat whistle moaned on the river, a melancholy sound that brought the past back so sharply to Jim that in spite of all he could do he found himself forgetting Mr. Aldus Willey and his multifarious trials and tribulations and remembering how it had been on those hot summer nights over thirty years ago in the old ramshackle cottage on the lake. Similar whistles had moaned on the lake there, while he was lying in his bed unable to sleep because he was so pleasantly excited about what had happened during the day and what was going to happen the next day. The sounds of sedate conversation drifted in from the verandah; his father and grandfather were playing cribbage, while his mother and his grandmother talked—about dresses, and last week's dancing party at the Boat Club.

All gone; just as if they had never been.

Jim got up abruptly to pour himself a drink, but glanced at his watch

first, then changed his mind. It was nearly one-thirty. He quickly
stuffed all of the remains of Mr. Willey back into his briefcase, put it
away on a shelf in the closet, then went in to take a shower and change
to fresh clothes.

A stuffy lukewarm wind was beginning to blow across the city now,
and the bathroom curtains stirred limply, then ballooned out for a
moment.

Jim wiped his face with a bath towel and cursed the heat. Had it
ever been this hot in late August when he was a boy? Not as he
remembered it, certainly.

Jim sat in his Ford waiting for Judy. He was turned half around in
the front seat, with his legs up, smoking. In a moment, the big golden
Volari's sign went off, leaving a much-dimmed street. There was a
faint hint of coolness in the air now as a mist moved in from the
direction of the river; and all the streetlights were wearing blurred
yellowish halos.

Now Jim saw Judy emerge from the side door of Volari's and got out
to greet her. She came toward him, with rapid grace, her high heels
tapping a loud tattoo in the stillness.

"Hi," said Jim; then he helped her in. "What's the big mystery?"

"You tell me," said Judy, as he got in.

He turned and looked at her. "I thought you said you had a surprise."
He felt vaguely, and rather childishly, disappointed.

"Oh, I have," said Judy. "I didn't know you meant that."

"What did you think I meant?"

"Oh," said Judy, "something's going on back there. I don't know what."

"At Volari's?"

"Yes. Al sent Gino home early. Don't ask me why. And Gus has been
in and out of Al's office all evening. I don't think Gus has ever so much
as been in there before. What's it all about, Jim?"

"How should I know?"

"Zena says you'd know. Says that you and Al have been cooking up
something."

"Zena's crazy," said Jim, irritably. "Where is she, anyway?"

"That's part of the surprise," said Judy. "Gino let her off about twelve.
She's going up to the lake with Mr. Mount for Saturday, Sunday and
Monday. Got a girl to take her place. Gone by now. So we'll have the
apartment to ourselves. But that's not all. Wait."

Jim drove off in the direction of Judy's apartment, feeling better
now—after all, there really was a surprise of some kind; and he'd had
none for a long time—no pleasant ones, that is; but he was a little
worried about all the commotion at Volari's. He was positive that it

had something to do with getting Tom Patton out of town, and he did not have very much faith in Al Patton's astuteness. Silly to cause so much talk among the help.

"Why don't you tell me about it, Jim?" asked Judy, rather reproachfully. "You can trust me."

"I don't know anything about it," said Jim, firmly. "Why do you listen to that rattle-headed Zena?"

"Frankly I don't know," said Judy. "But she can really get a person steamed up."

"It's probably nothing, anyway."

"Maybe not," said Judy. "That place is just like a small town. Rumors, rumors, rumors—and such gossip; from morning till night. The last bit was, that Al's broke and is closing the place."

"I heard that one from Tully," said Jim. "Al, I'm pretty sure, is far from broke."

Jim parked the car down the street from Judy's apartment, and they walked to the entrance arm in arm. "Feel that air?" asked Judy. "It's cooling off. Oh, it will be delightful up there."

"Up where?"

"Never mind. Surprise."

The little elevator shot them upward to the sixth floor. Judy handed Jim her key, talking rather excitedly; Jim unlocked the door and opened it, then turned to look at Judy in surprise. Mr. Mount, who'd been pacing back and forth in the living room, was staring at them blankly.

Zena rushed in from some place, almost tripping over three traveling bags on the floor.

"I thought you'd be gone," said Judy.

"And I thought you'd wind up at Jim's," said Zena. "Allen's been expecting a call the last hour or so. It's important."

"Well, no harm done," said Judy. "Come on in, Jim."

Jim entered, glanced at Zena but said nothing. He felt nervous, as he'd been completely unprepared for this unpleasant encounter. He'd never liked Zena, and he certainly did not like the looks of her new boyfriend.

"This is Mr. Mount," said Judy. "Mr. Chase."

The man shook hands gingerly. "They go on calling me 'Mount,' these girls," said Zena's new boyfriend, "but my name's Mond. Allen Mond."

"Oh, my God," said Zena. "Excuse me, Allen. Why didn't you tell me before?"

"It's no great matter. How are you, Chase?"

"Fine. You?"

"Damned irritated. We're trying to get away to the lake and this knucklehead that works for me … oh, well. I won't bother you with it."

Zena rushed out to make some drinks and Judy followed her to the Pullman kitchen.

Jim and Mond sat down, Jim on the sofa, Mond on a chair opposite him. Mond was wearing a beautifully tailored brown silk suit, a pale-pink silk shirt, and a narrow brown tie. Everything he had on was expensive, from his gold tie-clip to his handmade shoes. Jim's clothes were also expensive, but far from new, while Mond shone with newness from tip to toe.

He had an odd narrow pale face and slitted eyes, almost Oriental in appearance. His beard was heavy, and, closely shaved, it looked pale blue owing to the unusual whiteness of his skin. His upper lip was long, his mouth wide and very firm, as if he kept it permanently compressed. Jim couldn't make him out at all. When he looked at Mond he thought of gambling … or maybe the theatre, but only vaguely. It was something else … but what?

Just as Zena came with the tray of drinks, the phone rang, and Mond answered it at once.

"Mond here," he said, then listened imperturbably for some time. "Good. All right. You know where to contact me. Fine." He hung up, then turned to all of them with a smile that did nothing to light up his face. "Well, all's well that ends well. A stirrup cup and we'll be on our way."

They took the drinks from the tray and drank in silence, then goodbyes were said, and Zena and Judy hugged each other perfunctorily.

When the door had closed on Zena and Mond, Judy said: "Sorry, Jim. But I couldn't help it."

"It's okay," said Jim. "But that's an odd bird of some kind."

"Zena always winds up with odd birds."

"Probably because she's one herself," said Jim.

"Maybe," said Judy. "A funny thing. I'm surprised Zena didn't ask you what was going on at Volari's. She was so sure you knew."

"Maybe on account of Mond being here," said Jim. "She probably figured she'd hear it from you later."

"Yes," said Judy. "That must be it. And now for the surprise. Come on."

"Where?"

"Follow me," said Judy, laughing.

They left the apartment and walked down the hall to a door at the end. "Open it," said Judy, indicating the door. "It's heavy."

Jim opened the door and they climbed one narrow flight of stairs to another door. Jim glanced at Judy, who was smiling mischievously, then pushed open the second door. He felt a damp wind on his face, saw a string of blurred lights, far off. They were on the roof.

Judy moved past him. "Come on," she said, and he followed her to a corner of the roof, where there were three big comfortable deck chairs, a low metal coffee table and a little cabinet for drinks.

"Well!" said Jim, somewhat let down, not knowing what else to say, as Judy seemed so pleased with herself.

"We're good tenants," said Judy. "Have one of the best apartments in the place and pay on the dot. So the manager fixed this up for us. Nice? We can sunbathe without going all the way out to the lake. There's a canvas thing, right over there—we can stretch it across and make sort of a little room. We can sit up here at night, if we like—our own little open-air penthouse. Look how far you can see."

He had noticed many times how pleased Judy could be with simple things. At the moment he felt sorry for her, and at the same time irritated with himself. Why should he feel sorry for Judy, with her happy nature? And what was wrong with being pleased with simple things?

They leaned their elbows on the parapet and stood looking out over the vast, sprawling city. Streets angled off below them in every direction, the streetlights mere pinpoints of yellow, in regular patterns, like gold embroidery on an immense dark coverlet. Far to the north they could see the bluish-white glow of the North River Freeway and the dim-gold light garlands of the huge Upper River bridge. A vast solitude of silence hemmed them in on their height, punctuated at long intervals by vague sounds from below. A whistle moaned on the river.

"I like to hear the whistles," said Judy. "I used to like to hear them at home. Freight trains. The tracks were only about a half mile behind our house. One of my brothers was a brakeman for a while—Link."

Jim took out his cigarettes and they lit up.

"Oh," said Judy, "I forgot the liquor. I'll go back and get it."

"Never mind the liquor," said Jim. "Let's sit down."

"How do you like my surprise?" asked Judy, as they settled themselves side by side in the deck chairs.

"Fine," said Jim. "Nice up here. Cool, right now. Quite a relief."

The whistle sounded again on the river.

"It's almost like the freight train whistles," said Judy. "I don't like those diesel horns on the streamliners. Do you?"

"No," said Jim. "Not particularly." After a pause, he asked: "Do you think about home a lot, Judy?"

She looked at him in surprise. "What do you mean?"

"Well … you mentioned the train whistles."

"Oh, I see. Well, not so much anymore. Not like I used to when I first come here. But everybody thinks about home, don't they? No matter how lousy it was—and mine was pretty bad."

"Yes," said Jim. "Everybody does. Were all your people from the South?"

"No," said Judy. "My mother was from Marietta, Ohio. She came down to Memphis to work and met the Old Man. That was a sorry day for her."

"Where is she now?"

"She died about five years ago. I got out right after that. I couldn't take my Old Man and my brothers. Todd—that's my younger brother—came all the way to Cincinnati looking for me once. Funny thing. I saw him on the street and ducked into a doorway. He could have taken me back whether I wanted to go or not. He and the Old Man and Link—they were pretty rough."

"You never expect to go back?"

"For what?" There was a long silence; then she went on: "But I like to think about it. It wasn't all bad, especially when I was a kid and Mom was there. She took no nonsense from the men folks. Drunk or sober, they listened to her." A pause. "How about you, Jim?"

"I'm the last of my family, except for those two boys of mine. I don't even have a home anymore."

"And you miss it?"

"Yes. Sometimes."

A long pause, then Judy said abruptly: "I'm going to Southern California. All the money's out that way now."

This sudden unexpected statement surprised and worried Jim. "I never heard you say anything about going to California before."

"Well," said Judy, "there's nothing for me here." A pause. "I'm not kidding myself about us, Jim. I never have. It was crazy and wild and you were drinking and everybody was throwing money around like confetti, from Jake Webb on down. Now that's over."

Jim sighed and said nothing for a long time. "What about Zena?" he asked, finally.

"Oh, she'll go with me."

"I see."

"You don't see at all. It was my idea. Not Zena's. She likes this town. But if I went, she'd go. You don't know how she depends on me. Sometimes it's like she was a little kid."

"She looks like anything but a little kid to me," said Jim.

"I know," said Judy. "But maybe it's because she never really had any childhood. Her parents died in an automobile accident when she was six. The relatives put her in an orphanage. They were Old Country people—Poles, I think."

Jim did not know what to say. If Judy was serious about going to California, it would leave a definite void in his life, and he'd be even more lonely than he was now. A feeling of anxiety nagged at him. Leaning across Judy, he took her into his arms and kissed her.

"Why do you do that, Jim?" asked Judy. "It doesn't mean anything anymore."

"Doesn't it?"

"Does it?"

They fell silent. Jim got out his cigarettes and they lit up again. The mist from the river grew heavier and now they could feel it brushing their faces, like the touch of infinitely soft, invisible hands.

"Getting too damp for you?" asked Jim, as Judy remained silent.

"Yes," said Judy. "Let's go back to the apartment."

## 3: SATURDAY

Somebody was shaking him by the shoulder. Jim rolled over, opened his eyes, and looked about him foggily. Daylight showed at an unfamiliar window. He rolled over further. Judy, with a bathrobe held sketchily about her, was standing beside the bed, trying to wake him.

Jim felt depressed and with a strong disinclination to facing the new day.

"Somebody on the phone for you," said Judy, her eyes heavy with sleep. "I think it's Al Patton. But I'm not sure. It's only six-thirty." She seemed bewildered as she handed him the phone.

It was Al Patton, all right, but his voice sounded very strange. "Tried you every place, Jim," he said. "Just had to get you. Sorry to call you there. Come over right away, will you? And don't waste any time."

Jim stared at the phone blankly, trying to orient himself, then said. "Wait. Where are you?"

"Here," cried Al, as if Jim should know immediately what that meant. "At the place, for God's sake. Volari's. Come in the alley door—my office."

"All right," said Jim. "I'll be there."

He hung up slowly. Judy was studying him, her eyes showing worry. "You in some kind of trouble, Jim?" she asked.

"No, no," said Jim, hurriedly. "But I've got to leave—right away."

Judy repressed her curiosity, and started for the Pullman kitchen. "I'll make you some coffee. How about breakfast?"

"Haven't got time," said Jim, still half asleep and wondering what it was all about. "Just the coffee."

As he hastily threw on his clothes, he went to the window and looked out: a gray, coolish morning with a heavy river mist hanging low in the deserted street. To the south, a factory whistle blasted in the early morning stillness. Jim wished that he could go back to bed and sleep for hours, sleep till night had fallen again and the lights had come on all over the city.

As soon as Jim saw Al's face he knew that he was in the presence of a catastrophe. Al seemed to have aged and shrunken in a few short hours; his normally pink complexion was whiteish green, his plump cheeks sagged, and his eyes had a dazed look.

"What the hell is the matter, Al?" asked Jim.

"You've got to help me, Jim," cried Al. "You've got to help Tom. Look, the Administration was pretty good to you, boy, and if you've got any gratitude in your heart …"

"Al—wait," said Jim. "I'm working for you, remember? You retained me. It's not a question of gratitude. Now what's the matter?"

Al seemed vastly relieved and sank down at his desk. "Oh, it's a disaster, boy; a real disaster."

Jim sat opposite him. "All right, Al. Tell me."

Al picked up an unlighted cigar and began to shred it, obviously trying to get his thoughts together. "Well," he said, finally, "since Tom was going to be subpoenaed the only thing to do was get him out of town, fast. So Tom figured the best place would be San Francisco. We got cousins out there, in the salvage business. Tom just didn't want to go to some strange town where he didn't know anybody at all … Jim," said Al, suddenly, "did you know Ben Ziegler?"

"Who?"

"Our watchman. The guy who stays here at night. The ex-cop."

"Oh," said Jim. "I know who you mean. I've seen him."

"He had a good record on the force. And he's not like most watchmen. He's only forty years old. And we pay him good. Okay, wouldn't you say? And how about Gus? Wouldn't you say he was all right? A real tough, dependable kid?"

"Yes," said Jim, giving Al a bewildered look. "But what's this got to do with …?"

Al held up shaking hand. "Give me time, Jim. It's pretty complicated."

After a moment's thought, Al rose, pushed aside the huge Chinese screen, opened a hidden panel, which was very large and took up nearly half of the wall, and displayed to Jim's surprised eyes an enormous, impregnable-looking safe, completely out of place in Volari's, such as you might see in a small bank or a big expensive jewelry store.

Jim made no comment.

"Remember when I bought the place from Gino and redecorated? I put this in, then. When we were riding high this safe really carried a load, Jim. We did all of our business here in this back room. Well …

there's nothing much in it now, except tonight's receipts and a few lousy securities. This is where I kept Tom's getaway money. In cash. Two hundred thousand dollars. Getaway money did I say? Tom's roll, I mean, except for a piddling checking account. Don't have to tell you why we transacted our business in cash and didn't use the banks with all their goddamned records. Okay? You follow me?"

"No," said Jim. "Not exactly. Are you trying to tell me that somebody robbed this safe?"

"No," said Al. "I'm telling you I sent Gus and Ben Ziegler up to the lake to deliver that money to Tom. And it never got there. That was five hours ago. Drive should have taken forty minutes or less."

"Good God," said Jim, appalled. "Did they know what they were carrying?"

"No," said Al. "You think I'm crazy? The money was packed in a big black briefcase of Tom's, locked and sealed. I gave 'em a hell of a pitch about the important documents in the briefcase, law stuff, you know, and told them Tom's lawyer was up at the lake and they had to deliver the papers right away."

"Maybe they got in an accident."

Al's eyes lit up, then faded. "No traffic, and with a former squad car cop driving? Does that seem likely?"

"No," said Jim. "Did you report this to the police?"

"Boy, you're not thinking straight."

"Oh, I'm thinking straight all right. I just want to know all the angles."

"Of course I didn't."

"How about the car? Whose was it?"

"Ben Ziegler's. A new Ford."

There was a brief silence, then Jim said: "Well, we've still got friends. How about Cap Ryan?"

"Only if the worst comes to the worst. How could Gus and Ben do such a thing as this? I'd've bet my shirt on those two guys." A pause. "Cap Ryan's in a little trouble right now. Might be on his way out. Judge Weybrecht don't like him."

A long pause. Jim didn't know what to think or say for a moment. Finally he spoke. "What about Tom? He knows of course."

"Knows!" cried Al. "He blames it all on me. Thinks I should have let you bring the money up."

"Al," said Jim, after a moment, "neither one of us is thinking straight. The main object is to get Tom out of town. Can't you scare enough cash to …?"

"Sure, sure," cried Al, his face clearing. "I'm crazy. I'm an idiot."

"All right," said Jim. "Get the money together. I'll take it up to Tom and see that he gets out of town, right away."

"Oh, God, Jim," said Al, "you're saving our lives. We were just stunned, see, stunned." A pause. "Then you come right back here. I need you."

Jim had driven Tom to a good-sized town forty miles north of the city, and they were now at the airport barrier waiting for the Chicago plane to be called.

Tom stood shaking his head. He was taking the whole thing much better than Al, and his big face looked as pink and rosy as usual. "You can see what I've had to put up with for years, can't you, Jimmy boy? That lunkhead brother of mine makes a big deal out of delivering the money. A tough young bartender and an ex-cop, carrying a pistol. He could have sent it by Golden Arrow. He could have brought it up himself. Or given it to you. But, no, it has to be a big mystery, like on television. So what happens? These two guys figure if it's *that* important, they better look into it. So they did. And when they saw all that beautiful moola ... boing ... gone! Jesus, a guy can only stand so much temptation. I blame Al. Nobody else."

Now the flight was being called. Tom turned and shook hands with Jim, then said: "Here's the keys to my cottage. I cleaned it out good, but I was in a hurry. Look through it, will you? Burn any papers you don't like the looks of ... if I left any. And see if you can get that money back."

"What?" said Jim, astonished.

"I need it, I need it," cried Tom. "You think I'm going clear to San Fran and live on my relatives? And tell Al to keep sending me something every month till this thing blows over. What are you looking at? I'm hiring you. Ten per cent of every dollar you get back is yours. And that ain't sugar corn pops for a guy that's out. Well, is it?"

"No," said Jim, thinking how much twenty thousand dollars would mean to him at this all-time low point of his fortunes. "Do I just tell Al this?"

Tom thought for a moment, then he took a card out of his wallet and hastily scribbled a message with his fountain pen. "Here," he said. "And tell Al to do the best he can about the cottage. Either sublease it, or get out of the lease some way. That's his headache. Well, goodbye, Jimmy boy. I got confidence in you; always did have."

"Goodbye, Tom; and good luck."

They shook hands, then Tom turned and walked across the field with the other passengers, toward the plane, swinging his heavy shoulders like a young man, though he was in his late fifties.

Not too long ago Tom Patton had been known around the big town as the Kingmaker. Now he was through; an aging lamster in deep financial trouble. Jim wondered if it had all been worth it to Tom, wondered what his thoughts were as he set out alone on a long exile.

Jim stood at the barrier till the plane took off, then he walked slowly back toward his car. A little man in thick glasses grabbed his arm, startling him.

"Wasn't that Tom Patton?" he asked, excitedly.

Jim shook him off and walked on. The little man dug a worn-looking press card out of his pocket and displayed it.

"We may not be big-town up here," he said, "but we're not asleep."

"Maybe not," said Jim. "But what's that got to do with me?"

"The man you were with—who was he?" demanded the reporter, shooting out the question like a prosecuting attorney.

"My uncle," said Jim.

"Oh, you don't tell me, Mr. Chase," said the reporter. "On your wife's side no doubt."

"You seem to be mixed up all around," said Jim.

"Oh, sure, sure. You want me to print you were up here seeing him off?"

"Print what you like," said Jim. "Go on. *Make* an ass of yourself."

A shadow of indecision crossed the reporter's intent face. Jim hurried on, wondering how in the hell the reporter had known who he was. And then a possible solution occurred to him. The reporter had probably seen him and Tom getting out of the car, and, recognizing Tom—or thinking that he had—had checked the owner's slip in the car.

"All one now, anyway," Jim told himself.

Jim returned to Tom's cottage and checked things over carefully, but Tom, in spite of his haste, had done a thorough job. There wasn't a scrap of paper in the place.

Jim, feeling a little tired now, sat down and smoked a cigarette. His dream of recovering the money and making himself—and Larry—a cool twenty thousand dollars had already exploded. Gus and Ben Ziegler were probably out of the state by now, maybe in Canada. They could be anyplace, for that matter, and perfectly safe. Nobody was looking for them. Al, with his incompetence, had managed to engineer a real mess.

Suddenly a thought struck him and he took out his wallet and looked through it for a telephone number, hardly expecting to find it, because it belonged definitely to the past. It was the number of a shrewd little informer—Marty, who had been a great help to him during the old Administration. To his surprise, he found it.

"Who? Who?" Marty kept asking on the phone. "Jim Chase? For God's sake, Mr. Chase. Is it really you?"

Jim could sense the wariness, the caution in Marty's voice. "Remember the Dempster case—405?" asked Jim.

Marty laughed curtly. "It's you all right. What's up, Chief?"

It was idiotic and maybe a little pathetic, Jim realized, but Marty calling him "Chief" bucked him up considerably. "I want to see you, Marty; right away. Where?"

"As per," said Marty.

"Okay. Give me an hour."

"Like old times," said Marty, sounding pleased.

Just as Jim was getting ready to leave Tom's cottage there was a knock at the door. Probably a door-to-door salesman, a tradesman, the mailman … Jim didn't worry about it, preoccupied as he was running over in his mind what he intended saying to Marty. He opened the door abruptly.

"Yes?"

It was a man, whose eyes showed surprise, then were quickly veiled, when he found himself confronted by Jim.

"I'd like to see Mr. Patton," he said.

"He's not here." Jim studied the man, with the vague feeling that he'd seen him before. He was young, well-dressed, wore glasses. Jim looked off beyond him at a nondescript car parked at the curb.

"When will he be back?"

"I don't know," said Jim. "Now if you'll excuse me, I'm leaving for town."

Then all of a sudden it hit him. The DA's office. He'd seen this man around the Hall of Justice. The subpoena!

Boy, they'd just beaten the gun.

"You have no idea when he'll be back?"

"No," said Jim. "You could wait—in your car, I mean. I don't know what his plans are."

The DA's man did not know what to say or do. Jim watched him with secret amusement. Above all, the DA's man did not want to spill the beans.

"Well, maybe that's best," he said.

"Fine," said Jim. Then he went out and shut the door firmly behind him.

When he started back for town he could see the DA's man in his rearview mirror, standing rather undecidedly at the edge of the curb, smoking a cigarette.

When Jim drove into the big filling station on the southern edge of the west-of-the-river industrial district, Marty was already there, in one of the public phone booths, apparently engaged in an engrossing conversation. Beyond the filling station, which took in nearly half a block, loomed the grimy brick buildings of Polishtown. Jim could remember when this section was the business district and Downtown area of the city; now it had badly run to seed and was crammed with rooming houses, cheap stores, hole-in-the-wall bars, pool rooms, machine shops, dancehalls and round-the-clock movie theatres where weary bums snored the night away.

Marty opened the door of the booth and stepped out. His surprise on seeing Jim was well acted; they shook hands, talked animatedly, then lit cigarettes and leaned against the booth, apparently lost in amiable and harmless conversation.

Marty, an ex-lightweight, had a battered, rather stupid-looking face. But his dark eyes were shrewd and alive.

"If you hear of a real big score, I want to know about it," said Jim.

"Okay. What's with you?"

"I'm practicing law. It's for a client."

"Okay, Chief. What else?"

"Know anything about an ex-cop named Ben Ziegler?"

"Sure. Watchman over at Volari's."

"Anything else?"

"Never on the take, as far as I know. And I never had anything against him one way or another. Straight Joe."

"Ever consort with hoods?"

"No. Hell, no," said Marty, firmly.

"All right," said Jim. "There has been a big one. Big ones get around, one way or another. I'll give you my card." Jim wrote his home phone on his business card and handed it to Marty.

"How's it been going, Marty?"

"I'm starving. The Hall ain't what it used be. I'm on the crap list, I guess. Never get a jingle. Could I tap you for half a yard, Chief?"

"I haven't got it on me," said Jim. "I'll send it to you—cash. Would ten help now?"

"Like water to a guy on the desert. Be careful how you give it to me."

They talked for a while longer, then threw their cigarettes away. A moment later Jim offered Marty his pack again, slipping him a ten-dollar bill at the same time.

"Mail the half yard to Connor's Pool Hall in Kosciusko Street," said Marty. "I'm sweeping out now. Is that a yuck? But a guy's got to eat, Chief. I'll really give you some service for that kind of money. Man, it's been tough since you guys fell. Tough for all of us. Some of the boys who used to flash rolls are in the soup line at the Mission. Wow!"

Jim smiled wryly to himself. It was the same all over the city from top to bottom.

Al, still looking shrunken and greenish, examined the card Tom had given Jim, then handed it back.

"All right," he said. "That's your contract. Now, Jim, give me your honest personal opinion. How much chance have we got to see any of that money again?"

"Damned little," said Jim. "The way we're operating they've got all the advantages. If we called in the police it might be different."

"That's out," said Al, impatiently.

"I know. All right, Al. Let's get down to business. Have you got phone numbers for Gus and Ben Ziegler?"

"Yes," said Al. "I think so." He began to scrabble through his desk drawers, and finally swore loudly, and put on his glasses, as Jim watched him with some impatience, thinking what a bad break it was for old Tom to be saddled with such a brother and to be forced to depend on him in a crisis. "Here," said Al, finally. "In this book."

"Either of them married?" asked Jim.

"No," said Al. "Gus plays the field, I guess, and Ben's divorced."

"They live alone then."

"As far as I know."

Jim called Gus's number first and after a long wait a woman came on.

"Creider's rooming house," she said.

"I'd like to speak to Gus," said Jim.

"Gus Bailey? He's not here anymore."

"Are you sure? He was there yesterday, wasn't he?"

"Look, young man," said the woman with some annoyance, "I run this place. I know what I'm talking about. Gus wasn't here last night, and then a man came and paid his bill and got his clothes. Said he'd been called away."

"I see," said Jim. "What did the man look like who came to get Gus's clothes?"

"Oh," said the woman, "I didn't pay too much attention. Nice looking fellow in his twenties. An Italian, I think. No foreigner, though. I mean, American born. Very polite."

"I see," said Jim. "Thanks." He hung up, repeated the conversation to Al, then asked: "Know anything about Gus's friends?"

"No," said Al. "Nothing."

Jim now called Ben Ziegler's number, with exactly the same result.

"Well," said Jim, "I'll say one thing, Al. Gus and Ben didn't lose their heads. They thought of everything."

"I just can't get over it," said Al. "Those two guys, of all people. I'd've bet my bottom dollar on both of 'em. That's why I sent 'em in the first place."

Jim heaved a long sigh, then he got up and began to pace. "Al," he said, finally, "I want you to think back now. Anything at all out of the way happen here lately? Doesn't matter how little it was. Just something that struck you. Anything."

Al thought for a long time, his brow wrinkled and his lips pursed; finally he sighed and shook his head. "Nothing, Jim. Nothing. Hey, wait a minute. Yes sir, by God. And I sure thought it was funny at the time, then I figured maybe it was my fault. I'm kind of absentminded sometimes. That alley door was unlocked, early last night. I always keep it locked, always; except when I'm expecting somebody after the place is closed. Like when you came."

"I see," said Jim. He thought this over for a long time, then he asked: "Who knew about this safe, Al?"

"Nobody that I know of except Tom and Gino, and, of course, the guys who installed it, and maybe some of the workmen when I was redecorating. Hell, Gino's okay. You know that."

"Yes," said Jim. "We won't worry about him. Now, look, Al, when you got the money out and put it in the briefcase ..."

"But I didn't, Jim. It's always been in the briefcase, locked and sealed."

Jim gave a groan, leaned back in his chair and stared at the ceiling. "I'm stopped, Al. I was thinking that with the door unlocked, without you knowing it, somebody might have been watching you. Me being around here twice in two days after staying away for so long caused quite a lot of comment. Another thing, Al. The place was buzzing last night because you had Gus in your office a few times."

"Oh hell, it's always buzzing," said Al. "I hear all the silly gossip from Gino."

"Got a drink around here?" asked Jim.

Al tossed him his keys and indicated a cabinet on the wall. "I still don't trust myself," said Al, with a sad smile. "So I keep it locked. Silly, eh?—with the key in my pocket."

Jim poured himself a stiff drink and tossed it down. "Al," he said, finally, "there's only one thing to do. We need help. I've got to talk to Cap Ryan, tell him the whole thing."

"You can't, you can't," cried Al, holding his head. "It would bust wide open."

"Not officially, Al. Pat loves Tom. He'll help."

"He's in bad himself, Jim," said Al. "Just because he was such a good friend of Tom's. If those idiots in the City Hall now knew how much trouble that damned Irishman had given us ... honest as the day is long. And here them damned reformers think ... all right, Jim. Maybe you're right. He's a good guy to have on your side."

Jim picked up his hat and started to leave; then a sudden thought stopped him. "Al, what about Gus and Ben? What are you going to tell everybody, from Gino on down?"

"Oh, Jesus," groaned Al. "I never thought of that. What *can* I tell 'em?"

Jim thought this over for a while, then said: "Al, I think it would be a mistake to tell them anything. God knows that might come up later. When they don't put in an appearance tonight you'll be as surprised as everybody else. Have Gino call their homes. Let him be the one to tell the rest of the help. Okay?"

"All right, Jim," said Al, with a groan; then: "God, what a mess!"

"And, Al, keep trying to remember. Anything. Anything at all out of the way. If you do, call me; either at home or the office."

"Okay, Jim. Now I'm going to try to get some sleep. Boy, am I dead."

It was nearly noon when Jim got to the office. Larry was in the anteroom, going over some papers with Gert.

"Well," said Larry, "wow, you look beat."

"Come on in," said Jim. "I've got to talk to you."

Larry glanced at Jim quickly, worry showing in his eyes, and Jim immediately realized that it was one of Larry's apprehensive, unoptimistic days. Well … he'd have to tell him anyway, although it would probably spoil his sleep for a week.

"Any calls, Gert?" asked Jim.

"Yes," said Gert, smiling. "Your son called—Robert."

"What?" cried Jim, staring.

"Yes. Here's the message. I'll read it. 'Don't forget the fungoid bat.' Does that mean something?"

Deeply pleased, Jim laughed loudly and both Larry and Gert turned to look at him. They'd never heard him laugh like that before. 'Fungo' bat," said Jim. "Baseball. They're very light weight. You hit practice flies with them."

"Well, now!" said Gert. "I thought it was some kind of monster. There are two boys live down the hall from me and all they talk about is monsters. 'Fungoid bat' sounded pretty awful to me."

"Anything else?" asked Jim.

"Yes," said Gert, rather primly. "A young lady. Didn't leave her name. Here's the number."

Jim took the slip of paper and glanced at it. Judy!

"Give me a minute, will you, Larry?"

Jim went into his office, closed the door and called Alma's home. Lloyd answered the phone after a long wait.

"Oh, hi, Dad," he said. "Hey, we called you. Bob did, I mean. Wouldn't let me talk. About the bat."

"I'll get it just as soon as I can. I'm awful busy. What are you doing?"

"Eating lunch. Mom's taking a shower." Now a long argument broke out at the other end, there was a crash, then Bob came on: "Hi. We called you about the bat. But don't tell Mom. Andy says he'll get us one, but we said 'no', you'd promised."

"That's right," said Jim. "Just you sit tight."

"It'll be football season pretty soon, you know," said Bob; then the argument started again at the other end and Jim heard: "I'm the oldest, I'll do the talking. Now you stay away, creep, or I'll ..." Suddenly Bob spoke into the phone: "Oh-oh, here comes Mommy." Then Jim heard Alma's voice: "What is this? Who are you talking to?" There was a scraping, ringing noise, then: "Hello. Who is this?"

"It's me," said Jim; and there was dead silence at the other end. "I called about the bat. I'm going to get it for the boys as soon as I have a minute."

"Oh," said Alma. "Well, that's nice."

"Everything okay?"

"Yes," said Alma. "Everything's fine." Her voice sounded guarded but not unfriendly.

Jim laughed. "How's Ole Hoss?"

"Who?"

"Andy. He calls everybody 'Ole Hoss'. Didn't you ever notice?"

"Well, he doesn't call *me* 'Ole Hoss'," said Alma. "He's fine."

Jim wanted to say 'if you need anything call me'; he wanted to say 'why don't you bring the boys in and we'll have lunch, all of us'; he wanted to say 'maybe I'll drop by some Sunday afternoon'; but all he said was: "Well, I won't keep you. Glad everything's okay. 'Bye."

Alma hung up and turned to look at her two sons, who avoided her eyes. "Did you call him, or did he call you?"

Bob hesitated for a moment. "He called us. Didn't you hear the phone?"

But this was much too subtle for Lloyd, who danced about nervously for a moment, then said: "But we called him first. At the office—about the bat. He wasn't there."

Bob hung his head.

"Seems to me," said Alma, "that you are getting a little too smart for your britches, Bob. A little too smart for ten years old. Now listen, both of you. I don't want you calling your father."

"Why?" Bob demanded. "He's our dad, isn't he? Andy's not our dad."

Alma looked into Bob's angry young face in surprise.

"Well, who said he was?"

"I want a dad," said Bob. "At school they said where's your old dad; you haven't got any."

"Bob socked Eddie Priest," cried Lloyd, dancing about in delight. "Oh, man, did he sock him. One, two, three." Lloyd demonstrated, dancing on his toes and punching the air.

"I don't want you fighting, Bob," said Alma. "Fighting never settles anything."

"It sure settled old Ed," said Lloyd, giggling.

"All right," said Bob. "I'm sorry, Mommy."

Jim was talking on the phone with Judy now.

"Are you okay, Jim?" she was asking.

"Sure, I'm okay."

"Sorry about calling you at the office, but, Jim, really you looked awful when you got up this morning."

"Well, gee, thanks."

"No, I mean—so pale and drawn. You looked better after the coffee, but I just got to worrying, so … go to bed early tonight. Will you, Jim? And I'll get a good rest, too. It'll be rough tonight at Volari's—Saturday."

"Okay, Judy," said Jim, feeling both relief and disappointment. "Call you Sunday. Bye."

It was a good thing that Jim had insisted that Larry take a stiff drink first. He'd heard it all now and he was jumping about like a fly, as all-to-pieces, for the moment, as old Al Patton.

"But, good God, Jim! If this ever hits the papers … wow!"

"You want me to handle it alone? I mean, not make it an office matter at all. The way I see it, if I collect, half of it is yours. It would really set us up, Larry—get us in the black."

"Jim, you're kidding yourself. This is hopeless. Aside from that, you might get your head blown off. With two hundred grand at stake? Wow! Besides, Jim—think, man, think—those guys are in Canada or maybe even California by now."

"Then where's the harm in trying?"

Larry sank down at Jim's desk and took his head in his hands. "All right, Jim. All right."

"And put that tipster of yours to work if he's got any underworld connections. News of a big one travels around. These guys had help. At least there's a third guy, who picked up their clothes and checked out for them."

"My tipster's out," said Larry, sadly. "He's a police officer. But I've got a couple of other ideas. Let me think. Meanwhile, what about Aldus Willey?"

"I'm working on it," said Jim. "We've got all the time in the world with him. Hopeless, anyway."

"Wow," said Larry. "This was a nice quiet peaceful day till you showed up."

Pat Ryan had been more than a little surprised to hear from Jim, but had agreed to meet him in a back-room at Clancy's On-The-River, one of the oldest restaurants in town. Once it had been a hangout for out-of-work stevedores from the Hiring Hall on the corner; but the Hiring Hall had burned down over fifteen years ago, stevedore activity had moved further south, and now Clancy's was in the center of the honky-tonk, striptease district.

Clancy's, at least, had not changed, and it looked good to Jim, with its dark woodwork, its stained and misted mirrors, and its good beery, cooked meat smell.

Pat was waiting, with a stein of beer at his elbow, and eating a huge corned beef sandwich with obvious relish. About forty, he was short, wide-shouldered and swarthy, with Italian black hair and an impudent-looking, turned-up nose.

"Whatever it is, Jim," he said, "I can't help you much. I'm just hanging on by the skin of my teeth. A little bird whispered to me this morning I might be transferred to Smoketown, special security—and you know what that means. How about food?"

Jim ordered the same. Under the old Administration Capt. Pat Ryan had been the dreaded boss of the 17th Precinct Station. Lately he'd been moved back to Downtown and put in charge of homicide, quite a comedown. Now, apparently, the new bunch was cooking up worse for him, hoping he'd resign. They had probably found out by now that there were no charges on which they could fire him. Pat was very tough and had been criticized for it, but that was the most that could be said against him.

They talked desultorily till Jim's order came, then Jim laid his cards on the table and told Pat the whole story from beginning to end. Pat just sat shaking his head, groaning, and saying: "Oh, no!" quietly.

"Well, that's it," said Jim. "What do you think?"

"First," said Pat, "I think Al Patton is a fool. Always did think so. Second, I don't believe it in the first place."

Jim smiled in spite of himself. "You don't believe what, Pat?"

"There's something wrong with that story," said Pat. "Now let me say this. I knew Ben Ziegler pretty well. Of course, I'll admit I haven't seen him lately and he may have took to drink or cheap women or something; and I'll admit he did get a little insubordinate on the force and finally quit—he wasn't fired; or in any trouble. This just doesn't sound like him, Jim. Not the Ben Ziegler I know. He could have been had, you know."

"What do you mean?"

"This Gus guy. Guessing what was in that satchel—that briefcase—and knowing Ben wouldn't go for anything crooked, he might have blasted him, then dumped his body someplace."

Jim shook his head. "I doubt it. Gus has been working for Volari's for six or seven years. He was there before Al bought the place. A real nice fellow. I knew him pretty well. Besides, Ben was carrying a gun. Gus wasn't."

"As far as you *know*, he wasn't," said Pat. "Besides, this Gus might have had help. I know it was on the spur of the moment and all that, but according to your story Gus was in and out of Al's office a lot that night, and you don't know what Al said or how much he talked. I wouldn't trust Al to run a church social. I told Tom that once. He got very red in the face and swelled up—remember how old Tom used to do?—then he started to laugh and told me a long-winded story about when they were kids and Al, playing William Tell, shot the lady next door right in the bull's-eye with his arrow. Tom said you could hear her screech clear across the river." Pat laughed, shook his hand, and drained his stein.

"I don't buy this Gus story, Pat," said Jim. "I don't think he's smart enough and calculating enough to pull a deal like this. He's a tough kid, all right; but in a nice way, like a lot of pugs we've known, Pat."

"Well, you know him and I don't," said Pat. "But you'd be surprised in my business how many times that is a drawback. We pull in a rapist, or a child molester, and his wife shows up, indignant as hell. How could we ever think that her darling Bobby ... you know the rest."

"Could you look Gus up some way?" asked Jim, finally; realizing that Pat was right in regard to how wrong you could be about somebody you saw every day. "He might have a record."

"Yeah," said Pat. "I can do that for you, on the quiet. Give me all the data you've got on him."

Later, after they'd ordered a couple more steins of beer, Pat said: "You know there's something a little *too* smooth about all this. That young guy checking them out and taking their clothes, so nobody around where they lived would start asking questions. Does that sound like the way a couple of novices would work—especially when the score was a real big one? They usually panic. That's the way they get caught."

"Ben was a former cop, Pat," said Jim. "I didn't know him, but I've seen him around and he didn't strike me as the kind of man who would panic very easily."

Pat reached across the table and took hold of Jim's forearm. "Jim," he said, "believe me, I've got a nose for things like this and something smells wrong. We haven't got the whole story. I'd bet my bottom dollar on it. If I didn't know Al so well, I'd begin to suspect that he rigged the whole thing so he could grab Tom's two hundred grand; then hired you to make it look good."

Jim sat back and stared at Pat in consternation. "Good Lord, Pat!"

"Goddamn it, Jim," said Pat, "keep it in mind. Listen to me. Two hundred grand is one hell of a lot of money. Husbands, wives, daughters and sons have been killed for much less. Maybe that defeat shook old Al all up. Maybe he's a little off his rocker."

"It shook him up all right," said Jim; "but, Pat, if that's true how about Ben Ziegler? He'd have to be a part of it."

"I wouldn't believe it till it was proved to me," said Pat, "but it's not impossible. Nothing is, with that kind of money at stake."

They sat in silence for a long time; then finally Pat spoke. "Jim, all I'm saying is, there's something wrong with the story some place. It shows premeditation—planning—and yet there was damned little time for it. And according to Tom, neither Gus nor Ben knew there was any money in the briefcase. Jim, I just can't buy it." Now he glanced at his watch. "Got to get home and look at a couple of TV programs with my kids. Promised them. I'll look up Gus Bailey. I'll help any way I can, within reason, because I loved that old windbag, Tom Patton. But let me say this. You've got a wrong story of some kind. And I doubt very much if you ever see a cent of that money."

Jim's phone was ringing as he unlocked the door and entered his apartment. He felt dog-tired, nervous and depressed; he'd been on the go since six-thirty that morning. He could hardly hold his eyes open and all the way back from Clancy's he kept thinking about how good his bed was going to feel.

The phone quit ringing before Jim could get to it, which exasperated him so that he flung his hat on the floor and began to stomp and swear, before he realized that he was acting like a child, and stopped.

"Hell, I'm really bushed," he said. "I'd better hit the sack fast."

But the phone began to ring again, just as he had started to take off his shoes. It was Marty.

"I put the money in the mail this afternoon," said Jim. "Okay?"

"Okay. Chief, we better have a talk." Marty was speaking very low, his voice guarded. "As per."

Jim groaned to himself. "Tonight?"

"Anytime you say. I may have something. Big."

"All right Marty. But some place closer if you can make it. I'm bushed. RD?"

"Got it."

Jim hung up, groaning, and began to put his clothes back on.

"RD" was the old Rollerdrome, now condemned and about to be pulled down. It was around a mile and a half from Jim's apartment. As he didn't want to get his car out again, he picked up a cab at the stand of a small hotel on a corner near his apartment.

Half a block down from the Rollerdrome he had the cab park and wait. To his relief, Jim saw a dark figure pacing up and down, smoking a cigarette, in front of one of the darkened arcades.

"I got lucky, hitched in," said Marty. "Them buses … what schedules!"

"Did you hear something?"

"I did. Don't know if this is it. But it was one hell of a big score. A vault job. A new sharpie around town, and maybe two or three local boys."

"That couldn't be it," said Jim, "if you mean a break-in."

"That's the way I heard it. Hell, Chief, I'm sorry, but you didn't tell me …"

Jim suppressed his irritation and stood for a moment in silence, smoking. Marty kept glancing at him rather apprehensively. He didn't want the Chief sore at him. Hell, he hadn't made a score this big for months and months. He'd been going for ones and fives.

"Marty," said Jim, finally, "did you ever hear anything in particular about Volari's?"

"I sure did," said Marty; then he laughed. "Plenty of the boys have talked about cracking that place, but never could figure out how."

It had been a mere shot in the dark. Jim was so startled that he couldn't speak for a moment. "Cracking it? What do you mean?"

"Oh, hell, it was headquarters," said Marty. "So the boys figured the payoffs were made there, so they figured cash was kept around. But nobody ever tried it as far as I know."

"Any talk lately?"

"Not that I've heard," said Marty. "You want to brief me?"

"No."

"Well, you asked me about Ben Ziegler, remember? Now you ask me about Volari's. I'm getting the idea something's up. I'll keep it in mind. Am I on the payroll?"

"Yes," said Jim.

It was not much after nine o'clock when Jim finally managed to get to bed. He was so tired that muscles in his legs kept twitching and he found it almost impossible to relax. It was very warm, and the night sounds blared in through his open windows: the beeping of horns, the whoosh of bus air brakes, the bump and rattle of big trucks, and the tinny jangle of surface-car bells: solo voices, against a constant vague bass rambling, the true voice of the city.

Jim closed his bedroom windows to shut out the sounds but the room immediately became stuffy, so he opened them again and lay smoking a cigarette and staring at shifting patterns of light on the ceiling. One pattern, which moved erratically, darting here and there, slowly began to take on the shape of a little boat with sails ... the sky turned from gray to blue. It was very hot in the sun. Above, the sails bellied and whipped, and with a loud laugh one of the girls deliberately fell overboard. "Now, damn it," cried Hugh Ambrose, who, for some weird reason, had gray hair now, "why did she have to do that! Put her about, Jim." Then Hugh, in his immaculate white duck pants, dove off the stern into the quiet green water ... a ship's bell tolled faintly ...

Jim woke with a start, and looked about him for Hugh who should have come back aboard long ago. Then he groaned, fully awake, switched on the light and looked at his watch. A quarter of twelve. He couldn't believe it. It seemed to him that he'd just barely closed his eyes, and hadn't slept at all.

What had awakened him?

The night sounds were still coming in the windows, but with less volume as the hour grew late. Jim switched off the light and was just getting out a cigarette when the phone rang. So that was it! Vaguely he remembered having heard a faint ringing sound earlier, but it had seemed part of the dream.

It was Judy.

"Were you asleep, Jim?"

"Yes. I went to bed at nine o'clock."

"Sorry to bother you, but I thought you ought to know. I'm in the ladies' so I'll have to talk fast. I don't know what's going on here, Jim— but Al got you out of bed at six-thirty this morning, so I'm putting two and two together that you and Al have got problems. Well, Gus didn't show up tonight. Gino called his home and he's gone; moved out. Wait. Ben Ziegler didn't show. He comes in at ten-thirty usually. Gino called his home, and he's gone, too. Crazy. You should hear the talk around here. After all, something was going on last night, with Gus in and out of Al's office—I mean, it's causing talk ... Jim, I got to go. I hear somebody coming. Bye, honey."

"Bye. Thanks."

Jim hung up, then sat staring at the floor for a long time, lost in thought; finally he called Al's office. Al answered at once, sounding jittery.

"Al? Jim. Can you talk?"

"Yes, I'm alone, Jim. And is the fat in the fire!"

"Judy just called me about Gus and Ben. She doesn't know anything at all, of course. She just wondered. Al, this may be tougher than we thought. There may be a police investigation, if anybody makes out a missing person report. So we've got to have a straight story. Why was Gus in your office so much last night? That is what is causing the talk."

"Well, he ..." stammered Al. "I was giving him instructions."

"I know," said Jim. "But think up a story. It was very unusual for him to be there. Could it be something about the tabs? A lot of people owe you bar tabs, Al—like me. Would that do?"

"Yeah, yeah. Great," said Al.

"Business has not been so good," said Jim. "Put it that way, if necessary. Then say you were talking to Gus about extending further credit to some, like me, say—and shutting it off from others, making them pay cash until their accounts are settled up. Okay?"

"Wonderful, fine," cried Al, gratefully.

"Of course it may all die down," said Jim. "But if it doesn't we are prepared. Wait a minute. Better still. Get me in this. I'm your lawyer. You called me in to ask my advice about how to handle the collections— after all, it's a delicate matter, Al; a lot of big guys owe you. Okay?"

"Perfect, Jim, perfect," said Al. "I'm breathing easier already."

"Call me if you need me," said Jim. "I'm home. But let me sleep tonight if possible. I'm really bushed."

"I was thinking about calling you earlier," said Al. "But, hell ... I figured you'd had it for the day. A guy can only go so long. Call you tomorrow if anything happens."

Jim hung up, went back to bed and lay for a long time with his hands under his head, staring at the ceiling. This could turn into quite a mess, and might hit the headlines. If a missing person report was made, the police might take this opportunity to dig very deep into Al Patton's affairs, and Jim had absolutely no faith whatever in Al's ability to look after himself. In fact, if Al got careless and didn't keep his head this might turn into the big blowoff that the reformers had been looking for ever since they took office. They'd moved slowly, cautiously, guided by the astute old judge, Harley Weybrecht. At last, after all this time, they'd issued a subpoena for Tom Patton to appear before the Grand Jury—a very bad sign.

Jim felt confused. The issues at stake were just not clear to him. He had none of the black-and-white mentality of Judge Weybrecht, and of his own grandfather, old Judge Weldon Chase. A "perfectly clean" city— as the Reformers had put it during their whirlwind campaign—was a sheer impossibility, an idealistic dream, a doctrinaire fantasy, or nightmare. Human nature was human nature; wishing and yearning could not change it; nor could all the theories of all the well-meaning idealists of the world. As long as men wanted women for a night, there'd be prostitution; and where there is big scale prostitution there is corruption of venal police and officials. As long as men wanted to gamble, there'll be gaming houses and the "numbers" and bookies; a dedicated army couldn't stop it. Unpopular laws are almost impossible of real enforcement.

Jim, rightly or wrongly, felt more at home with Tom Patton, than he did with Judge Weybrecht, because, whether he liked it or not, Tom seemed much closer to common humanity than the Judge, therefore more realistic in viewpoint and better able to grapple with the basically insoluble problem of running an immense city. There was plenty of graft during the Tom Patton regime, but Tom knew it—took some of it himself—and tried to keep it from getting out of hand. Under the old judge, there would still be graft and corruption, only the judge wouldn't know about it until it was too late and his administration had got a sudden and completely unexpected black eye. To talk about a city of a million people as being without graft or corruption, was to speak as a child, or as a doctrinaire completely out of touch with the human condition.

"In other words," Jim told himself wryly, "I don't know right from wrong." This was a gross exaggeration, of course; but in a conventional sense, he could have been taxed with it.

Finally he slept, where little by little the sounds of the city died down to a vague continuous whisper, punctuated now and then by the hooting of a taxi, the shriek of brakes, or the blast of a tug whistle on the wide, black, slow-flowing river. The moon set; the stars went out one by one; a smoky pink showed in the east; then a vague gray light began to spread through the dark deserted city canyons, while high up the windows of the tall buildings caught the first red beams of dawn.

A new day. Jim slept on.

## 4: SUNDAY

It was after twelve noon by the time Jim had showered, shaved and had his breakfast. Sunshine was flooding in all of the windows; the sky was blue; and there was a cool breeze blowing up from the river. Church bells were ringing all over town. Summer ... as Jim remembered it from the past. Summer ... as it seldom was anymore; or so it seemed to him. There wasn't a cloud in the sky; and the wind had blown the smog away. Below him, the old street was checkered with sun and shade, and almost deserted; what little traffic there was moved leisurely.

Jim felt fine. The long sleep had set him up, and the usual morning worries had put in but a token appearance and then had vanished. He felt a strong desire to escape from the city; from Al and his worries; from Larry; yes, from Judy, too, though he'd hardly admit that to himself. One day of escape, one day of pretense that all was well and that there was a solution for every human ill, and that life was just "a bowl of cherries," as they'd said in the Twenties.

Snapping his fingers suddenly, he called Gert at home.

"Hi, Gert."

"Well, you sound bright," said Gert. "Just got back from church. Can you say the same?"

"No," said Jim. "Tell me something. Where do you think a man might find a fungo bat on Sunday?"

There was a brief silence at the other end. "A what? Oh yes, I remember. Try one of the big chain drugstores."

"Thank you, Gert. I don't know what we'd do without you. See you Monday. Oh, by the way, Larry said you were arranging for a call service. Is it arranged?"

"Yes," said Gert, and gave him the number. "I don't get it. You're not so busy that you have to be found anytime of the day or night."

"We might be."

"We hope."

Jim drove all over town, trying to find a fungo bat in various chain drugstores. He found bats of all shapes, weights and sizes, much to his surprise—but no fungo bats. He was assured on all sides that he'd have to wait until the sporting goods stores opened on Monday morning. But he kept trying, and finally in a chain store that was part of a huge shopping center in a far West Side suburb he found what he was looking for. He was so delighted that he bought three, just in case "the boys broke a couple," as he explained to the salesgirl, who thought he was a little dotty and was very bored with him before he left. "All that fuss over some old football bats," she said to another salesgirl.

Jim drove back to his apartment to make a few phone calls, after carefully locking the precious bats in the luggage compartment.

First he called Alma's house. She came on at once.

"Hi. It's me," said Jim.

"Jim?" said Alma, sounding faintly surprised.

"I got those bats."

"Those what? Oh. I don't believe it."

"Where are the kids?"

"They're out front, screaming and yelling."

"You going to be home this afternoon?"

"Yes," said Alma. "Andy might drop over, or he might not. He's playing golf. When he loses, he hates himself and doesn't want to talk to anybody. But we'll be here."

"Good. Don't let the kids get away and don't tell them I'm coming."

"All right, Jim."

"How about early supper? If I remember right, on Sundays in the old days ..."

"Yes, Jim, fine," said Alma, rather hastily, he thought, then she hung up.

Before he left for Upper River, he called Marty, Pat Ryan and Al Patton and gave them his new call service number in case they couldn't reach him at the regular places; then, just as he was coming out the front door, the phone rang. His first impulse was to ignore it, to get out and away from all claims and responsibilities, at least for one day. But finally, swearing to himself, he answered.

Judy!

"I thought you were going to call me, Jim," she said. "It's after two o'clock."

"Well, I slept late," said Jim. "Then went out for breakfast. I just got back."

"Then you got a good sleep. Fine. I kicked myself for calling you last night, after I'd told you to get a good sleep. But it was really crazy around Volari's. I'm sorry."

Jim felt like a heel. Didn't know what to say. "Oh, that's all right."

"Anything the matter, Jim? You sound funny."

"No, no. Everything's fine."

"Look honey," said Judy, "it's such a wonderful day—nicest day we're had for months, so why don't I pack up some vittles and you pick me up and we'll go up the river to one of those little parks and have a picnic? Okay?"

Jim groaned to himself. At any other time he'd have jumped at the suggestion. "Judy," he said, slowly, "I'm sorry. I can't."

"Why?" cried Judy. "It's Sunday. Don't tell me you have to work on a brief or something like that."

"No," said Jim, "it's not that."

"You mean I'm not going to see you?"

"Not till tonight."

There was a pause, then Judy spoke in a rather cold, curt voice. "Would it be presumptuous of me if I asked why?"

Jim hesitated for a long time, then made up his mind to tell her the truth. "Judy," he said, "I'm sorry, but I promised the boys I'd ..."

"Oh," said Judy, quickly, "well, okay then. See you around. Maybe Monday. We're going to be very busy tonight, and I'll be tired. Bye."

She hung up. Jim paced for a moment, then reached for the phone to call her back. After all, Judy—not Alma—had gone through all the rough part with him. But suddenly he remembered the laboriously acquired bats—and the kids.

"Oh, well," he said to himself, "I don't blame her for being sore. But she'll get over it. She always does."

All the same he did not feel right about it, and, in a sense, his day was spoiled.

That is, he thought it was, till he saw the looks on the faces of his two sons when he dragged not one but three fungo bats out of the luggage compartment of his Ford.

"Wowee!" cried Bob. "Neat! Neat!"

Lloyd's pale blue eyes bugged. In a moment the boys were quarreling over the bats, crying: "This one's mine. This one's mine."

Jim let them quarrel, but finally Alma broke it up.

"A fine spectacle this is," she said. "Three bats, two boys; and both of you want the same one."

"I'm the oldest. I get first choice," yelled Bob.

"Jim," said Alma, "put the bats back in the car. These boys aren't old enough for them yet. They are only babies."

"No, no," screamed Bob and Lloyd, appalled.

And finally things quieted down a little and the boys went inside and after a few minutes of dickering, Bob wound up with the "choice" bat, and Lloyd with the other two.

Jim thought this was very funny and kept laughing.

"Oh, we made some trades," said Bob, mysteriously.

They ate supper at a little place out over the water, about five miles north of Upper River. They were in the open air, with a big canvas marquee over them. Water slapped at the pilings just below them. There were candles in bottles on the tables and checkered tablecloths. The boys had never been there before. They thought it was very "neat".

Twilight drifted in over the river, and the lights of the far shore came on, making yellow zigzag reflections in the black water. One of the Sunday excursion boats, with all its portholes lighted, slid past in the middle of the stream. They could hear music playing.

"Hey, this food is okay," said Bob.

"Neat," said Lloyd, with his mouth full.

Jim sat back, finally, lit a cigarette and as he smoked, studied his 'family' with pleasure. He was proud of them; proud of the way they looked and acted. For a moment, it was almost as if he hadn't lost his head and thrown it all away. Maybe it was only a nightmare, after all!

"Dad," said Bob, "how about we go back and watch TV when we're through here? There's some keen programs on Sunday night."

"All right," said Jim. "If it's all right with your mother."

Alma had hardly said a word. "Oh, it's fine with me, as long as they are in bed by nine-thirty."

Later Jim helped put them to bed and joined in the roughhouse till Alma broke it up. Finally Jim and Alma returned to the living room. They were very awkward with one another, almost as if they were virtual strangers, alone together for the first time.

"Well," said Jim, "I guess I'd better get going."

"Yes," said Alma. "I generally go to bed early." There was a pause as Jim picked up his hat and stood hesitating. "Jim, there's something I think I ought to tell you."

Jim felt a quick stab of apprehension. "Yes, Alma?"

"Andy asked me to marry him."

Jim felt himself stiffening and wondered if he looked as pale as he felt. "Oh? And?"

"Oh, I know it's nothing to you Jim—you and your beautiful Southern Belle."

What a description of Judy!

"Yes?" He could hardly bring the word out.

"I'm worrying about the boys. They liked Andy so much and now all of a sudden they don't."

Jim felt like running in and kissing his two mighty sensible sons. "They don't? Why?"

"Oh, Andy's moody. Breaks his golf clubs. Gets in arguments with people. He doesn't mean it—but ... well, he's got a lot of responsibilities and ... Damn it, Jim; I don't know."

"What can I say?" said Jim. "If you are in love with him, marry him. You're only thirty-five years old. Kids have to take the bitter with the sweet."

"Did I say I was in love with him?" cried Alma, with startling asperity.

"Then what's the idea?" asked Jim.

"I like him. He's been very, very kind. I don't think he's such a clown as most people seem to think."

Oh, so she was catching on to Ole Hoss, finally!

"What do you expect me to say?" asked Jim.

There was a long silence, then Alma said wearily: "Nothing. I should have known better than to mention it. Go home, Jim. I'm tired."

"All right, Alma," said Jim; then: "Let me say one thing. If you don't love him don't marry him. It would be just no good. I know you, Alma."

"You don't know me at all," cried Alma. "You never did. I'm thinking about the future—my sons' future. Now does that clarify things?"

"A little."

Alma turned away. "Good night, Jim."

"I may be up again soon," he said. "I'll call in advance."

Alma nodded wearily. Jim went out, closing the door softly behind him. For the first time since Alma had insisted on divorcing him and getting custody of the boys, he had felt a faint ray of hope. Alma was a very strong-minded woman and very proud, but going it alone was beginning to take its toll. As for Andy ... well, Jim doubted very much if Alma would ever be able to bring herself to marry him. But there were other men in the world, many of them, who were not Andy Reeds—no clowns; and it was just possible that Alma might meet one of them and ... but Jim abruptly put the brakes on his imagination at this point.

Jim drove to the business district of West River, parked his car, and went into a big chain drugstore to use the pay phone. His call service informed him he'd had but one call; from a Mr. Ryan, who had left his number.

Jim put in a call for Pat, looking about him, through the glass doors of the phone booth, as he waited. What a place this drugstore was! Immense; a bewildering labyrinth of aisles and counters, and with an army of salesgirls. Practically anything could be bought in such places, even "fungoid bats!" And Jim suddenly remembered the corner drugstore when he was a boy; a narrow hole-in-the-wall, with its small, marble-topped soda fountain on one side and the prescription counter at the back, where lurked an odd-looking little man in thick glasses— Mr. Pawley, who was known as "Doc," and consulted on matters of health by half the people in the neighborhood. Jim would never forget the odor of "Doc" Pawley's; a mixture of chocolate syrup and drugs. But it was a friendly place where all the neighbors congregated, while the chain drugstore had the cold impersonality of a public institution.

Memories of the past were assaulting Jim more and more frequently of late and it worried him, because he could see in it the very same growth, of what used to be called "old fogyism," that he had noted in both his father and his grandfather.

He lit a cigarette and tried to turn his mind to other things. Pat finally came on.

"Don't like to bother you, Pat," said Jim. "But I thought I ought to return the call."

"We're just getting the kids to bed," said Pat. "It's a chore in the summer. No school, so they think they ought to be allowed to stay up to all hours. I called you about Gus Bailey. No local record, and since you say he's been at Volari's for six or seven years, looks like he's clean. At least in this town. Know where he's from?"

"I'm not sure," said Jim. "But I'm under the impression he's a local boy. I'm pretty sure he is, from his conversation."

"Then he's clean," said Pat. "Don't mean he couldn't go wrong, though."

Jim thought for a moment, then remembered something, and asked: "Pat, has there been a really big safe, or vault, job in the city the last week?"

"No," said Pat. "A couple guys hit a safe in Arnold's Sporting Goods store for about four hundred. And another bunch ran off with a safe from a trucking company but couldn't open it and left it in a field. Oh, yes. A bakery was hit for a couple hundred or so; but that may have been a sneak-thief job. And there've been half a dozen misses. No big ones, Jim. Why?"

"An informer told me he'd heard rumors of a real big vault job."

"Do you know your man?"

"Yes. I used him now and then, all the time I was with Jake."

"Some of those guys lie to make themselves interesting, or to be sure they stay on the payroll. He's wrong about a big vault job. The department pushes them hard, Jim; and I'd have all the facts. Wait a minute. After all, Al's money came out of a vault."

"That's right," said Jim, a little startled. "My man might have got only the tail end of the rumor, or misinterpreted it."

"It's a thought, at least," said Pat. "Keep on it. Anything else?"

Now the line seemed to go dead, then Jim heard Pat say: "All right, Mary; all right. Tell 'em I'll be there in a minute. I'm busy."

"Damn kids," said Pat into the phone, laughing. "Every night I'm home we got a routine. They save up all the riddles they hear and I've got to answer them before they go to sleep."

"I went up to see my kids tonight," said Jim, pleased that he could match Pat in this field. "They sure are hard to get to bed. Say, Pat— another thing; my man tells me there have been rumors for years that Volari's was loaded with cash—because of the administration—and that it would be a good place to knock over. Do you think this is significant?"

"No," said Pat. "But he's right. There's been a lot of talk. But there's been a lot of talk about Goldman's too—the Tiffany of the Midwest, you know—and yet there's never been an attempt on it. Jim, you've got a real doozy on your hands here. Don't get gray over it."

Jim hung up thoughtfully, wondering what some of the local malefactors would say if they knew that Pat Ryan had a hard time making his kids go to bed and had to answer riddles before they'd consent to go to sleep. Pat was feared and hated by the criminal element, and more than one of them had tried to get him busted, by charging him with brutality to prisoners. The thing was that Pat hated the malefactors as much as they hated him and would take no insolence or nonsense from any of them. When he was bossing the 17th, the criminals had walked carefully in that district. The word around town had been, "Stay out of the 17th or behave yourself there; if Pat Ryan gets his mitts on you, you'll wish you'd never been born."

Jim left the phone booth and started for the front door.

"Ole Hoss!"

Jim cringed slightly, then turned. Andy Reed, in golf clothes, his face brick-red from the sun and his forehead peeling, was coming toward him with an outstretched hand.

They shook.

"Up seeing the kids?" asked Andy.

"Yes," said Jim.

"Great kids! Yes sir," said Andy, emphatically." I was going to drop by but I had such a lousy day at Riverside!" His big face clouded. "Trouble is, I been taking lessons lately. Couple weeks ago I broke eighty-five, so this fellow says, 'Hey, Andy, Ole Hoss, you're getting good, so why not take some lessons and get *real* good—a little while and you'll be breaking eighty?' Oh yeah? So I take these lessons from the pro—and now I can't break ninety he's got me so goddamned mixed up! I'm just a natural golfer, see? Maybe I don't do things just right but I get the job done. Now I'm doing 'em right and I'm not worth a damn. Look, I'm a hell of a driver, right straight down the fairway. Now I'm hooking 'em into the trees, for Christ's sake. How am I going to get myself straightened out?"

"Stop taking lessons," said Jim.

Andy's eyes lit up. "By God, you're right. Say, you play the game?"

"No," said Jim.

"You don't play?" cried Andy, outraged. "Why the hell not? Why, Jim, you were a real good athlete at military school. Baseball and all. Course you were too skinny for football. Look—you ought to take up golf. Get out in the sun. You're too pale."

"I'm too busy trying to make a living," said Jim. "Can't take the time. Not like you, Andy—a plutocrat."

Andy chuckled and seemed to swell slightly. Oh, the whirligig of time! He remembered back when he'd been an awkward farm boy scared of everybody at the big military school. And there was Jim Chase, grandson of Judge Weldon Chase, with all the fellows flocking around him. He'd tried to model himself on Jim, but it was no use. He just could not acquire that easy, offhand manner and that quiet way of dealing with people and things. Worse yet, he had ended up on the Awkward Squad and the drill sergeant had yelled at him:

"Hey, clodhopper—hay-foot, straw-foot, belly full of bean soup ..." while Jim, a cadet lieutenant then, had lolled in the shade, laughing at him.

But now look!

"Well, if you ever change your mind, Ole Hoss," he said, magnanimously, "let me know. I'll put you up for the club. There's a waiting list. But, don't worry, I'll get you in."

"Well, thanks, Andy," said Jim. "I appreciate that."

Andy walked to his car with him, still talking, and then shook hands again as Jim got in.

"Good seeing you," Andy said, beaming, as Jim drove off.

It was a little past eleven-thirty when Jim got back to his apartment. Several times he was on the point of calling Judy at Volari's, but finally changed his mind. Judy was angry with him; and he decided that it might be a good idea to let her cool off till Monday—when Volari's was dark. After a good night's rest she'd probably feel differently and maybe he might have time to take her up the river for a leisurely dinner on her free day.

He called Marty instead and finally got him.

"Chief," said Marty, pleased by the call, "anything new?"

"You're wrong about the vault job," said Jim. "I had it checked."

"You mean the police are in this?"

"Not officially. Could you have misunderstood somebody, Marty?"

"I don't see how. Let me think. Outside sharpie, local boys. Big, a *real* big vault job. That's the way I heard it, Chief. Sorry."

"Well, just keep listening. You may be on the right track at that."

Marty sounded very relieved as he said goodbye and hung up.

Jim had such a good rest the night before that he did not feel like sleeping, so he got out Mr. Aldus Willey's papers and began to work on them in the breakfast nook, wincing from time to time at what he found there.

It was nearly twelve thirty now and Volari's was very busy for a Sunday night. A new bartender, Oswald, was having his troubles at the bar, and Gino, with a strained irritated look, was hurrying about from the bar to the booths to the supper room, ironing out difficulties and hurrying the help.

"We *would* have a new bartender and be shorthanded besides tonight," Gino said at the slot to Judy, who was waiting for Oswald to make up her order.

"It's not my fault that girl didn't show up to take Zena's place," she said, hot, tired and irritable, and just about ready to give Gino a piece of her mind.

"Did I say it was?" said Gino. "Anyway, it's Zena's loss. They're tipping big tonight. Right?"

"Yes," said Judy, grudgingly.

"It's the convention," said Gino. "They're staying at the Metropole. I guess my friend, Saunders, must have sent them over."

After quite a wait Judy finally got her drinks—Oswald was not nearly as fast as Gus had been—and delivered them to a wall booth up front. Just as she was turning away a big man came in from the vestibule and stopped her. She knew him slightly, as he was often around Volari's during the weekends: Mr. Draper, a traveling salesman who lived in their neighborhood someplace. He was always trying to date Zena and being perfunctorily brushed off.

"Why isn't she here tonight?" he asked Judy.

"She took a couple of days off, Mr. Draper. She's up at the lake."

"She is not," said Draper. "I saw her get out of a taxi in front of where you live. I was across the street. I called to her but she didn't answer or maybe didn't hear me. She seemed in quite a hurry."

"Was she alone?"

"Yes."

"Oh, you must be mistaken."

"Judy," said Draper, "I'd know that figure any place. It was Zena, all right."

Judy thought this over for a moment, then said: "Well, maybe she came back earlier than she expected. I thought she was going to stay till Tuesday morning."

"Did you ever put that good word in for me?" asked Draper.

"I told her I thought you were a nice fellow," said Judy.

"Well, thanks, anyway, honey. I guess I'm not her type."

He crossed to the bar and sat on a stool. Judy took another order and went to the slot. Gino had disappeared. He came in from the back, looking furious.

"Goddamn, it must be the weather or something," he said.

"What's the matter, Gino?" asked Judy.

"Shorthanded," cried Gino. "I say a word to him, he quits—right in the middle of serving."

"Who?"

"Tony," said Gino. Tony was the youngest waiter in the supper room and very good-looking and popular with the regular clients. "He's been sort of insolent the last few days. Now I say one word, he up and quits.

There's a hex on this place."

The night wore on. More people trooped in from the Metropole Hotel, down the street. Some of them were wearing badges; many of them were drunk; a few were obnoxious. At one o'clock the place was jammed nearly to capacity. Gino was forced to act as bar-waiter, then bartender, then supper room waiter, by turns. Judy didn't have a moment's rest. But occasionally little worries nagged at the back of her mind. Why had Zena returned so soon? A row with Mr. Mond—maybe? Xena would simply take no nonsense from men. And why hadn't Jim called? Merely because she'd lost her temper over the phone? She'd lost her temper many times with him.

And finally she began wondering what had got into Jim all of a sudden to want to go and see his boys? Why, he'd been so lax about it for a while that even she had suggested that he ought to at least call them on the phone once in a while.

But she did not have time to think clearly about Zena or Jim. Gino kept snapping his fingers at her; and she had to stay on the alert in the darkened bar to elude the playful hands of the conventioneers. One big man told her she was the prettiest girl he'd ever seen—"they don't grow 'em like you *downstate*, baby," he'd insisted; and asked her to marry him, to cheers from his friends.

Quite a Sunday night!

Chauncey, who had a beat-up old jalopy that seemed to amuse rather than irritate him, give Judy a ride home, and as she was going up in the elevator it suddenly occurred to her that if she'd done such a thing back in Memphis her brothers and the Old Man would have beat her good, then disowned her. Judy had been in the big town for such a length of time now that it no longer appeared odd to her that nobody seemed to care one way or another about such things; at least, none of the people she knew. She herself had not even felt in the slightest degree uncomfortable with Chauncey. He was just a rather nice and amusing young guy that she worked with.

She entered the apartment expecting to see Zena and hear all about why she had come back so soon. Zena was sometimes extremely funny on the subject of her various men. But Zena was not there. Judy, suddenly worried, turned on all of the lights and looked for her. Then she noticed that Zena's clothes were gone from the closet and even the huge dress bag was no longer in place; and Zena had cleaned out all of her dresser drawers—except for one item, and the finding of it gave Judy a sharp jolt. At the back of one of the drawers was a cardboard box and in it, protected by layers of tissue paper, was one of Zena's most prized possessions—a large gold mesh bag. Xena was so crazy about it that she never carried it, and took it out of its box only to admire and fondle it. Why would she pack and take away all of her clothes, even the old, slightly outmoded ones, and leave behind her precious gold mesh bag?

There was only one reason that Judy could think of. Xena had been wildly excited and upset, and had forgotten it.

Judy felt scared and called Jim at once. Jim, who was still working at the Willey brief, though it was nearly half-past two, answered the phone wearily.

"It's me—Judy. Did I wake you?"

"No," said Jim. "I'm catching up on my work. You lonesome all alone?"

"Yes," said Judy. "Come right over."

"Okay. But you sound funny. What's the matter?"

Judy told him, explaining about the gold mesh bag.

"Didn't she leave you a note?"

"No," said Judy. "Well, I mean … if she did it's not in plain sight. She could have called Volari's. Or dropped by. She was in a cab."

"I'll be right there," said Jim.

Judy looked all over the apartment for a note, but found nothing. Weary, hot, irritable and a little scared at being alone, with the silence of a late hour throbbing all about her, and wishing that Jim would hurry up and get there, she quickly took a shower, put on some lightweight lounging pajamas, and was just starting toward the Pullman kitchen to make herself some coffee when the door buzzer sounded.

She gave a cry of relief, thinking: "Jim certainly made good time getting here." She ran to the door and opened it.

"Hello," said Mr. Mond, smiling at her sardonically in the doorway.

Judy gave a wild start.

"What's the matter, honey?" asked Mond, coming in and closing the door. "Something bothering you?"

"I wasn't expecting you," said Judy. "I'm getting ready for bed. You can't stay."

"I want to talk to Zena, that's all."

"She's not here."

Mond's face hardened slightly. "What do you mean, she's not here? Say, what are you so nervous about? You been talking to Zena?"

"No," said Judy, feeling more and more scared. "I haven't seen Zena since she left with you."

"You trying to tell me she didn't come back here?"

"She must have, while I was at work," said Judy. "Her clothes are all gone."

Mond started slightly, then brushed past Judy, switched on the light in the bedroom and stood staring at the still open closet door. There was nothing left but a row of empty clothes hangers. He began looking through the drawers, slamming them back in roughly.

Little by little anger drove out Judy's fear. "Just make yourself at home," she said.

Mond turned and moved toward her menacingly, his face white and still, then seemed suddenly to change his mind. "You kids are all alike," he said. "Chips on your shoulders because you're good-looking and got the guys chasing you."

Judy's heart was still beating heavily because she'd been sure that Mond was going to hit her. His abrupt change of front bewildered her. Finally she asked, trying to make it sound light: "Did you and Zena have an argument of some kind? She's always arguing with people."

"Like a lover's quarrel, you mean?" asked Mond, eyeing Judy, studying her face as if he couldn't quite make up his mind about her.

"Yes," said Judy. "Like that."

"You might say so," he said. "Yes, you might say so."

He walked past her into the living room, lit a cigarette and stood staring thoughtfully at the floor. He still had his hat on. Now he removed it. Judy saw beads of sweat on his forehead.

"She didn't contact you, eh?" he said finally.

"No," said Judy, coming into the living room. "I came home and found all of her things gone. I can't understand it."

"You're either an awfully good liar, honey," said Mond, "or you are telling the truth."

"Thanks," said Judy.

He thought things over for a moment and asked: "Has she got any relatives in town?"

"No," said Judy. "None that I know of."

"Where would she be likely to go? Look honey. All right; we had an argument. Maybe I talked pretty rough to her. But I didn't mean it. I've got to find her, patch things up."

But Judy did not believe him, not for one moment. He was just not the type of man, in her opinion, who searched frantically for a girl who had run away from him, merely to "patch things up."

"I haven't the slightest idea where she'd go," said Judy, telling the truth. "We've been together for a long time—years; and she's never gone away any place before. I mean, like this. On short trips, yes."

"Where does she go on short trips?" prodded Mond.

"The lake," said Judy. "And twice to Chicago."

Mond could not seem to make up his mind whether to go or stay, or exactly what to do. Just as he was about to speak the door buzzer sounded. He appeared to repress a start, as if his nerves were on edge.

"That's Mr. Chase," said Judy. "I'm expecting him."

"Little late, isn't it?"

"He usually picks me up at two. Tonight he couldn't."

There was a brief pause. The buzzer sounded again.

"Well," said Mond, "I'll be going."

He walked to the door with her and stood aside as she opened it. Jim threw a surprised look at Mond, who nodded, smiled and offered his hand. Jim took it, puzzled.

"Hi," Mond said. "I'm on my way. Judy will explain. Good night—both of you."

Judy shut the door and they stood in silence till they heard the faint hum of the elevator, then Judy spoke: "I'm afraid of him, Jim. Something's very wrong. I know it."

Jim went to the kitchen with her and while she made a pot of coffee she told him about Mr. Mond's odd actions.

"I can believe that they had a fight all right," said Judy. "Knowing Zena. But why would she run away like this—move out? And why would he be so anxious …? He was white, Jim. Much whiter than usual; and very nervous."

But Jim was tired from hours of wrestling with the almost insane complexities of Mr. Aldus Willey's records and accounts, and did not want to force himself to think about the mysterious goings-on of Zena and her odd-looking boyfriend. He had far bigger fish to fry—Tom Patton's vanished two hundred thousand dollars.

They took their coffee into the living room and sat on the lounge.

"Jim," said Judy, "I'm sorry I snapped at you on the phone. I shouldn't have."

"It's no great matter," said Jim, sinking back wearily.

There was a brief pause, then Judy said, showing a slight embarrassment: "Honey, will you stay all night? I'm nervous. There's something about that man …"

"Sure," said Jim, stretching his legs and settling himself comfortably.

"What a night!" cried Judy. "Volari's was a madhouse, and I was just about ready to start yelling at Gino—and now this!"

Jim glanced at her quickly. "What was the matter at Volari's?"

"New bartender—Oswald; very slow. The girl that was supposed to take Zena's place didn't show up. And Tony quit."

"Who's Tony?"

"You know Tony. The good-looking waiter in the supper room."

"Oh, yes. Why did he quit?"

"Gino was rough tonight. Got on Tony. So Tony quit. Gino says he's been acting pretty insolent the last few days—but that proves nothing.

If you don't jump every time Gino looks at you he thinks you're insolent. He's always pinching Zena and Cecile and me ... to make us hurry. Zena says he's a sex maniac and likes to pinch bottoms—but that's just her talk. Gino's been square with all the girls ever since I've been there. You know, a man in his position, hiring and firing ... well, he could have his pick. It's a good spot, even now; big tips. But Gino doesn't play that way. He's got his wife and his kids and his big house out on the river."

Judy could have bitten her tongue. She saw Jim studying her and looked away. "Anyway," she said quickly, "It was a rough night."

Jim gave a long sigh and sank lower on the couch. "God I'm tired," he said. "I've been beating my brains out over a hopeless job for hours."

There was a long silence; finally Judy said: "I'm just not going to like it, living alone. I'm not used to it."

Jim gave her a surprised look. "What makes you think Zena won't be back?"

Judy sat bolt upright and stared at him. "I don't know," she said, with a worried, apprehensive look. "I just assumed ... why did I assume, Jim? I don't like this."

Jim patted her soothingly. "Come on. Sit back. You're tired. You've been working hard. Let's relax for a little while and let the world go by. Tomorrow will come soon enough."

"Tomorrow's Monday," said Judy, suddenly. "I'm so all mixed up I forgot."

"Yes," said Jim. "And we're going up the river for dinner."

"Good," said Judy. "Fine. Now I'm going to sit back, close my eyes and think what I'm going to wear."

In a moment Jim fell into a doze and the coffee cup would have dropped from his hand if Judy hadn't grabbed it. As he dozed, he dreamed that there was a crazy puzzle he was trying to put together; he could see its weird, jagged parts distinctly but none of them seemed to fit any of the others ... Larry sat down to help him, but knocked all of the pieces to the floor in his zeal. Jim leaned down to pick them up but another man, on his hands and knees, had beat him to it. The man looked up. It was Tony—the young waiter from Volari's.

Jim woke with a start. Judy was sitting sideways, looking at him.

"Dreams are crazy," he said, trying to laugh. "Weird." He felt deeply disturbed, but he hadn't the faintest idea what about.

"I know," said Judy. "I've had some dandies. Shall we call it a night?"

"Yes," said Jim. "Let's call it a night."

# 5: MONDAY

He had never seen Judy look better. She was wearing a plain black dress; her black hair was up, with a big bun at the back; and, due to a good night's sleep, the signs of strain had gone from her face, her pale complexion looked creamy and smooth, and her big gray eyes were brilliantly alive. He noticed quite a few people, both men and women, studying her, wondering, speculating. He'd known Judy so long that her undeniable good looks seldom impressed him. But tonight he was seeing her through the eyes of other people, strangers; and it took him back to the time he'd first noticed her at Volari's.

"You're looking mighty fine tonight, Judy," he said, over the coffee, and Judy shrugged and smiled rather sadly. "No, I mean it," Jim insisted.

"Well, thanks," said Judy; then, after a moment: "You know … a funny thing. People think we look alike."

"Us?" asked Jim, surprised.

"Yes," said Judy. "Even Gino. One night he said you looked like my older brother."

"I'm glad he said brother."

"Oh, you look young for your age."

"Well, I've got all my hair and no stomach," said Jim. "But aside from that …"

"It's funny," said Judy. "But you *do* look a little like Link. Oh, I've got two very good-looking brothers. Neither one of them is worth a damn, but they're good-looking. Always being chased by women."

They talked on, about nothing in particular, as if they were both trying to avoid more serious topics. Judy could not get the thought of Zena out of her mind. As for Jim, something kept nagging at him, some lead or hint or suspicion—he wasn't quite sure what; but the more he tried to grasp it the further back into the dark recesses of his mind it drew. It was maddening, like trying to recall the tune of an old song that you knew perfectly well and yet couldn't quite ever …

He glanced up. Judy was looking at him.

"I wish you'd tell me what's going on," she said.

"How do you mean?"

"At Volari's," said Judy.

"Volari's?"

"Oh, Jim," said Judy reproachfully.

They fell silent as the waiter came bringing their brandies. They were eating on the terrace at the Savoy-Plaza. It was dark now, and candles, in hurricane lamps, were burning on all of the tables. Below them flowed the big, black river, rippling and murmuring, and carrying on its wide bosom thousands of reflections of the city lights.

When the waiter left, Judy said: "I'm no kid, Jim. I know something's going on. First everything's all right. Then all of a sudden it goes haywire. Gus and Ben Ziegler leave without saying a word to anybody. Al calls you at six-thirty in the morning at my place. Zena goes away and gets into some kind of a jam. Tony quits…"

Jim was staring at her so strangely that she broke off, worried: "All right Jim," she said. "I won't say any more. You don't need to tell me anything."

"Let's get out of here," said Jim.

"Are you mad at me?" asked Judy.

"No, no," said Jim, hurriedly. "I'd tell you about it if I could. But it's better you don't know, Judy. Stay out of it."

Judy waited in the lobby as Jim hurried off to use the public phones. She felt nervous, tense, still disturbed by the strange look Jim had given her.

Jim phoned his call service and discovered that Pat Ryan had been trying to get in touch with him for the last half hour; also that Marty had been calling regularly.

He phoned Pat first.

"Trouble, boy. Trouble," said Pat. "Gus Bailey's girlfriend … wait a minute; I've got it here … Doris Kallen … has filed a missing person report. They'll act on it right away. Better phone Al and tell him to expect callers tomorrow. Sorry, boy. Anything new?"

"In a way. Can I see you tonight, Pat?"

"How soon?"

"About an hour. At Clancy's?"

"Okay. I'll be there."

Jim reached Al at his apartment and gave him the bad news. Al groaned. "You mean the cops will be coming up here tonight?"

"No," said Jim. "They'll be at Volari's tomorrow night during working hours so they can question all of the help. I'll be there early."

"Good boy," said Al, then groaned again. "And I thought I was going to get a real nice sleep tonight!"

It took Jim some time to get Marty, and between calls he went back to the lobby and sat with Judy.

"I hope I don't have to sit here alone much longer," said Judy.

"I'm sorry," said Jim. "But there are some things I've just got to look after."

"Well," said Judy, "I've been getting a few plays. I may be gone when you come back."

"Pick out one with money," said Jim. "That would be a relief, wouldn't it?"

Judy gave him a reproachful look, but Jim laughed and patted her on the shoulder.

He finally ran Marty down at Conner's Pool Hall. Marty seemed agitated.

"Chief," he said, "I can't talk good here, but this is important, so listen fast. I got a buzz on you tonight. Guy I never seen before sat down beside me in a diner, got to talking. Said Slim Conners had sent him over to see me, wanted to know a lot about the town; then he asked me if I knew you. I said I'd heard of you, when you was Chief Investigator for the DA. He wanted a rundown. I give him nothing, Chief. Just a lot of wind."

Jim was startled and somewhat worried. "I don't understand this at all, Marty. What does he look like?"

"Like nothing. Just an average-looking Joe; about thirty. No coat. Cheap sport shirt. Brown hair. Hard to describe. But, Chief, I got a feeling maybe we might be getting close to the knuckle. Wait. So I come back here and buzz Slim and he says he never heard of the guy. Nobody asked him nothing about me. It was a come-on. Someway this stranger knew I hung out at Slim's. Why me? I don't get it."

"You want out?" asked Jim.

"Naw," said Marty. "I don't scare easy at these prices. Chief, it's not private here no longer. Goodbye."

Jim hung up slowly, more than a little bewildered. Things seemed to be moving very fast now, and in different directions.

"What's the matter?" Judy asked, looking up at him.

"Problems," he said; then: "Look, honey. I've got to talk to a man down on the riverfront. It's no place for you, so ..."

"Oh, no, you don't," said Judy. "You're not going to take me home and leave me. I'll wait for you someplace."

"But wouldn't you be better off in your own apartment?"

"No, I would not," said Judy, emphatically. "It gives me the creeps."

Jim studied Judy for a moment. There was a pleading look in her eyes. It was obvious that Mond had given her quite a fright and that the disappearance of Zena had unsettled her considerably. He foresaw complications for the future, and groaned to himself. "My place?" he suggested.

"That's more like it," said Judy.

As they were walking across the lobby toward the front entrance to pick up a cab, Jim said: "By the way, do you know Tony's last name?"

She glanced at him quickly, suppressed a query, and said: "Yes. Fiala."

"Is he Italian?"

"He was born right here in the city, I think," said Judy. "But his folks were … what do they call them?" She tried to remember. "The reason I know is, Tony used to talk to me an awful lot. I didn't know he was on the make, but he was, as I found out, so I stopped with the polite conversation. Czechs! That's it. His folks were Czechs."

Jim nodded.

As they got into the cab, Judy said: "I'm not supposed to ask why, am I?"

"No," said Jim.

They rode in silence for a while. The boulevard paralleled the river, and they could see, far out in mid-channel, a powerful little low-slung tug towing a huge ore boat upstream. Golden reflections danced and dazzled in the freighter's wake. The tug's whistle blasted and a tiny puff of white smoke showed for a moment, then vanished. Far downstream a searchlight swept the black water at regular intervals.

"Judy," said Jim, "do you know where Mond lives?"

"That creep! Wait a minute. Yes. Regent Hotel. Or at least that's what he told Zena. She may have even called him there. As a matter of fact I believe I remember that she did—once."

Jim merely nodded. Judy glanced at him, hesitated, then turned away, curbing her curiosity. Jim was right. Best for her to know nothing; stay out of it.

Pat made no attempt to interrupt. He sat opposite Jim in the back room at Clancy's, with a stein of beer at his elbow, and listened in silence to the long recital. At first Jim had tried to take it point by point but soon found that to be impossible. In order to take something point by point there must be a certain degree of logic in it. There was no logic here at all. Like the puzzle of his dream, nothing seemed to fit. Finally he thought he had told Pat everything and then suddenly remembered the odd circumstance of Marty and the stranger. Pat glanced up sharply at this bit of information.

"What's the matter, Pat?"

"Got a gun?"

"Yes," said Jim, "I have."

"Carry it. And just keep this in mind at all times: there's two hundred thousand dollars at stake. A fortune, even in this day and age."

"I'll remember," said Jim, smiling wryly; then: "How do we check on this Mond fellow? Or do you think I'm reaching too hard?"

"I do not," said Pat. "What I mean is, something was happening at Volari's that bears looking into. Let me check. Be right back."

Pat went out. Jim rang for the waiter and ordered a stein of beer. The waiter and Pat returned at the same time. As soon as the waiter had gone, Pat said: "He was staying at the Regent all right. Checked out last night; no forwarding address. He was registered as from New York, Bannerman Apartment Hotel. I talked to Joe Carr, the assistant manager, an old friend of mine. He says Mond is a salesman for a chemical company. He didn't know what company. Mond ran up a big bill, and paid it in cash. It was the only thing about him that struck Joe as unusual. Bills that size are usually paid by check, traveler's check, or the client is billed—you know, the credit arrangement."

There was a brief silence, then Pat said: "This waiter Tony. What's your idea about him?"

"It's wild," said Jim. "But remember the young fellow who went to both Gus's and Ben Ziegler's to pick up their clothes? From the vague descriptions we got, it might have been him. I'm just reaching, Pat."

"Keep reaching. I told you the first time we talked that I didn't buy the story, that there was something wrong with it. I'm still in the dark, but I have a sneaking feeling we're getting someplace."

"Pat, what do you think about the Zena business? To me it doesn't make sense. According to my information, this girl just hated to be alone and she was very dependent on the girl she was living with. All of a sudden she just moves out, says nothing."

"I'd say she was scared of something."

"Mond. But why?"

There was a long silence; then Pat heaved a sigh and glanced at his watch. "Sorry, Jim; but I ought to be on my way. Keep plugging. We may unscramble this one yet, but that doesn't necessarily mean you'll ever see a penny of the money."

Pat glanced at his watch again and got up. They shook hands, then Pat started out but turned back. "Make sure you're not being followed, Jim," he said. "Might louse us up if we have to move all of a sudden."

"I'll watch it," said Jim; then: "What time tomorrow do you think the guys from Downtown will get to Volari's?"

"Early in the evening, about eight, something like that, so they can talk to all the help about Gus Bailey without interfering too much with the workings of the joint."

"I'll be there."

Pat left. Jim stalled around for a while, finishing his beer and paying the check, then he left also. It was getting cooler outside, and a thin mist was drifting in from the river, blurring the streetlights and dampening the pavements. The old familiar riverfront did not look so friendly to Jim tonight. The thought of being followed by criminal unknowns was very unsettling to him; he felt tense, nervous, and relieved when he'd reclaimed his car from the dark parking lot and was on his way back to the apartment.

He kept glancing into the rearview mirror as he drove along; but if anybody was following him he couldn't detect it.

When Jim got to his apartment he found Judy on the living room couch, asleep. He woke her gently.

Before he could speak, she said: "I've made up my mind. I'm going to move. I'll never be comfortable in that place again."

Jim sat down on the couch beside her and patted her soothingly. "Stay here tonight. Get a good night's sleep. Maybe tomorrow you'll feel differently about it."

"No I won't," said Judy. "I want out of that place, out of that building, out of that neighborhood."

Jim sank back with a sigh, got out his cigarettes, and they lit up. He'd been living at a tension for nearly a week now, struggling with problems that baffled and bewildered him, and this new development, though actually trivial by comparison, began to take on exaggerated proportions in his mind—finding a new place for Judy, moving her stuff, dealing with all the niggling little details that were inescapable …

"Judy," he said, "I'd think this over if I were you. Zena may be back in a day or so, and then what?"

"She won't be back," said Judy. "I feel it. I know it."

"Does that really make sense to you?"

"Yes," said Judy. "Good sense."

"All right," said Jim, rather irritably.

Judy turned and looked at him. "You think I'm silly, don't you? Well, maybe I am. But do you think I want that man barging in on me? You weren't there. You didn't see his face. As soon as you came in, he changed. Once I thought he was going to hit me, and if he ever finds Zena …" She broke off, scared by her own thoughts, then she took hold of Jim's arm and shook him slightly. "Jim, what's happening? What's this all about?"

"I don't know," said Jim. "I'm trying to find out."

"I'll tell you how I feel," said Judy. "I don't want to go back there—ever. Not even to get my things. I hate the thought of that place now."

She seemed so shaken, so disturbed, that Jim was ashamed of himself for having been irritated with her. "All right, Judy," he said. "I'll move you out tomorrow."

Judy gave a long sigh of relief, then turned and lay up against Jim with her arm around him. "Jim, you just don't know. I couldn't stand to be alone in that place for five minutes."

Jim patted her. "How are you rent-wise?"

"I'm paid up to the first, and that's only about a week away."

"Any idea where you'd like to go?"

There was a brief pause, then Judy said: "Around here someplace."

Jim avoided her eyes. Was she hinting that she wanted to move in with him? That would certainly be the simplest solution for her. And it was also what Jim had wanted during the first months of their love affair, but at that time Judy just could not bring herself to leave Zena all alone.

"She'll flip," she told Jim. "I can't do it." Zena was out of the picture now, but time had passed, much had happened since those first wild days, and Jim's feelings had changed—slowly, subtly, but unmistakably.

"I thought you didn't like this neighborhood," he said.

"I didn't," said Judy. "But I've changed my mind. It was so peaceful here when I was waiting for you. It reminded me of back home—old-fashioned, I mean—and, you know—comfortable, restful. I can't say exactly what I mean, but ..." A sudden thought occurred to her and she studied Jim's face. "Is that why you live here, Jim?"

"Yes," he said.

"I never could figure it out before."

She sank back and they sat in silence, smoking, for a long time, with Judy resting comfortably against him, while the rumble of the city came in through the open windows and tugs hooted on the big river.

Finally Jim spoke. "There are some nice little apartments on Weldon—it's a side street about a block from here. They've been done over. You might like 'em."

Judy glanced at Jim, then nodded slowly. "All right, Jim. Whatever you say."

Had she expected a different sort of arrangement? Jim wasn't sure, and did not want to pursue the point, even in his own mind. He felt guilty enough, all around, as it was.

## 6: TUESDAY

"Do you think one little drink would hurt me, Jim?" asked Al Patton. "I'm nervous as hell."

Jim shifted about uncomfortably. "Well, Al," he said, "you've been away from it quite a while. Might bounce pretty hard, and we've got to talk to the police in a few minutes."

"Why is he taking so long?" Al grumbled. "Last I heard, he was out in the kitchen, talking to Jacques, and even to the dishwashers."

"They're thorough," said Jim. "Al, let me do the talking as much as possible."

"It's all yours—and you're welcome, I'm sure," said Al; then: "How about a weak one? Maybe with some hot water—a toddy?"

"Go ahead," said Jim. "But be sure and make it weak. A hot drink always has more effect than a cold one."

Al made himself a toddy, using hot water from the tap and whiskey from his carefully locked cabinet. Jim watched him in silence as he sipped it slowly. Little by little color began to show in Al's rather flaccid-looking cheeks.

"Boy," said Al; "that really helps. Jim, you think maybe a half of a shot in my lemonade might be all right now? I been off it a long time."

"Don't ask me," said Jim. "Ask your doctor."

"Oh, that bastard!" cried Al. "You ought to see the diet he's got me on. Hell, I just don't get any joy out of living anymore. You think that helps a man get well? I don't. Makes him want to give up."

"Oh, come on, Al," said Jim. "You're just looking for an excuse to drink."

"Damn right I am," said Al. "Maybe I'll change doctors. That weak little old drink really set me up. I haven't felt this good for months."

Meanwhile, Detective Sergeant Gamble, from Downtown, went quietly and efficiently about his business, questioning the help at Volari's, from Gino on down.

At a little before nine, there was a tap at Al's office door, then Sergeant Harry Gamble stepped in. He was of medium size and stocky; his blondish hair was cut short and he had small pale-gray eyes that appeared not to blink. Jim had seen him many times in the corridors of the Hall of Justice, in the old days.

"Mr. Chase ... Mr. Patton," he murmured, his voice coarse and rather husky. "I know how busy you are, Mr. Patton, but would you mind answering a few questions?"

"No," said Al.

The sergeant turned to Jim. "Would you excuse us for a few moments, Mr. Chase?"

"Why?" said Jim. "I know as much about this business as Mr. Patton. In fact, I've been retained by Mr. Patton—on another matter, of course."

"That so?" said the sergeant. "Well, all right. I see no objection to your remaining. Now, Mr. Patton. Didn't you think it was kind of funny when Gus Bailey and Ben Ziegler didn't show up for work?"

"I did," said Al.

"What did you do about it?"

"Nothing—for a while. Then I consulted Mr. Chase."

"Why did you do that?"

"I wanted his advice."

"And why did you think you needed his advice in a matter like this?"

"I can answer that," said Jim.

"I prefer Mr. Patton to answer it, if you don't mind."

Al glanced quickly at Jim, sighed and seemed to shrink in his chair.

"Sergeant," said Jim, quickly, "I think you ought to know this. Mr. Patton is ill and under the care of a physician—Dr. Maudley. Actually he ought to be home in bed. The disappearance of these two trusted employees has upset him very much. I'd appreciate it if you'd let me answer the questions—that is, with the proviso that Mr. Patton adds whatever he thinks necessary to what I have to say."

"Yes, Sergeant," said Al, giving Jim a grateful look, "that might be better if you don't mind."

"All right," said Gamble, his face noncommittal. "Mr. Chase?"

"I'll begin at the beginning," said Jim. "Business has been falling off at Volari's for months now; over a year, in fact. Some very prominent men have run up big tabs which they have neglected to pay. Mr. Patton didn't want to dun them in the usual way. So he called me in to ask my advice; I gave it to him."

"Mr. Chase," said the sergeant, patiently, "I don't quite see ..."

"If you'll just let me continue. Please!"

Gamble nodded wearily. "All right."

"Thursday night I had a consultation with Mr. Patton. And again on Friday night. I gave him my advice on how to handle the tabs. He called Gus in several times to talk it over, so Gus would know how to handle this rather delicate matter at the bar. Gus was here till two o'clock on Friday night. And that is the last Mr. Patton saw of him."

Sergeant Gamble studied Jim's face for a moment, then asked "Why was no report made to the police? This is damned odd, you know, Mr. Chase."

"Well," said Jim, "I'll tell you. In the first place nothing was missing. Gus's accounts were in order. Ben Ziegler has nothing to do with money or accounts. In the second place I called Gus's home and also Ben's. They'd checked out. Their rent was paid up. A man had come and got their clothes."

"I see," said the sergeant, glancing from Jim to Al.

"Now if there are any other questions I'll be glad to answer them," said Jim. "Or maybe Mr. Patton has something to add."

"Mr. Patton?" murmured the sergeant, turning to Al.

"I can't think of anything," said Al, "except that I liked both Gus and Ben. They'd been with me quite a while. I can't imagine why they left. I'm pretty much upset."

"But you didn't report it," said the sergeant. "And if Miss Kallen hadn't ..."

"I thought I explained that," said Jim, mildly.

"But they'd been with Mr. Patton a long time," said Gamble. "Almost friends, you might say."

"Is that a question, Sergeant?" asked Jim.

"No. Merely a comment."

"Sergeant, if you'll excuse me," said Jim, "I'd like to point out something you seem to have missed. Two men, like Gus and Ben, must have had a very good reason for disappearing. As far as Mr. Patton could find out, it had nothing to do with him or their work—nothing to do with Volari's. As I told you, we discovered they'd checked out of their homes, taking their clothes. So why should Mr. Patton be expected to call in the police? I don't quite see your point, Sergeant."

Gamble nodded slowly to himself, then rose. "Well, thank you," he said. "Mr. Chase. Mr. Patton. I won't keep you any longer. I hope I haven't interfered with the routine here too much. I tried to work it out so as to cause the least friction. Good night, gentlemen."

He nodded, smiled perfunctorily and went out.

Al sank back with a long sigh of relief. "Well, that's that."

"I'm not so sure, Al," said Jim. "Gamble's tough; and he's got something sticking in his craw."

"I can't stand too much of this," said Al. "It makes me too nervous."

"Al," said Jim, "if the going gets rough, I'll have the doctor send you to a hospital for a long rest."

"Will you?" cried Al, eagerly. "Boy, that's just what I need. How about now? You take over, Jim. How about it?"

"Not yet, Al," said Jim, wearily. "Wouldn't look right."

There was a long silence. Al glanced up at the locked liquor cabinet several times, but said nothing. Finally there was a light tap at the door.

"Yes?" called Al.

"It's Judy Waggoner, Mr. Patton. Is Mr. Chase still there?"

"Yes, he's here."

Judy sounded very agitated. Jim rose hurriedly, went out into the little dimly lit hallway and closed the door behind him. Judy, whose face looked white and strained in the half-light, grabbed him by the upper arms excitedly.

"Jim! I talked to her—Zena. She phoned me."

"Was the Sergeant still here?"

"No—he'd gone. Jim, she didn't make sense. And I don't know where she called from—but I think it was out of town. She said goodbye and she was crying. I asked her if she was all right but she didn't answer and kept on crying. Then she said something about Chicago I couldn't get. I think she meant she was going there."

"Did she say anything about Mond?"

"No. Oh, poor Zena. What am I going to do?"

"What *can* you do?" asked Jim. "You have no idea where she is. Maybe she'll calm down and you'll hear from her later."

"Oh, I'm so glad you moved me out of that awful place, Jim. I'd have blown my top if I'd had to stay there. Will you meet me tonight?"

"Yes," said Jim. "I'll be around for a while, then I'll come back."

Sergeant Gamble and Lieutenant Kastner were huddled over their coffees in a squad room on the third floor at Downtown. It was late and very quiet, with many of the offices closed for the night. As it was still hot the windows were open and a damp, lukewarm breeze was blowing in from the direction of the river.

"… and your opinion, Harry …?" Kastner was saying.

"Is that all of the employees are telling the truth," said Gamble. "And Chase and Al Patton are lying."

"Why do you say that?"

"It's all too pat. Why would Al Patton call in a hotshot like Jim Chase to help him collect his accounts? Do you buy that?"

"I don't know," said Kastner. "I think Chase has had a rough time since the election. Al knows it. Maybe he's trying to throw him a little business, no matter what. Those guys are clannish, Harry. Don't forget it."

"I'm not forgetting it. I'm remembering it. All I'm saying is, let's not write off Volari's or Al Patton or Chase. There's something funny about this. Those guys just disappeared, for no reason. I mean for no reason that we can discover."

"How about their home?"

"Both lived alone, in rooming houses. We got a pretty good description of the guy who came to pick up their clothes and check out for them. The woman at Bailey's place is sure she'd recognize him if she saw him again. The woman at Ziegler's is not so sure. Said she paid no attention. Look, Gordon. Nobody at Volari's noticed that anything out-of-the-way had been going on—except for two things. Mr. Chase was there two nights running after having stayed away for months. The nights were Thursday and Friday. On Friday night Gus Bailey was in and out of Al Patton's office three or four times. This was very unusual. As far as the rest of the employees remembered, he'd never been in Al's office before. So? A lead, I said to myself. I go in to talk to Al Patton. Chase is with him. Takes over. Al hired him and so forth and so forth. Kills my lead. Don't that look like a set-up alibi to you, Gord?"

Kastner nodded slowly. "Could be. Chase is pretty good at such things, I hear. But, Harry, what about Gus and Ziegler—their private lives?"

"They weren't even friends," said Gamble. "Just saw each other at work. Nothing in common. This girl, Doris Kallen, was figuring on marrying Bailey. She gave us a good rundown on him; all about him; his friends and everything. She didn't know Ziegler; had never even heard of him. Another thing, if the girl's right, Bailey's a good square guy. No reason to run away. As for Ben, he don't seem to have had any friends at all. I used to know him. Liked him. Little too outspoken for the force. But aside from that, okay."

They heard footsteps in the corridor outside the door and Harry turned to see who it was.

"May have a surprise for you, Harry," said Kastner.

The door opened and a stranger entered—a stranger to Gamble that is. Kastner motioned him over to the table and got him a cup of coffee.

"Harry," said Kastner, "this is Leroy Stone—DA's office. Stone—Sergeant Gamble."

The two men shook hands and nodded to each other; then Stone sat down and sipped his coffee.

"How you coming, fellows?" he asked, and Gamble looked at him quickly.

"The Sergeant thinks Patton and Chase are lying," said Kastner.

"I don't think there's any doubt about it," said Stone.

"Brief the Sergeant," said Kastner.

"Well," said Stone, "the DA finally decided to subpoena Tom Patton. It was a pretty secret operation, but Chase or Al Patton must have a pipeline someplace and were tipped off. Chase picked up Tom Patton on Saturday morning and drove him to the airport at Alton—got him out of the state. The sad part was, we'd just that same day located Tom Patton's hideaway. We were just a few hours too late. One of our boys knocked on the door to give him the subpoena and Jim Chase opens it. Later we searched the house. Every scrap of paper had been burned or taken away."

"I see," said Gamble. "I knew there was something. Now what we have to do is fit Bailey and Ziegler into the picture."

"Stone's got a very interesting theory," said Kastner.

"Now you understand," said Stone, "that's all it is—just a theory. A lot of graft was floating around during the previous Administration, and it's common knowledge that Volari's was a kind of headquarters. Now you know Tom Patton wasn't putting all of his money in banks—it was coming in too fast; wouldn't look good. So I feel that he may have kept at least some of it at Volari's. Some way he got word of the subpoena. Al Patton called Chase and asked him what to do. Chase told him to get Tom out of the state—right away. Now don't forget Ben Ziegler was a tough man; and dependable. So Al sent Bailey and Ziegler to take the money to Tom Patton, which they did. On Saturday morning Chase got Tom out—with all the boodle in an innocent-looking briefcase no doubt."

Gamble seemed fascinated, and was leaning forward. "And what about Bailey and Ziegler?"

"I think they left by car," said Stone, "and probably met Tom Patton in Chicago. Maybe they're going to stay with him. After all Tom's nearly sixty years old, needs somebody. He can't come back, you know."

"What about extradition?" asked Gamble.

"We've got to locate him first," said Stone. "Even after we do, we'll have to prefer serious charges of some kind to get him back. And even then it's no cinch. The truth is, we've been outfoxed."

Gamble swore quietly and sat back. "And I was beginning to get interested in this one."

"Harry," said Kastner, "it's only a theory. We don't stop."

"I know. I know," said Gamble. "But it's a damned good theory. It covers everything. I buy it."

"I don't entirely," said Kastner, "and I'll tell you why. Gus Bailey and this Kallen girl were going to get married, right? You mean to tell me he wouldn't have said a word to her? Just beat it? Would you act like that?"

"No," said Stone. "But there's a possible answer. This was a very big thing, boys. So either Chase or Al Patton warned Gus to keep his mouth shut, told him exactly what to do. When things cool down Bailey can contact his girlfriend."

"Maybe, maybe," said Kastner; then he sat back and puffed smoke at the ceiling thoughtfully.

"There's something we can't quite dope out yet," said Stone. "Chase has been contacting a fink, named Marty Callison. One of our boys pretended he was an out-of-towner, a stranger, and tried to pump Marty about Chase, as a lawyer, but got absolutely no place. We've got a tail on Marty. We may put one on Chase. But the DA's against it. He says Chase will notice it and be warned."

"But what about the fink? Won't he notice it and tell Chase?"

"It's easier to tail a man in Polishtown, as you know, than in a more conventional part of the city."

"Stone," said Kastner, "if I know finks, this boy not only knows he's being tailed but he's already called Chase and told him he was buzzed about him."

"Yes," said Stone, "but in the underworld you never know who's tailing you. Why would it have to be the police? Lieutenant, these guys are up to something. Maybe they've already pulled it. Maybe there are loose ends. As far as they know, the underworld might be interested."

"I'm getting mixed up," said Gamble; then he rose and began to pace the floor.

"That's the trouble with theories," said Kastner. "They either quiet you down or mix you up. I say we go right ahead on the assumption that Bailey and Ziegler are missing and may have been victims of foul play or whatever you like—just like any other missing person case. There's only one thing. I won't buy double amnesia."

Stone laughed. But Gamble was thinking hard, trying to bring into some kind of order the chaos of the known evidence.

It was three o'clock in the morning and Jim and Judy were hanging pictures and putting other finishing touches on her new little apartment at 333 North Weldon, about one block from Jim's place.

"All right," said Jim, finally. "That's it. Do you mind if I wash my hands and sort of smarten up? I'm not used to this manual labor."

When Jim returned from the bathroom Judy picked up his coat from the back of a chair and held it for him. "Jim," she said, "what makes this coat so heavy?"

He got into the coat quickly. "It's my wallet with all that money in it."

But Judy patted his pockets. "Why, that's a gun! Jim, what in the world are you doing with a gun?"

"I'm breaking it in for a friend," said Jim.

But Judy did not laugh. "I wish I knew what was going on," she said. "That cop—Sergeant Gamble. What a cold-blooded fish. Did you notice his eyes? I couldn't look at him. He just kept asking questions and asking questions. Jim—tell me—has something serious happened to Gus and Ben?"

"You know as much about that as I do."

"Are *you* in danger?"

"No. Of course not."

"Then why the gun? I hate guns. My brothers had guns all over the place. They were always out shooting things; rabbits and squirrels and doves and ducks and God knows what else. Once the Old Man almost shot his big toe off, cleaning a gun. He was drunk, of course."

"Shall I toss it out the window?" said Jim, laughing at her, trying to calm her down.

The phone rang. Judy showed immediate apprehension. "Now who would know …?"

"Sorry, Judy," said Jim. "I gave my call service this number. I forgot to tell you."

He picked up the phone. It was Marty.

"Chief, trouble. There's a tail on me. And you know the guy that buzzed me about you? DA's office. I just got the tip from a friend. He seen me sitting with him in the diner. Thought I knew he was a copper. We got to talking just now, at Slim's. What do I do?"

"Nothing in particular," said Jim, "till I contact you again. I'll send you some more money—to Slim's."

"Okay. Fine, Chief."

Jim hung up. What did it mean? In a way he was relieved to find that it was the DA's office that had been asking about him and not some vague mysterious underworld figure; but even so it was very unsettling. And then all at once it came to him. The Tom Patton getaway! That was it. Had to be. So …? What could they do about it? He was in the clear. He had merely driven a free citizen to an airport.

But all at once a different aspect of this very complicated matter occurred to him. He turned. Judy was looking at him in silence, puzzled, apprehensive.

"Jim, you *are* in some kind of trouble, aren't you? Blackmail?"

"Why blackmail?" Jim demanded, surprised and irritated.

"Well, you said you'd send more money—to Slim's," she explained.

Jim laughed at her, then said: "Judy, I just had good news; I won't have to break the gun in for my friend after all. Now go in the bathroom and shut the door. I've got a call to make and it will just confuse you. The less you know, the better."

Judy hesitated, then did as Jim had suggested.

Jim dialed Pat's home number and waited, hoping that the call wouldn't wake Pat's kids.

Pat sounded very surly. "Yeah? Hello."

"It's me—Jim. Sorry. But there's something I've got to tell you—right now." And then he went on to explain that his informer was being tailed by the DA's office, and that it was possible that he himself was being followed.

Pat said nothing. There was a long silence.

"Pat! You there?"

"Jim, this puts me in a hell of a position. And it's not just me. I've got a family. Top Brass is after me, anyway. You know that."

"That's why I called you. Bow out, Pat."

"I hate to. I hate it like hell. But I've got to, Jim. A guy don't save much money on my pay. Sorry."

"Pat, let's try to anticipate the worst. I might have been followed to Clancy's. Why did we meet? Did you want to ask my advice about legal matters of some kind?"

"Yes," said Pat. "That's it."

After hashing things over for a quarter of an hour they finally made up a story that satisfied both of them.

"Night, Jim," said Pat. "I feel better now."

Jim called Judy in from the bathroom. Her face looked pale and strained. "What's the matter, honey?"

"Oh, all alone in there I just kept thinking about poor Zena. She sounded awful, Jim. Not like herself at all."

Jim patted her soothingly. "Come on, honey. We've been working hard getting this place fixed up. How about a drink? A nice long cool one. You sit down. I'll be the bartender."

# 7: WEDNESDAY

"Well, hello, stranger," said Larry, as Jim entered the anteroom, carrying his briefcase. "Don't you work here anymore?"

"Hi, Larry," said Jim, then he put his briefcase down on Gert's desk and began to take out a sheaf of papers. "I've got a raft of notes on the Willey case. They are in the form of rather extended paragraphs, all numbered. As soon as Gert can get them typed up for you, read them—and comment on each paragraph, by number. Makes it easier all around. Gert, how are you this morning?"

Gert smiled up at him. "I'm fine, Mr. Chase. Oh, no! Look at that pile of work. I suppose you want it all done by noon."

"Sooner, Gert, sooner," said Jim, then he motioned for Larry to follow him into his office.

Jim shut the door. "Well, anything new?"

"No," said Larry. "I'm afraid I'm not being much help to the outfit. My finks can't turn up a thing."

"Let me give you a rundown on what's happening," said Jim; "then there's something you can do for me."

Larry listened with mounting apprehension; then finally he said: "Jim! We might find ourselves right in the middle of the soup. You realize that, don't you?"

"Yes," said Jim. "I do. But look here." Jim took a check from his wallet and handed it to Larry. "I got a call early this morning from Al Patton. He's in bed; the doctor's with him. It's partly a stall and it's partly serious. I don't think Al knows which is which; and neither do I. But we're in full charge."

"Five thousand dollars!" cried Larry, staring.

"Retainer," said Jim. "That'll keep the pot boiling for a while. And an unlimited expense account; that is, within reason. We were already out nearly two hundred dollars. I didn't want to mention it, but Al is so scared and so anxious to get the cat off his back, that he thought of everything. Now, does that make you feel better, Larry?"

"Much better," said Larry, grinning. "With what I muscled Willey for and this, we are really in business."

"And now I can pay some of my bills," said Jim, "and be sure Alma gets her money on the dot. I was getting low."

"Low is hardly the word," said Larry. "Before Mr. Willey showed up I was getting ready to float a loan. Beth's a busy little woman in the home and I had to buy her a washing machine, a dryer, a new stove, a new refrigerator and God knows what all. Installment plan. And, God, how the months roll round. I'm cut up like a prize-fighter with four managers."

Jim laughed and said: "Now I can straighten out that four-fifty I owe you."

"No," said Larry. "I never did go for that."

Jim waved him to silence. "All right. We'll argue about it later." Now he took a card from his wallet. "See the name and address on the back? I want you to go there and see what you can find out. If my hunch is right, he may have skipped."

"Anthony Fiala. Who's he?"

"He's the waiter who quit. You're an insurance salesman. You've been handed his name as a prospect. Let's see. By Gino Volari. Can you handle it?"

"Handle it!" said Larry. "I sold insurance for a while when I was at State. What do you want to know?"

"If he's there and everything seems okay, nothing. If he's not, where he went and why."

"Will do. You know it's a wonderful thing how a check for five thousand dollars perks a guy up."

Sergeant Gamble poked his head into the anteroom and called: "Hey! Where's the lieutenant?"

"Down the hall. Men's room," somebody called back.

Gamble lit a cigarette and stood in the corridor, waiting. In a moment, Kastner appeared, carrying a folded-up newspaper.

"Hi," he said. "Did you see how they buried the story?"

"Yes," said Gamble.

"I thought with Volari's being in the picture and all it'd get more. But the finks'll see it; and that's the main thing."

"Good," said Gamble. "Joe Creel put me onto something so I took a run up the river to see Gino Volari. You ought to see the house that guy's got. Is he living it up!"

"Well, he sold out to Al Patton for a big figure, and he's making good money right now. So, what's funny?"

"Nothing," said Gamble. "I was just surprised at the tennis court. Hell, he's got a daughter who looks twenty-five. How the hell old is Gino?"

"He's been around a long time. Come on in."

They went into Kastner's little partitioned off cubbyhole of an office and sat down.

"I got something all right. I don't know what, but something," said Gamble. "Joe's been helping me, you know. Well, he picked up a list of employees that I didn't see. Gordon, there's not just two missing at Volari's, there's four."

"Aw, come on," said Kastner, skeptically.

"Listen, Gus Bailey and Ben Ziegler disappeared late Friday night or early Saturday morning. A hostess—or bar girl—Zena Myland, asked for a couple of days off Friday night. She was due back Tuesday night. She didn't show. On Sunday, Anthony Fiala, a waiter, quit. Joe's checking right now."

"H'm," said Kastner. "Could be coincidence."

"Yes—if they show up. But if they don't …"

"What did Gino have to say?"

"He just gave me the facts. Seems kind of bewildered. Oh, yes. Gino went home early Friday night. But that *was* a coincidence. Gino has a lot of trouble with his stomach. And it really kicked up that night. I checked with his doctor. Old Al Patton's sick, too—no stall. I checked."

Kastner sat shaking his head. "The more I think about it the less I like Stone's theory. Ignore it."

"I am," said Gamble.

Larry tapped at Jim's door, then came in.

"Well," said Jim, "how did we make out?"

Larry sank down into a chair, took off his hat and mopped his brow. "He's not there. He had a row with his father and left. His father doesn't know where he is. He's pretty much upset. Nice man, the father. A Czech from Prague. I was there during the war—in Praha, I mean. That's what they call it."

"What did the father have to say?"

"I could hardly get away from him, Jim," said Larry. "He wanted to tell me his troubles. Anthony—that's what he calls him—has been going wrong lately in his opinion. Never home; hardly spoke to his father. The mother's dead. There was a lot more, but I can't remember it."

"Try."

"Oh, about quitting his job. That's what caused the final row. He'd been making good money at Volari's, a choice place, his father said. The father's a thrifty Old Country type. I think he's sort of bewildered by this country. Maybe his son's okay. I only heard one side of it."

"Do you know when he left home?"

"Monday morning. Jim, another thing. I'm not sure about this. But I think I saw a plainclothesman ringing the doorbell when I was driving away. My car was parked round the corner. When I turned into the main street ..."

Jim suddenly snapped his fingers and jumped up.

"What's the matter?" asked Larry, startled.

"If they're checking on Tony they'll be checking on Zena soon and that means Judy."

"But I'm not sure, Jim."

"It figures."


Judy, wearing lounging pajamas and with her hair tied up in a scarf, was eating her lunch on a tray and watching TV when there was a quick tap at her door.

She started slightly, then sat still. She was expecting no one. The tapping continued. What could it be? Maybe a telegram from Zena. But no; they telephoned those. A Special Delivery letter?

"Oh, for heaven's sake," she thought, "what am I scared of? It's broad daylight."

She rose, turned off the TV, and went to the door. "Who is it?"

"Police, Miss," said a deep voice. "Don't be alarmed. Just want to ask you a few questions."

Judy didn't know what to do. She felt very nervous. Was it about Zena? Had something happened to her? Had they found ...?

"Just a minute," she said.

She tried to compose herself before she opened the door, but she could feel her heart beating heavily and wished that Jim was there. Finally, with deep misgivings, she turned the latch. The door was pushed open and she found herself confronted by a big, rather grim-looking man in a brown tweed suit.

"Sergeant Joe Creel, Downtown," he said, showing his credentials. "Can I come in?"

"Yes, come in," said Judy, standing aside.

Creel stepped in and closed the door. Judy had given herself a facial that morning and her complexion seemed to glow, and the orange scarf contrasting with the black hair and the pale gray eyes gave an impression of almost startling good looks. Creel stared at her admiringly, then lowered his eyes. Judy noted the look and felt a little easier.

"Would you like to sit down?" she asked.

Creel nodded rather ponderously, then lowered his bulk carefully into a straight chair. He didn't seem to trust the chair.

Creel threw the hammer and put the shot on the police track team. "He's even got muscles on his muscles," they said in derisive admiration at Downtown.

"I understand you are a friend of Zena Mylan," said Creel.

"That's right," said Judy, suppressing with difficulty the questions that rushed to her mind. Poor Zena! She was certain that something terrible had happened to her.

"When did you see her last?"

"Friday night when she left for the lake."

"You haven't seen her since?"

"No."

"Has she communicated with you?"

Judy hesitated. She didn't know what to say. Something was happening that she didn't understand; Jim was involved in it; and if she said the wrong thing it might get him into trouble.

There was a tap at the door. Judy stared, then rose. Could it be? It might be. "Excuse me, please," she said, and hurried to the door.

"Jim!"

Creel got up from his chair and turned. "Oh, hello, Mr. Chase," he said. His voice sounded friendly but his eyes showed definite annoyance, enmity even.

"Hello," said Jim. "Sergeant Creel, isn't it?"

"That's right."

"I suppose you've come to question Miss Waggoner again about Gus Bailey," said Jim, smoothly.

"Not exactly," said Creel. "It's about Zena Mylan."

"Oh, I see," said Jim. "She was Miss Waggoner's roommate. Funny thing about that, Sergeant; she went to the lake for a few days—that was the plan at least. She left on Friday night. On Sunday night she came back and without a word to Miss Waggoner, who was at work, she moved all of her clothes out of the apartment—and that is the last Miss Waggoner has heard of her."

Judy heaved a sigh of relief and avoided Creel's eyes.

"I see," said Creel, noncommittally, but thinking: "You slick bastard." Then he went on: "Mr. Chase, if you don't mind, let the little lady answer the questions from now on."

"Of course, Sergeant," said Jim.

But Judy had been given her lead and was well aware of it.

"Now," said Creel, "you moved in here yesterday, I believe. Right?"

"Yes," said Judy.

"Wasn't that sort of a sudden move?"

"I suppose so."

"Will you tell me why?"

Judy tried not to look at Jim. To help her in this, he turned his back and began to pace, smoking.

"With Zena gone, the other place was too large and too expensive," she said, choosing her words carefully. "Here I've just got this room with a daybed, an alcove and a little kitchen. There we had a good-sized bedroom, living room, and ..."

"I know," said Creel. "I saw it. I understand you've lived with Zena Mylan several years and that the two of you are very close friends."

"That's right."

"What made you so sure she wouldn't be back?"

"She took all of her clothes. If she was coming back, why would she do that? I was paid up just to the first. I didn't want to pay another month's rent. It's nearly twice as much as here."

"Had you girls had a quarrel, spat, anything like that?"

"No," said Judy. "We wrangled once in a while. But nothing serious."

"Okay," said Creel. "Now let's go back. She went to the lake for a few days. Did she go alone?"

Judy shifted about uncomfortably. Jim turned in his pacing and shook his head quickly before Creel could look at him, but Judy didn't know what he meant. Should she tell about Mond, or shouldn't she?

"Sergeant, excuse me," said Jim, "I don't want to interfere in any way here, but you just asked an embarrassing question. Tell me this. Has anybody filed a missing person report on Zena Mylan?"

"No," said Creel. "But apparently Miss Waggoner, as her best friend, should have."

"Under the circumstances," said Jim, "Miss Waggoner can answer the question or not, as she sees fit. To tell you the truth, Sergeant, I don't even understand the purpose of these questions, since no report has been filed. In fact, it might be said that you are exceeding your authority in asking them."

"I'm not trying to force her to answer anything," said Creel, his face showing a slight flush.

"However," said Jim, "since nobody seems to have any idea what happened to Zena Mylan, and none of us really know where we stand—including you, Sergeant—my advice to Miss Waggoner is to answer the question."

Creel gave Jim a surprised look, then turned to Judy. "Did she go alone?"

"No," said Judy. "She went with a man named Allen Mond."

"Do you know where they stayed?"

"No. I do not."

"Have you an address on him?"

Judy hesitated, but Jim had turned his back again so she answered the question. "Yes. Regent Hotel."

"Thank you, Miss Waggoner," said Creel; then he handed her a card. "If you hear anything from Miss Mylan, will you give me a call?"

"Yes, I will."

She went to the door with Creel and let him out. Creel merely gestured as he left without looking around.

"Oh, was I glad to see you," said Judy, turning. "I didn't know what to say."

"You did great," said Jim. "Any coffee around here?"

"I've got some Scotch."

"Too early."

"There's some coffee in that pot but it's probably cold. I'll make some fresh. Come on."

Jim followed her to the little Pullman kitchen and they talked as she worked.

"Want to hear something very unlikely?" asked Jim.

"I don't know," said Judy. "I've heard too many unlikely things lately."

"I'm your new boss."

Judy turned to look at him. "What?"

"I'm running Volari's now. Al's home in bed, and Dr. Maudley's sending him to Greet Memorial Hospital for a rest and checkup."

"You're kidding, of course."

"No," said Jim. "I'm dead serious."

Judy stood shaking her head. "I don't know. Sometimes I think I'll wake up and find out it was all just a nightmare. Jim—tell me the truth. Has something happened to Zena? Is that why that man was here? I just can't get her out of my mind for a minute."

"Not as far as I know," said Jim. "And that's not why he was here. It's just a follow-up on the Gus-Ben disappearance."

"You mean they think there's a connection?"

"I don't know what they think. But it's logical for them to look into it, isn't it?"

"God," said Judy; "this is awful. I'm always in a stew now. I was just thinking last night how peaceful it used to be before all of this happened, whatever it is."

"Was it?"

Judy turned to look at him again. Then she understood. "Well, no. It wasn't. I guess I mean by comparison."

The phone rang and Jim answered it. It was Larry, giving Jim a number to call. "Sounds urgent," said Larry. "How's Judy?"

"I got here in time," said Jim. "Tell you about it later." He hung up.

Judy called from the kitchen. "Who was it?"

"Larry. I've got to make a call. Go in the bathroom and shut the door."

"Oh, Jim; please. You'd think I was six years old. I know. I know. It's for my own good."

He heard the door shut, then he dialed the number.

Marty came on almost at once.

"I was waiting, Chief. Look. There's a big noise all over the place. Some boys pulled a big one—vault job, something; I don't know what—and something happened—I don't know what—and the boys fell out; some of 'em ran off with the dough; and maybe somebody else got rocked to sleep, if you know what I mean. A real big noise, Chief—but that's all I could get out of it. I'll keep trying."

"Good. Did you get your money?"

"I did. Bought a new suit. You wouldn't know me. Slim's got me racking up balls and selling cigars. Says I can't sweep in my new suit. Thanks, Chief."

As they sat down with their coffee Judy said: "I don't know what you'd do without a telephone, Jim."

"I wish I could use radar on this one."

Kastner, Creel and Gamble were in a booth at Barney's, across from Downtown, having a belated lunch. The place was almost empty, with just a few men at the bar watching a baseball game on TV.

"Well," Gamble was saying, "it's a funny thing, but no matter which way you turn you run into Jim Chase. Whatever this is, and it's beginning to look worse all the time, he's in it up to his neck."

"Yeah," said Creel, "right in the middle he walks in like the joint was bugged, or like he's got guys following all of us. And, oh, that doll of his!"

"Tell Gord the Fiala bit," Gamble prompted.

"I'm ringing the doorbell at Fiala's place," said Creel. "I look up. There's Chase's partner going past in his car. He'd been there; or I'm pretty sure he had. Some guy had been buzzing Old Man Fiala just before I got there."

"Does any of this make sense to you fellows?" asked Kastner after a moment's thought.

"It gets more senseless if anything," said Creel.

"I agree," said Gamble.

"Well," said Kastner, "looks to me like maybe Chase is trying to run down the same leads we are. What does that indicate?"

"I hate to say this," said Gamble, "but it might indicate that he doesn't know any more about what's going on than we do."

"Oh, please, Gamble," said Creel. "I could hardly sleep last night trying to get this thing straight. Don't mix me up. I say if we could get Chase to talk we'd know the truth."

"Let's go back to the Stone theory for a minute," said Kastner, and the other men groaned. "Just the money part. Let's say the two guys were sent to deliver the money and didn't deliver it, but ran off with it."

There was a shocked silence and Gamble and Creel sat staring at each other in consternation.

"Let's say," Kastner went on, "that the two guys took Zena Mylan and Tony Fiala in with the play. A bar girl would be all over the place and could keep her eyes open. The same for Tony, who later could pick up the two guys' clothes and check them out. He sort of answers the description. Right?"

"Right," cried Gamble. "Then you think Tom Patton went away without the money, merely to beat the subpoena."

"I don't think anything," said Kastner. "I don't know. But we've been grappling around in the dark. This lets the light in a little."

"It sure does," said Creel, mopping his brow. "It sure does."

"All right," said Kastner. "Now let's start trying to kick it apart."

It was late afternoon. Because of heavy clouds and a river mist, the daylight was fading early. Westward, there was a vague smokey red glow in the sky as the sun declined. Lights were on in all the office buildings of the Downtown area.

Jim sat slumped in his office chair, staring with unseeing eyes at the top of his desk. He'd had an abrupt letdown; all of his energy seemed suddenly to have vanished; and though vaguely realizing that he was tired, nervous, and not in a frame of mind for it, he could not prevent himself from taking stock of his life, present and future. What did he think he was doing? He'd been rushing around at such a pitch for days that he'd never stopped to consider; up to his neck in an extremely dubious and dangerous business that might mean, with a bad break here and there, his total eclipse in the city; disbarment, disgrace, bankruptcy. Why had he jumped in with both feet so eagerly? Was it out of loyalty to Tom Patton and the Old Machine? Was it because he smelled money? Or was it only irresponsibility, egoism, not giving a damn—as Alma had charged repeatedly when they were having their many quarrels before the divorce?

Once he'd had high hopes for a distinguished career in law or politics, or both; like his grandfather and his father before him. But he'd never really managed to get himself reoriented after nearly four years in the Army. He'd come back to a changed city and a changed world. He'd been introduced to Tom Patton by an old lawyer friend of his father's. The rest was local history. He'd risen to power with the Administration, which had managed to stay in office for nearly ten years, and he'd fallen with it, like a puppet with no volition of his own. Now what was he? "Shyster" was not too strong a term, defending the indefensible Mr. Aldus Willey, and obstructing and trying to defeat the purposes of justice by fronting for Tom Patton, in an affair that was actually none of his business at all.

It was a form of drifting, and he was fitfully aware of it, but as a rule he fought against acknowledging it even to himself. He'd been drifting since 1946, drifting for twelve of the most important years of his life. He'd drifted into the Administration, into a wild love affair with Judy, into divorce and loneliness. And now he was drifting into what? Almost certain disaster. Pat Ryan was a brave man, but he'd backed off—out of concern for his family, while Larry was being pulled along like a man in the wake of a comet. As he was himself.

Jim got up, went to the window, and stood looking out into the dismal reddish-gray of late afternoon. He'd never felt so low in spirit in his life before; not even in the Italian hospital during the War when it was thought for a while that he might lose the use of his right leg. What was ahead? A few more years of failure, then senility?

Just as Jim turned abruptly to get himself a drink there was a light tap at his door and Gert put her head in.

"Mr. Chase, excuse me," she said. "But you've got some distinguished visitors."

She opened the door wide, but nobody appeared.

"What is this?" Jim demanded, with such exaggerated irritability that Gert looked at him in surprise.

But at that moment grinning youthful faces looked round the doorjamb.

"Hi, Dad," said Bob.

Lloyd was so delighted at the success of their surprise that he didn't say anything at all but just jumped up and down and squealed.

"Oh, God, aren't they cute!" cried Gert, then she grabbed them both and hugged them fiercely.

The boys struggled hard and got away, glancing in embarrassment at their father.

"Oh, so you don't like women," said Gert. Then she laughed and went out, closing the door.

"Is she ... does she work for you, Dad?" asked Lloyd.

"Yes," said Jim, still not quite over the shock of their sudden appearance.

"Isn't she kind of old?"

Jim burst out laughing. "Well, she's not decrepit," he said.

"What's that mean?" asked Lloyd.

"Oh, never mind," said Bob. "Always silly questions. Won't you ever grow up?"

They began to bicker. Jim pushed them over toward the couch. "Sit down, boys, and tell me what you're doing here."

He pulled up a straight chair and sat opposite them.

"Mommy's downstairs," said Bob. "She's got something wrong with her teeth."

"Ole Doc Cromwell sent her in here," explained Lloyd. "He's our dentist and he's an old crab. Gives us lollipops, though."

"Mommy had to see a what-do-you-call-it," said Bob.

"A specialist?"

"Yes. Won't take her a minute. He just has to look and then call Doc Cromwell, or something like that. She might have to have two or three teeth pulled. Wow!"

"We can't stay long," said Lloyd. "We're supposed to see if you are here and say hello and go right back. She wasn't even going to bring us along; then she changed her mind."

"Just relax boys," said Jim. "Your mother knows where you are."

"She might get mad," said Bob. "She doesn't want us bothering you. She made us swear not to call you on the telephone anymore."

"I kept my fingers crossed when I was swearing," said Lloyd, and both boys giggled loudly.

They talked on. Time passed. Little by little Jim relaxed and pretty soon he was wondering what in the hell it was that had been disturbing him so before their arrival. Something about drifting and having fallen from a high estate and senility, and … hell, everybody got old. Could he expect to be an exception? He heard himself laughing loudly at one of Lloyd's remarks. You could never be quite sure whether Lloyd spoke out of innocence or slyness.

"How are the bats?" he asked.

"Neato!" said Bob. "You ought to see me whack that ball."

"He busted Mrs. Thomson's window," said Lloyd.

Bob gave his brother a reproachful look. "Now why'd you have to bring that up, snitch?"

"And he's so broke!" Lloyd went on, unperturbed. "He had to pay for it out of his allowance."

"How about you!" cried Bob. "Dad, he threw water all over Beverly Jane."

"Who's Beverly Jane?"

"Girl next door."

"A drip," said Lloyd. "She kept calling me Nasty Boy so I cooled her off."

"Her mother was going to hit Lloyd with a broom. You should have seen him run." Bob imitated the sound of a jet plane and demonstrated with gestures.

They roared.

In the outer office Gert was speaking primly into the phone: "Yes;

he's still in conference. I'm sure it is 'rather important,' Miss; but I can't disturb him. I'm so sorry." Gert hung up, then nodded her head once in grim satisfaction, as if to say: "So there!"

Later Alma phoned and told the boys to come down at once. She sounded a little put out, and Bob looked at his father and said: "Oh-oh! You've got us in a jam."

Jim took them down in the automatic elevator, which they admired very much and wanted to run, but Jim vetoed the idea. "How did you get up here?" he asked.

"Oh," said Bob, embarrassed and disdainful, "that old nurse had to bring us up."

Alma was waiting in the hallway.

"Boys," she said, "I told you to come right back. Now this is the last time."

"Wait a minute, Alma," said Jim. "It was my fault. They told me they had to go right back. I said it was okay to stay."

"But I don't want them bothering you, Jim. I know how busy you are."

"I wish they'd come in every day," said Jim.

Alma gave him an irritated look, then her face softened. The boys were dancing around laughing.

"It's not the last time, is it, Mommy?" cried Lloyd. "It wasn't our fault."

"We'll see, boys," said Alma. "We've got to go, Jim. I've still got work to do this afternoon."

"Okay, Alma. I'll be up one of these times."

He stood watching them leave. The boys carefully opened the door for their mother and stood aside; then they both looked back at Jim, waving and grinning.

Jim hated to see them go.

... "I'll put him on now, miss," Gert was saying. "The conference is over."

In his office, Jim picked up the phone. Judy was already on.

"Well, you're a busy man," she said.

"That so?" said Jim, absentmindedly, still thinking about the happy faces of Bob and Lloyd.

"This is the third time I've called you. You were always in conference."

"In con—oh! Yes," said Jim. "We're trying to catch up on the routine stuff, Larry and me. I've been out of here so much. Did you want something, Judy?"

Silence at the other end.

"Hello. Hello," said Jim.

"Do I have to *want* something to call you?" asked Judy, rather coldly.

"No, no. But you said you called three times, so I imagined that …"

"I just woke up from a nap and thought about you right away, and called. That's all. Nothing to say. I won't keep you. See you tonight."

"Okay, Judy. See you tonight."

He waited. Judy seemed to hesitate, then hung up. It was obvious that her feelings were hurt. Jim sighed and leaned back in his chair. He was sorry, very sorry, but at the moment he just did not feel like talking to Judy.

A heavy mist was rolling in from the river, blurring the city lights and dampening the streets until they shone like black glass. The huge golden diagonal neon sign at Volari's cast a sharp glittering upside down reflection on the wide pavement in front of the club and Chauncey walked back and forth across it, in silhouette, as he waited for patrons to drive up. He was wearing a hooded slicker over his Volari's uniform. His breath showed as small puffs of smoke in the damp air. From time to time he stamped his feet and grumbled at the weather. "What's she going to be like this winter?" he thought.

Inside, Alice, the check-girl, read a paperback novel, which she held below the level of the counter, and occasionally examined her teeth, her hair and her complexion with the aid of a little hand mirror. "Even in this pinkish light I don't look so hot," she told herself, irritated and dissatisfied.

Oswald, the bartender, who had picked up the Volari routine and was now at ease in his job, was at the slot having a conversation with the new girl, Clarice, who was very pretty, with blue eyes and thick chestnut hair. She had formerly worked at a big bowling alley and recreation center, Downtown, and was still bug eyed over Volari's, stunned at the size of the tips, and amazed and saddened by the elegance of some of the women.

"Did you see that redhead that just went into the supper room?" she was asking Oswald, and when he nodded, she went on: "That coat she was wearing—dark mink—cost maybe six thousand dollars or more."

"So?"

"So where do they all come from? So where do they get their money?"

"Baby, listen," said Oswald, "you don't see these people in bowling alleys." Then he laughed loudly.

Clarice looked at the bartender with compressed lips. "Okay, Ossie. Very funny."

Judy came up to the slot and gave her order, followed by Cecile. People were beginning to arrive now, in couples and parties. It was after eleven o'clock.

"Oh, kids," said Clarice, "I saw the new boss. Did you see him? He was right back there taking to Mr. Volari. He's so good-looking, don't you think?"

Cecile giggled and gave Oswald her order. Judy said nothing.

"Well, what's funny?" Clarice demanded, looking about her, sensing something, but not understanding it. "He is!"

Judy gave her order. Clarice turned to her. Judy was the only one who hadn't made Clarice feel like a fool on her first day. Judy had helped her.

"What's so funny, Judy?" she asked. "Have I done it again?" She was tired of causing unexpected laughter that she did not comprehend the reason for.

"No," said Judy. "He is. I agree."

"Well, then," said Clarice.

Cecile left, then Judy.

"That's her boyfriend," said Oswald, chuckling with delight.

"Judy's? My God!" cried Clarice. "I should have come to work here sooner."

Now she jumped and gave a faint, partly suppressed shriek. Gino had just come up behind her.

"Aren't those your booths at the back? Don't you see the people?" Gino demanded.

"It's so dark in here, Mr. Volari," she said. "I didn't see them come in. I …" She was very scared and abjectly apologetic. She didn't want to lose *this* job!

"Go, go," said Gino, then, as she hurried off, to Oswald: "Could we have a little less social activity, Ossie?"

"Okay, Gino. But the girls like to talk."

Gino merely looked at him, then turned and moved back toward the archway where Tully Burke was telling his three musicians a killingly funny story, or at least you would think so from the way they were reacting. But, of course, Tully hired and fired and there were a lot of musicians out of work in the city.

Gino waited till the laughter had died down, then he took Tully aside. "Could we please, Tully, have a little more music and fewer jokes?"

"Philistine!" said Tully.

"What?" said Gino.

"It's a pet name. It means I like you. And if you will be a very good boy, Gino, for the rest of the evening, I'll tell you the story I told the fellows. It's a real gasser." He turned back to his musicians, while Gino just stood there, his lips compressed, feeling frustrated as he almost always did after a brush with Tully. "Okay, boys. 'April in Paris'. But inconspicuously. We don't want nostalgia to stop the flow of digestive juices. We must protect the patrons at Volari's from their own emotions. A-one, a-two ..."

He broke the musicians up. Gino walked away in dignified disgust. And so the evening wore slowly away at Volari's.

Jim was sitting at Al's desk, looking through a stack of papers. Judy tapped and came in, carrying a drink on a tray. Jim got up at once.

"Thanks, honey," he said. "I need it."

He took the drink. Judy looked at him coldly.

"Gino asked me to bring it," she said, as she started out.

"What's the hurry?" asked Jim.

"We're fairly busy," said Judy, "and Clarice, the new girl, is still pretty slow and gets things mixed up."

"Judy!"

Now she burst out: "You haven't said a word to me all evening and when I called you at the office first your secretary brushed me off and then you did. I'll never call you there again."

"Oh, come on, honey."

"I mean it. Conference, conference! I'll bet. And here I woke up thinking about you, so I called right away. You and your secretary acted as if wanted to borrow money."

Jim stared at her in amazement. After all this time! At first, during the early days of their affair, Judy had always been getting her feelings hurt, and nursing them for hours. Usually as the result of fancied slights.

"Judy," said Jim, "my kids walked in on me unannounced. That was the conference. I didn't know you'd been calling. Gert didn't tell me."

Judy's lips quivered slightly, but she said nothing.

"Will you stop with this nonsense?" said Jim.

"Those kids," said Judy, finally; "all of a sudden they are pretty important to you, aren't they?"

"I guess so," said Jim.

"I remember when I used to try to get you to call them on the phone, and you wouldn't."

It was true and yet Jim couldn't quite make himself believe that it was. Anyway such things belonged to the past.

"I know," he said. "But ..."

"Don't go into it," said Judy. Then: "I can see it coming, Jim."

"See what?"

"You going back—with your family. Maybe that's why I'm so touchy lately."

"It's not possible," said Jim.

"It's possible, all right," said Judy. "In fact, it's a dead cinch, in my opinion. And I'm going away to California just as soon as things get straightened around. I told you before—and I mean it."

"Don't talk like that, Judy," said Jim. "You can't go alone."

She glanced at him quickly, then lowered her eyes. "I came here alone, didn't I?"

Jim reached out and took her in his arms. But she resisted and pulled away.

"No, Jim," she said, "that doesn't prove anything or solve anything. I've got to get back."

To his surprise she went out hurriedly, closing the door behind her with a sort of finality, as if that was that. Jim stood hesitating. He wanted to follow her, make her come back and talk things over, but all of the employees of Volari's had eyes like gimlets and he did not feel like giving them more occasion for gossip and speculation, especially now that he was nominally in charge.

The phone rang. It was Dr. Maudley, calling from the Greet Memorial Hospital.

"It's worse than I thought, Mr. Chase," the doctor explained. "He's been living under a terrible strain and apparently everything has piled up on him at once. It's a sort of nervous collapse. I hardly know what else to call it. Complicated, of course, by hypertension. He's a very sick man. He'll be in bed quite a while. I have no idea how long. Do you think you should contact his brother? He keeps talking about him."

"You mean you think he might …?"

"No," said the doctor. "Unless there's quite a change."

"Then I don't think we should worry Tom with it. He's got enough on his mind as it is. And in any case, he couldn't come back here. Tell Al not to worry about Volari's or anything else. I'll look after it. Tell him to concentrate on getting well."

"All right, Mr. Chase. If there's any big change I'll let you know."

It was nearly two o'clock. Jim, who'd gone out for a while, was back at his desk at Volari's. Gino would check the receipts with Oswald and the supper room captain, Anselmo, and then Gino and Jim would recheck them, and put the money away in the safe.

Jim began to wonder about Judy, and finally called the bar on the house-phone. Gino answered.

"May I speak to Judy, Gino?"

"She's gone. She and Cecile left together. The new girl stayed. There was hardly anybody here, Mr. Chase, so I let Cecile and Judy leave. Apparently they had plans."

Jim hung up and sat staring at the desktop. So Judy had decided to make a break. There was no other explanation. This was the first time, since the beginning of their affair, that she had done anything like this.

"It's probably for the best," he told himself, but that was easy to say. Actually he felt worried, apprehensive and depressed. What in the hell would he do with himself, day after day, without Judy?

# 8: THURSDAY

A dazzling ray of light slanting in through the slatted blind hit Jim full in the face and woke him. During the night a strong west wind had blown the clouds and mist away and the new day was bright, sunny and warm. Jim, only half awake, yawned, stretched and wondered what dark thing it was nagging at the back of his mind. As a rule the morning worries did not start until he was washing and shaving. He glanced at his watch—quarter till nine; then he remembered and sat up straight in bed. Judy! He hadn't heard from her. He reached out for the phone, then hesitated. She'd obviously been out late—leaving for a party or a date at two a.m.!—so why wake her?

Sitting on the edge of the bed with his head in his hands he remembered how, back in the days of the old administration, Gino had tried discreetly to warn him about Judy when it became apparent to everybody that the affair was not something to be taken lightly. "She gets around, that little girl," Gino had said. "Yes, she gets around; her and her girlfriend, Zena!" Well, it looked like Judy had started "getting around" again. And why not? Old enough to be her father, he'd monopolized her long enough. Judy was only twenty-five and looked younger.

He showered, shaved and dressed, trying not to think about Judy; then he went down the street to Allie's for breakfast. The same untidy middle-aged waitress seated him and as usual without the slightest flicker of recognition. Jim kept his eyes averted. Hers was not a pleasant morning face.

He was in the middle of his breakfast when a car stopped in front of the place with a wild shriek of brakes and the hiss of tires. Then a man came in hurriedly. Jim glanced up. Pat Ryan! What in the devil was he doing there?

Pat saw Jim, sat down opposite him without a word, and waved the waitress away.

"Couldn't find you any place," Pat explained. "Got your partner on the phone. He suggested this joint."

"Coffee?"

"No, thanks." Pat seemed excited and nervous, and moved about uncomfortably for a moment before he spoke again. "Jim, I'll give you my bad news first; then yours."

"What are you talking about, Pat?"

"I've been transferred to Smoketown as of this morning when I came in," said Pat.

"I'm sorry, Pat," said Jim.

"I wondered about it. I'd been expecting it, as you know; but why this morning—and so fast? As a rule things aren't done like that in the department. I smelled ... not a rat, an elephant. So I began looking into it. Well, they wanted me out today for a very good reason. A big murder case came up overnight, and they didn't want me in charge of it."

"Why not?"

"I'm coming to that, so hold on to your hat. Jim. They found those guys."

"What guys?"

"The guys you're looking for—Bailey and Ziegler. They were in Ziegler's car under about thirty feet of water in the river. Both of them had been shot."

Jim almost dropped his coffee cup.

"Shot?"

"Yes," said Pat. "Obviously somebody knew what they were carrying. Knocked them off and took it. As you know the DA's office was tailing you, so somebody must have seen us talking together. So they didn't want me touching this case at all. Lieutenant Sam Gorsuch is in charge and he's a tough cookie, as you probably know."

Jim was too stunned to speak. He could hardly believe his ears. Such a solution to the disappearance of Gus and Ziegler had never even occurred to him in his wildest gropings. Who could have known what they were carrying? And just a plain hit-or-miss robbery didn't make any kind of sense. Too far-fetched—too coincidental. No; somebody must have been laying for them.

"Where was this?" asked Jim.

"About halfway to the lake, just off River Boulevard. The banks are steep there and it was late at night; probably deserted. The robbers just tipped the car over the bank. A couple of teenage skindivers found the car at about six-thirty this morning. The police sent divers down with chains and they had the crate out of the water at a little after seven. Fast work. I was supposed to be in charge, you understand, as captain of homicide, Downtown, but nobody called me. I slept through it."

"I can't understand it at all," said Jim, shocked and bewildered. "It doesn't make sense."

"Jim," said Pat, "I hate to pile it on you all at once but here's another little item to put gray in your hair. Tony Fiala is dead …"

"What!" cried Jim, so loudly that people turned to look at him.

"Take it easy," said Pat. "Found in the street last night. Suspicion of hit and run. I didn't get the report till this morning." Jim said nothing; things were coming at him too fast now. "Jim, listen to me. I've come here to warn you and give you some good advice. This was done by big-time professionals. Don't play policeman anymore. Lieutenant Gorsuch will be around to see you. Tell him the truth from top to bottom. If the DA's men were following you, they may know you were looking for Tony Fiala. His disappearance was already tied in by the boys; you can bet on that."

"I can't tell the truth, Pat. We can't afford to acknowledge that two hundred thousand dollars. Look, add it up for yourself. Tom Patton was Commissioner of Streets and Highways for eight years at twelve thousand a year."

"Jim," said Pat, "that's his lookout. Besides, he's in San Francisco. You're here. You know me. I was a friend of Tom's. But why get yourself in a terrible jam over old Tom? Tell the truth. Back out of it. Leave it to the department."

"No. I can't."

"Why can't you? You don't owe those guys anything."

"I just can't, Pat. Tom needs that money. I am still trying to get it for him. I am also trying to make a buck myself."

"The hard way," said Pat. "Listen, if you don't tell Downtown the truth—I will, and take the consequences, prosecution for withholding evidence in regard to a felony."

"Pat!"

"I mean it. I'm damned if I'm going to stand around and see you get yourself killed or sent to the clink out of some kind of crazy loyalty to …"

Jim was thoughtfully silent for a moment, then he said: "You're forgetting one thing."

"What's that?"

"Your kids, Pat—your family."

Pat stared at Jim for a moment in consternation, then began to squirm but remained silent.

"Look," said Jim. "Give me a few days, Pat. You're all excited. Go back to work. Let Downtown handle their end. Why help them? They booted you out of it. Stay out of it."

After a long silence, Pat said: "All right. I'll be in the old 21st eating smoke with the Poles from now on. I won't even come to your funeral. But, Jim, listen to me first. The professionals must have had Tony

Fiala and maybe Zena Mylan stooging for them at Volari's ..."

"That Mond guy," said Jim.

"Yes," said Pat. "Either Tony fell out with them or they were afraid he'd talk and killed him. Xena—pretty smart girl—got scared and took a powder. That's why Mond was trying so hard to find her."

Jim nodded, then told Pat about the last rumor he'd heard from Marty the fink. "Could be," said Pat. "They might have had a fight among themselves. There's usually a fight of some kind when a group's got that much money to split."

Now Pat got up and stood leaning on the table looking down at Jim.

"I'll give you a couple of days. You're a good talker. But I'm warning you, I may change my mind."

"All right, Pat," said Jim, reaching up to shake hands with him. "Thanks for everything."

"They're expecting to walk in on you cold," said Pat. "So govern yourself accordingly. The story won't break till the noon edition of the afternoon papers."

Pat nodded and left. Jim sat staring into space, still suffering from shock. The waitress came over. He looked up. To his surprise she was smiling at him.

"Glad everything come out all right," she said.

Jim stared at her, wondering what the devil she was talking about.

"Oh, I can tell a copper a mile off," she said. "I had a little trouble with 'em in my younger days. I'm clean now. But I can still tell 'em."

Her whole attitude toward him had changed since she'd seen him harassed, as she thought, by a "copper." He gave her a big tip as he left—big for Allie's, that is.

"Thanks," she said. "And good luck."

"Same to you," said Jim.

Jim hurried to his office. First he called Larry in and explained everything to him, as quietly and calmly as possible, trying to cushion the shock, but Larry took it much better than he had expected and did not start to jig about and talk incoherently.

"This is going to make quite a noise in the newspapers, Jim," he said. "They'll rake up all about Tom Patton and the old Administration and hash it over."

"Yes. Roman holiday. Larry, look. I'll keep you out of this as much as possible. But Downtown may know that we were looking for Fiala; and they may know that you talked to his father. So let's not deny it. Here's the story. Al was worried about his employees disappearing. We were looking into it. We had a hunch Fiala might have been the one who came for Gus and Ben's clothes. You went to check on him. If

Gorsuch questions you, tell him the truth; everything the old man said and so forth. Right?"

"Yes," said Larry. "But I think I ought to drive home and prepare Beth. Not try it on the phone."

"Okay. Go ahead."

Larry got up to go, but hesitated at the door. "Jim, maybe you should listen to Pat at that. This could get pretty ... well, you know."

"We'll talk about it later."

As soon as Larry had gone, Jim called Dr. Maudley. It took some time to get him and Jim paced impatiently and finally went out into the anteroom where Gert was working on Larry's notes in regard to the Aldus Willey brief.

"Gert," he said, "I'm expecting visitors soon—from Downtown Precinct. A Lieutenant Sam Gorsuch. Keep him waiting. Tell him I'm on the phone—which I may be. And try the doctor again."

Hearing heavy footsteps in the corridor, Jim hurried back into his office and in a moment caught the murmur of voices in the anteroom; then his buzzer sounded and Gert had Dr. Maudley on the line for him.

"Jim Chase, Doctor ..."

"I'm glad you called. Two detectives came to my office about fifteen minutes ago; wanted permission to talk to Mr. Patton."

"That's what I'm calling you about. I don't think we should let them disturb him."

"Certainly not," said the doctor, impatiently. "I told them it was quite impossible. Mr. Chase, I didn't like their attitude. I'm a reputable physician. When I say a patient of mine shouldn't be bothered, I mean it, and I have a very good reason for saying it. They seemed to imply that Mr. Patton was malingering and that I was a party to it."

Jim smiled to himself. Things couldn't have worked out better in regard to Al Patton. There had never been the slightest question of Dr. Maudley's integrity. He had a fine reputation in the city. Now some thickhead from Downtown had made an enemy of him. Perfect. Jim decided to add fuel to the fire, clinching the matter.

"I'm shocked, Doctor," he said, "that anybody would even imply an accusation like that against a man of your standing. It's disgraceful."

"Yes," said Dr. Maudley, his voice trembling slightly, "that's my feeling exactly. Disgraceful! Unheard-of!"

"They'll probably be back, pestering you again, I'm sorry to say."

"They'll get no place with me, I assure you," said Dr. Maudley. "I almost threw them out of my office as it was."

"Refer them to me, if they give you any real trouble," said Jim. "I'll deal with them as Mr. Patton's attorney."

"I'll do that," said the doctor. "And thank you for your understanding and cooperation, Mr. Chase."

Jim hung up, then took out some papers and began to look through them; after a minute or so of stalling, he buzzed Gert. "Any calls while I was talking?"

"No," said Gert. "But there is a Lieutenant Sam Gorsuch waiting to see you."

"Have him come in."

In a moment the door opened and Gorsuch stepped in, followed by Detective Sergeant Boston. Gorsuch was a big heavy-shouldered blond man, about forty, with a tough, weathered-looking face. His blue eyes were pale and penetrating. There was an atmosphere of grimness about him, which was dissipated when he smiled showing strong white teeth. Boston was slight and dark and quiet, hardly more than a shadow of a man in comparison with the rough, robust lieutenant.

"Hi," said Jim. "Sorry if I kept you waiting. Sit down. What can I do for you?"

Gorsuch and Boston sat on the couch, and Jim turned his swivel chair around and faced them.

"Mr. Chase," said Gorsuch, "did you ever get a line on Tony Fiala?"

"Tony Fiala?"

"Yes. You were looking for him, weren't you?"

"Yes," said Jim. "My partner, Larry Jackson, talked to his father the other day. Yesterday, I think it was. I could check. Apparently Tony had a fight with his father over quitting his job and left home."

"Why were you trying to find him?" asked Gorsuch, who had already thrown a quick glance at Boston, which said: "He may be wised-up."

"A hunch," said Jim. "He answered the description of the man who came for Gus Bailey's clothes—also Ben's—and checked them out."

"And why were you so anxious to find Bailey and Ziegler?"

"Anxious is not the word, Lieutenant," said Jim. "Mr. Patton was concerned. He was also not feeling well and asked me to help him."

"Something wrong with the Police Department, Mr. Chase? That's what we are for. We run down mysterious disappearances."

"I explained all that to Sergeant Gamble," said Jim, patiently.

"I know. I know," said Gorsuch. "You are very good at explaining, Mr. Chase. But it still does not make sense to me."

"Do you want me to repeat my explanations?"

"No," said Gorsuch. "I've read all of Sergeant Gamble's reports. Mr. Chase, I don't have to tell you that withholding evidence in regard to a felony is against the law. As a lawyer you know more about that than I do."

"Yes, Lieutenant? What felony?"

Gorsuch hesitated for a long time, then he said: "Mr. Chase, do you have any objections to coming to Headquarters with me?"

"Yes," said Jim. "I've got work to do. I have to earn a living you know."

"What time would you be at leisure?"

"Oh, say, five o'clock."

"And you wouldn't mind coming over at that time?"

"Yes, I'd mind. But if you think it's absolutely necessary ..."

"It'd be a help. Tony Fiala's dead, Mr. Chase. And we found Bailey and Ziegler—in the river."

Jim said nothing for a long time, but merely looked from Gorsuch to Boston. "I'll be there, Lieutenant," he said, finally.

When they left, Jim got up and began to pace. Alone now, he was suddenly assailed by doubts. What did he think he was doing? One man against all the machinery that Sam Gorsuch and the DA could bring into play against him! What chance did he have? And yet ... he just could not bring himself to tell the truth. It would mean certain ruin for old Tom Patton, who was in enough trouble as it was, and it might mean the death of Al Patton. And anyway what awful purpose would it serve, aside from saving his own neck? Gus and Ben and Tony Fiala were all dead. Nothing could bring them back. As for justice ...? Justice was and always had been a cold abstraction to Jim.

Snapping his fingers at a sudden thought, he dialed Alma's home number, forgetting that she'd be at work at this hour.

"Hello," said a youthful voice. "Mars, here. Is that earth calling?"

Jim heard furious giggling.

"It's King Kong," said Jim. "How is it up there?"

"Dad!" cried Bob's voice. "How do you like our gag? We always answer the phone that way now."

"What does your mother say?"

"Oh, it's only when she's not here. She'd fracture us."

"She's at work, isn't she?" said Jim.

"Yes," said Bob. "You coming up soon?"

Before Jim could reply there was the sound of a struggle at the other end, and he heard Lloyd shrieking: "I want to talk to him. I want to talk to him." Then he heard Bob say, disdainfully: "All right, baby."

"Hi, Lloyd."

"Hi, Dad. You coming up soon?"

"I asked him that," came Bob's disdainful voice down the wire.

"Just as soon as I can, boys," said Jim. "You be good now and mind your mother. Don't cause her trouble."

There was dead silence at the other end and then he heard piercing whispers. "He did say that. He did."

Bob came on, "What was that, Dad?"

"I said to be good and mind your mother. Don't cause her trouble."

"Oh, okay, Dad. Mom thinks we're pretty good boys. She only whacks us now and then."

Jim had the feeling they were disappointed in him for suddenly playing the father, after all this time. Kids were funny, and very sensitive to changes of attitude and shades of feeling.

Jim tried to figure out how to retrieve his lost position. "If I get a good report on you boys," he said, "I may let you run the elevator the next time you come down here."

"Oh, boy!" cried Bob, then he repeated what Jim had said to Lloyd, who shrieked with delight. "That's neat! Neato!"

"Well, just wanted to see how you were," said Jim. "Got to go back to work. See you."

The boys both yelled: "See you," in the phone, then Jim hung up.

He felt heartened, and kept smiling to himself as he dialed Alma's number. He could tell that she was very surprised that he'd called her at work. This was the first time.

"Sorry to bother you, Alma," he said. "But there's something I've got to tell you. It may be in the evening papers; but probably not till morning. I think you'll see my name mentioned. Don't worry about it."

"What is it, Jim?" Alma sounded anxious, apprehensive.

"There's been a little trouble. I'm acting as attorney for Al Patton—Tom's brother. Remember? I may have to take the heat for a while. All I'm saying is, don't get disturbed. Don't worry. I don't know what the papers will make of it. That's why I'm warning you."

"Well, if you say it's nothing serious ..." She sounded doubtful.

"The thing itself is very serious," Jim explained. "But not my part in it. I called you at home by mistake; talked to the boys. Don't let them know I called there by mistake, okay? They sounded fine."

"They're pretty good boys, Jim," said Alma. "Pretty trustworthy for their ages."

"How's Ole Hoss?"

"Same as usual. Said he was thinking about putting you up for the golf club. What was he talking about?"

"Oh, I ran into him the other night. We had a cross-purpose conversation. How are you otherwise?"

"I'm fine, except I've been having a lot of trouble with my teeth. They say I should have three of them pulled, but I hate to. I may, though."

"Don't envy you that. Remember the trouble I had? Well, I'll call you, Alma. And don't worry."

He had no sooner hung up, than the buzzer sounded. Gert came on.

"There is a young lady ..."

Judy! He'd forgotten all about her.

"Jim? My you're getting hard to talk to. This is the fourth time I've called. First, it's conference. Then you're on the phone. Can you run out here? There's something I want to tell you." Judy did not sound like herself at all, but very distant, almost like a stranger.

"Yes," said Jim. "Right away."

Jim didn't know exactly what he felt as he hung up. Judy had deliberately made a break the night before. Did she regret it? Was it only a ruse to stir him up? What?

She hadn't sounded regretful, or much of anything else, over the phone except that there had been a slight touch of flippancy in her manner that certainly was not characteristic. Had it been only out of awkwardness? Last night she'd stated positively that she would never call him at the office again.

But before he would let Judy tell him anything, he told her as carefully as possible about the finding of Ben and Ziegler and Tony. Wanting to save her from the shock of suddenly running into it in the newspapers. She sat opposite him in longing pajamas, white-faced and still, occasionally gasping and exclaiming: "Oh, my God, Jim!" When he had finished, she got rather shakily to her feet.

"Jim … I … I … just don't feel well. I've got to lie down."

He helped her to the daybed, then mixed her a strong highball that she lay sipping.

"I think Zena got out just in time," she said.

"Yes," said Jim. "It looks like it."

"That's what I want to tell you about," said Judy. "I went to a party last night with Cecile. She knows a lot of these beatniks, who hang around Melton Stairs. You know; down on the river. Her steady boyfriend is a musician—out of work, of course; although Tully's thinking about taking him on. He's a wonderful bass player. Oh, what a collection, with the chin whiskers and all! Well, Cecile introduced me to this fellow named Shep. He's about twenty-seven or eight. Quiet. Never saw him in my life before, but he claimed that he knew Zena and kept trying to pump me about her. What happened to her, you know; and if I'd heard from her and where she was. He was very nice about it and kept talking about other things in between. I asked him where he'd known Zena and he said around Volari's. Listen, I'd remember him, Jim. He's tall and kind of good looking, with real pale blond hair, cut short. You think I'm imagining things?"

"No," said Jim. "Not necessarily."

"He wanted to take me home. But no dice. He kept hanging around but about three-thirty Tully showed up, then Shep let me be. I asked Cecile about Shep but she said she'd only seen him once before. So I told her to ask her boyfriend—Cliff—about him. Cliff said he'd seen him around; didn't know anything about him; not even his last name. Nobody knew anything about him. But with the beatniks that's par for the course. They don't know and they don't care."

"What did you tell him?"

"Just that she'd moved out suddenly without even telling me anything about it; that I hadn't heard from her and didn't know where she was."

"It might be on the square," said Jim. "I think you're forgetting how crowded Volari's used to be in the old Administration days. You couldn't notice everybody."

"Oh, it wasn't that far back," said Judy. "He talked like it was recently." A pause. "Well, I just thought you ought to know."

"Yeah," said Jim. "I'm glad you told me. Now listen, Judy. You'll have men from Downtown here. So tell them just what you told Creel. They've already read his reports."

"Why me?" asked Judy, showing apprehension.

"Everybody who works at Volari's, from Chauncey to Gino will be questioned. You've got nothing to worry about."

There was a long pause, then Judy held out her glass. "Will you freshen this?"

"Yes," said Jim. "Then I've got to go. This is my busy day."

Judy sipped the new drink tentatively and then looked up at Jim, who was standing over her. "I've made up my mind," she said. "I want to get around more."

"All right," said Jim. "I think you should."

"I thought you did," said Judy, smiling slightly.

"It occurred to me this morning how young you are, Judy. As a rule I don't think about it. Why should I monopolize you?"

"Yes," said Judy. "Why should you?"

After his divorce Jim had thought seriously of marrying Judy, but had never got around to mentioning it to her. This seemed fantastic to him now. They'd been together practically all the time. How had it happened that he hadn't once spoken of his intentions? But, of course, it was almost impossible to judge the wild, unruly, irresponsible past in the light of the sober present. They'd all been a little crazy, drunk with success and power, all certain that it would go on forever, so why worry about a little thing like marriage? There'd always be time for that.

And then the shock of defeat—and a changed world. Many of them had folded. Jim had managed to keep going and build a new life, such as it was. Reality had slowly interposed itself between Jim and his wild-headed affair with Judy; yet she had been aware of that fact before he was. From emotional heights they had gradually slipped down to a sort of friendly quietude; they were in the habit of seeing each other almost every day; so, without comment, they'd merely continued the habit.

"This whole thing has been mighty unfair to you, Judy, in some ways," said Jim, wanting to leave, feeling very uncomfortable, still not sure of his own mind by any means.

"Why?" asked Judy. "I was over twenty-one. I was no kid. I'm not complaining."

Jim shifted about for a moment; then took out a cigarette and lit it, his hand shaking slightly. "I've got to go, Judy. If you need anything, want anything, call me."

"All right, Jim."

He stood looking down at her for a moment, then he turned and went out, with the sensation that he was leaving an important part of his life behind.

Judy lay very still, almost rigid, without moving. "I've got to get used to it," she told herself. "I've just got to make myself get used to it."

Things were in a turmoil at Downtown. For hours Lieutenant Sam Gorsuch hadn't had a moment to himself, badgered on all sides by subordinates, men from the DA's office, photographers, and crime and political reporters. As time passed, he grew more and more irritable and uneasy. Good God! what a noise *this* was going to make? And although he would scarcely admit it to himself, he began to wish that hard-bitten Pat Ryan hadn't been removed and that he could turn to him for help and encouragement.

The newspaper men were the worst headache. They all smelled a huge, circulation-getting story, and showed him no mercy. What about Tom Patton? Al Patton? Jake Webb? What about Pat Ryan? Why had he been booted out to Smoketown just when a big one like this was about to break? Who had done what to who and why?

Sam did his best to be diplomatic. The newspapers had been at least partially responsible for putting the new Administration into office, with their scarifying stories on graft and corruption under Big Tom Patton and stooges! He just could not afford to offend any of them.

But, good God! When was he expected to work?

All day long a parade of people had passed through Downtown to be questioned one by one; Gino, Cecile, Chauncey, Anselmo and all of the supper room waiters, Judy, Tully Burke and his musicians, Jacques, the chef, and all the kitchen help, Alice the check-girl, old Mr. Fiala, Doris Kallen, Larry Packard, the keepers of the rooming houses where Ben Ziegler and Gus Bailey had lived, the teenage skindivers who'd found the car, traffic policemen who'd assisted in the salvage, two drivers, and nearly a score of other miscellaneous persons who were connected in some remote way with the case.

All were now gone from the station except one—Marty the fink. He was being held in a little detention room at the back of the place. Food had been brought to him and he had plenty of cigarettes and magazines. He did not seem in any way perturbed.

The photographers took Jim by surprise as he came up the front steps at Downtown. Three of them jumped out and began to snap pictures from various angles.

"Come on, boys," he said mildly. "I'm not that important."

"Who is important then, Mr. Chase, in regard to this case?" asked a political reporter Jim had often seen around the corridors of the Hall of Justice in the old days.

"I wouldn't know," said Jim. "I'm merely acting for Mr. Alfred Patton—as attorney."

"He been pinched yet?"

"Funny man," said Jim. "Mr. Patton is in Greet Memorial Hospital, very ill."

"Any other comments?"

"Yes," said Jim, "I hope Lieutenant Gorsuch runs down the men who killed Gus Bailey and Ben Ziegler with his usual efficiency. Very capable officer."

"Oh, please, Mr. Chase," said the political reporter. "Who do you think you're kidding? He'd have your head in a basket if he could."

"Well, that's news to me," said Jim. "I always got on very well with Sam."

Jim looked about him blandly, then went on into the station. The newspaper men shrugged, grimaced, and glanced at each other significantly.

"Don't seem to be worried much," said a photographer.

"That's the Chase manner," said the political reporter. "His grandfather's picture is hanging in the second-floor corridor of the Hall of Justice. That makes a difference."

"Yeah? He can get his hide nailed to the barn door just as fast as you or me."

"We hope. It would make such a pretty story."

Jim was ushered into the presence of Sam Gorsuch, who, in his shirtsleeves and with his blond hair mussed, was sitting astride a straight chair, looking out the window. His office was hardly bigger than a clothes closet and so dark that the lights were on round the clock.

"Sorry if I'm a little late," said Jim. "But something came up at the last minute."

"Have a seat, Mr. Chase."

Jim sat down and lit a cigarette. Now Gorsuch spoke while still looking out the window.

"I've been listening to testimony all day long and the picture is beginning to clear up a little."

"That so?" said Jim. "I wish you'd tell me about it. I'm pretty confused at this point."

Gorsuch turned his chair around and sat looking at Jim.

"Mr. Chase, do you know a man named Martin Callison?" he asked.

"Marty? Yes."

"How do you happen to know a man like him? He's got a record a yard long."

"You know very well how I happen to know him, lieutenant."

"Tell me."

"I'd be within my rights not to tell you, you know. But since this is no more than an informal talk, all right. He was the best informer I had during the old Administration."

"Talked to him lately?"

"Yes."

"Why? You have no official position now."

"Lieutenant, I'm a lawyer."

"I see. Still using him as an informer. Some case of your own, I presume."

"That's right."

"What case?"

"Lieutenant, you know better than to ask me a question like that."

"Suppose you are asked that question under oath?"

"My lawyer will object, of course. And he'll make it stick."

A long pause. "I can see you have no intention of helping us, Mr. Chase. You intend to obstruct, as you've been doing all along."

"Harsh words," said Jim.

Gorsuch got up and stood pulling thoughtfully at his hair. "Why do you think Gus Bailey and Ben Ziegler were killed?"

"I wish I knew."

"You haven't the faintest idea?"

"Why should I have?"

A long pause, then Gorsuch sat down opposite Jim and looked directly into his eyes. "This Allen Mond. What can you tell me about him?"

"Very little. I suppose you've read Judy Waggoner's testimony. Sergeant Creel took it all down. I was there at the time, and advised her to answer his questions."

"I know, I know, Mr. Chase," said Gorsuch with elaborate sarcasm. "And I appreciate that. Also I talked to Miss Waggoner herself about two hours ago. I'm asking you, Mr. Chase."

Jim hesitated for a moment, then gave Gorsuch a minute description of Mond, point by point; then: "I could never quite figure him out. I saw him twice; once at a distance, once I talked to him. According to Judy he seemed to have plenty of money, drove a big Alfa, and lived at the Regent. I'm sure you've checked all these points."

"And you have no idea where he's from?"

Jim hesitated. "No."

"Have you talked to Pat Ryan lately?" Gorsuch asked suddenly.

"Yes," said Jim. "Pat has been consulting me about a private matter. I'm a lawyer, you know, lieutenant."

"Did it have anything to do with Allen Mond?"

Jim saw what was coming now and winced inwardly. "Lieutenant," he said, "I can't answer that question. Just as I couldn't answer the question in regard to Marty Callison. Privileged."

"You'll answer it on the stand."

"I doubt it, lieutenant. But off the record I'll tell you something. Pat was trying to help me locate Allen Mond, because Miss Waggoner was so worried about Zena Mylan. The last Miss Waggoner saw of Zena she was in the company of Allen Mond. Pat called Joe Carr at the Regent. Joe is an old friend of his."

"And you just told me you didn't know where Allen Mond was from?"

"I don't," said Jim. "A man signing a register can write down anything, can't he?"

The lieutenant's trap had failed. He felt a sudden surge of anger and turned away from Jim; then, after a moment, he rose and left the room without a word. Time passed. Jim got up and walked to the window. Auto horns and police whistles were blasting on River Boulevard two stories below. It was the evening rush hour and one-way, four-lane traffic was roaring northward toward the River Freeway. It had clouded up since noon and the daylight was fading early. Lights were springing on here and there, many of them casting reflections onto the slow-moving, gray-green expanse of the darkening river. A squat white tug passed below, its bridge lighted, and with men moving about on its deck. Factory whistles sounded from the south. Far downstream a searchlight sprang on and started to sweep the water. In the gathering twilight the city began to take on an unreal, melancholy air to Jim, like a huge portentous stage set which dwarfed the futile posturings and irrelevant tirades of a ludicrously inadequate cast.

He turned away, depressed. The phone rang on the desk and after a moment he answered it. "It's for you, Mr. Chase," said a ghostly-sounding voice from somewhere.

"Hello. Mr. Chase. Gert."

"Yes, Gert."

"I hate to bother you, but an odd telegram was just delivered …"

"Hold it," said Jim, quickly. "I'll be there as soon as I can get there. I wish you'd stay, Gert."

"Oh, I will, Mr. Chase. No matter how late. I'll send out for my dinner."

"Thanks, Gert."

He had no idea what was in the telegram nor who had sent it. But he just did not want it read over a police phone at Downtown. You could never tell!

A door opened behind him and Sgt. Boston put his head in. "Mr. Chase, would you mind stepping down the hall to Captain Tryon's office?"

Jim followed Sergeant Boston down the corridor in silence. The sergeant opened the door for him and ushered him into a crowded anteroom. Lou Tryon, new boss of Downtown, was sitting on the edge of a desk, paring his nails. Grouped about him were Stone, from the DA's office, Creel, Kastner and Gamble from Missing Persons, and Sam Gorsuch of homicide.

Captain Tryon nodded to Jim then gestured vaguely toward the inner office. Sergeant Boston opened the door. A little bewildered, Jim went in.

Judge Weybrecht, the new DA, was sitting at the captain's desk, sideways, in the big swivel chair, staring out the window.

"Mr. Chase," he said, "sit down."

"Thank you, Judge."

After a pause, the Judge said: "I have seen many examples of misguided loyalty in my time, but this is the worst. Your grandfather must be turning over in his grave."

"I beg your pardon, Judge?"

"Jim," said the Judge, "I am no policeman. I'm not subtle. I do not intend to try to trap you. But in my opinion you are obstructing justice and compounding a felony. Why were those men killed? For money of course. Money they were taking to Tom Patton so he could skip town and evade service of a subpoena. Am I right?"

"It's a theory, Judge," said Jim, beginning to shrink slightly in his chair.

"Only a theory—from our standpoint," said Judge Waybrecht. "But you know it's true, Jim. You know it just as well as you know you are sitting there. Why not help us? Do you think you owe Tom Patton loyalty? For what?"

"I'm Mr. Al Patton's attorney, sir," said Jim.

"Don't you want those heartless killers run down? Do you want them walking the streets free to rob and kill again? What are you thinking about, Jim Chase? I'm ashamed of you."

A long silence. "Do you intend to prefer charges, sir?"

"I don't know," said the Judge. "It would be premature at this point, I think."

"Yes," said Jim, "and it might cause considerable criticism, sir. It's well-known in the city that the new Administration intends to *get* Tom Patton. It's talked about everyplace."

"And why shouldn't we *get* him, as you put it?" said the Judge. "He's a malefactor. He betrayed his trust in office. He was a symbol of graft and corruption. Why shouldn't we get him?"

It might have been his own grandfather talking. Right was right; wrong was wrong; no shades.

"Sir," said Jim, "maybe this is not the right way. If, as you say, a felony has been committed—two murders, a robbery—isn't that the important thing? To use it as a snare to trap Tom Patton seems to me to be ..."

"Sophistry," said the Judge. "All I want is your cooperation, and if, after you've thought it over for, say, twenty-four hours, I don't get it, I'll be forced to prefer charges, or at least hold you as a material witness."

"I understand, Judge."

The new DA swung around in his chair, turning his back abruptly on Jim. "That's all."

Jim, feeling a mixture of embarrassment, shame and annoyance such as he'd often felt after an interview with his grandfather, went out quietly. The buzzer sounded in the outer office and Lieutenant Gorsuch answered it and held a brief, enigmatic conversation with Judge Weybrecht, then he hung up and turned to Jim.

"Go ahead now if you like," he said. "But stay in town till further notice."

"All right," said Jim. "Goodbye, gentlemen."

As soon as the door had closed behind him, Sam turned to Sargeant Boston. "Call downstairs. I want the tail on him twenty-four hours a day. I don't care how many men it takes."

Boston got on the phone at once.

Captain Tryon heaved a long sigh, put away his penknife with which he'd been paring his nails, got down from the desk and said: "I like that Chase guy. Now how in the hell did he ever get mixed up with that Jake Webb-Tom Patton outfit?"

"He got mixed up all around, Captain," said Gorsuch. "Something wrong with him somewhere. Left his wife and kids for a bar girl."

"I don't get it," said Captain Tryon.

Gert was eating her dinner from a tray when Jim got back to his office. Before either of them said a word, she handed him the telegram, and then as he glanced at it, she said: "It was marked for delivery; not to be phoned. I read it because I thought it might be something very important. Was that all right?"

Jim nodded abstractedly.

"It seems to me something's been left out," said Gert. "Doesn't make sense—or not to me."

The telegram read:

### GENERAL INDIANAPOLIS BROKE ILL
(signed) Z

Jim thought it over for a little while, then his eyes lit up and he snapped his fingers. "Gert," he said, "go down to the drugstore. Use a pay phone. Call the General Hospital in Indianapolis and see if Zena Mylan is a patient there. If she is, get me a spot on the first flight out. If she's not, this may mean I'm to communicate with her by General Delivery."

Gert looked at Jim in amazement. "How in the world did you ...?"

"And Gert—you didn't hear any of this. All you did was hand me an unopened telegram."

"I understand," said Gert, stammering a little. "But why the drugstore?"

"There's a long chance this phone night be tapped. Also I'm almost certain to have a tail on me now." He noticed Gert's blank look. "I'm being followed and watched, so as soon as you complete your calls, stop at the fountain and have a soda; anything you like. Seem casual. Here's some money. I don't know how much the calls will be."

Gert went out, still looking a little bewildered. Jim sat on the edge of her desk and concentrated on trying to figure out the best way of losing the Downtown detectives he was sure were following him.

"She's there," said Gert, her eyes showing marked excitement, "and your plane leaves in forty minutes. I booked it in the name of George Brewster."

"Why George Brewster?" asked Jim, laughing.

"I once read about a man named George Brewster in a novel," said Gert. "He was lost at sea."

"Oh, fine," said Jim. "But you're a good girl, Gert. I should have told you not to make it in my name."

Jim took a cab to the Hotel Metropole. During the final hectic days of the old Administration, he had been followed many times; apparently by private detectives hired by the Reformers. Twice he'd thrown them off his track by means of the old Metropole. He was gambling tonight that the Downtown detectives would not know about the back way out of the downstairs men's room.

But whoever was tailing him was doing a very good job of it. He hadn't caught sight of them yet. He paid off his cab in front of the hotel, crossed the lobby leisurely and then went down the stairs to the shoeshine stand outside the entrance of the men's room. He got up on the stand, took a newspaper out of his pocket, and began to glance through it, as the colored boy slapped the cloths rhythmically and hummed to himself.

The first page was *literally* covered with items about the murder of Gus and Ben. The left-hand column was a hastily thrown together pastiche of all the known or guessed facts of the case and the names of the people who had been questioned that day. His own name was missing. In a big box in the lower right-hand corner was a succinct account of Tom Patton's career, dragged in with the excuse that Gus and Tom had worked for Tom's brother, Al. On the second page was a big picture of Judy and Cecile, with the heading: "Questioned Today." Judy looked beautiful; Cecile cute and appealing. Volari's was mentioned at least a dozen times, and Jim observed to himself: "It'll be booming there tonight."

Now out of the corner of his eye Jim saw a man stop on the stairs and light a cigarette. He was a stranger to Jim, but he had a smack of Headquarters about him. When the shoeshine boy had finished Jim paid him then stood talking to him for a moment about the local baseball team that was not far from winding up a disastrous season. Then, laughing at one of the boy's remarks, he turned and went through the swing-doors into the men's room. It was deserted. He stalled for a moment, washing his hands and combing his hair, but as nobody came in, he hurried down the last row of booths and found the familiar door. It was bolted on the inside and apparently had not been used in some time. He struggled with the bolt, cursing, expecting any moment to hear heavy footsteps on the tile floor; finally it shot open with a loud shriek of metal. Jim opened the door, went out, closed it quietly behind him, then climbed the narrow flight of cement steps to the side street above. Half a dozen taxis were at the curb, waiting to be whistled round to the front entrance of the hotel by the starter.

Jim had the taxi drop him off at the Regent Hotel, where he picked up another cab for the long ride to the Airport. As soon as the detective who had been following him discovered that he had found Jim's escape hatch, he immediately began questioning the taxi drivers at the Metropole cabstand. This way the trail could lead the detective to a dead end: Hotel Regent.

The air was bumpy but Jim was too tense and excited to pay very much attention to it, although on the whole he was not too fond of flying. He'd flown all over Europe during the war, often in crates that should have been condemned years before; and he'd had some bad scares and some narrow shaves. In short, as far as flying was concerned, he'd had it.

But after all this was a flight that you could do on your head; only a few minutes over two hours. He settled down in his seat and read the paper, from front to back. The brunette hostess reminded him of Judy, and he kept glancing at her. She had a fine, reassuring smile. He wondered why Judy didn't try such work. Why not get away from smoke-filled saloons and continuously upside-down hours? But probably there was a big difference in the money to be made.

He sat studying Judy's picture in the newspaper. A real pretty girl; and a nice girl, in spite of all that she had been through in her short but rackety life.

The hospital was huge and sprawling. A middle-aged nurse led Jim down a long winding first floor corridor, explaining about Zena in a low hushed voice. This section of the hospital was very old, dark and dismal-looking, and stank of human squalor and mortality.

"Who signed her in?" Jim was asking.

"Oh, she's in a charity ward," said the nurse. "She came to us, asked for help. She was on the verge of collapse. We had her in the psychiatric ward for a while last night. Then we moved her. She seems very weak and run down. We don't know quite what it is. But she seems better now, though very nervous."

There were huge double swing-doors at the end of the corridor. The nurse opened them and Jim followed her into a big, dimly lit ward, with two long rows of beds, some of which were screened off.

Zena's bed was at the front, almost entirely hidden by a screen. Jim caught a glimpse of another nurse, at Zena's bed. They waited. After a moment Zena's nurse came over to them.

"How is she?" asked Jim.

"Better," said the nurse. "She knows you're here. Saw you come in. I know she wants to talk to you, but make it as brief as you can."

Jim nodded, then braced himself a little. He had always been uneasy and awkward with Zena because of the unspoken enmity between them. They'd managed to avoid one another whenever possible. As far as Jim remembered they had never once talked alone together. Now the extremely unusual circumstances in which they were meeting added another disturbing element, and Jim felt definitely tense and nervous.

There was a straight chair beside her bed and Jim sat down at once. In the half-light Zena's face looked very pale and drawn, her green eyes veiled and sleepy, but her short red hair had been carefully combed and arranged, giving her an odd look of elegance, completely incongruous under the circumstances.

"So you figured it out," she said. "I thought you would. That used to be your business, didn't it?"

"Still is, in a way," said Jim; then: "Zena, we've got a lot to talk about so let's get at it. They said I wasn't to stay long."

"How's Judy?"

"She's fine. Pretty much worried about you."

A smile flickered at the corners of Zena's mouth, then was suppressed. "I'll bet—after all the trouble I've caused her. She's a jewel, that kid; but you wouldn't know about that, would you?"

To Jim's surprise and embarrassment, Zena began to cry, fighting hard not to.

"Come on," said Jim, not too gently; "take it easy."

There was a long silence. Finally Zena composed herself. "I saw about Gus and Ziegler in the paper," she explained, in a low, firmly controlled voice. "I flipped, and ended up here. I knew something had happened to them but I didn't know what."

"You want to tell me all about it, Zena?" asked Jim.

"Yes. I would have before, but I had to get out. Allen would have killed me if he'd caught me."

"Maybe we'd better start from the first."

Zena nodded slowly. "Yeah. It might make some sense that way, though I doubt it. I must have been crazy. Sometimes I wonder if I'm not. I get these spells, you know; nervous spells. Judy's the only one can laugh me out of them. Well ... ever since I was a kid I've wanted to have a lot of money. Everybody I knew was poor; just one jump ahead of public charity, year after year. I'm not excusing myself, you understand. I'm just explaining.

"When I was twelve I started working; and I've been working ever since—and that's a few years, never mind how many. A lot of girls thought I made good money at Volari's and I did—but how can you save anything now? Rents, clothes, food—all high not to mention the income tax, with the collectors gouging us on the tips, watching our reports like hawks. Good Christ, haven't they got anything better to do than that? They're murdering people like me. Taxi drivers, you know; people that have to depend on tips. How those poor bastards raise families I'll never know ..."

"Zena," said Jim. "Let's ..."

"All right, all right," cried Zena. "But there's a lot in my system I'd like to get out. Well ... I met this Mond guy. He kept talking big money. Pretty soon he had me sold on clipping the safe at Volari's. He said it was always loaded. Crazy? Seems like it now.

"Then he got Tony Fiala in on the act. Tony and me were always watching Al—getting a line on his routine. Tony was a smart kid. He figured out a way to get the back door to Al's office open and then lock it again without anybody knowing about it. There were three guys working with Allen, who was boss—or thought he was at the time. One of them was a safe expert. He used to sneak back in the alley and watch Al, through the door. Allen had a lot of trouble with him. He said the safe was too tough, wanted to back out. He was the key man in the whole operation ..."

"What was his name?"

"Nick, I think. That's all I know. I never saw him. Nick kept making trouble, so Allen hired a couple of other guys to help, keeping Nick in the picture, just in case. Allen said he was going to get that money no matter how. If they couldn't break the safe, he'd use these strongarm guys. They'd just come in through the back door and stick it up some night. Crazy, eh? That I'd stay mixed up in a thing like this. But I kept thinking about that money and all I could do with it. I just wasn't thinking straight ..."

"These two other men. What were their names?"

"Carl and Shep."

Jim started, but said nothing. Shep! It was the name of the fellow who'd been trying to question Judy about Zena at the beatnik party. He looked up. Zena was studying his face.

"Something wrong?"

"No," said Jim. "Go ahead."

"Well," said Zena, "there isn't much more and it's all mixed up. I don't know what happened. Tony found out something, called Allen right away, and that's all I know. I figure from the paper Ben Ziegler and Gus must have been carrying a lot of money and the strongarm guys got them."

"Think back, Zena."

"Wait. There's more. When we got to the cottage on the lake, the three guys were there—with the money. I didn't see them, you understand, but God knows I heard them. They had a big row with Allen—not only about the dough but about me. I'd heard about Nick before—his name, I mean. But I'd never heard the names of the other guys till that night. They kept yelling 'Carl' and 'Shep' and 'Al' at each other. Allen only hired them, you understand; put up all the front money. But I think they only cut him in for a quarter share, maybe less. What a row! Then somebody yelled: 'And what are you going to do with that goddamned broad?' I got out. I ran to the highway. A truck driver gave me a hitch. Big tough man; nice fellow. Told him a no-good-so-and-so was chasing me. He said: 'Lady, I'll break his neck.' I could hardly get rid of him. He wanted to take me home and wait for the guy to come after me."

"But you didn't come back that same night, Zena," said Jim.

"I know I didn't. Wait. The truck driver dropped me off at a highway motel. I was so scared I didn't know whether I was going or coming; and mixed up, real mixed up! I stayed there two nights. Couldn't figure out what to do. Then I happened to remember a tough taxi driver I used to know. He picked me up at the motel, drove me back to the apartment and came in with me while I got my clothes and some getaway money I had hidden. I guess you can figure out the rest."

Zena lay back and heaved a long sigh. "Oh, God, I feel good now I got that off my chest. Could I have a drink of water?"

Jim gave her one. "Zena," he said, "I hope I can protect you from the law. But I can't promise. You're in serious trouble."

"I don't care," said Zena. "I've had it. You catch those lice and I'll testify."

"Do you know about Tony?"

"Tony Fiala? What about him?"

"He'd dead."

Zena flinched, then calmed herself, stared at Jim for a long time in silence, and finally nodded slowly. "It figures. Allen was just playing Tony and me for suckers."

"Zena, look," said Jim. "I've got to get back and start things moving. I'll have them shift you into a private room."

"No," said Zena. "I like it here, with all these people. I'd be lonesome, and maybe scared."

"All right," said Jim. "Just relax. You're safe here. I'm not going to tell anybody. Not even Judy, till things clear a little. Okay?"

"Okay."

Jim rose and stood looking down at Zena. "Let me ask you a question," he said finally. "Why did you telegraph *me*?"

Zena hesitated for a moment before she spoke. "Because you and Judy are the only two people I've ever met that I trusted. And what could Judy do?"

"Thanks, Zena."

"Otherwise," said Zena, "I don't understand what she sees in you."

Jim smiled at her. She sounded like the real Zena; going down fighting.

"Now you just relax," he said. "You've got no worries, financial or otherwise, for the time being. Goodbye."

Zena raised her right hand in a perfunctory gesture.

Jim had a brief talk with the head nurse before he left.

"There's no reason for her to stay in that ward," he explained, "but she wants to, prefers it. Could we make arrangements for a night nurse for a day or so? She seems all right but she's very nervous."

Jim wrote a check as a deposit and handed it to the nurse with his business card. "Now I don't want anybody from outside to talk to her," he said. "And she's not to leave here under any circumstances unless you check with me first. It's very important. I'm Miss Mylan's lawyer."

"Yes, Mr. Chase," said the nurse. "I'll look after it."

On the plane back, Jim, knowing only too well that he'd had a change of heart, tried to review his thinking and check his growing emotional conviction that what he was doing was not only crazy but stupid. The picture he'd been carrying in his mind of the whole affair had changed radically since he'd heard Zena's story. These men had to be caught and sent to death row, where they belonged; they were no better than mad dogs. He wondered now at old Judge Weybrecht's patience with him.

And yet how could be reverse himself, after the stand he'd taken? Not only that, he was on Al Patton's payroll. It was his duty to protect the Patton interests to the furthest extent of his capabilities. But did that include obstructing justice, compounding a felony and maybe, with the best intentions in the world, inadvertently making possible the escape of deadly malefactors who should be shot on sight?

Jim squirmed in his seat. All the way back to the big town he wrestled with this problem, without even coming close to a solution.

"Mr. Chase!" cried Chauncey, as Jim got out of the taxi. "Am I glad to see you! Gino's been calling everyplace. Everybody's been looking for you."

"What's the matter?" asked Jim apprehensively. "What happened?"

"Sad news," said Chauncey. "Mr. Patton ... he ... died."

Jim was staggered. "Al?"

Chauncey nodded slowly. "I feel real bad. He was sure good to me. It's not going to be the same without him."

"When?"

"The doctor called Gino about an hour ago."

"I'm certainly sorry to hear it," said Jim, then he nodded to Chauncey, gestured rather vaguely and walked into Volari's under the huge golden neon sign which was lighting up the night as brilliantly as ever, as if things were as usual.

"Mr. Chase," cried the check-girl, giving a start and almost dropping her hand mirror. "Mr. Volari's been looking for you for ..."

"I know," said Jim, and hurried on into the bar.

Cecile saw him first and ran to call Gino. Judy was at the slot, getting an order. He saw her turn to look after Cecile, then glance over in his direction, peering through the semi-darkness. A stranger on one of the bar stools noticed Cecile's haste and Judy's peering look, then he turned and looked himself. Jim pegged him at once: the man he'd seen on the stairs at the Metropole. The tail had lost him and had now found him again. In a moment, the detective from Downtown left his stool and walked off toward the public phone booths.

"Jim!" cried Judy. "Where in the world have you been? Gino's had everybody looking for you. Did Chauncey tell you about ...?"

"Yes," said Jim.

"We were getting worried about you. You all right?"

"Yes," said Jim; but he was not all right—far from it. He felt dazed, disoriented. There was no time now for a change of heart. All of his thoughts on the plane had just been so much wasted energy. He'd have to go ahead as he had planned. There was nobody but himself to protect Tom Patton now.

"Terrible about poor Mr. Patton, wasn't it?" said Judy, studying his face. "You look tired, Jim."

He said nothing.

Cecile hurried up to them. "Excuse me, Mr. Chase, but would you mind going back to Mr. Patton's office? Gino would like..."

"Thanks," Cecile," said Jim. "See you later, Judy."

Judy nodded then hurried off with her tray of drinks, watching Jim over her shoulder.

Jim was surprised at Gino's grief. All signs of the suave frontman, the elegant maître d'hôtel had disappeared; Gino, slumped down at the desk with his head in his hands, his bow tie awry, his curly black hair mussed, his easy sophisticated air shocked out of existence, might have been just any stricken man.

"You don't know how I feel, Mr. Chase," he said. "For years now we've worked together. No bother. No strain. No quarrels about money. Never saw such a man. I just can't believe that ..." He broke off. "Sure. I knew he was sick, had high blood pressure. But when we get over fifty we've all got something the matter with us. I just never imagined ..."

Studying Gino, Jim was embarrassed that he himself seemed to be so little effected by the news of Al's death, but then he'd been under such a strain for over a week now that it was possible he was getting a little numb. And besides, he had decisions to make now that left little room in his mind for regrets over something that couldn't be remedied, something that was gone beyond recall.

"What did the doctor say?" he asked.

"Heart failure. All of a sudden. They tried everything. But it was no use."

"Have you done anything, called anybody?"

"No," said Gino. "I wanted to consult with you first. And now can you take over? I'm sick. My stomach's killing me. I've got to go home. It's almost one-thirty. You can close in half an hour."

Jim was surprised at Gino and a little disappointed. The burden, at the moment, was too heavy for him; he wanted to pass it on.

"Okay, Gino," he said. "Go ahead."

Gino got shakily to his feet and started out, then he turned. "I forgot to tell you. When we couldn't find you any place, we all got worried, so l came in here and called Captain Ryan. He's looking for you. Said he'd call in. Was that all right?"

"Yes," said Jim. "And thanks."

Gino stood looking at Jim for a moment, then he held out his hand with an emotional gesture. Jim shook it, a little surprised, then Gino went out.

Jim thought for a while, then he put in a long-distance call for Tom Patton in San Francisco. It would be almost midnight out there and it was rough for a man to be awakened with news like this; but Jim made up his mind that Tom, who was a rugged man and no shirker, should be told about it at once.

It took him nearly twenty minutes to get Tom, who finally came on, and started shouting down the wire, as if he felt his great distance away made this necessary. "Jim? Jimmy boy? What the hell is this? You know it's damned near four-o'clock? What's up?"

"Tom," said Jim, "I've got some bad news for you ..."

"I've been expecting it. That money's gone. You can only do so much, Jim."

"Tom, listen to me. Al's been very sick, you know; high blood pressure and with all this strain, and tonight ..."

"You mean Al died?"

"Yes, Tom."

"When?"

"About an hour or so ago."

"Where?"

"Greet Memorial Hospital."

"When's the funeral?"

"We haven't quite got around to that yet, Tom," said Jim, more than a little amazed by Tom's businesslike attitude.

"Monday, would you say? That's not too far off, is it?"

"No," said Jim. "Dr. Maudley and I will look after everything."

"God bless you, Jim," said Tom. "I ran out and left old Al holding the sack, didn't I?"

"Oh, I wouldn't say that, Tom."

"I'm saying it. I'll catch a plane sometime tomorrow."

"But, Tom—the subpoena!"

"For Christ's sake, Jim; you think I'm going to miss my own brother's funeral because of a lousy subpoena?"

Jim was staggered. "But, Tom … they'll nail you sure. At the funeral if necessary."

"I don't care," said Tom. "To hell with it. I just don't care. We'll fight 'em, son; we'll fight 'em. What the hell are lawyers for?"

"But, Tom—you don't know what's going on here. The money … the two hundred thou…"

"The money!" cried Tom. "I'll catch a plane tomorrow. Now do you mind if I go back to bed?"

Jim started to laugh, feeling a little hysterical, partly through surprise, partly through relief and quite a bit through admiration. Now he knew why it was that he'd always liked old Tom Patton.

"Send me a wire," said Jim. "And I'll meet you at the airport."

"Will do," said Tom. "God rest poor old Al. Since we were kids things have always been too much for him. Good night, Jimmy boy—and thanks for everything."

Jim hung up and sat staring off across the room. It was over. All over. The long struggle had been for nothing. Tom would be subpoenaed and forced to testify under oath before the Grand Jury. Where the money was, was now irrelevant. Nothing but a few loose ends left. All that remained was for him to take Lieutenant Gorsuch and Judge Weybrecht into his confidence.

But little by little Jim found himself rebelling. Tom was in no state of mind to make weighty decisions. There was no way now that Jim could stop him from coming back. But there was a possibility … more than a possibility that he might …

The phone rang and Jim answered it. Pat Ryan.

"Jim, where in the hell have you been? God, I was getting scared, with what *I* know!"

"I'd rather tell you face to face, Pat. You might as well make a night of it."

Pat sighed heavily. "My kids are beginning to ask their Ma what I look like. Be there in about twenty-five minutes."

"Back way," said Jim.

It was five minutes of two now and the last patrons were drifting out, as Tully and his boys kicked off a loud one—"exit music," as Tully called it, and Jim, with the help of Anselmo, checked up with Oswald at the bar. Judy, who had changed her clothes, came to the slot.

"Jim," she said, "I'm going."

"Another party?" asked Jim, seeing Cecile just beyond.

"No. I can catch a ride with Chaucey if I hurry."

"A man's coming here to see me pretty soon," said Jim. "I'll take you home, if you want to wait. Might be half hour or so, maybe longer."

"Well, that's nice of you. But I don't want to be in the way."

"If you have no other plans," said Jim, irritated, "cut it out. And sit down. I've got things to do."

Judy hesitated, talked for a moment with Cecile, who left, then Judy sat in one of the booths and lit a cigarette.

As soon as the bar receipts had been checked, Anselmo and Jim checked the supper room receipts, then Jim sent Anselmo and Oswald home, went to Al's office, made sure that the back door was locked, then opened the safe and put the money and checks away. Just as he had finished there was a tap at the back door.

"Pat?" he called.

"Yeah, Jim. It's me."

Jim let him in, then locked the door again.

"We've got trouble," said Pat. "The place is being watched. Downtown guys, I'm sure, though I couldn't get a good look at them."

"I'm sorry, Pat. I forgot. I'm shook up."

"Yeah," said Pat. "Me, too. Tough about old Al. I liked him. Not a mean bone in his body."

Jim got out a bottle from Al's liquor cabinet and poured them both a stiff drink. They sat down. First Jim told Pat about Tom's reaction to his brother's death.

"Nothing I could do about it, Pat. He's coming back and that's that."

"I admire him for it," said Pat. "I sure do."

"And I want to help him. Are you in on it, Pat?"

Pat shrugged and slowly shook his head. "I'm in on it now whether I like it or not. So why back up?"

Then, while Pat sat in silence with his head lowered, Jim told him Zena's story, carefully and at length, and when he had finished Pat slapped the table and said: "This might do it. The Nick she's talking about has to be Nick Cromany. A well-known peterman—safe guy, you know—with a long record. Shep and Carl I can't place. Probably cheap strongarm hoods. They sure operate like it. These promoters like Mond will never learn. You hire a slob and that's what you get. The real big timers operate on the square."

Now Jim told Pat about Judy's experience with a character who called himself "Shep" at the beatnik party.

Pat's dark eyes flashed, then he said: "Keep her away from places like that, Jim. It's no good. Some real maniacs hang out around Melton Stairs. But it's a lead."

"Think you can pick up Nick Cromany? Hold him in the 21st on some phony charge or other?"

"If I want to put my head in a noose! Also, I'll get a couple of boys to work on your friend Shep. He shouldn't be too hard to find."

"When do you start?"

"Right now."

"Call me, no matter what time it is, as soon as you get your hands on one of them."

"All right. Then what do we do? Damn it, Jim, we're bucking Headquarters, and Sam Gorsuch and Lou Tryon are going to blow their tops."

"If my plan works out we'll make Sam and Lou the big men."

"Wow," said Pat, sadly. "I hope you know what you're doing."

"I hope so, too," said Jim.

When Jim returned to the bar Judy was curled up in one of the big padded leather booths, with her eyes closed, smoking a cigarette. All of the lights were out except for a bluish night-light in the vestibule and one of the pinkish lights over the bar. The supper room was dark as a cave, with the stacked-up tables and chairs dimly visible, mere phantom shapes, touched here and there by a faint reddish glow from the distant bar light. Seen in this guise, Volari's looked completely unfamiliar to Jim, a place of shadowy mystery.

"Well," said Judy, opening her eyes and looking at him sleepily, "did you see your man?"

"Yes," said Jim, slipping in beside her as she sat up. "Judy, I want you to stay away from Melton Stairs."

Judy gave him an odd look. "Oh? Is that an order, Mr. Chase?"

"Judy!"

"Well, it sounded like it. Look, Jim. You run your life, I'll run mine. Isn't that the idea?"

Jim glanced at her, then turned away. Yes, frankly, that was the idea. So why not admit it at once and get it over with?

"I talked to a man just now who happens to know all about Melton

Stairs," said Jim. "Just thought you'd like to know."

After a pause, Judy said: "I appreciate it." Then: "What's going to happen here, Jim? Will the place fold?"

"I doubt it. I imagine Al took care of it in his will. Probably left it to his brother. Gino and I will keep it going till we hear."

"Did you ever think you'd be running a supper club?" asked Judy.

"No."

A long pause. "Jim," said Judy, "Sometimes when I can't sleep I blame myself for all your troubles."

"You know better than that, Judy," said Jim. "That's ridiculous."

"I know it is. But sometimes I can't help it. If I'd said 'no'—and I should have said it, I guess, you being married—you'd still be living at the Savoy-Plaza in that beautiful big apartment with your wife and kids. Do you ever feel like maybe it's all a nightmare and you'll wake up?"

"No," lied Jim. "Can we change the subject. What is all this?"

"Time we thought about it. Time we talked about it. It's all over, Jim; and you know it. Why don't you just face it—like me?"

There was a long silence. Finally Jim got out his cigarettes and they lit up. "Judy," he said, "did you ever think about being an airline hostess?"

Judy dropped her cigarette and Jim rescued it from the front of her dress, brushed off the sparks, crushed out the cigarette and lit her another one.

"It's a good thing you don't handle trays like that," said Jim.

"Well, you startled me so."

"Why?"

"Because I've been looking into it lately. Zena used to talk about it once in a while. But it's a long process. You've got to go to school and live cheap till you make the grade; if you do. I make three or four times as much at Volari's as I could as a hostess. Of course there's only one Volari's in town. You should hear Clarice. She thinks she has hit paradise. The other night someone gave her a twenty-dollar bill and told her to keep it. His check was around three-fifty. She flipped. But ... Volari's may fold. And I'm not going to work in some bowling alley, like Clarice, or in one of those horrible joints I was in till Zena managed to squeeze me in here. You just have no idea what they're like. Full of human animals, male and female." There was a long pause; then Judy asked: "How did you happen to mention such a thing, Jim? It's like you read my mind."

Jim hesitated. "I saw a hostess that reminded me of you. And I got to thinking about you hustling trays in all this smoke and noise, and getting to bed at four and sleeping till noon, and ... oh, I don't know!"

There was a pause, then Judy leaned over and patted his forearm. "Thanks, Jim," she said. "Thanks for worrying about me, when you've got so many things on your mind and all … Shall we get out of here? It's beginning to give me the creeps. I expect to see Dracula come out of the wall any minute."

As Jim was helping Judy out of the taxi, she said: "Better have him wait, Jim. We had a big night at Volari's and I'm tired."

Jim glanced at her but she kept her face averted. He asked the driver to wait.

They walked up to the door of her apartment house in silence and climbed the stone steps. At the top Judy paused. "There's something I forgot to tell you," she said, and when Jim merely looked at her, she went on: "Gino called your ex-wife tonight."

"Now why in hell did he do that?" asked Jim, with marked annoyance.

"Well," said Judy, "after he heard about Mr. Patton Gino was frantic. He didn't know what to do. All he could think about was finding you. He called everyplace, then he kept pestering me and insisting that I ought to know where to find you, so I tried every place I could think of. Nobody knew where you were including your call service. So I had a hunch you might be with your family, so Gino called."

Jim was worried. What in the hell would Alma think was going on?

Judy noticed his preoccupation. "I'm sorry, Jim. I guess I shouldn't have suggested it. But Gino was all to pieces and I couldn't think of any place else you might be."

"It's okay, Judy," said Jim.

They stood looking at each other in silence.

"You're going back, aren't you?" asked Judy, at last.

"I don't know," said Jim. "Frankly I don't know."

"*I* know," said Judy, then she patted his cheek lightly and without another word went inside.

Through the big glass door Jim saw her climbing the stairs to her second-floor apartment. He had the odd feeling that he was taking her home for the first time: a strange girl he'd met at Volari's, pretty, pleasant, enigmatic, not just "old Judy," as she'd once described herself to him after a quarrel over some fancied slight.

As Jim walked back to the taxi he felt pulled in different directions emotionally. The tie with Judy was strong—much stronger than he had imagined while all was going well; and yet on the other hand he was worried about Alma and what her reaction might be to a late call from a stranger inquiring as to his whereabouts. Alma did not like intrusion of any kind; and in the past he'd given her so much trouble; he'd embarrassed and humiliated her—not by intention, of course, but what did that matter?—and it was possible that she was thinking: "Is this going to start all over again?"

As soon as he got back to his apartment he called her. It was better to wake Alma now even though it was three a.m., than to let her wait until the next day for an explanation. Angered, she might make up her mind to some drastic course of action before he'd had a chance to talk with her.

But she answered at once. "*Yes*, Jim?"

"Yes, Alma," he said. "Sorry to call you so late, but I just found out that Gino Volari phoned you because he couldn't find me any place."

"Yes, and he seemed very much upset. I began to get a little worried so I've been lying here reading. I thought probably you'd call."

To Jim's surprise Alma didn't seem annoyed in the least, but rather anxious, so he explained that he'd been forced to go out of town on a case and that word of Mr. Patton's death had come through while he was away.

"I've been reading about those two men in the papers," said Alma. "It's a terrible thing. And the boys saw your picture—you know, the one on the steps. Bob cut it out and I let them pin it up in their room. Did Mr. Patton die as a result of ..."

"In a way," said Jim, wondering what her own reaction had been to seeing *Judy's* picture in the paper. "He's been ill lately. Well, Alma—I won't keep you. Sorry to put you to this trouble, but it wasn't my fault—for once."

Brief silence at the other end, then Alma said: "Well, I think I can go back to sleep now. With you mixed up in this terrible business—I mean, as Mr. Patton's lawyer and all ... well, I got a little worried. I almost woke the boys up just to have somebody to talk to."

"Alma," said Jim, after a pause, choosing his words carefully, "I hope after I get this business settled, that I can see quite a bit more of you and the boys. That once-a-month routine—by court permission—well, it always did irk me a little. Now don't misunderstand me, I'm not trying to excuse myself. But maybe you know what I mean."

"Yes," said Alma. "I think I do. Come when you like. We're almost always home at night—unless we go out to a show."

"Oh, I'll call first, of course," said Jim. "Now go back to sleep. You have to get up early. Good night, Alma."

"Good night, Jim."

He hung up, lit a cigarette, and sat staring off into space. Was it possible? Could it be that after all the quarrels, recriminations, and bitterness that he and Alma might pick up where they'd left off? Alma was lonesome. No doubt about it. He'd detected it in her voice, her manner. Naturally she wouldn't admit it.

As for himself … well, he'd been lonesome even in the midst of all the riot before the fall. And not once, in his heart, had he ever considered his life away from Alma and the boys as anything but an aberrant hiatus. He'd just drifted. Time the drifting stopped. Even Judy knew it.

# 9: FRIDAY

Dawn showed as a band of smokey pink over the grimy brick buildings of Polishtown.

Nick Cromany sat pulling at his fingers and trying to hide his nervousness as he waited on a bench in a dirty, evil-smelling corridor of the 21st Precinct.

Why had he been pulled in at a time like this? Who wanted him and for what? Couldn't get a peep out of the radio boys who had picked him up. Had they found the body? How? Jeez, it was like these bastards had radar.

Nick was a small, dark, nervous middle-aged man who would have been mistaken by practically anybody for a poorly-paid employee of some kind—probably a clerk. Actually he'd been in on some of the biggest knock-overs in the state.

A door opened down the corridor and a policeman looked out. "Nick! Come on. Captain'll see you now."

Nick got to his feet, wondering. Captain? Risko? What the devil was old fat easy-going Captain Risko doing at the station at this hour of the morning? Nick began to feel easier. Old Cap Risko had never seemed too bright to Nick, and far from a strongarm copper. Maybe this was nothing to worry about at all; just a routine drag-in. Maybe some Hoosier shopkeeper had complained of a rifled safe and so they were rousting him just to show that something was being done!

But when Nick saw who the "Captain" was he began to wilt. Pat Ryan! What in the hell was he doing in the 21st Precinct? A Downtown beef? Good Christ, maybe this was really IT after all. "Oh no," Nick groaned to himself. All along he'd been worried about this one, worried about that over-slick little junky promoter, Mond, and his two small-time goons; worried about the girl the promoter had dragged up to the cottage with him; worried about the rip-and-tear knock-over and the headlines—wow, what headlines; worried about the promoter's squabble with the goons over the take—the whole thing had been a wrong one from top to bottom. And now, as of last night, the promoter was in the river with his head knocked in … and a murder rap was in the offing.

Why had he agreed to meet the promoter? How had the goons got word of it? And here he was in a lousy mess—maybe—over a knock-over he'd had nothing do with—except as a spectator. The two guys from Volari's, that was something different. Try and prove it. But this last rip-and-tear rubout—on a public pier, with people not too far away ... wow!

"How do you do, Captain Ryan," he said politely.

"Shut up and sit down," said Pat roughly.

Nick sat down abruptly.

Pat glared at him in silence for a long time, then he asked: "You want to talk?"

"About what, Captain?" asked Nick.

Now Pat shook his finger at him, like a weapon. "I'll give you one more chance. And don't say about what. Answer yes or no. Do you want to talk?"

Nick cringed and squirmed, then finally in a faraway sounding voice he said: "No."

"All right," said Pat. "I see I misjudged you. I figured you for a real professional, an expert who knows his own business, does it, and keeps his nose clean. Never thought I'd pull you in on a murder rap, Nick."

Nick hesitated, appalled, then yelled: "I had nothing to do with it, Captain, so help me God. All I did was meet the guy. Them goons trailed me and knocked him off. Me, I almost got it myself."

Pat did not have the faintest idea what Nick was talking about but his expression did not change. "Oh, hell—that's just your story, Nick." Now he took a shot in the dark. "Maybe Shep and Carl tell a different story."

Nick's face paled visibly and his jaw swung loose for a moment. "Them lying, thieving, no-good, cheap ..." he stuttered.

"Two to one, Nick," said Pat.

"You talked to 'em?" cried Nick.

"Maybe," said Pat.

A policeman put his head in the door. "Captain, could I see you for a minute?"

Pat stepped out into the hallway and the policeman closed the door. "We got 'em," he said. "The real big one—Carl—put up a hell of a fight and the boys gave him quite a lacerating. The other got hit in the belly and quit."

"Put 'em in separate cells," said Pat. "Then come get Nick. Stick him in one of the detention rooms and watch him. I got some figuring to do before I talk to him again."

It was nearly nine o'clock that morning before Pat was able to disentangle the mystery of Nick's surprising admissions. A body had been found half submerged in the shallows of Pier 7, and later tentatively identified through cards in an empty wallet as that of Allen Mond. Taking no chances with the identification, Pat had Joe Carr, assistant manager of the Regent, driven down to the morgue to have a look. "It's him, all right," Carr had said.

By twelve noon nearly one hundred and forty thousand dollars of Tom Patton's stolen money had been recovered, due to the fact that Pat had played Shep Still against Carl Becker and Nick Cromany against both of them.

Jim had been kept advised of the moves by telephone and shortly after one p.m., Pat called and said: "Well, I'm up to my neck in the soup now. But I've got all three of them nailed, for robbery and three murders. Nick will sing the best; he's the smartest. So I tap Nick for State's Witness. So far as I know nothing has leaked in Downtown. So now what do we do?"

Jim explained at some length, and finally Pat laughed sardonically and said: "Okay, son. See you in jail."

Lieutenant Gorsuch and Captain Tryon listened to Jim in ambiguous silence, not quite trusting him but even so feeling a rising excitement at Jim's intimations that if they cooperated with him, in some manner not as yet specified, he might dump the solution of the sensational Ziegler-Bailey case right into their laps.

"… and on top of that," Jim was saying, "it's possible that I may have two State's Witnesses who will absolutely clinch the case for the DA's office. Besides, I may be able to lay my hands on the man you want for the killing."

"Mr. Chase," said Gorsuch, "as I warned you before, we have laws about compounding felonies and withholding vital information from the police. I could hold you right now."

"But we're just talking informally, gentlemen," said Jim. "For all you know I may just be pulling your legs, to see what your reactions might be. I'm not under oath."

"All right, Jim. All right," said Lou Tryon. "I got a faint idea you can deliver the goods. Now what do you want from us?"

"First, Lou," said Jim, "I want you to set up a date for me to talk to Judge Weybrecht. Soon as possible. Right now if necessary."

"That's easy," said Lou "This case is number one to him because of the odd Patton tie-ins. What else?"

"I want both of you men to go to the front with the DA for Pat Ryan, one of the best and most honest public servants in this town or any other. Get him out of the 21st, get him back in the 17th, where he belongs."

Lou and Sam glanced at each other, Sam nodded, then Lou said: "All right. We'll do our best. We don't have the last word, you know. Now what?"

"The money," said Jim.

"What money?" asked Lou, glancing sideways at Sam.

"You know what money as well as I do," said Jim. "You've figured that all out by now."

"Okay," said Lou. "Ziegler and Bailey were delivering a wad of money from Al to Tom so Tom could skip town and beat the subpoena. They were killed for it."

"Yes," said Jim. "Let's say for the sake of argument that the money has been recovered. It's to be returned to Tom Patton. Nothing is to be made of it in regard to Tom's past."

Sam and Lou stared openmouthed, astounded.

"Are you crazy?" cried Lou. "Why do you think the DA's so anxious to clear this one up?"

"I know," said Jim. "But where's Tom Patton? What good is all this without him?"

Gorsuch and Tryon looked at each other in silence, then Gorsuch turned away to light a cigarette, leaving the play up to his superior.

"And you might deliver Tom, is that it?" asked Tryon. "Or have I got it figured all wrong?"

"You've got it right. I'm his lawyer. If my conditions are met, he'll accept the subpoena and appear before the Grand Jury. If not ... not!"

"Jesus, I don't know," said Tryon. "Like Sam said, we could throw the book at you, Jim. But, still ... on the other hand ..." He began to scratch his head.

"You got any other news for us?" Gorsuch said.

"One of my witnesses," said Jim, casually, "is Zena Mylan."

"You finally found her?"

"Yes," said Jim. "Just as you finally found Allen Mond. The difference is, she's alive and she's got a pretty story that you'd like to hear."

"Give us a hint," said Lou, sardonically.

"Oh, I suppose you've figured out by now that Mond engineered the robbery and the killing of Ziegler and Bailey."

"It was a theory," said Sam.

"He was a fool and a drug addict," said Jim, "and the guys he hired finally hit him on the head and threw him in the river."

Tryon and Gorsuch exchanged quick glances.

"So if you had the men involved you'd have them on three separate murder counts. DA couldn't fail to get a conviction."

"And your other witness?" asked Tryon.

"That's a touchy subject," said Jim.

"One of the guys?"

"That's as good a guess as any."

There was a long silence. Tryon and Gorsuch were slightly shaken by the unexpected ramifications. Finally Tryon spoke: "If I understand you, Jim, you want me to go to the DA with this, tell him what you've told me, see if he'll listen."

"I want you to do more than that," said Jim. "I want you and Gorsuch to make him listen. It's a good deal, boys. Downtown gets the credit for the solving and the arrests; the DA gets a sure conviction of an important case—important in the newspapers anyway. Tom Patton accepts his subpoena and appears before the Grand Jury. He also gets his money back without it being used as a weapon against him."

"And you get yours," said Gorsuch, sarcastically.

"That's right," said Jim. "I get mine."

Tryon scratched his head for a while. "All right," he said. "It's the craziest thing I ever heard but Sam and me—we'll make it strong to the old Judge. We'll go see him right now. You stay here. If the answer is 'no' you're in trouble."

"And so are you," said Jim. "What the DA wants most of all is Tom Patton in front the Grand Jury. Remember that. He won't get him if you blow it."

Half an hour later the phone in Captain Tryon's office rang, a secretary answered it, then called Jim, who had been sitting with his chair tipped back, reading a magazine.

It was Lou Tryon. "Come right over," he said. "Judge wants you."

"How did it go?"

"He never said a word one way or the other. Just listened. He'd have made a great poker player, except he don't believe in gambling. Coming?"

"Be right over."

Jim found Judge Weybrecht siting behind a littered desk in an office that was only too familiar to Jim; he'd been in and out of it thousands of times during the old Administration when it was the sanctuary of His Highness, Jake Webb. Judge Weybrecht, to whom surroundings meant nothing, hadn't made a single change; same drapes, same pictures, same carpet—even the gadgets on the desk were the same.

The Judge motioned Jim into a chair opposite him. His face was noncommittal but there was a somewhat steely glint in the eyes behind the shell-rimmed glasses.

"Mr. Chase," he said, "I have the feeling that you are a little confused. There was an election. Mr. Jake Webb is no longer here. It's a new regime. We are not in the habit of allowing ourselves to take part in the chicaneries of the past. Do I make myself clear?"

"I think so," said Jim. "You do not like my conditions."

"Mr. Chase," said the Judge, "you are understating it. I do not like anything at all about your proposition and I am about to ask for a warrant for your arrest."

"On what charge?"

"Obstructing justice; compounding a felony; withholding vital information."

Jim got to his feet. "Well, then, sir, I won't take up any more of your valuable time."

"Sit down," said the Judge and when Jim had obeyed, he went on: "Mr. Chase, whatever gave you the idea that you could walk in here and dictate terms to me? I make the terms. Oh, you were very clever about it, approaching Lieutenant Gorsuch and Captain Tryon first. They have only one thing in mind: to clear up the case. So, on the whole, they were favorable, as you know they'd be. But did you really think I'd agree to anything like this? Have your sense of values become so blunted by past association …?"

"Excuse me, sir," said Jim. "Tom Patton is nearly sixty years old. This is all the money he's got in the world. I was trying to save it for him. That's all." Now Jim rose and stood leaning on the back of his chair. "I don't quite understand your talk about values, Judge. But just let me tell you something. You don't have to make any deal with me to get Tom Patton. All you have to do is wait for Al Patton's funeral and then send one of your men over with a subpoena. Tom'll be there. Judge, Tom knew absolutely nothing about this deal I've been proposing. It was all my own idea. As soon as Tom found out his brother was dead he didn't care about the lost money, he didn't care about the subpoena. All he cared about was the funeral. He'd be there in spite of hell or high water. So, Judge, sir … you can see that I'm a little confused in regard to values."

Judge Weybrecht took out a handkerchief and polished his glasses, then he put them back on, picked up a notebook and a pen, and asked:

"The name of your first witness is?"

"Zena Mylan."

"Where is she to be found?"

"General Hospital, Indianapolis."

The Judge kept writing in the notebook without looking up.

"Nick Cromany. He's in jail. 21st Precinct."

"The other men?"

"Carl Becker and Shep Still. In jail. 21st Precinct."

"They were arrested by?"

"Detective Sergeants Baker and West, on the orders of Captain Patrick Ryan, of the 21st Precinct."

"Now in regard to the money."

"A large part of it has been recovered and is being held at the 21st Precinct."

"Original amount?"

Jim hesitated for a moment. "Two hundred thousand dollars."

"How much has been recovered?"

"A little over one hundred and forty thousand."

The Judge closed his notebook and glanced up briefly. "You are acting as Tom Patton's lawyer, I presume?"

"Yes. And I'll represent him before the Grand Jury in conjunction with Mr. Martin Cowan, if I'm not in jail at the time."

"I'd prefer not to serve him at the funeral. Will you make some arrangements to accept service?"

"I will, Judge."

There was a long pause. "Well," said the Judge, "I imagine that will be all, Mr. Chase."

Jim nodded and turned to go.

"Mr. Chase," called the Judge, "I want to say this. Your clearing up of this case was an amazingly efficient piece of work. It is too bad it had to be tainted with ... well, with an attitude of mind reminiscent of the old Administration. Putting that aside, I think your grandfather would have been very proud of you."

"Judge," said Jim, "like most men I have to make a living. I don't want to kid you; or have you kid yourself. Ten per cent of that recovered money was to be mine."

The Judge flushed but said nothing. Jim turned and went out.

Gorsuch and Lou Tryon were waiting in the corridor. Jim ignored them, and hurried to the elevators. Tryon glanced after him, then went into the Judge's office.

As Jim was crossing the big Hall of Justice lobby a girl called to him from the cigar counter. "Mr. Chase! Phone!"

Jim answered it at the counter. It was Lou Tryon. "Jim—what the hell did you say to him? Goddamn it, when we talked to him he hit the ceiling. Now it's okay. You've got your deal. Lieutenant Gorsuch is already talking to Pat on the phone at the 21st."

Jim was so shocked that he just stood there with his mouth open. He saw the counter girl looking at him. "Oh," he said. "So it's okay. Well, fine." He hardly knew what he was talking about.

He wandered out into the street in a daze and stood on the corner, waiting for a taxi. So it was over. All over. He'd made it.

Four-lane, one-way traffic roared past him on the boulevard. Eastward, the huge buildings of the Downtown area towered starkly up into the gray, overcast sky. Heavy clouds of whitish smoke were drifting in from the south—Smoketown—where at that moment good old Pat Ryan was talking on the phone with Sam Gorsuch.

Looking about him at the remorseless tide of traffic, at the weathered, grimy city—hearing the grinding and screeching and honking—smelling the dust, the smoke, and the carbon monoxide, Jim wanted to escape; if only for the afternoon, if only till it was time for the arrival of Tom Patton's plane from San Francisco. After that there'd be no time for escape, as he'd be living day after day in a feverish atmosphere of public hearings and legal bickering, and newspaper publicity and all the rest ... this was his last chance.

Finally he managed to corral a taxi, and as he got in he gave Alma's address in faraway West River. Maybe suburbia was not such a bad place after all.

THE END

## W. R. BURNETT
## BIBLIOGRAPHY
## (1899-1982)

NOVELS
Little Caesar (Dial, 1929)
Iron Man (Dial, 1930)
Saint Johnson (Dial, 1930)
The Silver Eagle (Dial, 1931)
The Giant Swing (Harper, 1932)
Dark Hazard (Harper, 1933)
Goodbye to the Past (Harper, 1934)
The Goodhues of Sinking Creek
    (Raven's Head, 1934)
King Cole (Harper, 1936)
The Dark Command (Knopf, 1938)
High Sierra (Knopf, 1940)
The Quick Brown Fox (Knopf, 1942)
Nobody Lives Forever (Knopf, 1943)
Tomorrow's Another Day (Knopf,
    1945)
Romelle (Knopf, 1946)
The Asphalt Jungle (Knopf, 1949)
Stretch Dawson (Gold Medal, 1950)
Little Men, Big World (Knopf, 1951)
Vanity Row (Knopf, 1952)
Adobe Walls (Knopf, 1953)
Big Stan (as by John Monahan; Gold
    Medal, 1953)
Captain Lightfoot (Knopf, 1954)
It's Always Four O'Clock (as by
    James Updyke; Random, 1956)
Pale Moon (Knopf, 1956)
Underdog (Knopf, 1957)
Bitter Ground (Knopf, 1958)
Mi Amigo (Knopf, 1959)
Conant (Popular Library, 1961)
Round the Clock at Volari's (Gold
    Medal, 1961)
Sergeants 3 (Pocket, 1962)
The Goldseekers (Doubleday, 1962)
The Widow Barony (UK only;
    Macdonald, 1962)
The Abilene Samson (Pocket, 1963)
The Winning of Mickey Free
    (Bantam, 1965)
The Cool Man (Gold Medal, 1968)
Good-bye Chicago (St. Martin's,
    1981)

SHORT STORIES
Across the Aisle (*Collier's*, Apr 4,
    1936)
Between Rounds (*Collier's*, Aug 30,
    1930)
Captain Lightfoot (*Argosy*, UK, Nov,
    Dec 1954, Jan 1955)
Dr. Socrates (*Collier's*, Mar 23, 1935)
Dressing-Up (*Harper's*, Nov 1929;
    *Ellery Queen's Mystery Magazine*,
    June 1947)
First Blood (*Collier's*, Apr 23 1938)
Girl in a Million (*Redbook*, Jan 1938)
Head Waiter (*Cosmopolitan*, Sept
    1931)
High Sierra (*Five Star Western
    Stories*, July 1941)
The Hunted (*Liberty*, June 28 1930)
I Love Everybody (*Argosy*, UK, July
    1943)
Jail Breaker (*Collier's*, July 7, July
    14, July 21, Aug 4 1934)
Little David (*The Saturday Evening
    Post*, Feb 15 1947)
Mr. Litvinoff (*Collier's*, July 18 1931)
Nobody Lives Forever (*Collier's*, Oct
    9, Oct 16, Oct 23, Oct 30 1943)
Nobody's All Bad [Billy the Kid]
    (*Collier's*, Jun 7 1930; *Ellery
    Queen's Mystery Magazine*, Dec
    1953)
Protection (*Collier's*, May 9, May 23
    1931)
Racket Alley (*Collier's*, Dec 16 1950,
    Jan 6 1951)
Round Trip (*Harper's*, Aug 1929;
    *Ellery Queen's Mystery Magazine*,
    Dec 1950)
Suspect (Collier's, July 4 1936)
Throw Him Off the Track (*Argosy*,
    Dec 1952)
Traveling Light (*Collier's*, Dec 7
    1935; *Ellery Queen's Mystery
    Magazine*, Sep 1951)
Vanishing Act (*Manhunt*, Nov 1955;
    *Mike Shayne Mystery Magazine*,
    Aug 1964)
War Party (*Lilliput*, May 1954)
Youth Is Not Forever (*Redbook*, Feb
    1939)

ESSAYS
Whatever Happened to Baseball?
  (*Rogue*, June 1963, article)
The Roar of the Crowd (Potter, 1964)

SCREENPLAY CONTRIBUTIONS
The Finger Points (1931)
Beast of the City (1932)
Scarface: The Shame of a Nation
  (1932)
High Sierra (1941)
The Get-Away (1941)
This Gun for Hire (1942)
Wake Island (1942)
Crash Dive (1943)
Action in the North Atlantic (1943)
Background to Danger (1943)
San Antonio (1945)
Nobody Lives Forever (1946)
Belle Starr's Daughter (1949)
Vendetta (1950)
The Racket (1951)
Dangerous Mission (1954)
I Died a Thousand Times (1955)
Captain Lightfoot (1955)
Illegal (1955)
Short Cut to Hell (1957)
September Storm (1960)
Sergeants Three (1962)
The Great Escape (1963)

UNCREDITED SCREEN
CONTRIBUTIONS
Law and Order (1932)
The Whole Town's Talking (1935)
The Westerner (1940)
The Man I Love (1946)
The Walls of Jericho (1948)
The Asphalt Jungle (1950)
Night People (1954)
The Hangman (1959)
Four for Texas (1963)
Ice Station Zebra (1968)
Stiletto (1969)

Made in United States
Troutdale, OR
12/24/2024

26185477R00186